Dear Mr. Mulroney,

I had a dream.

I dreamed I would publish a novel. Now, that dream has become a reality. But, I have often thought, along with the page traditionally set aside for acknowledgements, there should be one set aside for "in spite of".

I send this copy of my novel to you as a gift of encouragement from one Canadian to another. You are misperceived by many who dismiss economic and multi-cultural realities as rhetoric, and wanted to let you know, I think you and your team are doing a bang-up job. My humble message to you is, "in spite of" the critiques, HANG ON, HANG ON, HANG ON. Some Canadians very much appreciate the oft-times thankless job of running the country in these challenging times.

Here's to dreaming and having the guts to see the mission to the end,

I am,

Keith McKinnon
MAY 1990

The
Rempal
Inquest

by
Keith McKinnon

Highway Book Shop
Cobalt, Ontario POJ 1C0

ISBN 0-88954-329-1

Canadian Cataloguing in Publication Data

McKinnon, Keith, 1959-
    The Rempal inquest

ISBN 0-88954-329-1

I. Title.

PS8575.K5R45 1989   C813'.54   C89-095473-9
PR9199.3.M35R45 1989

Dedication

TO SHANNON DAWN STEIN
and the ongoing crisis
of her love
in my life.

Acknowledgements

I am greatly indebted to Betty Laffferty for her patient and thorough editing. Also, I wish to thank Shirley Kayes for her enthusiasm and encouragement. To my parents, Ron and Isabel McKinnon, thank you for roots and thank you for wings. Above all, I appreciate the understanding and support given me by my spouse, Shannon.

Keith McKinnon
October 1989

Prologue

(From the personal journal of the Greek slave-scribe Rempal, 22 B.C.)

Another orgy of violence. Brutal and senseless. I am sick of it. The world has gone mad. And Rome is the centre of madness.

Marcellus returned yesterday from his expedition in the East. He claims that his Legion was attacked and he commanded his soldiers to defend themselves. Attacked? By whom? Peasant women and old fishermen, children and sheep perhaps—were these the enemy? Did they cut so deeply with their defiant looks and proud faces that he could not stand to bear their resentment without raising the Roman Standard and smashing their skulls to prove his authority? My good friend Petra passed me a scroll late last night on his way to the city. In it I read the truth of the massacre. Hundreds line the roads, hanging from crosses, their eyes weeping tears of hopelessness as parents watch daughters and sons die beside them, their only crime a desire to be free of Roman rule.

So then why am I here, pen in hand, preparing to write a victory song for Marcellus? I know he is no victor. He and the swine he leads are children let loose, wild animals. But I will say he is great and his father will slap him proudly on the shoulder when I have finished and drink to his health. I am deeply ashamed.

I also know that I have no choice.

Who does? These Jews—does their stubborness mean anything? Their corpses hang from olive trees leaving rotted meat for the scavengers. What difference does it make? All they do is provide an outlet for the frustrations of the army.

I suppose, if it were not Marcellus and his armed savages crushing an uprising of religious fanatics in Judea, then it would be something else. The Senators must have an issue to debate and the soldiers flesh to dull their blades. After all, what would be the sense in governing the whole world if there was nothing left to conquer? Now that Augustus has distributed the booty of Egypt, the people are beginning to hunger for something else to celebrate. So, Marcellus will be proclaimed a hero for his latest escapade and the beast of arrogance will be appeased for another short time. How utterly mad is mankind!

These are only words I write. Empty syllables. I talk like one who has the power to change the world and I have not even the power to change my clothes without permission. A slave, even a scribe such as I, must obey or die. There is no luxury of opinion permitted. I must stand and sing my poems portraying the grace of the countryside and the grandeur of Rome. Virgil is paid for his pretensions. I am obliged with my life.

At times I abhor my existence. My mind craves free expression. When the words THE GLORY OF ROME *pass my lips, I feel a layer of skin has been torn from my flesh as slave tax to the Empire. I have thought of killing myself and perhaps Marcellus or his father in the process, but I am too much a coward.*

As I prepare to write a poem for Marcellus, a final thought has occurred to me. Poetry is a blasphemous art because it is idealistic. And humanity is too barbaric to be spoken of in ideal terms. I would rather have been born a carpenter or a mason. At least, even as slaves, they can avoid the most blatant forms of hypocrisy...

I

December 1995

Baden-Baden, West Germany. It is evening. Regulars have begun to arrive, talking softly amongst themselves in pairs as the opponents move about on the huge park chessboard, lifting and arranging pawns, knights and castles by the handles attached attractively to the head of each delicately crafted piece.

The game is about to begin.

The wooden benches placed around the perimeter of the two-hundred-square-foot gaming area start to absorb the warmth from the bodies of the solemn men and women who have come to quietly enjoy the challenge of the evening.

The players step from the gameboard. One is nervous and quick. The other—older, more experienced—strolls comfortably from one end of the board to the other, thinking as he goes. He gives the impression of a man confident in his ability to surprise, to outthink, and calmly conquer.

One spectator sits alone. From a distance one would think he too were focused on the players in front of him, but from up closer, a shift in body posture reveals that his concentration is now directed to the park entrance. What is he really looking at? Perhaps he is bored by the first common moves of the game. He looks distracted...young...impatient...serious—not like the curious and respectful spectators who frequent the board every Wednesday and Friday nights.

Closer inspection would reveal more oddities. A click. He whispers a few words. He nods. He speaks in a low tone. By now it is clear that this spectator is present to a different game. His eyes follow the limousine rolling slowly to a halt three hundred yards away. For the first time since he was seated he looks directly at the magnificent building that stretches for half a block against the dark wooded area of the park.

The game is about to begin.

1

Inside the palatial structure another man meets his gaze through a small opening in the separated curtains that fall in lacy ripples from the top of the oval window almost to the floor. He holds a phone to his ear, half concealing himself behind the royal velvet drapes that frame the huge window. He nods in understanding. Jerking the lace curtains closed, he places the receiver quietly on its antique pedestal and turns to face the main room of the casino. He walks deliberately past a wave of upper-class gamblers who have begun setting wagers equal to the national debt of a small country, and heads directly to the south-east corner. He waits impatiently as his superior concludes a conversation with a visiting entrepreneur. He feels the pressures of diplomacy and of his assigned task pulling at his gut, and is relieved when the tall, stately gray-haired gentleman shakes hands in farewell with his guest and turns to meet him.

"The minister has arrived, sir."

"By all means show him in, Franz," replies the man in a light, almost jovial tone. "Table number seven. He is to enjoy himself until he risks three hundred. Then tell him the manager wishes to speak with him. He is not to be embarrassed."

On his way from Ottawa, the Canadian Minister of National Defense had worried about how he could meet the demands of his NATO commanders. Political tensions in Europe had risen drastically over the preceding eight months, and leading political analysts had been quoted in almost every daily publication in the country as believing that Canada's contribution to the defence of West Germany was insufficient. The Minister had been ordered to commence discussions immediately on the procurement of planes and possibly tanks for NATO forces in Europe.

The Minister had been expecting that his meeting with General McDonnell, Deputy Commander for Canadian Forces Europe, would be difficult. It was. But not because the military and the government could not agree on a budget. It was demanding because General McDonnell was almost never available for his scheduled meetings.

Excuses had been offered. A crisis of some kind was alluded to each time the Minister insisted on knowing why he was being kept waiting, and it never seemed clear to him how such a subject

2

as the purchase of military hardware could be vital one moment and of only secondary importance the next.

In the end, a kind of truce was achieved with the Minister being invited to an evening of leisure in Baden-Baden before the long flight back to Canada. As he reflected on these things during the fifteen minute drive from Canadian Forces Base Baden to the casino, the Minister decided that perhaps things had turned out for the best after all. Whatever was dumping on the General's parade, at least he was preoccupied enough that the government did not have to take more funding from the farming budget or increase taxes, to keep the military out of the news before summer. And, the Minister thought to himself as the young private turned into the park toward the front doors of the casino, I feel lucky tonight. Maybe I can put together a little nestegg at roulette before the night is over....

In the entrance hall Canada's Defense Minister was greeted with quiet but thorough ceremony by a well-dressed and pleasant commissionaire who assured Colonel Timmens, the Minister's aide-de-camp, that a comfortable and secluded area had been secured for the evening's activities. The Minister's host was accustomed to the demeanor and timing required to make dignitaries feel at ease with their addictions, and Colonel Timmens was visibly relieved to see the Minister smile appreciably at the young man's comments.

"We are expecting great things tonight, sir. We have heard that Canadians enjoy roulette almost as much as their winter sport of hockey."

"I should like to think that we are less famous for our vices than our accomplishments," replied the Minister with mock drama. The commissionaire smiled warmly.

"Surely one risk is as entertaining as another, sir? I personally am more intrigued by the drop of the die than the drop of the puck. But then I am European and have grown accustomed to a climate more conducive to one than the other." The Minister laughed openly. He liked this chap.

"We shall see if I can do justice to your analogy. I am more than willing to test your hypothesis at any rate."

3

From his vantage point in the corner the tall gentleman watched the Minister enter with his aide and their helpful attendant.

The pawn is in place.

For a moment he felt a twinge of anxiety, realizing the importance of this stage in The Plan. This might be the last time Canada's Defense Minister would be in Germany for many months. He reached for the medallion that hung about his neck and absently fingered its edges between his thumb and forefinger as he was wont to do when nervous. He watched as chips were set in front of the Minister and the wheel spun for the first time. What he saw removed any last doubts he may have had that they had made the right move. The Minister's face lost its air of nonchalance and took on the careless excitement of the insecure and the addicted. As he had done countless times before, the man with the medallion watched as another man silently prayed for his dreams to come true, for his number to turn up. With a strange mixture of disdain and fascination he observed the unveiling of another. He saw this Canadian, a leader of people, a diplomat and politician, expose his humaness as surely as if he had shed all his clothes and danced on the table he was leaning on.

"Number 22, black." The Minister's first stroke of good fortune had been orchestrated with the flawless precision of a surgeon's scalpel. The tall man in the corner could feel the tension drain from his shoulders.

"Long live the Senate..." he whispered.

The game has begun.

***

Friday night in Baden-Baden is like Friday night in many places all over the world. Young people dance and eat pizza and race on the Autobahn, proving who is fastest, most capable, the best. They compete with each other and their parents, who compete with their neighbours and form governments that compete with each other. And everywhere, all over the world, there are winners and losers.

The benches at the chess board have long since been deserted for the night. The younger man lost as was expected. He risked too much too quickly. He allowed himself to be vulnerable. He

4

was **blind** to the obvious. For him, there is always next week. **Maybe** then he will win. And if not, he has only lost for one **more** week. The stakes seem important, but he can return to try again.

The park is quiet. Most of the high rollers have left. It's been a long night for coatcheck workers and the bartender who had to work double shift because his partner was sick. People all have their bad days. Some have them real bad....

Canada's Minister of National Defense had been spared the embarrassment of having his aide-de-camp present at the final spin. He had instructed the Colonel to have the car warmed up and ready to leave immediately.

There had been moments. But the moments were so few and the winnings so elusive. By night's end he was no longer excited but worn and afraid. The manager of the casino had informed him that his diplomatic position gave him access to an almost unlimited bank of funds should he need it. Unfortunately for him, and although he could not know it at the time, possibly the entire world would be affected by his actions.

People rationalize. A common defense. He signed loans and lost track. He rationalized ten thousand more when he won two thousand back. By the time his aide returned the Minister had signed for $340,000 and was facing the end of everything he had ever cared about: thirty years of political involvement, a family of four children and a country who would disown him as a national embarrassment

"You look haggard, Mr. Minister. Understandably so. You have had an unfortunate turn of luck this evening." The tall man spoke gently, with empathy. Canada's defense representative was oblivious to his speech, the luxurious furnishings, the chair in which he sat and the scotch and water that had been provided for him. He felt every day of his fifty-three years. He felt old. His mouth was dry and he thought he could taste death. Smell it, maybe.

"I am sure you are aware that debts are as important to this facility as are winnings to the public. I cannot express my condolences to you and...," he hesitated, "your country, sincerely enough. I am assuming, sir, that this unfortunate

5

circumstance can be put behind you with time. If you would just sign a cheque for the stated amount, I'm sure..."

"I haven't the funds. I haven't got one hundred, much less three hundred thousand. I haven't got the money." Silence. This time the Minister was sure. He could smell death. Every door was closed. He felt mortal and finite.

"I'm afraid I don't understand, sir. I am sure you were made aware that any losses or winnings would be accounted for at the end of the evening. Your aide has called for you and I have told him that you would be along shortly. It may not be so simple if what you are saying is the truth."

"It is the God's honest truth. I...I didn't know how far behind I had become. The numbers had been turning up all night. I thought maybe a few thousand..."

"I sympathize with your memory, but I am sure you must understand, sir, what you are saying means that we have an international crisis here. My country has invested in this complex for the entertainment of her citizens and visitors. However, any money raised at the tables belongs to the people of West Germany and their government. If you are unable to meet your commitment, I would have no alternative but to inform my superiors."

"Is there any way I could have some time? Even a few weeks perhaps...I have friends who could help me...."

"It has been done for others, Mr. Minister, and I should feel happy to oblige you as well. But never for such an amount. My accountants would not allow it. I am afraid we have no alternative.... Pardon me." The sound of the phone ringing startled the Canadian diplomat.

"This is most unusual. Are you sure you mean the whole amount? On what grounds? Very well. Just one moment." The manager covered the phone with the palm of his hand and spoke, his medallion reflecting the light from the chandelier as he pivoted lightly to face the Minister.

"I do not understand, sir, but neither is that any of my business. Apparently there is someone here who has heard of your predicament and is willing to pay the full amount. Do you wish to speak to him?

For a moment the Minister neither comprehended the question nor its meaning. Then it dawned on him: Somehow, someone—an old friend perhaps?—had heard of his difficulty and was willing to loan him the money. Yes! That must be it! With an absurd mixture of curiosity and panicky hopefulness, he tore the phone from the relaxed hand of his host. The manager left him to converse with his destiny in private.

"Good evening, Mr. Minister. I know this must be a difficult time for you. Perhaps I can be of some help." The voice sounded warm and sensitive. Soothing, almost.

"Who's speaking, please?" The Minister was confused and frightened. No one could have convinced him six hours ago that he would find himself so vulnerable to a strange voice, a voice that knew of his weaknesses and his debts. A nameless voice that held power over a powerful man in his moment of desperate need.

"You can call me Mr. Millar, if you wish. It doesn't matter so much who I am but perhaps you would be interested in what I can do for you. I have access to funds that could liberate you from your inconvenient and highly undesirable political predicament. I know your career has been long and hard won. It would be disastrous to have so much emotional and intellectual investment destroyed by a simple change in the weather, so-to-speak."

"I can assure you I would be most grateful for any help that you could give me, er-Mr. Millar, if I knew to whom I should thereafter be indebted." The Minister listened, and had begun to let his political mind control his speech. Find out what he wants. What's the cost. How does his influence as Minister of National Defense warrant a card worth $340,000 from a man he has never met before?

"Let me be frank with you, Mr. Minister. I know you are no fool. Even in your distress you can see that I have knowledge of your recent loss and am offering you total and complete indemnity. Surely your experience would suggest that I would expect something of equal or greater value in return for my financial leverage." The caller paused to let his words sink in. His direct and candid approach had a strangely calming effect on the Minister; he always felt more at ease when negotiators were up front with their expectations.

7

The voice continued. "I would also expect you to be wary of any such offer, especially in a position as influential and necessary to the security of your country as that of Defense Minister."

"I am listening."

"You have access to a piece of land that I want. It is practically worthless as real estate, but would have enormous investment potential for me if I could be granted permission to use it for independent research and development. I am working on a computer program that I believe will eventually allow me and my colleagues to predict the weather to a degree that would embarrass and fascinate even the most optimistic meteorological experts of our day. It is only a matter of time before I succeed, regardless of whether or not you feel prepared to cooperate. However, the land I wish to occupy in your country would give me the isolation and geographical position that could take months and possibly years off my research. As the saying goes, Mr. Minister, time is money and I plan to make a lot of it."

"I appreciate the straightforward nature in which you have explained your interest," replied the Minister. "But you can understand that I am left with many questions that could not possibly be dealt with over the phone. I would need to know exactly where this interest is located, how you would use its resources, and I would have to have some insurance that national security was not at stake. Regardless of the consequences I might face in my present position, I am not a traitor." Muffled laughter could be heard on the other end of the line.

"I am sincerely impressed by your impartial appraisal of the situation, Minister, but now we have come to somewhat of an impasse. You can probably tell that I am calling long distance which means that an immediate conference would be impossible. I must also mention that in matters as delicate as these I do not delegate responsibility to even my most trusted employees. These factors alone limit our options. I need not remind you that you too are under certain restraints, given the need for restoration to be paid in a way that would not prejudice what might already be called strained international relations. If a layperson knows of your debt so quickly, surely the West German government is also curious as to how you will be paying your dues to the people who so graciously offered you entertainment this evening." These remarks, spoken clearly and succinctly, did not lose their intended effect on the Minister. He was cornered and was being offered a way out. But was it truly a way out or a deadly path into something that could not be foreseen?

"Surely you are aware, Mr. Millar, that any decision I made tonight would not be immutable, regardless of your good intentions or the extent of my good fortune at having been offered such a proposal. I am the representative of my government, but only its representative. Except for affairs that deal with allocations of equipment, manpower and financial planning I am only the figurehead of the parliamentary process. I may have limited or even negligible influence where land appropriations are concerned."

"In this you are mistaken, Minister, to the inestimable benefit of both your national image and my plans to acquire fame and fortune. My sources informed me several years ago that the Canadian military was to be auctioning off prime real estate to the highest bidder. The closure of your military radar sites throughout the country may have been a tremendous loss to those who served in their maintenance and functioning for so many years, but was a stroke of unfathomable fortune for my organization when the bidding was publicly announced."

The mention of Canada's radar sites brought vivid memories to the Minister, of public debate and parliamentary standoff. Long before his appointment as Defense Minister, he had seen the difficulty which the government had in deciding to close the majority of the sites. The economic burden imposed on the Canadian people far outweighed any strategic advantage the sites may have once represented. Most of the instrumentation and equipment was so outdated that replacement parts could only be acquired from other countries. In one case "other countries" meant that a certain vacuum tube essential to the functioning of the radars could be purchased only from the Soviet Union.

Problems with the sites were not limited to the irony of replacing or maintaining equipment. Serious debate centred on whether or not the sites even provided sufficient warning of an initial attack given the advancements made in intercontinental missile technology and satellite monitoring systems. It was a case of an instrumental and strategic military investment outgrowing its usefulness. No one would argue that the money could be used elsewhere. Then again, there were constituents to be considered. Salaries and services from the military communities which supported the radar sites contributed greatly to the economic survival of many rural businesses. Closing the stations meant cutting off cash flow. As well, those military personnel who specialized in radar technology or administration would need to be relocated. Not least of all, was the question of what to do with the stations themselves. All necessary equipment to feed, house and entertain the personnel were permanent structures. What does the government do with structures that cost so much to maintain? One of the solutions was to sell to the highest bidder.

"But as we both know, Minister, not all sales were completed. Your government ceded to public pressure, as might be expected, and some of the sites were maintained for minimum security prisons or used to develop native community centres. For me this was a particularly painful and untimely change of events. I offered your government twenty times what any other bid may have offered, but I received no part of these ideal properties."

"What is past is past, Mr. Millar. I should not have wished to be so weighted with the fruits of my leisure at any time, but formerly we may have had something to bargain for, had it been necessary. As you have said, my government would not budge once those lands had been allocated and those decisions made public. I do not see how this changes our ability to barter in the least."

"I would wager, if you'll pardon the expression, Mr. Minister, that you still have considerable influence in this area. In the last two months there are three stations that have been added to the list of those to be closed. It is with some considerable excitement that I discovered one of these last three could also serve my purpose. The disappointing part is that this very same station will soon be occupied by a community of highly motivated native people given a decision made two weeks ago today. I am also aware that there remains a small contingent of military personnel on the station which is helping the new

10

occupants become accustomed to the demands of total self-sufficiency and will be there for at least another six weeks.

"What I require of you is very simple, Mr. Minister," continued the impetuous caller. "I have no illusions of being able to own what has been allocated already. All I want is the freedom to occupy sixteen hundred square feet of useless radar housing to hold my computer and meteorological equipment. There would be no personnel on site except for maintenance and occasional cleaning every three months. I would be willing to give my word that these visits would be arranged as inconspicuously as possible. You, Minister, would be free of debt and embarrassment, and I would be on my way to the recognition and fruits of scientific labour that I deserve."

"I am impressed by your keen interest. The apparent reliability and accuracy of your information also deserves some applause. But how am I to know that you are telling me the truth? As innocent and self-serving as your plan could be, I have never met you and have no reason to trust you other than the fact that I have a debt that needs to be paid."

"As complicated as it could be, it is as simple as that. I have the money you need to be free of debt. You have sixteen hundred square feet of land that is worth more to my research than pure gold. If you are unsure of my motives, you need only check the records. You will find numerous attempts on the part of a J.E. Millar and Company to purchase these very lands legally, and were your aboriginal peoples not so adept at lobbying I would not need your assistance at all. It is a case of us both being in the right place at the right time. You only need say the word. The money could be wired to the casino in less than ten minutes. I challenge you to find a better compromise for your morals and judgment than this, Mr. Minister."

II

Warren Cross had never seen himself as a rancher, even a modest one, but then, twenty years ago, he hadn't foreseen where his military training would lead him or how long it would take for him to understand that there were more things in life than foreign policy, espionage and the CIA. Cross could recall vividly the final brutal act that ended his career as a field agent.

It had begun innocently enough. He was having coffee with one of his buddies from Information when the subject of a recent operation was discussed. News was that Level One had destroyed a touring vehicle at a railway crossing. The goal was successfully accomplished: Three small packages containing eyes-only documents were completely burned. Along with them were seven innocent teenagers.

On hearing the news, Cross totally lost his "perspective" and with it his career as an active field agent. Dissident opinions are one thing, but Cross had gone too far. He threatened to expose the whole operation if responsibility was not claimed by the Agency and some type of restitution offered to the grieving families. The organization thanked him for his concern by shutting his file and threatening to "lose it" if he talked any more about buses and teenagers.

It was a hard decision for management. Cross was one of those field agents who had a predictable and very personal sense of moral duty. On the one hand he could follow instructions without questioning, whether it meant maiming or even terminating the source of "conflict". At the same time he had also earned the reputation of someone who would refuse a task or assignment if he didn't trust the team he was chosen to work with.

In a way the timing for his retirement was good for Cross. He had begun to feel his touch becoming shaky in the last couple of jobs. In Venice, three months before the tour bus incident, a misplaced cipher book had almost cost him his life, and no amount of rationalizing could make him feel comfortable with the way things were headed. He had thought about asking for a few weeks R and R in Tokyo, but the thought of hanging up his passports for good never entered his mind. Within a year he was no longer gainfully employed by the CIA and was pensioned off to raise sheep or cattle or drink his life away if he wished. As long as he minded his own affairs and left his past where it belonged.

Cross had heard what it was like to be out after twenty years with the Agency. Some of his friends didn't make it and either killed themselves or faded into the bottom of a bottle with nothing to keep them sober. Field agents understand that relationships and a home life are the first casualties of peacetime warfare. But no one makes it clear how you're supposed to cope without them once the ride is over. Some just can't adjust.

That was almost three years ago and although there were times when the loneliness became almost unbearable, Cross had etched out a tremulous transition to civilian life by taking an old farm and working sixteen-hour days, twelve months of the year, to keep his mind full and his body moving. He never asked himself questions and he avoided philosophy. Thus far, he was still sane and breathing, and that was an accomplishment.

There were some things he had even become attached to. The people in the surrounding area had an unpretentious and down-to-earth way about them, always ready to lend a hand or offer a piece of advice to a newcomer. They were suspicious too, but Cross's ability to reciprocate a good deed and to mind his own business had earned him a reputation as one who could be trusted. In the wide open plains of Wyoming, nothing meant more.

Today had begun as any other. At 5 A.M. Cross arose to begin the basic chores that kept his eleven head of cattle comfortable and healthy. He checked Bess for any last traces of the hoof rot she'd been limping with for the last week, and started loading the truck for the forty-five minute ride into Chesterville for supplies. He found it hard to admit to himself, but he looked forward to these trips. He'd caught himself enjoying a serious conversation with the chickens in the back pen last Saturday and knew then he had to start socializing more. It was something he didn't want to think about. Socializing usually meant women and women meant only one thing to him. Bridget. And when Bridget came to mind, twelve years dissolved before him: her bleeding head was once again in his hands, a victim of his work. It was an accident, but what difference did that make now that she was gone? Three grams of telflon-coated steel had punctured a small bullet hole between her eyes, a bullet that should have killed him instead. Maybe that was the beginning of the end. But since that time, he had never really looked at a woman, though he had slept with many faceless women and had even been loved by some.

But Cross wasn't destined to make it to Chesterville this morning, so he needn't have worried. Tracy-Jo, his youngest female, decided that nature's timing had every right to insist he stay and witness the one thing that never ceased to amaze him. She was about to give birth to her first calf.

"I don't know what's the matter, Warren, I can't get her to move." Gary Fletcher, Cross's closest neighbour and a steadfast support in the first years of his new life, spoke from the barn floor where he knelt beside Tracy-Jo, his hand on her swollen belly. "I've run my hand all over that young calf from the nose to the tail and I know she's not breached." Tracy-Jo wailed and strained, but all that could be seen of the new calf was the front hoofs. The mother-to-be had been struggling for nearly an hour and in the time it took Fletcher to speed over in his '67 Ford from his farm twelve miles away, there had still been no progress. Cross was worried.

"I'd like to say you're right, Gary, but what the hell else can it be? I'm no vet but she's been pushing like that since before I called you and nothing's changed. You don't suppose she's holding twins?" His neighbour looked up and smiled warmly. Cross sounded every bit as serious as if he were discussing the birth of his own children.

14

"No sir. I've felt the insides of a lot of young cows, and this lady's carrying just the one." Tracy-Jo grunted and shook her head. She looked at Cross as if to ask him to get a move on. "I have an idea what it could be, but if I'm right you're gonna have a handful till noon. She might've been bred to too big a bull. She's young and healthy but she's small. If that's true, that calf won't move at all unless we help her. Her mom'll die tryin' but she'll not have it on her own."

"What do we do?"

"Get the block and tackle from the tool box on my truck. I'll try and get her to stand. We'll see if we can help ease the little fella out of her when she contracts."

For the next hour and a half Cross and his companion worked rigging the block and tackle to the beams of the low ceiling and firmly but gently pulling on the front legs of the calf. Twice the momma tried to lie down and twice Fletcher kicked her back to standing. It was hard for Cross to see her being bruised in this way, but he understood she had to stay up if she was going to have this calf and live to bear another. He wondered, as he watched Fletcher move quietly and confidently, if he would ever seem this comfortable in his new life; if the belly of his cow would ever feel as secure as the handle of a gun.

To Cross the ordeal seemed like a lifetime, but shortly before lunch the calf began to move. With him and Fletcher pulling firmly on the rope and pulleys and Tracy-Jo breaking his heart with her effort, a new life was led onto the straw-covered floor of his barn. Cross couldn't remember the last time life had impressed him that way.

Cross invited Gary in for a cup of coffee after they'd seen to the comfort of the newborn and its mother. He wasn't much of a cook, but after a little practice Cross had learned to turn out edible biscuits. With these and some homemade strawberry jam purchased at the market the week before, Cross served his friend a noonday snack.

"So what are you gonna call the little fart?" Gary asked his much relieved and hardworking associate. "I'd be hard-pressed to find a name that would suit the pressure he put on his dear ole dad. How about *Seizure* or *Panic* maybe?"

Cross was not embarrassed by Gary's remarks. He knew that running the farm was a completely new lifestyle for him, and he

15

had grown accustomed to the teasing and ribbing that accompanied his acceptance as a newcomer.

"I wouldn't be so quick to poke and ridicule," answered Cross, shaking his head. "If I was Tracy-Jo I'd have long since lost faith in your examination and begun to think you had your hand up my behind for other reasons."

Gary's response was lost on Cross. In the instant it takes to recognize the familiar, the dreaded, Cross had forgotten Tracy-Jo, her new-born calf, his biscuits and his lifestyle. Cross had seen the flash through the kitchen window of a government vehicle turning onto his property, and its meticulous and plodding approach toward the farmhouse left him feeling sick to the stomach, his mind racing to find an explanation.

He had talked with Gary a few times over drinks about his past: never detailed, and never compromising his need to stay as far from his memories as possible, but enough for Gary to know there was a hole in his friend's life, a part of Warren Cross that was radically different from the plains of Wyoming and the dust of the barnyard.

Gary could remember the first time he saw a glimpse of the past, and he knew enough not to ask anything more about it. Cross and he had gone for drinks after harvesting grain and a local had tried to pick a fight with Cross over some trumped-up insult. Cross asked the gentleman to back off and finally warned him to drop the issue. What had happened next still buzzed the bar when they entered for an evening brew. Without warning, Cross reached behind to where his challenger stood scowling and grabbed him by the wrist. Pulling him forcefully into the edge of the bar with both hands, he drove his knee into the man's groin and slammed his face on a bar stool. Gary watched as the limp form slumped to the floor and blood oozed around the man's crushed nose and rapidly swelling eyes. Cross shook his hands of the blood that had splashed upward from the stool and asked the bartender for a rag. Then he apologized to Gary and finished off his beer without a word.

Gary had never asked him what he had seen or lived that let him act that way, but he saw the look. And when he glanced up from his laughter at the kitchen table to see Cross staring out the window, he saw it again. Long explanations weren't necessary

"I've got some visitors," said Cross in a low tone, still watching the car move toward the house. "I'll probably be busy here for a while. Why don't you have a beer for me at Carl's? I'll bring your tackle over as soon as I can. Thanks for your help, Gary."

It was eerie to see the concentration on his face. Gary had the distinct feeling that Cross was talking but that his mind was totally elsewhere—as if he had become a machine with two separate tasks to perform: the simpler one handled with courtesy and coolness, the second occupying the focus and energy of a piercing intellect, muscles taut, breathing even.

Fletcher did not ask any question or make small talk. He said he understood and walked to the truck. As the old Ford whined into life, he pushed it into first and rolled down the window.

"Call if you need a hand." Cross nodded a common understanding without taking his eyes from the car which had now stopped near the fence opposite the porch. Fletcher bounced unhurriedly over the dusty driveway toward the highway.

Through the settling dust Cross could see that his first impression was not incorrect. The three men in the car were in no hurry. They paused until the truck crawled onto the highway before opening the doors and walking toward the fence where Cross had straddled a post. Patterns. People are creatures of habit, Cross had learned. Study them. Learn their patterns. Two young men; the weight, the safety net. A third, older, experienced: the courier. Cross had seen the pattern and played it out countless times. He was not mistaken. When they had come to within ten feet of the fence, the lead man signaled his escorts to standby. Slipping his hands into his coat pockets and shifting his hat, he sauntered over to the fence and leaned lazily on the railing next to Cross. He played with a stalk of straw between his teeth and turned to face the fields opposite the fence.

"Beautiful place you got here, Colonel," began the courier. "Some land, some beef. A real nice way to slip away and be forgotten."

"Speak your piece."

"I guess you could say I've been told to offer you a proposition."

"Not interested."

17

"I'm not surprised," answered the courier, shrugging his shoulders. "But let me finish. If you don't they'll just send somebody else and then another. The quicker I'm off your land, the quicker you'll know what's expected of you.

"You're a closed file, Cross," he continued. "That means nobody wants you or even wants you to be remembered unless there's a damn good reason for stirring up shit. The word is you're needed. Simple as that. Some high-ranking general in the Pentagon asked for you by name. Said he used you in a search and find in '81 and won't take no for an answer."

"And you told the general to go fuck himself."

"Not exactly. You know how the management feels about pissing off the State Department when it's not necessary, but they made it clear you were *retired*. The general pressed his point and he was told of the circumstances of your retirement. He still insisted. So here I am, on a free weekend, choking on the dust of this bald-ass prairie to recruit a man who I just knew would not be interested." The courier glanced at Cross and for a moment Cross thought he saw a mild sympathy. Perhaps this one was close to his own retirement. Or maybe the news got worse. Maybe both. "You're some kind of field messiah as far as this general is concerned." continued the courier. "And I for one have learned not to fuck with the religions of the rich and famous."

"Get to the point."

"Well, it's like this. Seems that there has been a little shipping problem with the latest consignment of intermediate-range missiles and one was—er...diverted en route. Temporarily, of course. At least that's what the State Department wants pretty badly to believe. It's bad enough that they've lost one but the cruncher is that these missiles were headed for West Germany, and boy, I don't need to tell you what that means."

To Cross, it was clear. For a number of years the United States and the U.S.S.R. had been honouring a treaty signed in 1987 that banned intermediate-range missiles in Europe. Political tensions had escalated due to some serious misunderstandings during the past six months, and the Chiefs of Staff must have decided to send an emergency shipment of the missiles to Germany in case the Russians invaded the West German border.

Such a scenario would have seemed unimaginable as recently as 1990, but the mediteranean conflict of 1991 shocked the world into a state of anxiety many had believed would never again be necessary. The political optimists of the late 1980's were horrified. The proponents of continued vigilance and nuclear deterrence on both continents were quickly promoted.

Now, should the Soviets learn that the U.S. had begun shipping missiles to Germany contrary to the '87 treaty, the resulting political damage could mean full scale mobilization. Possibly war.

"Don't get ahead of me, farmer," said the courier, noticing the wheels turning in Cross's mind by the expression on his face. "It gets worse. The person or persons responsible for this particular diversion of military hardware have contacted the Pentagon and demanded they release the arming code for the missile. If they do not receive it within fourteen days, they have pledged to divulge the location and previously planned destination of the missile to the Soviets. Result? You guessed it. War. And probably not the Saturday-night-at-the-movies version. The Reds are angry, the American public is angry and everybody's looking for an excuse to pounce. Wouldn't take much these days."

"And so your general wants me to find your toy and the universe will continue to unfold as it should. Makes no sense to me, and as a footnote to your whole message, I wouldn't give a shit if it did. You've wasted the taxpayer's valuable money and the Pentagon's budget of time. Go hunt someplace else."

"Even before you hear the end of the story? You must be getting rusty, Cross, sitting out here under the deep blue sky with nothing but wind and horseshit for company. I wouldn't have even told you this much unless the whole goddam organization wasn't sure you'd follow up. I'll make it clear. Your old man is dying. He's in the Harris Methodist Hospital in Fort Worth and is diagnosed as terminal. Some type of cancer. Level One says they've got a serum being worked on that's pulled from the immune cells of chimpanzees and that they can probably cure your dad. It'll cost the Department about seven million dollars and they've been told that if the general gets his messiah, your dad will be started on it right away."

19

Cross was now fully attentive. Somewhere in his chest he could feel an emotion, a mixture of emotions boiling, ready to explode in tears, in blood, in screams that said 'No Dad, not yet!' and 'To hell with him!' in the same instant. He did not, could not reveal the depth this messenger had reached until he knew more.

"God help you and anybody else involved if what you're saying is not true."

The veteran courier felt the cold steel of a determined and trained killer staring at him. He shuddered involuntarily. "I'm not stupid, Cross. I know how cold the field can be and I wouldn't snow you about family. For some of us it's all we've got. I've been told you and your dad haven't spoken in quite some time. But if you want to check it out, you can call the hospital and speak to him. Even fly to Fort Worth if that's what it takes. But it's true—the missile for your dad."

Cross jumped from the post and walked directly to the house. It must be true, he thought to himself. Dad would never cooperate with them even if he knew what was at stake. He's hated me and the U.S. government for stealing his football star from university scholarships and him and Momma from their dream of grandchildren. It never was good. But six years ago it was finished. They'd had the biggest fight he could remember since Momma died and they hadn't spoken since. And now he's dying. It must be true.

The phone call confirmed it. His dad was weak, but the voice was unmistakably his father's. He talked about a possible treatment that might be started on Monday. He would be moved to a special hospital and stay there for at least a month. Could Warren forgive an old man his arrogance? Could he see his son soon? Sure, Dad. I have to do some things for the government in order to help pay for those special drugs the doctors talked about. It'll take a few weeks. Sure, Dad. I love you too....

It was true.

Cross stood at the doorway to his living room, one hand still on the receiver. He stared at the phone on the wall. His eyes followed the coiling wire from the mounted dialing box to the black piece of plastic in his hand. A sharp staccato of beeps erupted from the ear piece. It was then that he recognized he hadn't yet hung up. He lifted the receiver and placed it carefully in its place. The beeping stopped abruptly. The house was quiet.

But Cross could hear sounds from the past. Far away. A piano hammered out an old favourite as his mom stumbled through in her broken soprano, his father sitting next to her and clapping his hands. When was that...last Thanksgiving? Or was that the time Mom's rink won the regional curling championships? There were an awful lot of people at that party. Hell of a celebration, Cross thought. Everybody together. Everybody getting along.

Not knowing how he got there, Cross found himself seated at the kitchen table next to Gary's unfinished biscuits. He glanced out the window. The courier was still leaning on the fence. A courier? *"Your father is dying..."* Cross looked down. His fingers moved lightly over a brown-coloured photo album. He opened it. The following was written in his father's fine script:

Remember us, Warren. Wherever you go, whatever you do, there's always family and there's always memories.

Love, Mom & Dad

Slowly, painfully, Cross flipped through the pages of the huge album. He hadn't gone through his pictures in over ten years. When his mother died it was too disturbing to be reminded of happier days. After the fight with his father it made less sense than ever to think about the past, to believe that memories of his family could mean anything. But now Cross needed to know something. He wasn't sure what that was, but he knew he would find it in his album, if it could be found.

Cross forced himself to look, to recognize, to feel. Waves of nostalgia swept over him. There was the first bass he had landed on his own. No bigger than a small perch, but his dad had insisted they mount it anyway. And this? Christ, Cross thought, a smile creeping to his face. Anne Hewett, his first date. She had the face of a camel but was game as hell. He learned a lot that night. And here, my sixteenth birthday. Cross looked closely. His father was proud. His smile was warm and genuine. It was a look Cross had forgotten. An expression of paternal affection for his only son.

21

Twenty minutes passed. Cross reached the last page and when he looked at it, tears came from a place that he had run from throughout his adult life. It was a family portrait.

The picture reminded him that there were deep scars of love in him...places in him that had made caring relationships a liability and a danger to his profession, and now in retirement, a threat to his sanity. The picture before him brought those dangerous emotions into clear focus, and Cross was tempted to run again. He didn't. He knew there would be nothing left to hide behind if he tried. He didn't give a shit about who or what was dipping into the government's missile stockpile, but he knew one thing. As long as there was a chance that he could keep his dad alive he'd do whatever was necessary to find the goddamn thing. And maybe, when it was over, there would still be a chance for them to really work things out...

When he opened the screen door of the porch and stepped down to the hard clay, Cross noticed for the first time how that door creaked. He thought to himself he would have to put some oil on those hinges. Maybe buy new ones. He was feeling the weight. The weight he hadn't felt for almost four years. The goddamn weight.

"You've got yourself a field man," Cross said to the courier with a flat voice and eyes that hid the turmoil deep within. "But tell your supervisor it will be on my terms. I'll call him from my hotel tomorrow afternoon in Washington. I don't know how the codes have changed but tell him I'll be using the GD-4 linkup. If he can't find it in his files, find it for him."

The government vehicle made a slow and awkward U-turn in the driveway and headed back along its trail like a big and clumsy elephant throwing dust at every pothole and rock it encountered. Cross watched it speed south along the highway and remained staring into the distance for a long moment. He was reminded of the present by the bawling of Tracy-Jo and her calf in the barn, complaining about the room service. Tracy-Jo and Gary Fletcher. That's the kind of people I can deal with. Down to earth. But these slippery government bastards...

There would be a lot of preparing to do before his plane left the next day and Cross knew from experience that putting it off didn't make plans run any smoother. Once the decision is made

22

to go or to do, emotions don't really count. You go. You do.

He decided on the spur of the moment that talking to Gary would help take one worry off his mind. He realized just how much he had grown to trust the man, and knew without a doubt that his cattle and his farm would be in good hands until he returned. He spent some time soothing Tracy-Jo and complimenting her once again on the newborn she had just given to the world. A kind of sadness came over him then as he remembered how much destruction and cruelty the world has ready for the innocent. On impulse, Cross turned toward the back of the barn as he was leaving, for a last talk with the chickens.

III

"That's your version, Corporal Girard. Given the occasion I feel as tolerant of you as I might of a young school boy strutting his first home run on the school baseball diamond. But anyone sincerely interested in knowing how this station maintained its sanity during the setup of the golf course in '85 will hear the Senior's side of the story. Harken if you have ears!"

The servicemen and women seated at the table where Master Warrant Officer Smith stood to make his final remarks, burst into laughter. The lower ranks took the opportunity to vent some frustrations in the more relaxed atmosphere of this closing Mess Dinner by throwing napkins and grapes at their beloved and well-respected Station Warrant Officer. MWO Smith received their applause and their heckling with the benevolence of a true patron. Unspoken affections and the deep-rooted bond of a close-knit military community were clearly evident. Tensions and biases had slipped away in past weeks as station personnel prepared for the final closure of Canadian Forces Station Miniwagin. For all their differences, it was as if everyone somehow understood they were seeing the end of an era.

For some, those who had managed one way or another to extend their postings over many years, it would mean the end of a lifestyle whose loss would be grieved for the remainder of their careers. For others, the young people with no desire to spend the weeks at a time isolated from the distractions of urban nightlife, the closures across the country would be a relief. One thing was certain. The government's decision to fold had a profound effect on all 237 members and their families in CFS Miniwagin. Some would be transferred to new trades after ten or twenty years as Radar Technicians. Others would be encouraged to retire early. All of them would have their own personal goodbye to say. Tonight they said goodbye to each other.

"As you may recall," began MWO Smith, "the idea was conceived, as are all and any ideas of merit, at the bar in the Senior NCO's Mess. Sergeant Collins boasted that he had scored an eagle twice in one day and Warrant Officer Gingras bet him one hundred dollars that if there was a golf course within a day's drive from the Station, he could beat him two games out of three. Needless to say, maps were speedily collected from various dusty glove compartments on the Station and sides were chosen with bets laid on both champions by nearly all members.

"Just when a course had finally been agreed upon, Sergeant Peters flippantly suggested that we could build our own golf course with the money we had put on these two characters. Someone else said Why not? and we finally agreed: To hell with the competition, let's bulldoze some of Her Majesty's vacant woodland and haul in some sand. What you see before you, ladies and gentlemen, is the end product of creative engineering genius and thorough delegation. Your NCO leaders have every right to take full credit for its completion and only confide upon the lower ranks some token acknowledgement due to their participation in its construction."

"Participation! More like bloody slave-driven hard labour!" retorted a private from a dark corner of the room. His friends cheered his spontaneous response to MWO Smith's point of view. The laughter and stories were to continue for many hours.

Alcohol flowed freely. After a few drinks, as men and women are apt to do when given license to share more of themselves, tears too were added to the agenda. There was the story of young Normand Pelletier, a local nine-year-old who was lost in the woods near the Station in 1982, and of the four-day search that discovered him, badly shaken but still living, eleven miles north in the deep bushland outside the Station perimeter. Tragedies were remembered. An automobile accident in 1978 had claimed the lives of two servicemen and three children on their way to a hockey tournament. Station personnel were like family, and even those recently posted could sympathize with the surviving families and friends.

Working eight or twelve hour shifts with the very same people day after day was difficult enough. These people were also the same ones who played baseball, ran the stamp collectors' meetings and organized field trips for the Boy Scouts. Needless to say, living on a military radar station tended to polarize the station community such that you either liked or disliked someone. There could be no luxury of indifference. Those who couldn't handle the lack of personal space didn't stay long. Over the years those who remained were there because they loved it.

All this was to change radically in a few days. Deciding to take a stroll around the Station, MWO Smith had donned his fall jacket. In spite of his years of experience and the control he commanded over the lives of his subordinates, he was a man who needed time alone, time to think and reflect.

The Mess Dinner had been enjoyable. Heart-rending and nostalgic in some parts, but pleasant. He had ordered the other NCO's to turn their heads if they saw anyone pulling plaques from the walls or slipping an ashtray into their pockets. Everybody coped the best way possible, and he knew that for some, it would be difficult to leave without taking some small token with them.

The officers had their say and their explanations. A good enough bunch this time around, he decided. Stayed out of the way when there was real work to be done and a few even had the guts to take the heat if it was necessary. That type he could do something with. But the young ones he never did get used to. There was the odd lieutenant who knew he was here to learn and aligned himself with the NCO's as soon as possible. The others were a pain in the neck at best and downright dangerous if they got out of hand. Four years of academics, parades and weekend warfare and they arrived with the idea they were in charge. He had found a simple solution. Let them be in charge until the roof caved in and bruised them up a bit. Then clean them off, cover them with a blanket, sit them down and tell them to stay out of trouble until they learned enough about their people and their place in the organization to be of some help to somebody other than themselves.

It was a cool night for September. He pulled the collar of his jacket up around his neck and tugged at his cap, tightening its

26

soft grip on his graying military haircut. He didn't really notice the cold all that much. His actions were a reaction more than anything. He was already elsewhere in his mind.

Smith was back at the drawing board, trying to convince the Canadian Government as he had a thousand times before, that the closure of this particular station, his station, must be a mistake. Years had passed since the other stations had been closed. The strategic importance of its location and the need to train qualified technicians in an operational setting should far outweigh any political pressure from the public that it cost too much or could be used for other purposes. But these efforts to block the closure never went anywhere. His ruminations had become a running nightmare, but he couldn't help himself. At the time when the majority of his colleagues from the Regiment was begging to be relocated from the stations back to the field, MWO Smith had volunteered and re-volunteered to maintain his status and his responsibilities. The administration often had a difficult time understanding why but it didn't hurt his career any. And if they knew half the truth, Smith probably would have taken a demotion if he had to, in order to remain in Miniwagin. Where else can a man raise a military family this close to hunting and fishing and weekend camping?

There was the job itself as well. One thing that stood out as more important than anything else to him was that he believed in the role he had so diligently supported and helped develop over the years. Even if the Russians never flew over the Pole once during the entire year, Smith felt he had the responsibility of making his people believe they *could* and that meant being prepared to give the country enough time to plan and execute retaliatory measures and organize a defense.

It was an attitude, he would tell them. Attitude is everything. If you think you've made the military a career so you can smile at forty-six with your twenty-year pension and say to hell with the nation that has hired me and fed me, then you're not cut out for this outfit and I'll do my damndest to see you don't make it past corporal. Attitude. When you sit at that console staring into the north for six or eight hours, you bloody well stare and know what you're looking for. And if I find out that some Russian Husky has nuked my favorite fishing hole without enough warning for me to move my boat shed, I'll be ver-r-r-y irate! And so they learned attitude. Although he was a hard man to work for at times, his mixture of toughness and good humour had won him the admiration of young people and officers throughout the forces. Yes, at least these things I did to the best of my ability, Smith thought as he rounded the POL fueling point, absently scuffing at the gravel on the side of the road. At least I did the best I could.

People sometimes wonder if a leader lives what he teaches; if the Captain who screams "over the hill" would truly be prepared to do the same if the time came. Anyone who held questions of this kind for MWO Smith should have been on that road beside him. Attitude, he'd tell them. It was all attitude.

Just as Smith rounded the point, he heard the grind of a truck changing gears. From the distance it seemed like maybe someone was stuck. But 3:10 in the morning? Don't tell me Private Johnson has stolen the five-ton for a joyride again, has he? Smith decided to slip off the road and wait. There are fun times and there are limits. This is still a military installation, and God help him if he's behind the wheel after drinking like a fish all night.

From the shadow of the POL tanks Smith could see what was making the noise. It wasn't Private Johnson or a military five-ton transport. Moving slowly toward the graveled road incline that led to the recently abandoned radar dome sites were two civilian transport trucks. Smith realized with concern that they must have come through the entrance to the logging road because no civilian vehicles were permitted on the station after hours without his direct approval or that of the Station Commander. The station CO was in Ottawa this week finalizing transfer details so no trucks would be, should be moving anywhere near this area without his knowledge. That meant illegal entry. Illegal entry meant there was something somebody wanted on the hill.

Smith figured he could do one of two things: Make his way carefully back to the station's central grounds and round up some personnel to confiscate the vehicles, under force if necessary, or follow them up the road and find out more about why they're here, before alarming anyone. Had ninety-nine percent of the station not drunk their way to oblivion, Smith probably would have chosen the first. But he also had a personal stake in handling this affair. Until the CO's return the following week, any intrusion was his direct responsibility. Knowing the present government, politicians could be looking for souvenirs of their own without even telling him to expect a visit. Best to keep it under my hat until I know the scoop, he decided.

It was to be the most disastrous decision of his distinguished career.

There were only two buildings on the hill. The radar dome itself, and the small shed beside it where tools were stored. By this time the lead truck had already parked around behind the huge dome whose red and white checkered colours could barely be seen against the clear night sky. Its sister was slowly following to a place where the back end protruded from behind the maintenance hut. Smith kept low and followed the perimeter fence, staying slightly out of earshot. It was frustrating, being unable to hear the conversations but one thing was clear. Whoever was dropping in so unexpectedly must have known exactly what to look for.

Four men jumped down from the trucks and moved to the rear doors which were unbolted and swung open. Smith noticed what happened next with increasing alarm. As three of his companions hoisted themselves from the delivery platforms and into the trucks, one man walked straight to the dome door and proceeded to remove the seal that had hardened only two days ago. With a crowbar he completed his task, and pulling a flashlight from his belt, entered the man-made cave with a knapsack over his left shoulder.

Smith couldn't put his finger on it but he sensed that what he saw was more than just illegal. It seemed planned with uncanny precision. Military precision. The hair on his neck stood up. Having no more than his pen knife in his belt he realized he had make a mistake. What now? Should he turn back and risk being discovered only to return after damage was already done? No choice. He had hung himself out on a limb and he had to at least find out more information before they left. Make the best of a bad situation. He realized too, with a strange kind of embarrassment, that his knees and back were getting sore from trying to move in a crouched position for so long. Forty-eight years old. The goddamn irony of it all, he thought: Never a missile sighted in almost thirty years of service and on the night we're closing up shop we've got a military threat on our hands and a crippled old man for the possible defense of the country. Shit.

The four on the hill were well-suited to their task. With dexterous movements and few words spoken, they began moving equipment of various sizes and shapes from the trucks into the radar dome. The first man to enter had not come out in some time. His cohorts had begun to place instruments of various sizes and shapes throughout the area immediately surrounding the dome.

By the time Smith had succeeded in scrambling along the fence to a position east of the parked vehicles and within hearing distance of the men, another twenty minutes had passed. It seemed they were nearing completion. Smith was sweating now. For all his concern a part of him actually hoped they were stirring up trouble. He'd love to get his hands on something that could bear the brunt of his frustrations around the closure of the Station. If someone thought there was something so important on the hill, maybe the Station might even be reopened. Just the passing thought of such a possibility made him determined to find something to hook his teeth into before the trucks moved away.

"Is there something here that interests you?" The man standing behind Smith startled him so badly he lost his balance. Focusing more clearly on the heavy-set man who had surprised him, he remarked with increasing alarm and a tightness in his throat, that a gun was pointed at him. Evelyn...The kids...

"Don't worry, old man. I won't wash you until you've had a chance to get your questions answered. A funny thing about technicians. We all love to have people admire our work. Up the hill. And don't try to bolt. I'll get real nervous and have to end our discussion with a lack of ceremony."

He looks like a fucking wrestler and talks like one, Smith thought to himself. Be damned how he snuck around behind me carrying that kind of weight. The big man answered his gaze as they moved toward the dome. "They should have trained you never to jump to conclusions. If you're close enough to see, you're close enough to be seen. And when you've done enough assignments, even carrying a little extra muscle won't get in the way.''

They reached the largest of the two trucks, just as another technician was leaving the dome. "So Demetrius," he said, startled to see his cohort leading someone at gunpoint. "What have we here? Let me guess. This is Canada's first line of defense against the relentless and insidious Russian Bear who will stop at nothing to eliminate the capitalist cancer from the world. What a pity our organization did not have the necessary technology to pack such an honourable task into such a compact form. Does it speak?''

"Yes, I speak," answered Smith defiantly. "Jokes do not become the simple-minded. I find it usually serves only to heighten the glare of their ignorance.''

"And it speaks with courage! Well, the least one could do is to offer you an explanation for your troubles. I would love to be able to leave you with the illusion that the long-distance enemy has finally attacked, but we are not Soviet. Neither are we interested in the petty struggles that occupy the time and financial energy of most of the world's terrified population. My colleagues and I have the good fortune of belonging to a sector of society that is trying to do something about the abysmal state of the world. The world has become one great library with nations playing hide-and-seek with each other behind endless volumes of useless philosophy. Thank the gods that history repeats itself. We may yet improve on the past. Your house on the hill will help us.''

"You sound like you've just come from a fascist revival, young man. I feel sorry for you.''

"And I, you. I won't confuse what you believe about the destiny of mankind by boring you with rhetoric. But come and watch. You may learn something. Our evening's work is sure to impress you at any rate. Paulus? Bring the transmitter and set the dish on that iron ring at the door to the dome. Good. Switch it on.''

As instructed, the younger man removed what appeared to be a miniature satellite dish from an aluminum carrying case. It was constructed of a dark screen material and was about twenty inches in diameter. Placing it on the iron pedestal near the door

31

to the radar dome he' touched a button near the base. A soft humming sound could be heard.

"And now, your private demonstration." At a keyboard the apparent leader of the expedition tapped a numbered sequence and paused. He keyed in another sequence and removed a small square disk from his glove, about the size of a postage stamp. This he placed into a slot at the top of the keyboard. One more key was pressed.

"What you have just seen is a communication link with our headquarters. In the time it takes you to say your name, four billion pieces of information about the atmosphere, the land and the electromagnetic field of the Northern Hemisphere will be transmitted halfway around the world. It is only proper that you be aware that your station will soon become an integral link in the chain of knowledge that will return discipline and sanity to the affairs of men."

"The affairs of men deserve to be handled by the men and women they affect. I have no idea what your dish does for you, but it gives me the impression that somebody somewhere has decided he knows best what should happen to the world. The last person who thought that ended up committing suicide after killing millions of people. Just for the record, you're trespassing on Crown Land under the protection of the Canadian Department of National Defense. I also think you and your headquarters are full of shit."

Almost three full days passed before someone on the search team thought to look around the docks. Pandemonium had broken out around seven-thirty when his wife Evelyn called the Station Duty NCO to report that her husband had not returned from the Mess. The whole station participated in combing the area surrounding the Station for three miles in every direction. No sign of Smith was discovered.

On the afternoon of the fourth day his jacket was found in the reeds about a quarter of a mile west of the boat house where he had spent so many pleasant hours with his family and friends. His body was brought to the surface the next morning and no one could understand how such a tragedy could have happened. The Station CO was immediately recalled from his duties in Ottawa, and after the funeral, promised an inquiry into the night of the accident. The only information gained was that someone had heard Private Johnson fooling around in the five-ton again up on the hill. Private Johnson said he honestly couldn't remember if he had or not. He said he was too drunk to remember anything at all....

IV

Washington. 8:43 A.M.

There could be more fulfilling positions for a twenty-two year veteran of overseas field work, but George Dion chose not to complain. Seven more months of this courier bullshit and he would be heading for a villa on the coast of Spain. The debriefing was always the worst part. Barry Wallace was the most abrasive Level Two office chief he had ever had the misfortune to deal with. He would want to know every single detail about Warren Cross and their brief conversation. Dion often wondered if Wallace harboured some deep-rooted fetish around insignificant items. Maybe he kept a shoe box of his favourite notes close to his bedside and stroked himself to sleep with a fistful of yellow message slips jammed up against his nose? Yeah, that's it, he likes the *smell* of bureaucracy. Dion smiled. Wallace is an asshole.

"Mr. Wallace will see you now." Wallace's secretary interrupted Dion's thoughts. Dion checked his watch. 8:45. Right on the nose. What an asshole.

"Have a seat, Dion. I'll be with you in a second." Turning his attention to the telephone, Wallace dialed a number and paused, tapping a pencil on his desk as he waited for an answer. "Marty? Yeah, it's Barry. I know. You've been busy and it's been a long summer. Well, to hell with the summer and your list of somatic aches and pains. I told you four days ago that Cross was top priority. Since then I haven't seen a single sheet. What do you want me to do, make your day? I want a printout by noon or you'll be sorting paper clips with Bugs again, and not because he needs the help. Do you understand?... No. Just single copies." Wallace rarely said goodbye. Message passed. Receiver fell like an auctioneer's gavel. End of conversation.

Wallace looked up from behind his desk, momentarily interrupting his shuffle of papers to inspect his courier. That's what it felt like, thought Dion, a fucking inspection. He takes just long enough to let you know he's seen the ketchup stain on your cuff. A man spends three minutes in this guy's office and he's convinced he's got shit for brains and will never amount to anything. I feel sorry for the young guys. Every working man's resurrected nightmare of a demanding and inflexible drill sergeant. How the hell he ever made it to Level Two is a bureaucratic miracle.

"What are you waiting for, Dion, a written invitation? What have you got?"

Heartburn and a pain in the ass for breakfast, thought Dion. "Not a hell of a lot, Mr. Wallace." Dion opened his briefcase and pulled out his six-page report. "Geographical specs, clothing, verbatim conversation are all here. What else did you want to know?"

"Information would be helpful. How did he react? Did he buy that bit about his old man? How did he check it out?"

"I think I mentioned on the phone, sir, that he agreed to take on the assignment."

"I know that. For all I know he could have said that just to get you off his property. How can you be sure?"

Dion recalled the shiver he had experienced when Cross had warned him he had better not be lying. "I'm sure," replied the veteran field agent simply. Dion met Wallace's gaze evenly. The message was clear: Bellow all you want, but don't tell me I don't know my job. Wallace heard him.

"Was there anyone else with him when you arrived?"

"One man. Late thirties, early forties. Name is Gary Fletcher. He's clean. Looks like they've done some farming and drinking together. He never hung around to ask any questions, and didn't seemed alarmed or in any hurry to leave when we showed up."

"Find out where he's from anyway. There's something about Cross that unnerves me. I wouldn't be surprised how far he'd go to fuck up this assignment given his past history for digging into things that are none of his business. I'm up to my ass in red tags from the Secretary of State and Secretary of Defense to find a missile that should be in the ground facing Moscow by now and the only man they'll hire to find it is the last man I'd have chosen. Fuck. Just like the goddamn Morrell Inquiry of '82. All the fucking responsibility and no control whatsoever." This man is more than halfway to an early grave, mused Dion. I wonder what makes him get out of bed in the morning? It must be at least twice as miserable for him to be living with himself as it is for me to be sitting in the same room with him.

"Yes, sir, I'll get right on it."

"And another thing. I want his room wired. Use some imagination and put it where it might take him more than fifteen minutes to find it."

***

"Please extinguish all smoking materials and place your seats and lunch trays in the upright position. We will be landing in Washington in fifteen minutes." Cross opened his eyes and glanced up the aisle. Nice legs, he thought. A hammered-on smile eight hours a day, kids puking all over your shoes, living out of a suitcase for weeks at a time. With that kind of stamina and those legs, that's a lady I could call in sick for.

Call in sick. That's an expression for normal working people, Cross reflected, turning his head toward the window as the pilots began their descent and the motors adjusting the flaps began to whir under the wings. It's been so long I'd pretty well forgotten I was anything but normal.

There was no emotion of recognition for Cross as he stood in line to receive his suitcase from the conveyor belts. He'd seen this airport and just about every other major airport in the world maybe twenty times during his years with the CIA. The only one that meant anything to him was Chicago O'Hare. That's where life had begun to mean something for a while. That's where he had met Bridget. Even now, even today, the memory was so clear....

"Pardon me, sir, but do you know where I could get a refund for a cancelled flight? I'm afraid this is my first time in Chicago and I've had a hard time just finding the ladies' washroom." Cross had looked up from his magazine with a mixture of impatience and anger. He was in the middle of an investigation that had taken him across the ocean twice in two weeks and had little energy for himself, let alone for a curious stranger. "Sorry," the young brunette had continued, "you look even

36

more tired than I am. But could you please point me to the nearest Information desk at least? I'm lost." Cross could not remember the last time he had seen a woman who impressed him on first sight as this one had. She had the kind of smile that communicated a remarkable lack of self-consciousness or pretension. He was even more intrigued when she opened her coat to pull out her ticket. "See? Eleven-forty. It's eleven-thirty and they announce that it's cancelled. I've travelled almost four hours to take a cancelled flight. What a pain! Now what do I do? I've no relatives in Chicago and no money for a taxi to the train station. So I've got to turn in my ticket for a refund and start the whole thing again next week some time. That's why I've bothered your reading, sir, if you could simply point the way." She smiled again and Cross stood up. She had power, this lady. And I'll be damned if she's not completely unaware of how potent that smile of hers can be. Cross took a look at the ticket and shrugged his shoulders.

"It's my first time to Chicago too," he lied. "I guess I'm just lucky enough to have a flight that's leaving as scheduled. I feel bad for you. Why don't we take a greenhorn's tour of this complex together and see if we can get your money back?" Cross had a winning smile of his own when the situation warranted it.

"What about your magazine?" Right, thought Cross. What about that thrilling magazine that's occupying my otherwise exhausted mind?

"To tell you the truth," he lied again, "I was beginning to tire of 'Dear Abby meets the President.' I'd love to go for a walk if you'd like some company." He smiled. She smiled back, only this time a little differently. A little longer than the first time, maybe?

"Thanks. If we get lost together remember, it was your idea." The thought of getting lost with a woman who seemed as fresh and genuine as this one was more than mildly distracting.

They walked and talked along the way. They ended up in a bar, staying for nearly three hours before Cross realized he had missed his flight. By that time it was also clear that Information could wait. He called in "delayed" for the first time in his career, and they stayed in Chicago for four days before saying goodbye at O'Hare the following week.

Cross remembered how there hadn't been sex right away. He was more surprised at his own desire to wait than the fact that Bridget had made it clear that she needed to take her time when she first met a man she liked. In fact they had never become intimate that way until the third meeting four months after that bright Friday morning. It was the most beautifully passionate and fulfilling experience Cross could ever remember. It was then that he became really afraid. Afraid because he knew what this kind of relationship did to a field agent and because he was deeply aware of what life had been like without it. He had even come to the realization after a year and a half that he soon had to make a decision one way or another. He had fallen in love with Bridget and espionage could provide no life for either of them, together or apart.

These days, airports and baggage and flight schedules only depressed him. Every time he stopped to pick up a magazine before a flight, he felt a profound sense of loss. The pain had lessened over time, but the memory of that joy-filled Friday in the empty life of young Warren Cross continued to remind him of his loneliness.

Cross often felt surprised, in a kind of distant way, that he had reacted the way he did to Bridget's tragic death. Most men might have left the service and mourned their loss in the civilian mainstream. But Cross had turned his grief into vengeance, becoming tireless in his duties, rarely asking for time off and choosing the most hazardous assignments. Some of his closer friends held the opinion that Cross was a living Death Wish; that he was so good at his job simply because he didn't care anymore. Maybe it was true. Whatever the reason, Cross rose quickly from the Ivy League of CIA field investigations to full-time espionage and internal security. And he was very good.

The streets of Washington looked familiar and predictable. There were new structures and new faces, but the patterns were there as they always were: young urban professionals and academics lobbying for power and influence in the Grand Central Station of American politics. Cross promised himself two things before the day was over: A hot shower and a brew at Kent's Bar and Grill. At least there was one place where people minded their own affairs and did not make money from policy or policy for money. He glanced at his watch. 11:46. Still time to do some hunting. He'd need a reliable communications net including someone to make calls for him. Time to pull in some unused favours, thought Cross. Like it or not, I'm back.

***

"That's all I have on him, sir. That's my report," finished Barry Wallace. Wallace had spoken for nearly thirty minutes. He was sweating visibly and appeared on the verge of getting sick at any moment. As much as he tried to look organized, the main impression he succeeded in conveying to his Level One supervisor, Vince McKay, was that he was nervous and needed very much to please his superiors. McKay was torn between an urge to pat him on the head and kick him in the ass. The latter was quickly gaining ground in his frustrated and overloaded mind when a quick knock at the door interrupted him.

"Yes?"

"He's here, Mr. McKay," spoke his assistant in a cool tone.

"Send him in."

Cross had spent part of a busy afternoon speaking briefly with Wallace on the GD-4 linkup and arranging a three o'clock meeting with McKay. It had taken him all of ten seconds to size up the first contact as mentally disturbed, and he refused to answer any questions until the afternoon meeting. He had promised himself after hanging up the phone that he owed it to the organization to talk to someone about Wallace. If this is what has happened to the CIA in the last three years, he thought, God help us all.

When Cross first stepped into McKay's office, two things stood out. McKay had positioned himself directly in front of his desk facing the door. Up front, thought Cross. He liked that. And secondly, he was almost certain he had seen the man before.

"Introductions are hardly necessary, Cross. Whether or not you remember me, I was part of the nightmare that became Velvet, the second-last assignment you worked on. Welcome back."

Cross remembered. Under the jacket and tie McKay would be sporting a deep scar stretching from just below his right collarbone to the base of his neck where a machete had almost severed his shoulder from his body. Tough and up front. Maybe Cross would get some answers after all.

"I didn't necessarily want to leave at the time, McKay. And I sure as hell had no intention of returning. You've changed uniforms since the last time we worked together but I'll assume you haven't softened so much behind the desk that you don't know I mean what I say.

"I'm not on assignment for you or the organization or the American government. I don't need a welcome back. I'm here because some fuzzy-haired biochemist has the soup that will cure my father. This is personal and it's going to stay that way."

"Whatever anyone has told you about what is required of you, Cross, you have my word that as soon as we received the green light yesterday, the process began for the treatment of your father. Likewise you will be handled as a 'special commodity' which means you have the access and flexibility you require to get the job done. But let's all be clear about why you were recruited in the first place. Somewhere in the world there is an intermediate-range nuclear missile that belongs to our government which threatens not only the political image of our nation but the safety and security of the entire world. We have very little time to bicker about rights and wrongs or to indulge in the luxury of political philosophy reserved for the youngsters. I also want to make it clear to you that I am not interested in the least how you were retired or how well the farm is doing. If you get fed-up and decide the ride is not what you bargained for, I'll be the first to remind you that the serum for your dad's cancer can be cut off as quickly as it was begun."

"Sounds like my services are indispensable, Mr. Supervisor," said Cross, knowing full well the chances were very good that he might not return from the task regardless of its success or failure. "Does that mean I get a hero's welcome when this is over?"

"The reality hasn't changed, Cross. There's no sense in playing games. At the place where the choices are made, your ticket came up and that means you're the man. But that might

40

mean the first of many. And if you don't come back, there won't be much time spent in mourning.''

"There's one question I want answered right away," said Cross, moving to a chair on the far side of the office and sliding nonchalantly into it. "How do I know that the serum will continue if I don't?''

"No guarantees. Seven million dollars is a hell of a lot of defense money that needs to be explained to someone, penny for penny. We both know that the moment you check out, the government is going to forget your dad and his precious monkey-made antibiotics. You might say there's an incentive to carrying the torch as far as you can.''

"Bastards.''

"Blame your dad's illness on us or God, I don't give a shit. Just remember. This is personal for you, but a possible world-wide crisis for the rest of us including your dad and your cattle. We may as well work together.''

"Who do I see and where do I start?''

"Cliff. The lights.'' McKay pulled a chair from beside his desk, and his assistant handed him a control switch for a slide projector as Cross turned his chair to face the side wall. "This is Canadian Forces Base Baden, West Germany. As you know, our bases in Europe and particularly in West Germany have been using Canadian aircraft and warehousing in Baden and Lahr for a number of years for the storage, maintenance and transportation of classified materials and personnel.

"This is Brigadier General McDonnell, Deputy Commander of Canadian Forces Europe. He has been directly involved with the displacement and transportation of men and materials for our government since his first appointment to NATO forces in 1988. He will be the man you will need to meet with in Baden when you first arrive. He is stationed in Lahr, but has arranged a number of staff meetings to coincide with your arrival tomorrow afternoon their time. He'll be in Baden for three days. Baden will be expecting a time and place once we have completed your briefing.''

"What will he have for me?''

"Not a hell of a lot more than we can tell you, other than showing the actual storage area for the missiles that arrived

41

safely and answering any administrative details about their transport that might seem pertinent to you."

"Who's that shorter man on the left?"

"That's the Canadian Minister of National Defense. These pictures were taken about ten months ago when he was meeting with General McDonnell about Canadian armaments in NATO."

"A timely meeting."

"It was meant to be, but on the day the Minister arrived, McDonnell was caught up in other matters which he, and the CIA, found more threatening than lack of funds. Apparently one of General McDonnell's chief aides, Colonel Walter Newcombe, was caught photocopying top secret information about the delivery and dispersal of the missiles. This would not have been so unusual except that this aide was a full Colonel working for the British Secret Services and was doing his photocopying at two-thirty in the morning, under the light of a small flashlight. And he neglected to sign the register upon entering the building as well as the photocopying records. He was caught in full video colour from a camera behind the venting grill. Ironically enough, it was his office that installed the equipment, only he was away during the week when the work order came down from General McDonnell."

"Any motive? Where does he fit in?"

"This is the part that seriously disturbs all of us. This particular Colonel was apparently a loving and devoted father and husband. The day after he was arrested he was found hanging by his belt in his cell along with a goodbye note to his wife."

"Not unusual,"volunteered Cross with a shrug of his shoulders. "I'd be embarrassed too, if my career just folded before my eyes. I might not pull the pin, but if I was depressed enough about it, the thought might occur to me."

"My sentiments exactly," agreed McKay. "But take a look at this." He handed Cross a photocopy of a handwritten note, obviously part of the last communique this Colonel would leave the world. The words in bright yellow liner said it all: "...and although I know there is no way you could possibly understand, Lillian, believe me as one who has loved you and shared life with you for over a quarter century: I did what I did because of my

42

commitment to my ideals; my unfaltering confidence that one day, mankind will succeed in leaving the mediocrity of his fears and insecurities and move toward the great and eternal truths of a long and happy life that have been passed to us by the conquering stoics of our rich past. So many people have died needlessly in wars around the world since the beginning of time, and for what? So that new politicians can replace one kind of oppression with another? But there *are* eternal truths, dedicated to the betterment of mankind, and I have seen them in action! Obedience, self-denial, honesty, hard work, physical and intellectual training—these things allow us to build and structure our society, not rape it with greed or sodomize it with quarrels over petty differences. 'Not every man was born for leadership, but no man was born for dishonour.' Rempal spoke of that hundreds of years ago. I believe it is as true today as it was when Augustus was the proud leader of a noble and honourable world. Today you may not forgive me, for I have left you alone and confused for the first time in many years; and this time finally. But when the glory of civilization as that of ancient Rome, repeats its heartbeat in the cycle of modern history, you and our children will be there to celebrate what small part I may have played in its fruition. Lovingly and forever yours, Walter.''

"What the hell does all that mean?"

"That, Cross, is the frightening and integral question we are all asking each other. Everyone from the State Department and the Chiefs of Staff are convinced that if someone of this man's caliber killed himself in a premeditated action designed to protect an ideal, then we may be up against something far worse than one stolen nuclear missile, if that is possible. It doesn't stop there.'' ·

"I was certain you'd save the fun for last."

"The Russians, for all their frenzy over embargoes and NATO military exercises on every border of the Kremlin, are sounding strangely authentic in their belief that there is a third destabilizing force emerging in the world political scene. Twice in the last six months the red phone at the White House has awakened the President and his translator over issues that were sensitively orchestrated and timed to induce fury in the Soviet people, but had nothing to do with American policy. After heated discussion and quite frankly to the credit of both governments, international crises were averted with both superpowers feeling helplessly manipulated by someone or some organization that appears to operate independently of the influence of both nations. I don't need to impress upon you the delicate position our government is in, over the loss of this missile. Both nations have agreed upon a transitory allegiance over the past two months, in an attempt to pinpoint where information leaks and destabilizations may be originating. Chiefs of Staff and the Soviet Military have begun to share information with each other which would have startled and even amazed leaders as recently as one decade ago. It's what one might call a halting but frank and trusting relationship between the two nations that, under different circumstances, might be of great benefit to the world.''

"But all the Russians need to know is that we have begun to place illegal missiles in Europe and the fragile trust is blown,'' summarized Cross.

"Precisely.We can debate all we wish over what is necessary for deterrence being fully aware that they are engaged in the same tactics to protect their interests. But the timing for this type of deception at this stage in the communication process would be the end of it all. There would be pressure for our government to provide an explanation to the Soviets that it could never sell to its own honourably motivated but deluded population, and the Russians would be forced by their own mandate to uphold the Marxist hand of justice.''

"Is there any idea who or what might be behind this 'destabilizing force'? Surely the reams of info gathered here have shown some type of pattern during the past year that points somewhere.''

"We've got our best people on it and all they've come up with is this: the organization has access to highly classified military and scientific secrets and considerable power—financial, technological and now, God bless America, this. Cliff?'' With that the slide projector was shut off. The men sat in darkness and silence for a moment. Soon the sound of a film projector began. The image was, Cross noticed with some irony, a farmhouse and barn. It appeared to be early evening.

"Living on the plains of Wyoming, you've probably encountered a bad wind from time to time. One of the most dangerous things about tornadoes in particular, is that they are just about impossible to predict. When we were given the ultimatum by teletype for the code on the missile, included with it was a second 'motivator'. We were told that this particular abandoned farmhouse would be destroyed by a tornado at precisely the minute, hour and day specified. We humoured whoever sent the message with a filming of the location, beginning fifteen minutes before their specified time. Three minutes before it was to occur, what you will see here, began to unfold. I swear to God, Cross, this is no hoax."

Cross watched transfixed as black clouds in the distance began the dreaded dance that sometimes results in the most destructive of nature's windstorms. Within ten minutes, dread turned to fascination and horror as Cross watched a full tornado sweep in from the distant east and touch down over an area two to three miles from the farm house. Even those in the room who had seen the film before were jolted by the complete destruction of the farm house as the tornado swept through the property and into the western sky.

The room was silent for a full minute when the lights returned, Cross thoughtfully digesting the possibilities of such information and of the person or persons who held it.

"If you've got questions, go looking for answers. We've never seen anything like that in the history of this agency. Even the A-bomb was predicated by twenty years of worldwide research. Nobody we know anywhere can touch this kind of thing."

"Was it a prediction, or a creation?"

"Like I said, we don't know. We'd like to be optimistic and say prediction, but the coordinates were so exact....It may be that someone out there has his hands on something that would paralyze the modern world, if he wanted to use it. Which leaves us more confused than when we first started. If this was created, why steal a bomb in the first place? Why negotiate? Why give us two weeks to come up with the code they've asked for? At times one gets the feeling we're being toyed with. One thing is damn sure. We're in deep shit.

"And when in trouble, do one thing at a time," continued McKay. "To management, right now that means buy time." McKay stood and walked to his desk. Picking up a folder, he looked at it briefly and then pointed it at Cross. "From you, the CIA and the State Department want only one question answered."

"What's that?"

McKay tossed the file into Cross's lap. "Where the fuck is our nuclear missile?"

V

Strasbourg. Situated near the border between France and West Germany, this commercial Alsatian city—like many of her sister cities in France—possesses an architecture and culture that are living mosaics of modern industrial development and lingering socio-cultural elegance. She challenges her inhabitants to compete in the world market, yet pleads with them not to be seduced by its fleeting distractions. One will find here oil refineries, iron ore and steel industries. Here too are immigrant street peddlers, small smokeshops and bakeries. And the romantic need not worry: They can leave the refineries at night to converse in the informal luxury of a sidewalk café, or ponder the meaning of life in the solitude of her Gothic churches.

Cross greeted her without ceremony, without curiosity. He was tired. He wanted a hot shower and something more nourishing than freeze-dried mashed potatoes and ham reheated in the belly of a 747 whale six miles above the Atlantic Ocean. He knew he could have had these things in Paris when his flight landed, but there were people in Strasbourg who had information and papers he would be needing. He decided then, that it was better to wait and refresh once he arrived in Strasbourg. No amount of clear mountain air or raising cattle would let him forget what he needed to succeed, to survive. For now it was simple, and for that he was grateful. Some questions, some paperwork. Then food, then rest.

Cross parked his rented car next to the curb. He glanced at the door on the passenger side to ensure it was locked and felt for his passport in the inside pocket of his sports jacket. Reaching for the button to release his seat belt, Cross noticed something move quickly in the rearview mirror. The pattern was out of place. Curious tourists, on a lazy afternoon in Strasbourg, usually moved quietly, enjoying the sights and sounds. This movement was tense. Awkward. The outline was not clear. A hat? A beard? Maybe it *was* a tourist. In a hurry perhaps. *Wait. Stall.* He stretched his hand toward the glove compartment and opened it. Bending lower, as if searching for something inside, he watched in the sideview mirror for another glimpse. Was his mind playing tricks on him? Why did his muscles feel so taut?

If there was a tail on him, two things were obvious. One, the man was inexperienced, nervous; his patterns stood out as those of a man who either tried too hard or was charged with a job he didn't feel ready for. Two, someone in Washington was playing both ends of the field. The only people who knew his plans for the next three days were the briefing team. And if there was a leak at that level, his assignment just graduated from dangerous to damn near suicidal.

"Are you all right, monsieur?" asked a passing pedestrian from the open window. Cross realized he must look like he had collapsed in the front seat.

"If I can find my street map, I will be fine, thank you," Cross answered with a smile. Gotta loosen up, he thought. I've still got one leg in the barnyard by the look of things.

Closing his car door firmly, Cross looked both ways before entering the street. This is no way to start a fucking undercover investigation, he mumbled to himself, running his hand through his hair. Back on track. Let's move away from the paranoia, ole boy. One thing at a time. Papers. A post office.

The door to Charlie's Merchant Warehouse opened with a squeak. Small bells hanging from the ceiling near its hinges chimed his entrance. The moment he stepped inside, Cross was transported back half a decade. The small shop where three quarters of all his European paperwork had been created or expertly duplicated over the years still smelled of Old Spice and pipe tobacco. "La Maison Charles" was one of a kind.

"Est-ce que je peux vous aider, Monsieur?" Smiling from behind antique round spectacles that settled softly but firmly on his nose, a short, elderly gentleman carefully examined his customer.

"Perhaps," answered Cross in French, masking his usual American accent with ease. "But I am looking for the master. I do not deal with peasants."

The old man had recognized his client by this time. But he was a professional. If his visitor did not ask right, even this one could be refused service. "Peasants work hard like the rest of us, monsieur. Only some of us are better paid and perhaps more fortunate to be born with the ability to organize and to lead."

"Then take me to your leader. I have work for him to do." Cross smiled. The shop owner smiled in return. They regarded each other for a moment.

"What kind of work do you have for him, sir? He has been ill of late. His hand is not as steady as it once was." Cross could sense some sadness in his friend's voice.

"Even the hand of this master at his deathbed would more than suffice for the work he is renowned for." The warmth of Cross's compliment was received with dignity. Charles nodded.

"You have not lost the touch of a true gentleman, Mr. Cross, although one might say you would not be a true gentleman if you had. I heard you were retired. I am glad to see you again. How can I be helpful?"

"I will need three books, possibly four. I am in Europe for a week but I have no idea where I may be headed from here. Probably east. We are both aware how careful one must be in those areas. Can you prepare them for me?"

"I can bring you the world on a golden plate, Monsieur Cross, if I am given the time to do it. When must your passports be ready?"

"Early tomorrow morning."

"You are busy."

"Yes."

"Very well. It will be twice the usual plus five hundred. I need my sleep. When I miss it, it must be repaid or I cannot live with the resentment." Cross agreed. "Is there anything else?"

"I need to know where I can buy a cup of coffee, Charles. I have heard that Reuben's is no longer in business." Charles knew that Cross was looking for information. (His last informant had died several years ago in a bombing incident near Paris. It was a perilous profession.)

49

"I know of a place near the Strasbourg Cathedral called Chez Michel," began Charles. "You will find coffee and a martini if you wish. But be careful. No one can be sure who this man works for. He is said to befriend only his own interests. For that reason you may trust his information but not his actions. Once he has spoken with you and given you what you need to know, he will turn to the next person and tell them the questions you asked, for twice the price. He does not understand loyalty."

"My mail, Charles. Can you have someone hold it?"

"I will give you a box number when you return tomorrow morning. Sleep lightly. I have heard that something is boiling in the kitchen. If it gets much warmer, I may decide to leave myself. Good day, Monsieur Cross."

A tour guide was beginning to address a small crowd of eager tourists gathered near the Strasbourg Cathedral. "The structure was damaged during the Second World War, but has been carefully restored and remains today one of the finest examples of fifteenth century architecture in the city. If you would like to follow me to the church entrance, we will begin our tour. I must remind you again to keep a hand on your purses and wallets when the clock strikes the hour in the cathedral, as there are unfortunately numerous pickpockets known to frequent the area when it is crowded. This way please." Cross had followed a tour very similar to this one almost twenty years ago. He had long since lost his fascination with the intricate works of the huge astrological clock in the church that provided an entertaining several minutes chiming through the afternoon hours, but still often wondered who would be caught without their wallets when the show was over. The tour guide would remind them three times during the tour, and once again just before the clock struck, to be careful with their pocketbooks. It was rare when no one was a victim.

Sometimes there were more than one.

The breeze Cross had felt when leaving his car at the corner near La Maison Charles had softened to a whisper. The afternoon sun had begun to add to his thirst for something cold. Good timing, he smiled to himself. He stepped across the street from the church and headed for the café half a block west.

50

The scene inside Chez Michel had the unmistakable air of pseudo-French: slightly overdone and with melodramatic tones that would help a tourist feel at ease with his fantasy of the French. The only French word Cross could distinguish was "monsieur", and occasionally, "merci beaucoup". Otherwise Cross was in what might be called an all-American watering hole. Clips of various conversations Cross could easily overhear, told the story.

"And what makes you the authority on English or French or fucking Bohemian culture, for that matter, Mr. Cooper? You pay a hundred francs for a six franc wallet and think you've become an international fucking expert!" Slightly inebriated and fully blown with his own sense of righteous mission, a tall muscular man with a moustache and receding hairline spat across the table at a middle-aged man in a sports jacket who seemed very uncomfortable with the company. His girlfriend didn't help. She was leaning on her hand and seemed to be staring at the man with the moustache, a kind of distant hunger in her eyes. This was probably the most excitement she could expect for the entire trip and she wasn't about to miss it. "If you asked me, I'd say you spend your time trying to impress people with money you don't have no idea how to spend. Ain't that right, darlin'?" The girl nodded with a smile that was as seductive as Cross had ever seen.

Cross allowed his eyes to roam as they adjusted to the artificial darkness. Near the bar stood three young men, early twenties. Their glasses sat on the bar like little fenceposts, the alcohol helping keep inside the loneliness and frustration that even travelling across the ocean doesn't tame. "Three more cool ones for me and my buddies here, missure, and don't spare the horses. Ain't another goddamn thing to keep a man occupied in this foreign country but booze and women." Cross was always amazed at how young people could travel overseas and still find nothing to spark a curiosity about the history and culture of the host country. Some of the hotels they'd be staying in were dated as far back as the fourteenth century.

Cross could see to the far end of the room. Without thinking he began his pattern—a habit he had repeated countless times before, in bars and social meeting places all over the world.

Number of tables: seven, four against the wall, then three. Five occupied. Couples: six. No, make that seven. Those two females aren't holding hands to share grief by the look of it. Windows? None. Bathroom—far left hand corner. Emergency exit blocked by cardboard boxes. Against the law, but who would report it? Cross didn't like closed doors. One single man at a corner table. Red flag, thought Cross. Just the spot I would choose. Features? Undistinguishable. Slim. One glass of beer in front of him, half finished. But an ashtray full of butts. Looks like he's been here for a while and wants to appear like a drinker. Maybe bored. Maybe trouble.

The bar. The three young men, arguing now about whether the German custom of not tipping in restaurants or the French custom of exorbitant tipping made the most social sense. And then, of course, what does one do in a border town like Strasbourg? Two females talking softly. The bartender (Is that him? Is that Michel?) moves over to the men who are arguing quite loudly by this time, and whispers something to them. The biggest of them laughs and says something back to the bartender. He smiles and says three or four words. A standoff. The drinker says an audible "fuck you", slaps a bill on the counter and turns to the doorway, his buddies following behind him.

"Looks like you put up with the worst of it in here," Cross said to the bartender, stepping up to the bar and pointing to a draft tap.

"We get young ones and old ones, monsieur. Impolite people come in every size and shape. I like to keep a quiet place. They can raise hell somewhere else. Anything besides the beer? We can fix you a nice sandwich. Take it on the outside tables maybe? It's a warm day."

"Thanks for the offer, no. Maybe you could help me with something else." The man smiled and reached for another glass to dry. "I would like to speak with Michel."

"Michel is well known, monsieur. Why not just step up to him and talk? He is always ready to talk to people."

"For one thing I don't know what he looks like," answered Cross, aware that he now was speaking to a cautious and bright informant. "I am visiting, but I am not new. I have spoken to others before him. Reuben was a good friend of mine, until his accident."

52

"I did not know Reuben. He was a strange man I am told. He was known to be involved in matters that, how do you say, were not healthy, not legal perhaps? I run a legitimate business, monsieur. If there is any way I might be of help to you, ask. But please do not dishonour my humble establishment. I do not allow trafficking or peddling and neither am I interested in fencing the most precious cargo. I run a café. I am content."

"It's too bad," replied Cross, turning away from the bar and leaning his elbows on the edge. "You are content. But are you wealthy, Monsieur Michel? I have twenty thousand francs that I must spend this afternoon or my government will take it in taxes regardless. What is a man to do with twenty thousand francs?"

"That amount would certainly buy a lot of draft beer, monsieur," said Michel in a lower tone. He stepped closer to Cross. "What do you see on the shelf? Can you be specific?"

"I have heard that there is heat. Some people are in trouble, and others are causing the discomfort. I am very much interested in general knowledge. I am looking for answers to why people must be made to feel so uncomfortable."

"I see you are an artist, monsieur," said Michel, placing the glass aside and leaning over the inside edge of the bar closer to Cross's ear. "You have perfected the art of asking for all information without disclosing any specific interest. How is one to be sure you are not here to cause *me* discomfort? You can understand that not everyone I meet wishes me health and good fortune."

"I offer you only fortune, Michel. Your health and your comfort are none of my business. I know of other cafés. I am tired from my journey and do not wish to battle small streets and frustrated policemen halfway across the city. But I will get my information. And someone will be twenty thousand francs richer."

"Very well, monsieur. I will speak to you as one stranger to another. Should you forget your wallet, or twenty thousand francs of it, I would not complain." Cross pulled out one thousand francs and laid it gently on the bar. Then he turned away again.

"There is a lot of money at the border," Michel began, his voice clear and firm. "I mean millions of francs. I have heard that hundreds of thousands of American dollars have been financed through Baden alone, sometimes several times in one evening. The source is unknown.'' Cross turned and set five thousand more francs on the bar. ''Were you to leave one hundred bills in front of me, I would have no name for you, monsieur. His name and face are a mystery. But it is said that the casino in Baden-Baden has moved most of it. Payment for huge debts, and often to men and women of considerable influence.''

Cross nodded. ''Continue.''

''The governments and black market organizations are worried. We are well accustomed to competition, both legal and illegal. But so far there has been no demand placed on any of the leaders on either side of the border. No government inquiries, no night raids. No underground murders out of place. There is a gathering storm, but no wind to show its presence. The lack of knowledge makes even a reputable businessman such as myself, very nervous.''

''You make these people out to be ghosts. Is that it? Perhaps there is a fairy godmother working miracles for her delinquent children. I have not known a human who does not leave a trace. I need more.''

''Everyone needs more. My little café sits on the border of two nations that will be destroyed by the political paranoia of the United States and her rival in the East unless someone can gain more information than that which I have provided you. Oui, monsieur. There is much heat. I should be grateful if you or anyone else could make it more clear. I might be persuaded to pay fifty thousand francs myself for that kind of knowledge.''

''Here is twenty-five,'' said Cross, slipping a handful of French bills toward the bartender. ''This is to demonstrate my integrity in this matter. I have no personal interest in you or your business. But I have money. If you hear anything worth more, you are to leave a chalk mark on the post that holds your café sign. Either myself or another will return for it.''

''Your generosity impresses me and worries me. I have never known the need for information to be so great from so many people.''

''I'm sure you are impressed,'' finished Cross, turning to face the bartender and regarding him thoughtfully as he drank the last of his draft. ''But I do not believe you are so worried. Good day, Michel.''

"Bonjour, monsieur."

Cross turned to survey the room again, the last of his pattern. The man at the back had ordered another beer. There were more butts. One couple had left. But he felt uncomfortable again. The sense that he was being watched. Had something else changed in the bar that he hadn't noticed? He tried to shake the feeling as he headed for the door. Cross recalled a psychologist friend telling him that sixty-five percent of high ranking generals in the military could be classified as clinically paranoid. They managed to stay there because of it. Was it his imagination? Or had he seen or heard something that registered in a place he couldn't reach right now?

Cross went outside. He shaded his eyes from the glare of the afternoon sun and looked around. Another bus load of tourists was gathering near the entrance to the church. Again the feeling. I'm being watched, he thought. This time he felt certain. Certain, not because he saw anything different, but because his gut insisted. Cross had learned an important lesson of survival those years in the field. Query feelings—Look around—Listen, but if they persist, stop asking questions. Trust your mind and the tuning of your intuition. Move. *Now!*

Cross stepped from the front of the café and turned, walking slowly along the sidewalk. The adrenalin began to pour into his stomach and neck, tensing muscles that had just begun to relax in response to the small amount of alcohol he had just ingested. The sensation of being followed by someone who could not be seen or heard was an unsettling stress Cross had learned to forget. As sure as he could be without being introduced, he was aware of someone watching him. No more wondering or daydreaming. Retirement and cattle be damned. The business he was hired for had just stepped out from the shadows of uncertainty into the light of an imminent threat.

Put him on my terms. Cross had engineered this many times, but that was a lifetime ago. Could he follow the lead of his mind, a mind full of worry for his father, enough to stay alive even through his first night on assignment? *Carry the torch as long as you can.* McKay's words burned their way into the part of Cross's body that formed priorities. *The serum can be turned off as quickly as it was begun.* Bastards. I have to think. Put some heat on the hunter. Make it hard for him to tail, hard to keep covered. When he moves from his cover...

Cross picked up his pace, stepping briskly from the sidewalk and into the street. His mind on full alert, he clarified and eliminated his choices. The church? I'd probably lose him, but I'd never have a chance to be sure who was so interested in me, or why. Back to the bar? Not enough room to move around. The market? The market.

To the north and south of the church, street peddlers created an informal market throughout the day, wooing unwary tourists into purchases they neither need nor want. A small fortune in money is exchanged daily for penny goods of much smaller value made with cheap labour in countries where a salary to be thankful for is a dollar a day.

Cross moved quickly. He bumped into an older woman searching her purse for funds and had no time to apologize. Without looking back he knew whoever was following him couldn't be far behind. The lady had just increased the tone of her complaints from indignant to angry. "What kind of country is this? People just barge through...Hey! You big brute! Watch where you're going!"

You big brute. That's it! The guy with the moustache at the first table! *He was gone when I left the bar.* That's the piece that was missing. *You big brute.* Son of a bitch. I don't want that hulk cornering me, Cross reflected.

Cross took two seconds to confirm his theory. He glanced over his shoulder as he edged his way by a couple who were admiring artwork on the sidewalk. There he was. Their eyes joined. The same quick movements Cross had noticed in his car near La Maison Charles. Of course. Big people find it harder than anyone to mask a quick movement. It wasn't a beard or a hat he saw. It was a moustache.

Once he knew Cross had spotted him, the uninvited shadow became more intense and consequently, more clumsy in his pursuit. This was the cue Cross had hoped for. The pieces were forming an outline for him now; young man, eager to perform, impatient. For a moment Cross thought another person had impressed him with those same questionable but highly motivated qualities not long ago. Washington? He couldn't quite put that piece in place. Later. At least now he had leverage. And he planned to use that same energy and motivation to knock a few walls down. Preferably ones closest to where his uninvited guest was standing.

The big man's clumsiness began to attract attention. Someone threatened to call the police. Cross decided to use the publicity to his advantage. The next three peddlers had their tables knocked over and their merchandise scattered. By the time the man with the moustache reached the mess Cross left behind, it was he who received most of the flak. He took no time to defend himself. Tripping over the tables, chairs and merchandise Cross conveniently strewed in his way, his frustration turned to anger. Cross stopped in his tracks and gave his pursuer the finger. A peddler noticed the gesture and suggested to the crowd that the man with the moustache had maybe lost his girlfriend for the night? A number of tourists laughed. This was the distraction Cross had hoped for. The hunter was enraged. He shifted his anger and embarrassment toward the crowd and shoved a little boy out of the way as he passed. The jovial atmosphere ceased. Two men tried to grab him. Another shouted how easy it was to pick on children, why not try someone your own size? And Cross had disappeared....

Cross could see the confusion on the young man's face through the window of the chocolate shop he had slipped into. Cross explained to the store manager that he was running from his lover's husband. The manager shook his head and talked of better days, when faithfulness meant something to people. Cross assessed the situation. Now that he knew exactly who was after him one thing was clear: The hunter must become the hunted. But how?

"Could you please tell me if there is a short cut from this street to the Cathedral?" Cross asked the shop manager who was still mumbling to himself about the shamelessness of modern relationships.

"Do not involve me in your squabbles, sir," he said, shaking his head again in a gesture of righteous judgment. "You have cooked this soup. Do not ask me to take the bowl from your lips."

"I'm not asking, I am purchasing assistance," replied Cross pulling five hundred francs from his pocket. The manager looked at the money and glanced around like a boy with his hand in the cookie jar. He quickly grabbed the money and shrugged his shoulders.

"She must have been a beauty, monsieur. Your business is your business. Follow this street west to the shop called 'La Carte Blanche'. Turn north for two blocks and you will find a service alley that leads to the side of the church. Perhaps you will say confessions for us both."

Without replying, Cross swung open the door to the shop and, pretending to lose his balance, slammed into an outdoor menu sign for the restaurant next door and cursed. Immediately the cat snapped his head about. He's biting, Cross thought, playing the irresistible mouse.

Sirens could be heard from the far end of the market area. To stop the nuisance that was disturbing an otherwise profitable afternoon's peddling, someone had called the police. More incentive, smiled Cross to himself. Given a choice between talking to the authorities and following me, I'd put my money on him tracking me to hell and back before stopping.

Cross turned right at "La Carte Blanche", slowing just enough at the corner to insure the hunt would continue into the alley. The sound of the sirens began to die away. Cross was aware of his own heavy breathing and realized that this was probably the most he had run in nearly four years. Thank God he never was one to put on weight. His legs did the work. His mind put up the effort.

Cross could hear footsteps behind him. And soon, one final reminder that he was back in the field. A gun.

A short snapping whisper was followed by the all-too-familiar zip that caused Cross to tuck his head instinctively as his assailant fired three rounds in rapid succession toward the darting target in front of him. The Cathedral! Cross could see it now. He realized that he hadn't been inside a church since a friend's wedding over six years ago. Once, when Cross was a teenager, he had dated a religious girl who had convinced him that there just might be a loving God out there, who cared for His children. Their relationship ended when he joined the military, but he continued to struggle with his beliefs. Then, near the beginning of his career as an agent, he learned about an oriental snuff ring who dealt in kid murders. The hardest to swallow was the fact that parents were selling their kids at black market prices, many of them fully aware that their children were going to be killed in the prime time arena of child pornography. He hadn't been able to eat for days. He stopped wondering if there was a God who cared, for he had seen the most innocent die for nothing. The fact that he was now headed for the sanctuary of a church as part of his own immediate salvation, had not lost its irony on him.

Another two shots were fired, the last narrowly missing Cross's left shoulder. Cross would later discover a burn mark on his jacket which would bear testimony to the fact.

No entrance appeared on this side. Cross knew that there would be only one choice to make: either left or right. Often the back end of the church was blocked in one direction by a hallway or porch connecting the priests' quarters with the rear vestibule of the church. If he chose the wrong way...

Maybe it was a shadow on the wall from the sun, or the kind of intuition that makes people believe in mystery enough to go on building churches. But Cross chose left. With relief, he could see a lineup of tourists, possibly just beginning their tour, at the front of the Cathedral. A glance over his shoulder sent a cold chill across his back. Behind him, on a right turn from the alley, was a garden of flowers and a fountain to the Sacred Heart of Jesus. A crucifix hung behind the fountain, on a wall fifteen feet high that connected the church on one side to a warehouse on the other. He would have died against that wall. Mystery or luck? No time for debate or gratitude. Cross arrived at another lineup of tourists just as the tour guide was starting his hourly spiel about the origin of the church and the need to be careful with purses. He plunged unceremoniously through the centre of the crowd and made his way into the church by the front doors.

Cross knew two things—in a crowd he would have time; in a building like this he would have cover. Could he lure the big cat with the silencer to a place where he could turn it around? His thoughts were interrupted by mumbles from the crowd, announcing another disturbance. He's persistent, I'll give him that.

Cross gambled another few seconds. He glanced about him and tried to remember the layout of the church from his visit years ago. A dark place. A small place. That's what I need, he reasoned.

"Many of you who are visiting Strasbourg for the first time will appreciate the ingenuity and remarkable mechanical creativity of the engineers who designed and pieced together this magnificent clock..." the guide continued.

Behind the clock. That's it! Cross moved to the east aisle of the church trying to move quickly without drawing too much attention. A lot of people had gathered already for the four o'clock chimes. He checked his watch. 3:54. He knew the section that housed the clockworks fronted a small access area where the workmen would maneuver ladders and tools to maintain the mechanism of the clock. The dance of the figurines and the bells that tolled the change of hours would give Cross time to get some answers, if he survived long enough to corner his pursuer.

Getting to the front of the crowd was the hardest part. Cross's watch now read 3:56. He looked behind him. His enemy had taken the opposite aisle, probably hoping to cut off another exit. Squeezing past a couple who were hastily attempting to load their camera for the change of the hours, Cross moved quietly to the edge of the altar area. 3:57. Cross reached the curtains at the side of the altar which prevent the congregation from seeing into the workspace. Separating them he found a door and tried the handle. To his relief it opened, but stiffly. The hinges creaked, reminding him briefly of a door and squeaking hinges on a farm thousands of miles away.

The buzz of anticipation in the crowd made it hard to hear. Cross felt his way to a place close to the door and wrapped his fingers around a two-foot section of pipe found leaning against the wall. The air behind the clock smelled musty, damp. Although he couldn't see them, Cross could hear the wheels and pulleys begin to move as the crowd fell silent. 3:59.

Like an actor on cue, the door opened, showing the form of a man, his shadow spreading on the side wall by the dim light from the altar. He paused. Cross wondered if his breathing was as loud as it sounded. For a moment the two stood frozen: Cross poised, breath held and pipe gripped tightly in his hand; the other, angry, frustrated but wary, with one hand on the door and another extending a long-barreled pistol into the darkness.

"We remind all of those touring with Global Bus Lines to be sure you have at least one hand on your purses...."

The pistol entered first, like a hand-held antenna, monitoring, protecting. Then the face showed. Sweat formed a stream on the side of his face that trickled like a small river between his hairline and his chin.

"You will notice in particular the costumes of the dancing ladies and their partners. Each article of clothing and the painting of the figurines were hand crafted..."

Four o'clock.

"And there, ladies and gentlemen, the show you've been waiting for..."

As the huge clock struck the first of its chimes, and the crowds sighed in appreciation, Cross's primitive weapon crashed down on the wrist of his pursuer, crushing bone and staggering his posture. Stepping forward, Cross swung open the door with his right elbow and smashed the pipe into the side of the bigger man's face, staining his bewildered expression with blood and grease. Without pausing to introduce himself, Cross leveled a third blow just below the rib cage, bruising muscle and damaging kidney. The shadow on the wall sank slowly to the floor.

"It might have made more sense to just walk up and buy me a beer," said Cross, pushing the moaning form from the doorway with his foot and partially closing the door. "I tend to get frustrated and mildly irritated when a complete stranger starts firing shots at me without telling me what he's looking for."

"You're nothing, Cross. You and your people and your big overseas assignment don't mean shit."

"And you and yours are, of course, relevant and contemporary," returned Cross. "I may not be shit to your boss but I sure as hell had better mean something to you." Cross paused to wipe the blood off the pipe on his adversary's jacket and pulled up a small stepladder to sit on. The flash of cameras could be seen around the edges of the back of the clock. "How did you know I was in the bar?" asked Cross, sitting on the top step of the small ladder. The slumped man coughed. He seemed to have trouble swallowing. "I asked you a question," said

61

Cross, poking him in the head with the end of the pipe.

"What? Fuck you. Do you think old Charles is the only one who knows that Michel sells information? I knew you'd show up sooner or later."

"Obviously too soon for us to be properly introduced. And unless I get some answers real fast, Bruno, it'll be too late to strike up a friendship. I can be a mean little prick, if I do say so myself."

"So this is the part where I'm all intimidated like, and share the story so that you can go back to the office in Washington and get on with raising cattle? Fuck, Cross. This situation is bigger than a small-town mugging behind the local church clock. Get it over with."

"No such luck. I know a man who runs a little chemistry shop and who loves to stick hollow pins in people. His experiments tend to bring out the most in people, know what I mean? You and I have some walking to do."

The moustache creased slowly into a smile. "You'll not get me near drugs, Cross. This is the last waltz. I'm just a bit sorry I couldn't have caused you more trouble before I dozed off."

"There's a lot of places in a man's body that hurt worse than a bump on the head," returned Cross, eyeing his opponent steadily.

"And dead men don't tell tales, remember that one?"

"I plan on keeping you fresh for at least twenty-four hours. Suit yourself. It's talk now or talk later."

The smile pulled slowly away from the moustache, now tinged on one corner with blood from the ugly cut. He coughed and looked up. "You've got a good reputation, Cross. Not bad. The church, the dark room. But I had time to take my medicine. You tidied up, closed the door and pulled up a chair. I took a bite on my collar. Not much of a counterattack but I bet you'll be kicking your ass well into the weekend."

"What the hell are you talking about?"

"You know, I've never been much of a philosopher, Cross. I was never great in school. Been in trouble with the law most of my life. But I've finally done something good for once, you know? Like the man says, history repeats itself. When the books record it, I'll be there. I did the best I could. So long, Cross..."

As he watched, the big man heaved and tore one more gasp. It looked like he was stopping in mid-breath, but there was no breath left to take: He was dead.

"And the final chime, ladies and gentlemen, marks the start of another set of gears, which will carry the clock through the next hour. I hope you've enjoyed this legacy from our forefathers. This way please."

As the crowds began to shuffle from the front of the church, Cross reached over to check the pulse of the man who sat in front of him. It was simply a reaction. The eyes had already glazed over. Cross knew he had died. Poison. Three, maybe four seconds to close the door and pick up the stepladder. The big boy with the moustache and a way with the ladies had bitten the top button of his shirt containing enough of the lethal drug to kill three men his size, effectively closing the door on Cross and himself.

Cross was not accustomed to this kind of combat. For every enemy, there usually seemed a place you could hurt, a place you could use to scare them, make them move. It was a dirty game, but the overwhelming desire to live, the instinct of survival, the willingness of even the most courageous to give anything for another precious breath of life—these things made weakness understandable, confessions nothing to be ashamed of. For the second time in as many days, Cross was confronted with a threat that claimed the lives of its own for an ideal. It didn't seem human. And it scared the hell out of him.

Cross went through the motions. No surprises. Not one piece of identification on him. The only thing he noticed was the ring he wore on the small finger of his left hand. It bore an eagle with the inscription: TO THE GLORY OF ROME.

63

VI

The country club was jammed today as usual. Dion was not surprised. If I were sixty-five, well-off and bored, this would be the kind of place I'd hang out, he told himself. Dion shifted uneasily in the seat of his rented car and glanced at his watch. 3:46. Cross's old man was almost twenty minutes late.

This wasn't the kind of job Dion enjoyed. He would have been content to do the last seven months before his retirement like the rest of the old boys and pick up his ticket for Spain like he had planned. Courier service was monotonous but it was "uninvolved", as they say; at least there was no blood and consequently no need to forget something else that the department decided had to be done, regardless of who or what was targeted. When Vince McKay approached him the day before with an offer to advance his retirement date by six and a half months plus twenty percent bonus on his pension for life just for the convenience of this last hit, he half wished he hadn't been considered for the job. It was not that he would cry for the people who would grieve their loved one, or that human life suddenly held for him some mystical place in the scheme of things. Morals were not the issue. It was just that Cross was already putting his own life on the line for the department, and that, after they had treated him like shit for simply speaking his mind. It didn't seem...well, nice; it wasn't polite, somehow. But Dion finally decided it may as well be him. Somebody would do it. McKay's offer of the extra time, and money to enjoy it with, made the idea of silencing Cross's father that much easier.

There had been considerable discussion by the "management" staff at Level One whether or not killing Cross's

64

father would make much difference one way or another. On the one hand, it was argued, his lifestyle had not brought him anywhere near his son in over six years. It was not likely that Mr. Cross would try to contact his son in the foreseeable future. Cross's mission was not expected to last more than a few weeks to a month. Does it make sense to kill a man on the slim chance that he might suddenly change his pattern of behaviour and try to reach his son? How can the variables be reasonably debated? The life of an innocent American citizen is at stake here, after all. But the stakes were much higher than that, it was finally decided. Warren Cross was recruited to find the missing missile at any cost. The search for that missile represented the fine line between precarious peace and full-scale war. There could be no mistakes. Once the father's body was discovered, there would be a news blackout concerning the incident; the body would be "handled" by Agency personnel and the usual cover-up procedures implemented. Cross would not need to know the tragic reality of his father's "lost battle with cancer" until long after his own usefulness had expired. Only Level One, Bugs—the chief administrative officer in Information—and Dion would know the truth. They would succeed in making the truth a tragic drama. There would be sadness and mourning in the department for the death of Cross Senior, the official report would say. Especially when it first appeared he was responding so well to the treatment for his illness.

Dion smirked and shook his head when the man he was assigned to terminate opened the front doors and walked from the exclusive Chateau Pacifique of West Los Angeles toward his BMW in the parking lot. It seemed strangely ironic to Dion that the department would have staged a terminal illness for Cross's father. Even at two hundred feet from the entrance where Dion sat waiting, it was evident that Mr. Cross was in excellent shape for a man his age. He walked with the bounce of someone who feels tired yet energized by a good game of tennis. As Dion watched from the corner of the parking lot, Mr. Cross reached his car and opened the trunk. The assassin cringed involuntarily as the unsuspecting target threw his sports bag and tennis racket into the trunk and slammed it shut. Dion exhaled slowly and nervously straightened his tie. It would have been difficult to explain to the head manager of the Chateau Pacifique what an

800-gram plastic explosive was doing, ripping holes in the cars and asphalt of his clubhouse. It would have been equally difficult keeping the accident out of the papers. But the impact of equipment on the floor of the trunk did not jar the sensitive timing device Dion had placed under the tank. Mr. Cross climbed into his car and closed the door with a thunk. Moments later the engine roared into life.

Dion checked his watch again and lifted the remote programmer from the seat beside him. It was now 3:58. He set the timer for 4:35. By that time, he reasoned, Cross Senior would be well out of the suburbs and on his way back to his country retreat. All was ready. For a moment Dion paused, his finger hovering gently over the "send" button. The act, he knew, would be irretrievable. The innocent man's death, certain. Dion thought about Cross the day they had met at the farm in Wyoming. He remembered what he had said to him about family. This was the hardest kind of job, he thought. The world is one mixed-up fucking jungle. Shaking his head in a final gesture of frustration, Dion pressed firmly on the button and started his car.

VII

"Your name, sir." The guard at the gate was firm but pleasant.

"Colonel Warren Cross, United States Rangers. I'm here to speak with General McDonnell."

"The General told us you'd be arriving today, sir. I'll need to see your passport and travel orders."

Cross handed the guard his papers and surveyed the entrance road into Canadian Force Base Baden. Trees lined both sides of the road. The sky was overcast; it was difficult to see any distance, for a haze had rolled in during the night.

"Thank you, sir." The guard returned Cross's passport and travel orders. "Please place this sticker on the lower inside corner of your windshield. Here is your mess card and the key to a Staff Officers Suite, number 3A, in the Officers Mess. Will you be requiring an escort, Colonel?"

"No, thank you. I'll find my way around."

"One final thing, sir. The General asked me to give you this envelope and to pass on the message that it should be reviewed before you meet with him at 09:30 hours. If you have any questions, please don't hesitate to contact the Base Duty Officer. He has been briefed on your visit and can be contacted from any base telephone at the number on the back of your Mess card."

"Thank you, Corporal."

"Have a good day, sir." The Corporal saluted sharply and Cross returned the gesture, mildly aware that he hadn't performed that little military ceremony in years.

Cross peeled off the back of the temporary permit and stuck it to the corner of his windshield, flipping on the intermittent wipers to clear the mist that had begun to settle. He slowly pulled away from the guardhouse and noticed the Corporal leaving his shack to lower the rail that blocked access to the Base. Cross was alone with his reflections. Only the occasional whine-thump of the wipers interrupted his thoughts.

The trees reminded Cross of vacations he had taken through the Black Forest. Far from the tensions and conflicts that occupied the time and energy of so many people, hc and Bridget had spent three beautiful weeks near Pforzheim. They had walked. They had shared hot coffee during cool evenings in front of a glowing fireplace; other times, they shared each other in touches and moans of pleasure, lifting one another through the joys of sexual intimacy, holding one another afterward, not wanting the present moment to ever go away. Whine-thump. Mist. Running in the rain one night after eating at a favourite restaurant in Pforzheim, they had collapsed on the doorstep of their cottage, laughing until Cross was actually in pain, the feeling that you can't take it any more, it feels too good...

This was how it always seemed to be for him. In the heat of the moment, his mind assumed control; the machine moved and struck, demanded, coerced. Then came the quiet. In younger days there were fantasies to keep him occupied and distracted. Done everything you can with one woman? Do it with two. Tried beer and wine with cottage cheese? Try them with vodka or grass or sleeping pills. Any goddamn thing to keep the quiet away. Then came Chicago and Bridget, and Cross discovered that quiet could be warm; that life wasn't just one steeplechase after another; that a man could slow down once in a while and still wake up sane. And then? A bad shot. A stray bullet. An accident.

Why? When he replayed it all, time and again he could find no answer. Why her? Why Bridget? Nothing. More terrible than before, the quiet always returned. Once, he never believed it could be filled, and it was. Now it was empty, and the running game did nothing to dull the pain. Sometimes, Cross had long ago decided, ignorance is safety. As the proverb says: "He is not poor who has little, but he who desires much." She had made him *want* so badly.

Cross didn't think twice about the burial of his adversary in Strasbourg, the parents or siblings who would mourn, or the mountains of paperwork some detective would have to complete to put a tag on this nameless American and his bloodstained moustache. He did what he had to do, and he'd do it again if the situation arose. And maybe his old man would live a few years longer, and he might even get to see Tracy-Jo have another calf the following spring if it all worked out. All that would make clear sense to him, if he could leave it at that. But as always, the quiet came—the place where Cross had let love pour in and fill the hole that needed a reason to keep breathing. Goddamn it. Relationships. Why bother setting yourself up for a kick in the head? Nothing lasts forever. Why did I let her get inside? I loved her so much! I loved her so fucking much...Whine-thump.

Cross slowed his car to a complete stop at the intersection northwest of the Officers Mess. It was almost eight o'clock. He could see a number of young officers on the sidewalk, leaving the Mess. It was good timing for breakfast, Cross reflected, guiding his rental into a parking spot at the far end of the lot. Most of the officers would be finished their meal and heading for eight o'clock appointments. He would have time and space to review General McDonnell's briefing notes over a second cup of coffee without having to explain his presence to regulars.

Walking to the doors of the Mess, Cross felt a bit dizzy. The trip from Washington had taken its toll, as usual. It would be fully three days before Cross would be feeling anywhere near normal. He had tried special diets, experimental drugs, sleeping before leaving, not sleeping before leaving—you name it. He finally decided that jet lag was like a bad case of the flu. Do whatever you can to get comfortable and let it run its course.

Breakfast was filling. Cross was satisfied that he could make it through his meeting with General McDonnell without collapsing. He figured whoever had brewed the coffee that morning must have been born under the same sign as he. It was strong and black.

He seated himself at the far end of the lounge in a chair that faced the entrance. Not that he had anything to be worried about here, but habits are comfortable. He broke the seal on the envelope he was handed at the gate and perused the information General McDonnell had left for him. It began:

69

GOOD MORNING COLONEL. I TRUST THE SERVICE HAS BEEN ADEQUATE AND YOUR JOURNEY FROM WASHINGTON WAS WITHOUT MISHAP. DURING YOUR STAY MY STAFF HAVE BEEN INSTRUCTED TO OFFER YOU EVERY ASSISTANCE AND TO ASK NO QUESTIONS. GIVEN THE POLITICAL CLIMATE OF LATE, THEY ARE LIKELY TO EXPECT ORDERS FOR MUNITIONS AS WELL AS MEALS. I ENCOURAGE YOU TO OPERATE FREELY AND TO CONSIDER YOURSELF DIRECTLY RESPONSIBLE ONLY TO YOUR SUPERIORS ON THE CONTINENT. I HAVE BEEN INSTRUCTED ON MY OWN NET TO PROVIDE YOU WITH APOLLO CLASSIFIED INFORMATION. THAT IS CLEARANCE ENOUGH FOR MY COMMAND TO BE PARTICULARLY SENSITIVE TO ANY REQUESTS YOU MIGHT DEEM APPROPRIATE FOR THE SUCCESSFUL COMPLETION OF YOUR TASK.

ONLY MYSELF AND ONE OTHER OFFICER HAVE HAD UNLIMITED ACCESS TO INFORMATION THAT MAY HAVE PROVED SEVERELY PREJUDICIAL TO THE POLITICAL POSITION OF NATO FORCES IN EUROPE OVER THE PAST ELEVEN MONTHS. YOU ARE AWARE OF THE TRAGEDY THAT ENDED THE LIFE OF THE OFFICER I REFER TO. UNTIL ANOTHER NATO OFFICER HAS BEEN APPOINTED TO WORK ON THIS DELIVERY WITH ME, I AM SOLE DIRECTOR OF THE OPERATION.

THERE ARE FIFTY-NINE PARCELS IN OUR WAREHOUSE AT PRESENT. IT IS NOT NECESSARY TO ELABORATE ON THE ODD NUMBER. THE ONLY TRUE LEADS WE HAVE TO ITS DISAPPEARANCE WERE EFFECTIVELY REMOVED BY THE DEATH OF COLONEL WALTER NEWCOMBE. THE FACTS AS WE KNOW THEM ARE AS FOLLOWS:

ON AUGUST 19TH, AN AMERICAN DESTROYER DELIVERED SIXTY PARCELS TO A PRESET TRANSFER POSITION OFF THE WEST COAST OF SCOTLAND. FROM THERE THE SHIPMENT WAS TO BE TRANSFERRED TO GREENWICH ENGLAND AND FLOWN BY CARGO TRANSPORT TO CFB BADEN FOR TEMPORARY STORAGE, TECHNICAL SERVICING IF NECESSARY, AND EVENTUAL UNDERGROUND DISPERSAL. ALL TRANSFER DOCUMENTS WERE CERTIFIED AND PRINTED BY COMPUTER, KEYED THROUGH A CODE KNOWN ONLY BY THE PRESIDENT OF YOUR COUNTRY. AS WELL, A PHYSICAL COUNT WAS CARRIED OUT AT THREE SEPARATE LOCATIONS, EACH COUNT

70

COMPLETED BY TWO SENIOR OFFICERS AT DIFFERENT STAGES OF THE SHIPMENT PROCESS. THE PARCELS WERE CAREFULLY WRAPPED TO CONCEAL THEIR MILITARY AGENDA AND SIXTY PARCELS ARRIVED HERE ON AUGUST 26TH AS PLANNED. WHEN THEY WERE UNWRAPPED ONE BOX WAS FILLED WITH IRON SCRAPS.

THIS IS THE PART WHICH IS DIFFICULT TO BELIEVE. THE PHYSICAL CHECKS BEFOREMENTIONED INCLUDED AN X-RAY SCAN WHICH WAS PROGRAMMED TO CORRELATE RADIOACTIVE SERIAL NUMBERS STAMPED TO THE PARCELS WITH A SPECIFIC CHECKLIST ON THE MASTER DELIVERY PROGRAM. ESSENTIALLY WHAT THIS MEANS IS THAT THE X-RAY VERIFIED EACH PARCEL TO ITS LABEL AT EACH TRANSPORT STATION ALONG THE ROUTE. THIS LEAVES US WITHOUT SO MUCH AS AN HYPOTHESIS AS TO WHEN OR WHERE THE PARCEL IN QUESTION MAY HAVE BEEN APPROPRIATED.

SEARCH-AND-FIND IS A MILD TERM FOR THIS ASSIGNMENT, COLONEL CROSS. YOU HAVE BEFORE YOU WHAT APPEARS TO BE THE ILLUSION OF MAGIC. I WOULD NOT BE SO FLIPPANT IN MY CHOICE OF ANALOGIES WERE I NOT SO ANXIOUS TO BELIEVE THAT THE SOLUTION COULD BE AS SIMPLE AS PULLING FLOWERS FROM THE SLEEVE OF MY UNIFORM. GOD HELP US ALL IF THERE IS NOT A CLEAR LEAD WITHIN THE NEXT FIVE TO SEVEN DAYS.

MY DRIVER WILL BE AT THE MESS TO PICK YOU UP AT NINE-FIFTEEN.

BRIGADIER GENERAL MCDONNELL
DEPUTY COMMANDER
CANADIAN FORCES EUROPE

"Pardon me, sir. Are you Colonel Cross?"

"Yes, I am."

"I'm your driver, sir. General McDonnell instructed me to pick you up at nine-fifteen."

"Thank you, Private, I'll be out in a moment." The young man smiled slightly and saluted. Watching as the soldier pivoted toward the lobby, Cross reflected that he had probably spent twenty minutes practicing his entrance. How clear and uncomplicated to have only one's belt buckle and shoes to be responsible for.

Cross had been startled by the interruption. He had spent the better part of an hour attempting to piece together the information he had been given since his arrival in Washington three days ago. All he could focus on were the gaping holes in logic that had left the best analysts of the CIA and many political figures groping in the dark like scared children who have good reason to be afraid of what they cannot see, cannot understand. Somewhere, someone had devised a plan that was so clearly directed and so sweeping in its ramifications that it had succeeded in enlisting people who were willing to kill themselves in order to protect it. This, coupled with the apparent ability of its directors to access top secret documents and perhaps to create biological disasters, had left Cross stunned with his imagination of the possibilities. By the time he began narrowing the facts toward a conclusion which considered an invasion of alien intelligence as one plausible explanation, he knew he had reached his own hypothetical limitations. Someone else was clearly in control of this game. He or she appeared to have sympathetic supporters in every conceivable level of international influence as well as technological expertise and considerable financial wealth. This last was an assumption, of course. It could be that the money Michel had spoken of in the bar was totally unconnected to the disappearance of the missile; perhaps the lead to the casino in Baden-Baden would provide Cross nothing more than an expensive evening's entertainment. But secrecy and commitment do not come cheaply. Cross would not be surprised to find that many paths were connected in the labyrinth he had discovered, including the paying of debts at a world-famous casino.

Cross pulled the ring from his suit jacket pocket and studied it for the tenth time since breakfast. TO THE GLORY OF ROME. Cross tossed the ring and grasped it tightly, throwing it back into his pocket.

Cross's first impressions of General McDonnell were not unlike those he had experienced the first time he went to Disney

World. He was curious, but also suspicious. The General's handshake was firm and warm, but Cross had come to suspect everyone. He still had not decided how he would maintain contact with his supports in Washington. Someone there had prepared a welcome for him in Strasbourg that had not been pleasant. Could he take this man at face value?

"Pleased to meet you, Colonel. I've heard good things from CIA Headquarters in Langely as well as personal recommendations from General Forsythe. Apparently you impressed the hell out of him on a search-and-find some years back."

"I'm afraid I've never met him, General. I did my job. I was successful. Someone had a lot to be thankful for, so I'm told."

"The story is almost always bigger and uglier than you suspect, Colonel. In that case the man you were instructed to locate was instrumental in the development of Allied Chemical Warfare. His abduction could have been disastrous had he been found by the Russians before we did. At the risk of sounding heartless, for us it would have been less complicated if he had died when the plane crashed. As it happened, your finding him first prevented the necessity of seeing to it that he not work for anyone at all."

"I'm not totally surprised," replied Cross. "I do my best not to extrapolate the motives of my superiors. I'd never get anything accomplished." He wasn't sure yet, but Cross began to relax. He noted no contradictions. His experience told him this officer was speaking cleanly.

"In this case, you are encouraged to assume and infer all you wish. The more minds burning candles over this file, the better our chances of jogging something loose that might be of help to us." General McDonnell closed the door to his soundproof office and took off his jacket. Loosening his tie, he sat on the edge of his desk and handed a file folder to Cross.

"That's the rest of it. I wasn't about to assume that even our lowly corporal at the gate did not have a hand in the pie when I passed him that envelope for you. I've spent a lot of years in this business, Cross, and I've seen more fuckups and treachery than the free world would want to ever hear of. Lost bombs, stolen codes, planned assassinations against our own people and church leaders. But at least there were leads. Eventually someone's ass was locked in a jar and shipped out and we learned our lessons for the next time. The scariest part of this crisis is that we've got no one to blame it on. Some disagree."

"Meaning?"

"Meaning that hardliners are apt to hide behind their blind belief that every evil menace in the world has a red flag and a communist party card in his wallet. While following their noses after the communist threat to democratic freedom they end up sticking their heads in the sand when it comes time for innovative thinking."

"And what's your opinion?"

"My opinion isn't worth shit because I haven't got a goddamn thing to back it up with. But I've got a right to it and until somebody proves me wrong, it's where I'm spending my money and my time." Cross's defenses gave him the green light. This guy was pulling no punches.

"You've got an audience, General."

"Back in 1974 I was attaché to the British ambassador for nineteen months. During that time we wined and dined just about every visiting dignitary on the political circuit of the day. It was a boom time for politicians. There were politcial and personal fortunes being made in oil and minerals, and the ambassador was adept at the social game of introduction and seduction. I was amazed at how much energy was concentrated on forming personal relationships with men and women of financial influence. Secrets were exchanged and bartered for investment information. You might say it was my initiation into the international financial community.

"There was one evening where the ambassador had arranged a private conference with a man who had made his money in computers and the development of computer technology. I was present at the meeting. His name was Roman Caspersan." Lights went on in Cross's mind. He had heard of Caspersan; a university genius; dropped from sophomore studies at MIT in the fall of 1968 for conspiring to procure NASA classified information regarding the moon mission through computer taping. Claimed he was planning to use the information as a thesis on the colonization instinct of man and his irrepressible drive to explore and conquer.

"Undoubtedly you can recall the furor which accompanied his arrest. Some of the press hailed him as a national hero who should be thanked for his ability to reveal gaps in the security of NASA information systems. Others wanted him permanently imprisoned as a threat to national security.

"He was tried on charges of treason, but acquitted on the grounds that the information he obtained could be proven as having been used solely for the development of his thesis on colonization. He spent eleven months in minimum security prison for tapping classified information without authorization and effectively dropped out of the limelight. Nothing was heard from him for years."

"So why the meeting?" asked Cross. "I wouldn't have been surprised to hear of him again, but not in the office of the British Ambassador."

"Caspersan had come up with some astounding results in his private endeavors to develop microchip technology from silicon that would double the density most companies were experimenting with at the time," answered General McDonnell. "As I recall, it had something to do with three-dimensional microprocessors. Anyway, the ambassador scheduled a private meeting to avoid the press but ended up laughing the man from his office, in effect telling him that he should stay with his social theories and avoid commerce. It was Caspersan's reply that stayed with me. I can't remember it word for word, but his message was basically this: He told the ambassador that the present advancements in computer technology were lazy, that they lacked the kind of circular thinking which would, for example, allow machines to eventually communicate freely with people. He said that Einstein was completely correct when he theorized there was one law which governed and was directly associated with each and every force of the universe. Social, political, electromagnetic, gravitational and physical forces played on each other, he said, and that one day he would demonstrate to the world how the never-ending cycles of the sun, of history and of finance, each represented one aspect of the law he called the Law of Circular Physics. He quoted some Latin phrase which the ambassador waved off as an eccentricity and stormed from the suite."

"And?"

"That's the point, Colonel. And—nothing. Caspersan dropped out of sight and has not been seen or heard of since. Official documentation begins with his birth in Maine and ends about two days after his departure from London. I can find no further trace of the man."

"Assuming, by some miracle, Caspersan didn't simply do away with himself or run off to the Himalayas, what makes you think he might have anything to do with this missile business? That incident you quoted occurred twenty years ago. I'm sorry General, I don't see any connection."

"That's exactly the point. There is no connection. There are no leads. There is no file that points to a pattern of behaviour which is familiar to our governments or which would explain the seemingly erratic behaviour and demands we've seen in the past year. I began looking for exactly that. A 'no-file', an eccentric. And I remembered Caspersan.

"I'm not looking for a pat on the shoulder, Cross. This file is part of the briefing. You might look at this as an indication of how close to the bottom of the barrel we've come in trying to find an explanation for this thing. But it's a hunch that feels warm. I haven't got anything but what's in that folder to back me up. At least I'm looking outside the Kremlin. Right now I believe the traditional focus is becoming a sore waste of time. Either Caspersan or someone like him is playing us all for fools, including the Soviets. There's just enough vengeance, veiled threats and eccentric playfulness in this picture to fit a brilliant man who has been burned badly by people from whom he may once have sought acceptance and possibly praise for his ingenuity and creativity. Maybe Caspersan was right about his theories. If he was, a tornado in the middle of the Texas badlands wouldn't be as far fetched as we might think."

Cross tried to catch some sleep before supper. He lay on his bed for half an hour, tossing and turning, commanding his brain to turn off and his system to shut down. Nothing worked. He decided to stop fighting the impulse to think, and put his hands behind his head. Staring at the white tiled ceiling, he reviewed in his mind the files General McDonnell had briefed him on.

Most of it was a rehash of the information Washington had provided. Dates, places, unanswered questions. But Cross was intrigued by McDonnell's account of his meeting with Caspersan. Roman Caspersan. TO THE GLORY OF ROME. Was it possible?

Cross did not share with General McDonnell the ring he carried from the dead body of his assailant in Strasbourg. He had decided for himself to begin tightening his own net, carefully screening information from people he wasn't absolutely certain he could trust. For the time being, that meant making sure Washington didn't have more to work with than they already had access to. Cross had played it over for himself a hundred times and he came up with the same answer. There had to be a mole at the top. Strasbourg was only one of several points he could have chosen to draw up his paperwork. The main reason he had finally settled on the border town was its proximity to Baden. No one could have foreseen his travel plans without prior knowledge of his destination.

Cross swung his legs over the edge of the bed and checked his watch. 5:37. Supper at six and an evening with the rich and bored from eight 'til eleven. He walked over to the mirror above the sink in the corner of his suite, running water for his second shave of the day. He wondered if the casino would yield any leads. Maybe the money funneled through was European and meant to appease foreign displeasure at Germany's fumbling of the recent talks in Geneva? Maybe everyone was looking in the wrong direction, and the casino was a dead end altogether? Cross slipped his hand into the water and let out a short scream. Might make a little sense to add some cold to the boiling hot, he chided himself. Whew. It's pretty obvious, he thought. Your mind is elsewhere.

Either Caspersan is involved or he's not. Either the fucking "Romans" are a clue or they're not. Here's my card, he said to himself, wetting his blade and pausing to smear shaving cream on his stubble. I'm preoccupied with this Roman shit. Either it's in or it's out. It's time to make up my own mind, one way or the other.

By the time they had reached the park in Baden-Baden, Private Mitchell had risked speaking with the hotshot from Washington on everything from international politics to his favourite

77

companions at the local brothel. He was cautious not to ask the Colonel his business, but had finally broken the normal courtesy of keeping silent until spoken to, by spouting his prowess and knowledge.

Cross was preoccupied. Had he been in a mood for silence, Private Mitchell would not have had the opportunity to ask directions much less carry on a one-way conversation with his charge. But Cross let him talk. Maybe seeing the private work out his nervousness reminded him it was human to be uptight from time to time. And that's what Cross was feeling. Surely by now word would have reached someone of the death at the border. If he was wanted and the casino had anything to do with the stolen missile, Cross would feel the heat before the end of the evening.

Cross noticed a small crowd had gathered for a game of chess on the outdoor chessboard. The game had never held much interest for him, but he was curious about those who enjoyed it. Especially when that recreation motivated people to build a board big enough to play basketball on.

"There you are, sir," said Private Mitchell, bringing the limousine to a smooth stop. "I hope I haven't disturbed you or bored you with my talking, sir."

"That's fine, Private. Don't worry about your stories. You can be sure I'll keep the news of your exploits to myself."

"Thank you, sir." The soldier waited as Cross quietly surveyed the entranceway and pulled on his gloves. "Will there be anything else, sir?"

"No. I'll be taking a taxi back to the base. Thank you for the ride."

"No problem, sir."

At the door Cross was met by an attendant who insisted on holding his passport and checking the guest list before he was permitted to enter.

It had been nearly ten years since Cross had last gambled here, but it hadn't changed at all from what he could see, As the huge oak doors closed behind him, he was mildly intrigued by the variety of uniforms, evening wear and languages spread out before him around the tables. Cross was startled by a voice from behind him.

"You are impressed by our games room, sir?" Cross turned to see a tall, thin, gray-haired gentleman speaking to him. He seemed proud of the casino. A manager perhaps.

"As I have been each time I've visited."

"Ah. A return customer! Does this mean we are indebted to you or should be wary of your skill as a gambler?" His smile was practiced, but Cross sensed the veneer would crack if he moved too quickly in the wrong direction. He regarded him for a moment and returned his attention to the crowds in front of him.

"I would say you are to be neither pleased nor cautious. When I gamble lightly I lose for the fun of it. I gamble more when I am more certain to win."

"I would be delighted to watch, Mr. --er--Cross." Caught momentarily off guard, Cross turned to face him. The passport. Cross relaxed and looked the taller man in the eye before responding.

"You are welcome, Mr..."

"Mr. Leblanc. My friends call me Joseph. You are free to choose whatever name you are most comfortable with." Cross nodded and began to slowly walk away. Doesn't take long, he thought. Somebody's nervous. That welcome was too greased and too warm. There is a connection. Someone here thinks I know more than I do. Time to play it up a bit.

Cross made his way through the crowds, occasionally standing over a diplomat as an unusually high sum was won or lost. He showed no particular interest in any one game. Others did not feel comfortable with his wandering.

After his initial greetings, the manager had slipped into his office to make a call. He was reporting as usual. Nothing to be concerned about.

"I cannot say for sure, Senator, but I am certain he will gain nothing here that will be of any use to him. Certainly. I do not know. This may not be the place to cause such a disturbance, Senator. Very well. I will see to it." The manager laid the receiver gently on its pedestal, and walked to a oneway mirror that faced the casino from the wall of his office. He watched as Cross introduced himself to a number of people at a blackjack table and reached for his medallion, absently fingering the edges.

"Hi." Cross smiled at a young woman who had just lost two hundred dollars on the dealer's blackjack. She looked up and smiled a weary smile. "Is there anyone sitting here?"

"Yes, there is. My date. I guess you'd call him a date. More like company. Have a seat and keep it warm for him. I think he's gone to call his banker." She smiled another tired smile, this one seeming to Cross sad and bored as well. Too bad, he reflected. She was very beautiful. Short blonde hair, firm figure, and makeup artfully applied. An athlete maybe.

"Do you always have this much fun when you go out?" teased Cross, waving five hundred dollars at the dealer.

"When I go out is when I'm not working or travelling and that is rare. Maybe if I had more practice I'd be better at amusing myself."

"And when you're bored you gamble thousands of dollars away and carry on conversations with perfect strangers while they keep the stool warm for your partner."

"Whoa. He's no partner. My mother would never forgive me. And sure. Stranger or no stranger you said hello." She smiled. To Cross the gesture looked like a touch of amusement, maybe gratitude. If this is the most exciting her evening has been, someone is playing the wrong game. The fellow who gained her company might well be spending more time entertaining and less at the bank. She was lovely. "Speak of the devil, here he comes. He may not be much, but Baden's a small city. Thanks for the diversion."

"Anytime." Cross gathered his chips and allowed the man who had escorted this new acquaintance to take his stool beside her.

For the past hour Cross had been aware he was being watched. He gambled at various tables. He had noticed almost immediately that the room had four bouncers. Each was appropriately dressed for the occasion, but seemed more comfortable with the occupation than the dress code. Their hulking forms contrasted noticeably with the softer lifestyles their guests advertised.

Cross was waiting for the time to start pushing buttons. General McDonnell expected him back at the base by early morning, but Cross had insisted on being given the freedom to move on his own. He agreed to inform the General if anything unplanned came up, but he flew solo. The General agreed it was his assignment and his choice and supported him fully. Now Cross wondered how his questions might backfire. Would he be up against those four wrestlers alone? Maybe he could outrun them. He smiled. No use putting off the inevitable. Time to move.

Cross positioned himself at the blackjack table opposite the beautiful woman he had conversed with so briefly. For one thing he liked the view. It also gave him a clear field to engage who he liked while keeping an eye on the muscle should things start to warm up.

"Pardon me." Cross spoke to the dealer in hushed tones as he began shuffling cards for another round.

"Yes, sir?"

"I'm wondering if you could tell me how to find a Mr. Roman Caspersan. I've heard he often gambles here." The dealer looked up at Cross with a mixture of surprise and horror: like a man who sees himself sleeping with his mistress on National Television. He lost his hold on the cards and dropped half the deck on the floor. In an instant the six years of training and experience that had landed him the position with this casino began seeping from his grasp. Cross looked on innocently as if still awaiting an answer to his question. "Should I maybe ask around?" The dealer attempted to regain his composure.

"Why, not at all, sir. I will ask the manager if he has seen anyone recently by that name." Picking up the remaining cards and calling a pit boss for new decks, he excused himself. Now Cross was sure. General McDonnell was on to something. By the look on the dealer's face, something significant.

Talk about service, mused Cross. Here comes my friend the manager. Cross could tell the heat would soon be real warm in the casino. His instincts made him look for an open door, a ticket out. A small whine from the table opposite gave him an idea. The blonde woman had apparently just lost more money. In one of those moves that follow intuition rather than common sense, Cross scribbled a note on the back of a pack of matches and eased his way from his stool to the blackjack table where the woman was playing. The manager had stopped and asked two of his bouncers to stand by. Cross figured he had about thirty seconds.

81

"Pardon me, I don't think I got your name." The woman smiled at first, and then, noting the concerned expression on Cross's face pulled back, confused. "My name is Warren." He place the remainder of his chips on her table and the matchbook in in her hand. "I'd like to thank you for your advice on that silver mine in South Africa. I believe it will be well worth these chips." Cross squeezed her hand firmly and held her gaze. The woman looked at him. Half scared, half fascinated. "What's your name?"

"Claire. Claire Monty."

"It's been nice meeting you, Claire. I'd like to talk more another time."

"Mr. Cross, I see you have made an acquaintance," interrupted the manager. "I feel ashamed that I must pull you from such an attractive companion, but I'm afraid there is something rather urgent that has come up that needs your immediate attention." Cross could see he had two companions of his own, together weighing well over a quarter ton. Two more had their eye on him from the doors.

"I assume there is no way I could convince you to hold my calls until I'm finished here."

"I'm afraid not."

VIII

Claire did not pay much attention to her date most of the way home. He had interpreted her indifferent nods and smiles as consent to spending the night with him. Being somewhat drunk and quite confident of his charm, he finally caught her full attention by slipping his fingers inside her low-cut dress to cup her firm breast.

"What the hell do you think you're doing?" Claire shoved his arm from her so quickly he cracked the face of his watch on the ashtray protruding from the back of the front seat.

"I'm feeling your tit—what do you think I'm doing? You just agreed to come home with me, for fuck's sake."

"Like hell! Not only do you drink too much, but you smell like you haven't washed since last weekend. Driver, let me out at that café." Ignoring protests and apologies, Claire Monty left the taxi, frustrated with her lack of enthusiasm, and hurt somehow. She knew he wasn't the type she'd marry, but even a little male company for a night shouldn't be so humiliating. Then this stranger comes up, throws a book of matches in her hand, and gives her the message that she's got to do something important for him. Make some kind of phone call. Shit.

Another taxi finally dropped her off at her apartment. Three o'clock in the morning and nothing to show for a night out but a splitting headache and some guy's name on a matchbook cover.

Claire fumbled with her keys. Imagine! *'Hi my name is Warren. Is there anyone sitting here? Do you always talk to strangers? Oh, by the way, could you please phone a General McSomebody at this number and let him know Cross needs help? Gee, thanks a lot. You've been a real pal.'* Claire opened the door and threw her keys on the bookcase. It was the only place she could put her keys and know for sure where to find them. Losing her keys was a constant pastime. In a way it was the epitome of Claire's dual life. At home she couldn't even consistently locate the can opener.

Claire was a loner, a person who loved the outdoors, sports and movies. On the other hand the girls at work were always teasing her that she was the most organized person they had ever known. And as a computer programmer for American Hi-Tech's West German subsidiary, she was organized. Organized, efficient, productive. A kind of supervisor's dream. No program she couldn't turn out, no project she wouldn't take on. A workaholic. A damn good one. Her high school guidance counselor said she had an IQ of 176. Her Aunt Joan told her she could be Miss America if she took the time to fill out an application. Claire looked in the mirror each morning before breakfast, thankful that her acne had completely cleared up before she left high school and unaware that she had a face and a figure that some men would give anything to seduce.

Some had tried to win her. On one occasion Claire had even tried to cooperate. But it didn't work out. It was third year university. He forced her to choose between their relationship and the university's Computer Programming Club. Bad move. He lost. Even Claire could never completely understand why her work always seemed to take first priority with her.

Claire whipped off her shoes and headed for the bathroom, dropping them in a corner and peeling stockings along the way. Maybe men were threatened by her abilities? Or maybe she found most men too insecure or insensitive to be any challenge? She turned off the sink taps and pulled her purse from the door handle where she had hung it. Here. Take this one, for example. A matchbook cover, for God's sake. Like something out of a Humphrey Bogart movie. "Call General McDonnell at Canadian Forces Base Baden, ext 4426. Tell him Cross is in trouble." *Tell him*. Not even the courtesy of *asking* me to call. *Tell him Cross is in trouble*. Humph. Maybe I should call just to find out if this is another pickup hoax....Claire was embarrassed and mildly confused by her reaction to the note. He was actually quite charming and polite when he introduced himself, she remembered. But there sure wasn't any fat on his message. *Call this number. Tell him...* So what if I do, Claire asked herself,

84

rinsing the sweat and smoke from her face. It's either a hoax or it's not. What can it hurt? Here's what I'll do—I'll call. I'll tell this General, if there is one, that this acquaintance I met at the casino asked me to call and leave it at that. Surely to God I can make an anonymous phone call without getting all perturbed about it. That's it. I'll just dial the number, feel good about doing some stranger a favour and forget it. Why, then, Claire asked herself quietly, do I sort of hope it is just a hoax? Why am I excited that maybe this stranger gave me a novel way of getting back to him? Forget it, sister. You're thirty-six years old, no serious relationship and about as interested in romantic mystery as Russian Opera.

Claire Monty finished cleaning up and threw on her housecoat. She moved with a soft and bouncing step that betrayed her love for outdoor sports, and sat cross-legged on the bed with a pillow on her lap. Claire always felt more secure on the phone if she had a pillow to keep her company. She dialed the number and leaned back on the headboard playing with the extension cord.

"Good morning, Canadian Forces Base Baden, bonjour."

"Hello?" Claire was disappointed, and frightened. Should she have called sooner? Should she be calling at all?

"Good morning, CFB Baden, can I help you?" The woman's voice was clear and sounded helpful.

"Hello. I'm sorry to be calling so late..."

"No problem, ma'am. This is my turn for graveyard, what can I do for you?"

"I'm afraid there's been a mistake. I—well, is there a General McDonnell there?" Claire had begun to clutch the pillow closer to her. The apartment suddenly seemed like a very lonely place to be spending the night.

"I'm afraid that's classified information, ma'am. If you have a message for a General McDonnell, I'd be willing to have it taken care of." Unsure of why she began to feel more anxious, Claire insisted.

"No, I think I need to speak with him immediately. I have a message from someone who has asked me to contact him right away on an urgent matter."

"Were you given an extension, ma'am? Otherwise I'm afraid the message will have to wait."

85

"The extension I was given is 4426."

"Yes, ma'am. I'll put you through immediately." The Corporal at the switchboard sounded tense. Claire's throat felt terribly dry.

"General McDonnell."

"Is this a real General? I mean, are you—is this extension 4426?" Claire was embarrassed and very nervous. She pulled her housecoat closer around her. *Tell him Cross needs help.* Claire felt terribly irresponsible. How could she have known the situation was what he said it was? What a strange way to meet an honest man.

"Pardon me? Yes, this is extension 4426. My name is General McDonnell. You must have some reason for calling, Ms..."

"Claire Monty. My name is Claire Monty. I'm calling for a man named Warren Cross. I think that's his full name. He just handed me this book of matches..."

"I realize you are probably confused and frightened, Ms. Monty, but any information about his man you refer to is of the utmost importance. Please continue."

"Well, all he wrote was 'tell General McDonnell Cross needs help'."

"Did he say what kind of help?"

"No."

"Did anyone at the casino see you with him?"

"We had only spoken for a few minutes. I—I don't know. I mean I'm not sure..."

"Ms. Monty, I want you to listen very carefully to me. I understand that you could not have any idea what this information means or who this man Cross represents. But I'm afraid it is absolutely essential that we meet."

"Well, er—General, this business has kind of taken me by surprise. I've just come from a long evening out and..."

"I am aware that your outing has been disturbed. I assure you, Ms. Monty, you will be fully compensated for your time. Could I ask you to be ready in about twenty minutes? I'll have a staff car sent for you right away."

"General, with all due respect, this is not really any of my business. I'd need a few moments to think it over."

"I can understand your need to sort out what is happening. I must inform you, madam, that you have become involved, albeit

86

without prior consent, in something of national and perhaps international significance. If I could call on your benevolence and patience, I would be prepared to explain more when we meet.''

"Very well, General,'' replied Claire, coming to her own conclusion for the moment. By God. Any man with the audacity to hand a perfect stranger information that would result in her being hauled from the comfort of her home at three-thirty in the morning owed her more than a simple explanation. Mr. Warren Cross had better be prepared... "I'll be ready in twenty minutes. This is my address...''

***

For Cross, the bouncer in the back of the sedan was not the problem. It was the driver. No sooner had his escort covered his bloody nose and begun to slump in the seat beside him than the driver had squealed the car hard right to a complete stop, fully discouraging any further antics by a blow to the side of Cross's head with a billy club that left his head throbbing.

"You are incorrigible, Mr. Cross, truly. Surely you do not believe that I would allow you to slip away like sand in the hand of a child when you have left me with so many interesting questions to ask, so many things to discuss.'' Joseph Leblanc was standing next to the door of the shed, his hands clasped in front of him like a young boy receiving his first holy communion. The small building Cross had been driven to, was dark and empty except for a bare light bulb and a wooden table with two chairs. One of the bouncers, standing off in a corner, occupied a full quarter of the room. He carried a pistol in his right hand that looked to Cross to be the size of a small rocket launcher. So much for the "really-can't-stay-for-coffee'' routine.

"For a manager you certainly take an avid interest in visitors to the casino, Mr. LeBlanc. I daresay you are hiding something. Come now. This is no love touch I'm sporting. What do you really want from me?'' Cross rubbed the side of his head and looked at the tall man with a mixture of amusement and feigned innocence. Mr. LeBlanc began playing with his medallion and laughed shortly.

"Very good, Mr. Cross. Your portrayal of the captured soldier who uses humour and disguised insult to frustrate his captors is most commendable. Am I to assume you will offer me nothing more than your name, rank and serial number after all the trouble I've gone through to make you comfortable?"

"The trouble with you is your approach, Mr. LeBlanc. There is a definitive lack of social grace in the way you invite people to share your hospitality. There I was, standing at the blackjack table looking for an old college buddy of mine, and the next thing I know I'm whisked off to the tool shed for interrogation. Not really professional, Mr. LeBlanc. Not professional at all." Mr. LeBlanc walked to the table and pulled out the second chair. Sitting down opposite Cross he looked at him for a moment. He smiled. "Cuff him," Leblanc said, waiting until one of the bouncers handcuffed Cross and tied his arms to the chair, before speaking.

"This could be a long and drawn-out process, Mr. Cross. I am at a loss to explain how surprised I was to hear you asking for someone who has been assumed dead for well over a decade. My curiosity was such that I was compelled to detain you until I got some answers. I can assure you I am not so patient that I can wait forever."

"Hell, I can make it simple for you. Roman and I were college roommates in '67. He helped me with physics, and I helped him get laid. It was a viable and highly profitable agreement for us both."

"Don't anger me, Mr. Cross. I know that you have recently been involved with activities near the Franco-German border that resulted in the death of a dear friend of mine. Our reports conclude that he chose the honourable route of self-sacrifice. It is only my own commitment to history that prevented me from having you dragged away and shot when I first learned of your arrival at the casino. You will not live, Cross. You know that. Your cooperation might influence the manner in which you die, which is the most I am prepared to offer you. You are not in a position to bargain or challenge my assumptions."

88

"Very well. As you wish. I am actually a real estate agent looking for investment possibilities in the new Roman Era. If you'll be so kind as to give Romie my card, I'll give him a call next time I'm in Baden..." The manager's anger flared. He stood and struck Cross with the back of his hand.

"Don't *dare* speak of him or his ideals with the impudence of North American arrogance! We are not toying with history here, Mr. Cross, we are in the making of it!"

"I am relieved to know why you and your dead colleague have so much in common. I was beginning to believe that maybe it was just a dreadful coincidence. Two idealistic morons living within three hundred kilometers of each other."

Mr. Leblanc pulled at the corners of his tuxedo and straightened his hair. "You are a singularly courageous man, Mr. Cross. The only other possible explanation for your fulgurous presentation is complete idiocy. I tire of your slander. You and the government you represent have come to the end of an age. The human race has been living an indulgent and hedonistic existence for almost two thousand years. Most men cannot see a vision of true civilization because they have become bogged in the marshes of laziness and indolent leisure.

"Perhaps you think we could be convinced that your theory of Mr. Caspersan's involvement is shared by those who sent you to find the stolen missile? Now I will present you with true arrogance—the kind that is based on knowledge: We know that all levels of government in your country are confused and have no clear hypothesis regarding the loss of the missile. We know that neither the Soviets nor the Americans have any idea who or what is behind the frantic international stresses that have been initiated in the last twelve months. You have no one you can trust. Your attempts to save the life of your father are commendable, but you are alone. You are alone, and your death will be of little consequence to anyone."

"I'm not so brave," returned Cross, pushing his chair back from the table with his feet. "I want to live, just like the next guy. I don't know who your source is, but you're right. I am alone. Maybe there is something I can offer your cause."

The manager smiled, feeling in control of the process for the first time. "I might have once thought you could be useful, but not now. You're too unpredictable, Mr. Cross. You would turn on your own government if you discovered some personal reason for disagreement with your superiors. We do not run an organization based on free-agent espionage. We are building the future of the human race the way it was meant to be structured— on hard work, vision and obedience.''

''Where does that put me?''

The manager shrugged his shoulders and moved toward the door. ''I'd like to say something comforting, Mr. Cross, but you are a grown man. You deserve the right to know your immediate destiny if not that of the world beyond. Mr. Lewis here will be escorting you to a gravel pit where you will be shot in the head. Any other questions?''

''You. What's your destiny?''

''I like to travel. I will be carrying news of your demise with me to a celebration in Istanbul, where the last move on the gameboard of nations will be played.''

''I'd love to be there to celebrate with you.''

''I'm sure you would. One of the greatest comforts of this journey will be the knowledge that I carry with me a ring that proves I have disposed of the man who murdered my friend Carl Peterson.''

''The man in Strasbourg.''

''Goodbye, Mr. Cross.''

***

Claire Monty had tried her best to remain livid with resentment and righteous fury over being dragged into something that had nothing whatsoever to do with her. But she couldn't help feeling excited and more than mildly curious about her sudden involvement with the military. General McDonnell must have ordered top speed to the driver, for he arrived at her doorstep exactly twenty minutes after she had hung up. The alarm and seriousness with which she was being treated felt strange and exotic. There was a pervading sense of being caught up in a wave of mystery and suspense, like being thrown into a fast-moving river, not knowing where it might take her.

''Driver, what can you tell me about Mr. Warren Cross?''

"I'm sorry, ma'am, I'm not authorized to speak with you on any subject whatsoever."

"Can't you just give me an idea why I'm being hauled down to CFB Baden at four in the morning? Surely to God..."

"Please ma'am," the young soldier interrupted. "I'd like to be more helpful, but I'm just doing my job. I'd ask that you be quiet until we reach the base."

So much for courtesy. Shit. This is all a mistake, Claire mumbled to herself. All this drama and General McDonnell is probably looking for Cross because he was supposed to return his daughter after dinner and dancing and forgot her in a bar downtown.

"Good morning, Ms. Monty. My name is General McDonnell." The office was comfortably furnished. General McDonnell looked like he was in the middle of a day's work, surrounded by papers, clean shaven and dressed in full uniform. Claire returned the handshake a bit more firmly than she had intended to.

"Good morning, General." There was a period of silence while he gathered some of the papers he was working on and placed them in his briefcase. It seemed like an hour. This was very strange, Claire thought. I'm a computer programmer who's afraid of relationships and likes to mountain climb. What the hell am I doing here?

"I know you have many questions, Ms. Monty. I will try to be as clear and concise as possible. Hopefully you will not be detained for longer than necessary." Detained? What the hell does he mean—detained?

"I came here voluntarily and intend to leave here as soon as I begin to feel uncomfortable, General. Let's be clear about that right off the bat. If anything, I'm doing you a favour." Despite his ability to socialize with diplomats from around the world, General McDonnell had forgotten what it was like to be directly confronted by an ordinary civilian.

"Very well, Ms. Monty. I can hear your position. If you would be so kind as to hear mine.

Mr. Cross was assigned a very important task in Baden-Baden this evening which may have placed him in considerable personal danger. He has not contacted us since his departure and his message to you leads us to believe he may require immediate assistance. Could you please tell me how he happened to choose you to pass this book of matches? Had you met him somewhere before?"

That's a damn good question, Herr General. Why did he choose me?

"I can't answer that, General, because I don't know why. He stopped by my table about an hour before. We talked, at the most, for five minutes. He seemed to be looking for a seat to play blackjack. My date had left for a moment and this Cross person kept his seat warm. We never spoke again until he stepped up and pressed the note in my hand." General McDonnell could clearly see why any wandering male, on assignment or otherwise, would find himself gravitating toward a woman like Claire Monty. It was past four o'clock in the morning, she was dressed in a T-shirt and jeans and still she was lovely.

"What was going on at the time he passed you the matches? Did he leave with anyone, or leave alone?"

"As a matter of fact, the casino manager came up and told him there were 'urgent things' Mr. Cross needed to take care of. Then he got up and they left together."

"Did you happen to see where they went?"

"I was curious so I watched them walk to the entrance, but once the big doors swung shut, that's the last I heard or saw of him."

"This is the book of matches?" Claire was folding and unfolding them as she spoke. She nodded.

"May I see?" General McDonnell quickly read the note. He threw them on the desk. Claire was angered, for some reason. After all, Warren had given them to her. Warren?

"Was there anything else, anything at all you noticed tonight in the short time you were with Mr. Cross that might be of help to us in trying to locate him?"

Claire shifted her attention momentarily from the dizzying questions and inner emotions that were beginning to contribute to a headache even worse than the one she had brought home from the casino. She tried to envision Cross. She flushed. All she could see was the side of his face when he turned to leave her table.

92

"I'm afraid that's all I can tell you, General. I wish I had spent more time with him. I mean, I wish I knew more."

"What you've given us confirms for me that he was desperate."

"Desperate?"

General McDonnell looked up from the small pad where he was jotting down notes of Ms. Monty's contact with Cross. He smiled. "I don't mean desperate for company, Ms. Monty. I can say with complete confidence that he would have chosen to introduce himself to you regardless of whether or not he thought you might be of some help."

Claire was embarrassed. "I—I didn't mean that, General. I was just er—worried at the seriousness of this matter."

"It is serious. And I know that both my own government and others are indebted to you."

"What happens now?"

"For you, it's quite simple. If you can, please return to your suite and get some sleep. It would also make sense to put this terribly inconvenient string of events out of your mind. I always feel awkward at involving civilians in such matters. Thank you very much for your help."

"Whoa, just a minute," said Claire, raising her hand slightly as if she were stopping traffic. "I think I have a right to know a bit more than you've shared with me, General. It's one thing to be involved in something that does not concern you. It is another thing altogether to be expected to just let go of the whole experience without any explanations. I feel I deserve at least that for my troubles."

"I'll be frank with you, Ms. Monty, and tell you that I was concerned you'd want to know more. The one thing you feel a need to understand, I can tell you nothing about..." Claire seemed about to interrupt but General McDonnell continued. "...and there can be no discussion or bargaining. Much like having a stranger ruin a new dress by splashing water on it while driving through a puddle, I'm afraid this is just one of those things."

"Is there any way I could maybe call Mr. Cross at some time and..."

"I am almost certain you will never see him again, Ms. Monty.

93

Please do not think me rude when I say that I can understand you feeling intrigued and maybe caught up in a fast lane. But this is not late night entertainment. Your encounter with Mr. Cross was an incident that would best be forgotten."

"Just like that?"

"Just like that."

Claire knew she would get nowhere here. The Armed Forces be damned, she thought to herself. I've got a computer and ten years of experience getting at information that doesn't belong to me. We'll see who gets access to what.

"Very well, General," said Claire with a shrug of resignation. "It is embarrassing to know that you may have remarked some interest in Mr. Cross on my part, but I guess that is normal. He was a charming individual in the short time we conversed. I would have liked to get to know him better."

"No need to feel embarrassed, Ms. Monty. I'm sure he would be complimented. I'll call my driver to take you back to your suite."

***

There hadn't been much discussion once Mr. LeBlanc turned to leave. Cross was untied from the chair and brought to a waiting vehicle outside. He could hear cars speeding on the Autobahn. The bouncer pointed his .44 Magnum at the back seat, and Cross climbed in.

Cross knew that any diversion would have to be aimed at distracting the driver first. He was the same one who had clubbed Cross earlier. Cross was also aware that he might only get one chance, if at all. There was no reason for anyone to treat him gently. The trip to the gravel pit was to be a trip to his grave.

The driver had spun from the shack and turned immediately toward the woods, taking a left, then a right over a dirt road. Reaching a highway that seemed to run parallel to the Autobahn, they sped southeast toward Reutlinger, the wooded area of the Black Forest on their left and farmers' fields on the right.

"Your distinguished career will soon be colliding with the Great Beyond, Mr. Cross. A man as adventurous as yourself must be looking forward to it," the driver commented, occasionally glancing at Cross in the rear-view mirror.

"I don't believe in the great whatever," answered Cross, gazing out the window and feigning indifference.

"You should," answered the driver, mocking seriousness. "My grandmother lived to be ninety-four. She swore that she owed it to her faith in God. 'Trust in God' she'd say, 'and don't let anything worry you'."

"Fuck your grandmother," answered Cross.

"Good, Mr. Cross. Ventilate. You will die with a sense of victory. When your friends find you a week from now, you will be bloated and stiff, but if I'm ever asked, I'll tell them you truly shared your feelings before you died." The driver began to chuckle. "Eh, Brutus? Do you think maybe our friend here will..." Now, thought Cross. While the bouncer had turned to respond to the driver, Cross threw all the weight of his arm and shoulder into the kidney of the big man seated next to him with the point of his elbow. In the same movement, Cross reached for the Magnum with both hands and squeezed off two rounds, one boring a hole in the side of the door, the other embedding itself firmly between the liver and left lung of the man driving in the front seat.

The bouncer had reacted to Cross's initial attack with surprise, amazed that he would dare try anything. Surprise turned to rage as Cross lunged for the pistol, but it was too late. By the time he had control of the handgun, the car had already begun to swerve violently to the left. It hit the edge of the road, and rolled, knocking both him and Cross unconscious.

Cross awoke to the smell of gasoline. He needn't have worried about struggling against the bouncer. When the car rolled, the edge of the car's rear door had struck against a boulder and chiseled its way into his huge neck, severing three quarters of the man's head from the rest of his body.

Cross knew it was only a matter of time before the car blew up. He managed to push out what remained of the rear window and crawl away from the wreckage. There wouldn't be time to celebrate. Scrambling across the road and down into the ditch, his pant leg had become caught in old barbed wire. Cross stood there for a moment, breathing heavily and trying to free himself from a rusted section of the fence. The handcuffs had begun to slice dull cuts in his wrists and salt from the sweat ran down his forearms, stinging bitterly. The BMW sedan exploded. Cross covered his face with his arm. He swallowed hard and coughed. Thank God they had handcuffed his hands in front of him, he thought. Ripping the trouser cuff and splitting flesh six inches along the side of his calf, Cross finally disentangled himself and began running again, stumbling over harrowed fields toward the base.

IX

"What's this, Claire? Weekends too?" Thirty-four years old with the stature and voice of the boy next door, Robert Forester smiled his warmest smile at the sight of Claire. He had harboured a deep and unshakable fantasy of bedding down with her since they were first introduced three years ago. Refusing to see his glasses, his height, or his inability to choose a tie that matched his sports jacket as an impediment to his dream of having her, he used every encounter as an opportunity to impress Claire Monty with his sincerity. He hoped she'd eventually see behind his cool act and simply ask him to put his nose between her breasts and get on with it. One day at a time, he told himself.

"Hi, Bobby," teased Claire, returning his smile. "I can't help it. Everyone else in the office is out humping their way through the weekend in chalets across the country, and my only successful seduction is at the keyboard. I guess I keep coming back where I feel most comfortable."

Try me! Try me for fuck's sake! "Yeah, I know the feeling," returned Bob, parking himself on the edge of her desk with a styrofoam cup of coffee in his hand. "I like to get caught up a bit on Saturday afternoons sometimes. I get bored with the nightlife. There's only so many brothels a man can go to without feeling there must be something better in life."

"Isn't that just the God's honest truth," agreed Claire, amused as always at Forester's attempt to impress her. She thought once that if he kept up his present track record, she might just sleep with him one night before she left Europe. Under all that disorganization and nerd-like outer shell was a warm heart. Putting one elbow on her desk, she leaned on her hand and gave him her full attention.

97

Forester beamed. "I just thought I'd finish up the flowcharts for the Nelson-Coleman paycheck sheets. I figured old man Girard would want to preview them Monday morning, even though we didn't even get the contract until Thursday afternoon. What are you working on?"

Claire raised her eyebrows and turned back to her screen. "To be honest, Bob, I'm doing a little undercover dirty work."

"That's half of what we're paid for," joked Forester. It was true, in a manner of speaking. Although not directly condoned by management, programmers were encouraged to tap data banks wherever and whenever they could to scrounge for faster and better programs. It also helped them develop computer protection systems for their own contracts. It could be dangerous, however. Any programmer actually caught by the authorities was required to take full responsibility for their "initiative".

"This one's a bit more personal, Bobby, I'm trying to connect with someone who owes money to a friend of mine, but he's not answering phone calls," Claire said. "She wants me to see if I can figure out when he arrived in Europe and where he's staying."

"Do you need any help?"

"Not at the moment. But I'll tell you what. If I get stuck, I'll head right for your desk."

Forester smiled shyly. "Okay. Great. Hey, by the way, how about dinner tonight?"

Claire wished she had kept count. This must be close to the tenth time Forester had risked himself by asking her out.

"Sorry, Bobby. You know the rules. No fraternizing with guys from work. It just keeps my life uncomplicated."

Defeat. Again. "You know, Claire," began Forester in a rare display of frustration. "You really can be one hell of a hard person to get close to. Has anyone ever told you that?"

"I've told myself that a million times," agreed Claire, running smooth fingers through her dusty blonde hair. "Maybe I'm just scared that somebody will actually like me. When you've spent thirty-some years keeping men at arm's length, it gets to be a habit, you know?" Claire was suddenly surprised by how candidly she had spoken. Forester was too.

"I guess so, Claire. If you ever want to practise, just dial 772 on your modem. I'll be hanging over the edge of your cockpit before you've got a chance to type your initials on the message."

Claire's "initiative" became a frustrating cycle of leads and no-leads, with protection services or disconnected modems closing doors for her before she had a chance to do any real digging. It finally dawned on her that she was going the long way about it. Instead of trying to slide her way past more sophisticated controls at the Armed Forces Base, why not begin with international airports. Maybe Cross didn't even fly in by military transport.

Bingo. Cross, W.G., Flight 463 from New York. Arrived Paris at 12:17 local. Son-of-a-bitch! No connecting flight. No return. So he's been in Europe for three days. He must have stopped over somewhere. Hmm. Flights were arranged privately. No hotels booked. Here. Phoned ahead from the aircraft. Mercier Car Rentals. No specified time limit. No specified drop location. Shit!

The afternoon dragged on. There were a few surprises. Claire learned that Cross carried an American Express Gold Card. Its use over the past four months showed an occasional taste for beer and pizza. Hmmph. Pizza night? My guess is it's a front for regular drug use. God only knows who he spent those nights with. Probably turns on the charm every third week just to keep in practice. Claire stopped typing and stared over her console at the clock on the far wall. Look at yourself. You've been here for almost seven hours. What are you doing this for? And even if you could figure that one out, do you have the right? Don't you feel that slightest tinge of guilt or embarrassment, prying into the private affairs of a man you talked to for less than five minutes? Where's your professional ethics? *Call this number. Tell him Cross is in trouble*...the hell with ethics. You got me into this, Warren Cross. Let's play ball.

It was now 7:30 P.M. Claire had taken twenty minutes to share a pepperoni and mushroom with Forester. Maybe she was trying to prove that eating pizza with someone of the opposite sex could be harmless. Whatever her motivation, Forester was thrilled at the offer, until a slight accident interrupted his racing fantasies.

His third slice of pizza slipped off his hand and slid three quarters of the way down the front of his shirt. He decided, at that point, that it might be better to quit while he was ahead, and insisted he had to leave. And Claire, after taking a few moments to wash the grease off her fingers, dove back at the screen for step two. Making contact.

Claire had learned early in her career that information could sometimes be added to an existing data bank much easier than it could be retrieved. In some ways she found it hard to understand why a lending institution, for example, might spend $75,000 for a system that would almost guarantee protection of existing accounts, but would apply little or no money insuring new accounts weren't simply created and then drawn from. Maybe it was the fear of the common depositor who demanded absolute protection of personal funds that made the difference. Whatever the motivator, Claire was grateful. In an hour, she had succeeded in screening a cursor for **CFB BADEN** that awaited her input.

> A: "TO: *(what do you call this character?)* Guest-Cross, W.G.
> ACCOMMODATION: Officers Mess *(best guess)*
> FROM: Headquarters
> MESSAGE: Mr. Cross is requested to contact Ms. Claire Monty at 842 Duveltstrausse, 49-228-12345 as soon as possible for an urgent personal message. If machine replies, please leave number. She will return your call."

For a long time, Claire paused. In a way the message didn't really seem very military. But maybe it wasn't only military people who had access to the computers on base. She debated. Should she put 'urgent personal message', or 'urgent message'? She decided 'urgent message' would seem more formal. She pressed the enter button on her keyboard and waited. No turning back now, she decided. One way or another, I'm involved.

***

It had been a very long night for General McDonnell. Once the tragic suicide death of Colonel Newcombe had come and gone, he was convinced that he had experienced every shock the military could throw at him. But the last two days made him question his assumption. A forty-five minute air search had located Cross approximately thirty kilometers northwest of the base at 06:10 hours. He was bruised, but not seriously.

General McDonnell shook his head and turned on the cold water tap in the kitchen of his Staff Officers Suite. He let the water run for a few minutes, and reached for a glass on the counter. Saturday hadn't been much better. There was the long conversation with Wallace in Washington about the Caspersan theory. Funny how he had insisted on knowing where Cross was and what he'd be doing. *I don't feel totally comfortable with him,* thought the general. *He's too nervous. Like he's hiding something. Come to think of it, he made one hell of a fuss over knowing all the details before I talked with McKay. Something about McKay insisting that he not be disturbed until Sunday. Soviet propaganda or some damn thing. I'm going to have a talk with McKay about that son-of-a-bitch as soon as it's dawn in the States.* The loud ring of the phone interrupted his thoughts.

"General McDonnell?"

"Speaking."

"Sorry to bother you, sir, but we've just had a red flag show on our printouts that concerns Colonel Cross. I think you had better come take a look at it."

"Be more specific, man, is it a directive or related information?"

"It's, well, it's hard to tell, sir. I—I think it's a personal message, sir."

"A what? What do you mean a personal message? On our Delta Printouts?"

"Yes, sir. It concerns a Claire Monty."

Miss Claire Fucking Monty, you are in deep shit, mused the general, as he hung up the receiver and threw on his uniform jacket. *Who would have thought she could slip her way into a Delta? This computer bullshit has got to go. It's getting pretty bad when any civilian can simply turn on her computer and send her mail priority post through top secret military communication channels.*

The General's car was waiting. As usual, it was prepared to leave at a moment's notice. Transport had received the phone call from Communications only two minutes earlier, and already the propane-powered vehicle was spinning its way toward the Officers Quarters. The sergeant in charge of the Transport section complimented Master Corporal Duschenes, on his way back to the office. Sergeant Russel never had to worry whether or not Senior Staff cars would run when needed. Duschenes was a good section commander and an expert mechanic. A bit of a weird duck, though. Six months ago, returning from a five-week vacation in Italy, he had decided to change his name from Pierre to Julius. Julius Duschenes. He was teased by his friends, but appeared serious as hell about the whole thing. It hadn't changed his ability as a mechanic, though. Duschenes was up for sergeant himself. One of the best his NCO's had seen overseas in years. A natural.

General McDonnell crawled into the heated car. He tapped the driver on the shoulder for emphasis and told him to beat it to Communication HQ. Half-way between there and the Exchange Supermarket, the overcast sky was lit up with an explosion that busted windows from the Junior Ranks Mess and burst trees into flames on both sides of the service road for fifty feet in both directions. General McDonnell was dead.

X

Cross was startled by the sound of the explosion. For a moment the throbbing in his head and the flesh wound he had endured were forgotten. He stood at the window of his room only long enough to see several pieces of twisted, smoking metal spread themselves on both sides on the road. Clouds of smoke rose from the bomb site like macabre incense, quietly, softly. In an instant, two lives were extinguished, the threat to an organized worldwide crisis reduced to one.

"Hello, dispatch? I know there's an emergency. This is Colonel Cross. I am attached to General McDonnell for special assignment. What happened?" The Master Corporal on the other end sounded stressed, confused. Sirens could be heard wailing in the vicinity, creating an echo through the phone line and again through the window of Cross's suite as the Base Fire Crews sped to the scene.

"I can't say, sir. It's not certain. General McDonnell was just picked up at his quarters. It could have been his vehicle. We're not sure. Hello? Sir?"

Cross had heard enough. Istanbul. He would need transport to Turkey. He would have to leave right away. McDonnell had assured Cross that only Level Two and above would know of his experience at the casino the night before. That meant...Barry Wallace! Cross *knew* there was something strange about him. He must have wanted to silence the theory about Caspersan and had arranged to have McDonnell killed. That left only one complication for Wallace's people. Cross would have to be next.

Picking up the phone, Cross heard a dial tone and then a click. Tapped. Someone was listening. He replaced the receiver. He

103

grabbed his jacket. Cross realized he'd have to walk to the hangers and drag a pilot from the night list at random, praying to God he'd find one that wasn't somehow involved with Caspersan. He moved toward the door and hesitated. What was that? Cross could swear he had heard the quiet screech that accompanied the opening and closing of the fire doors in the entrance to the hallway, three rooms down from his suite. There was no sound of footsteps. His imagination? He decided not to take any chances. Turning off the lights Cross moved quietly to the window facing the roadway. He tried to open it. Stuck. This time he heard someone moving in the hallway. His head was throbbing again. What now? Stay with the window, or move to a position behind the door and take my chances there's only one? Maybe it was intuition again. Maybe instinct. Cross chose the window, trying to loosen it by shaking the handles. It moved. Heaving it upward, Cross threaded his body through the opening and hung by the tips of his fingers. He glanced down: Three stories, too dark to see the ground.

A heavy knock could be heard at the door. "Colonel Cross? This is Communication HQ. Sorry to bother you, sir, but we have an urgent message for you." A short pause. "Break it open." Cross let go just as two Corporals braced themselves and threw their shoulders into the door of his room. The lights flashed on. "There he is!"

Cross could be seen heading toward the Military Police Headquarters, away from the hangers, away from his only chance of escaping.

Cross could feel the sting of his breath tearing oxygen from the air for the second time in twenty-four hours. Nearing the road where General McDonnell's car had exploded, Cross noticed a military policeman standing off to one side. Leaning on the roof of his vehicle, he was speaking into his radio. "Ten-four, Sergeant. Area is secured. Returning to Headquarters. Out." As he finished his message and turned to place his microphone back on its receiver inside the car, Cross stepped out from behind the trees on the edge of the road and grabbed him by the collar. Swinging the surprised young policeman fully about, Cross doubled him with one fist and left him unconscious with a knee to the head. Dragging him aside, Cross opened the corporal's jacket and pulled the service revolver from its holster, slipping it into his belt.

"Car forty-seven, come in. Car forty-seven, this is dispatch, come in. Where the hell are you, Jimmy?" Cross started the car and jammed it into reverse. The car slid off the edge of the road and threw bits of grass and dirt fifteen feet into the air as Cross began to speed from the scene toward the Private Married Quarters.

Cross knew by now that someone somewhere must have drummed up charges against him in connection with the General's murder. Cross had arrived on the Base in a vacuum, his mission unclear to anyone but himself and General McDonnell. It would not have been difficult to fill that vacuum with falsified information designed to focus attention to him after McDonnell was taken care of. By now the policeman Cross had assaulted, and his colleagues, would have something else to back up their assumptions. Exits would be already blocked as Standard Operating Procedure, until the investigation into the General's death was well under way. Cross figured his only way to a flight deck and away from the base would be to find a pilot and "convince" him it was in his best interests to cooperate. Where do you find a pilot at nine-thirty at night, in the middle of the Private Married Quarters?

Cross was certain that finding a pilot in the military housing complex without actually knocking on the doors and interviewing families would be just about impossible. His luck began when he noticed a model F-18 painted under the house number on one home. A quick search in the unlocked car in the driveway turned up two unsubmitted travel claims and a nametag. Cross was just about to invite himself in the house when other circumstances made it easier than he would have dared expect. Even from the driveway the tense voices of two adults fighting inside the house carried clearly.

"Don't start that again, Theresa, for Christ's sake. I told you an overseas tour was not a paid vacation. Sometimes we're told to go, and that means fucking go. I don't plan the flight schedules, and I'm not the fucking CO of the Squadron."

"That's right, big man, raise your voice! The kids will wake up in time to hear you spice your explanations with all the filth you keep giving them shit for. You and your duty. Carol told me where you and Jake took your bloody duty the last time you flew

105

to Lahr over the weekend, and I never said a goddamn thing. All I want is for you to spend some time with the kids and show a little responsibility. That's not asking too much, is it? For God's sake, Tom, grow up. That's it, walk out the door and leave it all behind. Dad was right. I should have left you the first time you walked out and never looked back."

Captain Tom Morris slammed the door of the house behind him, and strode to the car parked in their driveway. There was only so much bickering he could put up with. His fault, her fault, he didn't give a shit. He just wanted half an hour on the Autobahn or maybe in a field somewhere. Just a half hour's peace of mind. Fumbling with his key ring, Captain Morris finally located the key to the ignition and opened the door. He crawled in, and rolled down the window.

"Good evening, Captain Morris," said Cross, in a heavy whisper, reaching in through the open window and placing the policeman's revolver next to the pilot's ear.

"What—Who the hell are you? What do you want?"

"I'm a fucking Martian and I want to go home. When I open the back door to this sedan, I expect you to sit still. Otherwise your wife is going to have one hell of a cleaning bill getting what's left of your head off the front seat." Moving quickly, Cross swung open the rear door and climbed in. "Listen carefully. I'm only going to say this once. The authorities on this base are looking for me, and my guess is that they don't feel very friendly. I could spin a sob story for you but I won't waste your time or mine on details. Here's what I want from you. You are going to drive, nice and relaxed, toward the Air Movements Unit and prep a two-seater jet aircraft for an extended flight. You will then relay a last-minute flight plan with the tower and fly us both the hell out of here. In this situation you have two choices. One, you do as I say and survive to tell your fly buddies all about it or two, I blow your fucking brains out and find myself someone who will."

Captain Morris was a good pilot. He was no hero and that worked out fine for both him and his passenger. Within an hour they were airborne and heading south toward Italy. The small two-engined jet aircraft would not carry enough fuel to reach Turkey directly. Cross planned to "detain" his new

106

acquaintance in Rome if necessary, until he could figure out a way to procure transportation to Istanbul. Cross sighed. Rome. The only thing that city had ever meant to him before starting this assignment was a place to hang his hat on stopover.

Cross figured Morris must have taken him at his word when they spoke in the Captain's driveway because there wasn't a hitch. Morris covered the sudden flight to Rome through the tower as a need to book twenty hours before Monday. He even played it up a bit, calling the air traffic controller by his first name and mentioning the flight was also an excuse to leave his wife behind. Cross and his captive talked very little until Captain Morris cleared military airspace and had climbed to cruising altitude.

"Do you mind if I ask a few questions?" queried the pilot, checking his instruments as he spoke.

"Not at all, Captain. You've been an admirable hostage; couldn't have asked for better."

"What the hell brings a stranger, half beat-up and carrying a service revolver, into the P-M-Q's looking for a chauffeur?"

Cross smiled and looked out over the clouds below them. He was amazed how relaxed this chap seemed to be. "There are well-intentioned but highly delusional military authorities who seem to believe I had something to do with the explosion that occurred about twenty minutes before I crept up onto your doorstep. I've got business elsewhere and couldn't stay around for the paperwork."

"Did you do it?"

"No. There was a man killed in the explosion. Someone needed to believe I might have been connected to it. I'm as military as you are. I simply work for people who can't admit I'm employed. Not exactly the best benefit/protection package for a soldier, but life's a bitch."

"You on some kind of spy mission? Terrorist or something?"

"You might call me a cross between Batman and the Lone Ranger. I'm supposed to be retired. Fucking retired, if you can believe it."

"When my pension starts, I'm just gonna fade away," Morris returned. "To hell with government and die for your country and all that patriotic horseshit. All I want is my two cheques a month and a boat that doesn't leak. The rest is none of my business.".

"That must be why you haven't just crashed into the sea and killed us both in some gallant military gesture. You're a nine-to-fiver," summed up Cross.

"A nine to whatever, but that's where it ends. You know, my old man was a Brigadier General. He loved it. He breathed it and shoved it down our throats ever since we were old enough to memorize the words to the national anthem. If the military had legs with any shape and a place to shove his cock, he'd have fucked it on his days off as well." Cross laughed.

"Sounds like commitment."

"Nothing to admire, as far as we were concerned. I hated him for always making the family take a back seat. Swore I'd never do the same to mine."

"So why the big fight? Sounds like momma was lacing poppa pretty good in there. I was half expecting you to come flying out the window, never mind walking out for a breath of fresh air."

"We've got our differences. I guess I need more space than she does, I don't know. One thing's for damn sure. If I had to make a choice, even with her complaining, I'd let the military drop first anytime."

It was just one of those things. Like a rainstorm in the middle of a dry season, Cross lucked out and just happened to find the right man in the right frame of mind. By the time the aircraft touched down in Rome, Captain Morris was ready to bounce again and carry through if Cross gave the word. Hell, all he had to say was that the man held a revolver at the back of his head and threatened to kill his wife and kids. Cross weighed the pros and cons. Eventually whoever wanted him dead would find out where he was headed and what he was looking for anyway. Istanbul would be no secret.

"That's as much as you need to know to make up your mind," finished Cross. "Any more detailed than what I've told you and you would be in danger. I'm on my way to Istanbul. Fuel up or call the embassy, Tom, it's your choice now. I figured the least I could do was let you know what you might be getting into. I forced you this far because there was no other way. I don't mind saying I've enjoyed the ride. In a different place I might have

108

even had you over for steak and potato salad."

There was a short pause. "What the hell. I'm in, Colonel. My first child was born because I didn't have the common sense to pull out when I should have, but I've never regretted it. Let's do it."

Cross wouldn't have believed it if someone told him an anecdote that came anywhere near his own experience of the last ten hours. He felt indebted to Tom Morris, and Morris was not insensitive to the struggle Cross seemed to be facing. Before reporting at the Canadian Embassy in Ankara, Morris agreed to stay and wait for two hours while Cross made the necessary contacts in Istanbul. Friendship takes root in the strangest of places.

Western papers in Istanbul held frightening news. The subject was made to appear complicated, but the overall message was clear. NATO officials were assuming Soviet involvement in the murder of General McDonnell. Aparently CIA investigations were pointing to communications that had been interrupted by satellite that contained allusions to the assassination. The communiqués were in Russian, on Russian radio wavelengths and emanating from Soviet Bloc countries surrounding West Germany, particularly East Germany. The Soviets firmly denied any involvement and were so candid as to concede that the frequencies mentioned were indeed Soviet, but that they also had no idea how or why the communiqués in question were transmitted. Tensions continued to escalate, the papers said, with Canadian and American citizens demanding restitution. The reporter finished the article with a frightening question. How much more of the back and forth could international diplomacy tolerate without declaring war? There was great apprehension of retaliation from some quarter of the NATO Alliance.

Cross folded the newspaper. Retaliation. NATO Alliance. Good God. Leblanc talked about the "final move on the gameboard of nations," scheduled to occur in Istanbul. Turkey had become part of the North Atlantic Treaty Organization in 1952.

There might not be much time.

***

109

Cross made his way through the streets of Turkey's largest city for the first time in almost fifteen years. It hadn't changed much. Its people were still struggling to form a national identity which would allow for the Western influence that had so dramatically changed the socio-political climate of the country since the 1920's, while maintaining respect for and allegiance to religious traditions that were such an integral part of her pride and heritage. Istanbul's population of over 5,400,000 people reflected a courageous attempt to marry those two influences, without one simply annihilating the other.

The afternoon passed quickly. Cross was surprised to learn that his access to funds had not been terminated by the mole in Washington. He carried enough cash with him to buy favours from anyone who might prove helpful, and split the rest between four reputable international banks. Cross still hadn't decided whom he should contact to inform the CIA that he was alive and continuing the investigation. He could count on his right hand the number of times his father's illness crossed his mind. In the past four days there hadn't even been time to sleep properly.

In an older section of town, Cross passed a market where men and women continued to sell and barter. He came upon a stall where water pipes were being sold, and for a moment was sure he recognized someone. From behind her he could see she was slim and had short blonde hair. Then it came to him. Claire. The woman he had seen at the casino. Could it be? The lady raised her hand and shook her head. Too expensive, she said, turning away from the table. Cross laughed. The woman was much older and had a scar on her left cheek. Claire. Cross wondered what had happened to her since he had dropped the book of matches in her hand. He remembered having thought about what she would be like to get to know. God knows he owed her a drink for getting back to General McDonnell and saving him the thirty-odd kilometer hike back to the base. It wasn't just that. She seemed pleasant and straightforward, with the kind of simplicity that he had fallen for in Bridget. Come to think of it, the kind of simplicity that he had rarely seen in any women, but always admired.

Cross checked in at a clean but inexpensive hotel. He remembered at least three locations which might yield information, if they still existed and a person had the money to buy it. But before walking another step, he promised himself a damn good shower and a hot meal. Maybe even a few hours sleep.

After picking up his room key, Cross wandered to the pay phones and decided to phone his answering service in Strasbourg. The "mail box" Charles had referred to was actually a numbered code which would signal the person at the switchboard to relay any messages under the code to the caller.

"Courrier International, bonjour."

"Z436-295."

"Three messages, sir.

#1: HI WARREN STOP HOPE YOUR TRIP THROUGH THE ROMANTIC CITIES IS GOING WELL STOP JUST THOUGHT YOU MIGHT LIKE TO KNOW THAT TRACY JO AND HER LITTLE ONE ARE DOING FINE STOP NO PROBLEMS ON THE FARM STOP IF YOU NEED ANYTHING JUST CALL STOP GARY FLETCHER STOP END OF MESSAGE

#2: CALL WASHINGTON SOONEST STOP REQUIRE CONFIRMATION AND DETAILS STOP FATHERS CONDITION IMPROVING AND SERUM CONTINUES STOP CALL LEVEL ONE ONLY STOP 473-2424 STOP END OF MESSAGE

#3: YOU BASTARD STOP I HAVE BEEN THROWN INTO THE MIDDLE OF SOMETHING THAT HAS NOTHING TO DO WITH ME AND AM NOW BEING TRANSFERRED STATESIDE WITH NO EXPLANATION AND TWENTY FOUR HOURS NOTICE STOP I INTEND ON FINDING YOU AND CONFRONTING YOUR LACK OF ETIQUETTE REGARDLESS OF WHAT YOUR GOVERNMENT THINKS IS BEST FOR YOU OR THEIR TOP SECRET MISSION STOP PISSED OFF AND DETERMINED CLAIRE MONTY STOP END OF MESSAGE

***

111

XI

"Senators of the Aquarian Age. Do not mistake the present moment for a fleeting fantasy of years gone by, or deny yourselves the pride and righteous satisfaction that comes from watching the fruits of your labour unfold before your very eyes. We will see repeated for us, this afternoon, the exercise that has been practised and carried out with precision and unerring devotion by our Legions throughout the entire world. It will appear simple. The recording housed in our noble libraries will show modesty and restraint. There will be no music. There will be no banquet. But we thirty, together with those who have volunteered their youth, their energy and their resources in the service of humanity; we will grow old with dignity remembering the glory of this moment. It has been for us like the building of a great museum, one small stone placed upon another. But soon, our duty will be fulfilled. Then we shall decide the fate of mankind, and history will bear no grudge on the process we have designed. Augustus. Open the windows."

On his command, a soft buzzing sound could be heard. Light began to pour into the oval chambers from the end facing south. It revealed within, an auditorium, seated around its edges by men of varying ages and nationalities. They sat proudly, supported by simple benches. Their garb was woven from one seamless garment, a toga, the single ceremonial indulgence permitted by the Court of New Magistrates. Even this was chosen to remind each and every Senator of the glory that was Rome, and the responsibility which history had placed on their shoulders to fulfill.

The view from the Senatorial Chamber was barren. Soft winds carried dust and tumbleweeds across their field of vision. In the distance, against the lush spring marshes of Australia's outback, a small, twin engine passenger jet sat idling, with only the smallest blur visible from her rear engines. The ladder extended from the fuselage and touched gently on the dry terrain. A moment passed. Two. Without music, without banquet celebration, four young men could be seen walking from the left edge of the window toward the aircraft, each carrying with him an aluminum briefcase. The men gathered regarded the boarding and subsequent departure with gravity; reverence almost. No one spoke until the jet had taxied to the end of the runway and, turning its slim neck into the wind, completed its run up, steadily gaining altitude over the trees and wetlands until it disappeared beyond the horizon to the east. Roman Caspersan spoke once again to the computer. "Augustus. Close the windows and bring up sufficient light to converse." Another slight buzzing sound could be heard as the windows closed. At the same moment, hidden fixtures threw soft light into the chambers. Caspersan moved to the centre of the auditorium, and spoke.

"These are the last four dishes to be delivered. Within twenty-four hours, Augustus will have a completed network of over seven hundred satellite communication devices providing him with the geophysical and meteorological information that, combined with our Northern Hemispheric Centre in Canada and the Southern Centre to the west of our complex, will enable us to deal fairly and quickly with the scattered peoples of the world. The testing phase of the Rempal Inquest draws to its conclusion. The unfortunate complications in West Germany which necessitated the removal of General McDonnell yesterday, have provided us with an unexpected but welcome momentum which will contribute to the speedy conclusion of our debate. We will soon know whether the world, as we know it, has the tenacity and integrity required to survive the stresses its political excesses have brought upon it. Once we have heard from Senator Leblanc in Istanbul, we will know what steps must be taken to intervene. My assumption has long been that there would be no doubt. There are some of you that have disagreed. Let history be the true judge, therefore."

***

Collinsville was like most small New England communities. There were permanent residents, many of whom had been born and raised in this town of four thousand people, and in the summer there were the seasonal folk. Wealthy and private citizens who paid taxes year round for the privilege of calling Collinsville home for four months of the year.

Fall was particularly beautiful here. Whether one's pastime included hunting or painting or simply strolling in the woods, it would be difficult to find a place more hospitable than the Northeastern coastal region of the United States to enjoy the quiet and cool days of September. Many seasonal residents had partially winterized their summer cottages with insulation and wood burning stoves or fireplaces, enabling them to linger on the lakes and hillsides. It was not infrequent that some cottage owner would wait too long and awaken one morning to discover his pipes had burst from a severe frost the night before. Permanent and seasonal citizens alike reluctantly relinquished their firm hold on summer. Some just held on a bit too long.

Douglas K. Woodsworth had never stayed so long on the lake that his pipes froze, but he enjoyed the month of September to its fullest, dreading the last day of his retreat to the countryside and spending most of his waking hours on the paths through the woods that crisscrossed Collinsville's surrounding district. He had retired from a difficult but prosperous career in law, selling partnerships in two firms and investments which secured him a worry-free future, a long sought and well-planned goal of his and his wife Joanne. That was three years ago. He had heard how some people seemed to wither when they retired. He and Joanne were grateful for every moment. Many times they talked about how the struggles had been worth it. Now that their three children had been raised and given the educations they desired, they felt they deserved a comfortable season. It was only right that the rest come after the harvest. Even more so, for they had kept an eye on their habits and they had their health. God knows they had seen enough of their friends slip away without so much as a summer of leisure to call their own, to appreciate this greatest of fortunes. Time to reflect, to talk, to travel. It was a good life.

After returning from church in town, Douglas threw on his fall jacket and picked up his walking stick from behind the porch door. Joanne had invited some friends over for brunch and Douglas decided he would stretch his legs on the acreage behind their cottage for a half hour while the bacon sizzled and Joanne prepared a fruit salad. He enjoyed the Thompsons but they were not as keen as he was on walking, exploring. He felt he had better take the opportunity to enjoy the coloured leaves and gathering squirrels before they arrived. The sun set earlier these days. He might not get another chance during the evening.

It was on this walk that Douglas came upon a curious sight. Collinsville was not a fast town, politically or technologically. Douglas had learned how to operate computers in his law practice, never interested enough to apply them to his daily life. To be honest, he couldn't see what a home computer could do that a piece of paper and a pencil couldn't accomplish just as well. He was always ready to learn, however. An open mind is an open world, an interesting world.

"What's this, young man, E.T. call home? Seems like a strange place to be installing a satellite dish," said Douglas, approaching the young man in the clearing. He was arranging what looked to Douglas like a series of panels, maybe mirrors on the base of a transmitter. Douglas smiled warmly and kept a respectful distance. The young man was startled by his approach. He didn't seem prepared to offer much explanation. Leaning on his walking stick, Douglas looked around and breathed a full draw of fresh fall air. "I guess television is what keeps some people occupied. These days I could live without it. My name is Douglas Woodsworth," he said, extending his hand. The man rose slowly. He didn't return the handshake. He looked around and wiped his hands on his denims.

"Are you alone?" he asked, a thick accent making his words seem rough, unfriendly almost. Douglas dropped his hand slowly.

"I'm not a woodsman, if that's what you mean," replied Woodsworth, trying to find a subject that might help his new acquaintance feel more at ease. For some reason he felt a twinge of anxiety at the stranger's question. Perhaps it would be better to err on the side of caution, even in rural New England. "My house is just beyond that spring over there." Woodsworth pointed and straightened his posture. He poked the ground with his walking stick a few times. Strike two. The young man seemed more tense than before. Douglas knew when to back off. "I won't bother you any further. Have a pleasant afternoon, sir." Douglas Woodsworth, retired attorney, father, husband, turned to leave.

Mrs. Woodsworth became very worried when an hour and a half had passed. Forty-six years of marriage had taught her a great deal about her husband's habits. She knew he would never leave guests waiting for over an hour without calling. She convinced Brad Thompson, her friend's husband to look for him. God knows, maybe Douglas had broken his ankle somewhere. Brad left the two women at the cottage and took a stroll in the woods calling for Woodsworth. When twenty minutes passed and there was still no sign of his friend, Brad sped into town and rounded up a party of searchers. Even if it was only a bruised leg, the night could be pretty cold in Collinsville during the month of September.

"I never would've believed it, Fred," the old man said to his barber on Tuesday morning. There was no better place in Collinsville to share some serious gossip than Fred's barber shop. "After all them years his coming here every summer for two weeks at a time and telling everybody how he'd walk through them woods 'til he dropped as soon as he turned sixty. A young man and healthy at that. What a shame."

Fred shook his head. The barber's duty was to disagree, but just a little; just enough to keep the conversation flowing. "I'd have guessed somebody would wander near the old mill someday and find his way to the bottom of some hole. It was only two years ago that the Millar kid nearly cut his leg off when he fell from the beam over the old cutting table in the mill. I'd have to say I'm just not that surprised."

"I can't agree, Fred. A man don't retire at sixty with a house in California and another in New England just to end his life in some fall down an old mill well. Somethin's fishy about this whole dang business, if you ask me."

116

"The local police say there were no footprints, no sign of a struggle. Just the lawyer's walking stick and coat. Maybe he leaned over a bit too far for a peek down the well? I suppose we'll never know."

XII

Cross awoke to the sound of a motorcycle's busted muffler passing in the street below the window of his second floor room. Man, how those muscles ached. He sat up, rubbed the circulation back into his face with the palms of his hands and, rising slowly, made his way to the window. It was late evening. He checked his watch. Cross had been sleeping for almost four hours. An hour or two would have been a luxury. Four was like rolling over and playing dead for a week. The rest felt good.

The streets were beginning to change masks. The bustling crowds of workers and investors mixed with stubborn villagers and devout Muslim worshipers were beginning to give way to the slower, less hectic flow of Istanbul night life. Cross watched for a few minutes as the evening sun reflected off the mosques of the city, their golden orbs reaching into the evening sky, doggedly refusing to relinquish their ancient hold on the hearts of the Turkish people. A single man appeared on the balcony of a nearby mosque. Gathering his breath he began his chant, the last of the day's prayers. His voice carried clearly over the rooftops, rising and falling, a symbol of Muslim spirit and faithfulness in the midst of change and political upheaval.

Cross wandered back to the bed and sat. Glancing at his watch again, he planned ahead. He figured it was safe to allow four to five hours for a complete survey of the local brothels. He smiled at the thought, and shook his head. There was once when surveying a brothel in Istanbul meant tying your wallet to your chest and wearing a jock cup. A single man was not so bad. He could purchase a "date" and a beer and be ready to leave in an hour. On the other hand a bus load of GI's created a stir that wasn't always welcome. Rounding up the ones who were lost or beat-up and tossed in an alley was what really took time.

Cross left his memories beside his shoes and soiled pants as he peeled off clothes that had begun to feel like an unpleasant second layer of skin. A shower and a change of clothes and he'd feel more human. Even a lady of the evening had a right to social pleasantries. It wasn't that Cross needed to get laid. But one good deed deserves another. In this business, Cross learned, appearance means one hell of a lot. Smelling good and looking good could mean the difference between gaining valuable information and leaving a brothel poorer and no wiser for the effort.

By the time the last of the sun's rays had gathered and fled beneath the skyline, Cross was descending the wooden steps of the hotel and heading for the wharves where waterway traffic and the brothels that served it, traditionally provided the most recent and reliable sources of information. In a contradiction of sorts, the wharves represented to many the more secluded, less vulnerable area of town; a place where a man or woman could service weaknesses of the flesh or an insatiable appetite for gambling large sums of money, without too much concern for authorities. In fact, some sections of the wharf were frequented with almost the same religious devotion as the mosque. Still, the traditions which governed the bars and meeting houses were no less fraught with forceful sanctions. A stranger was not advised to wander alone.

Cross was accustomed to the dangers. He was prepared to discover new laws, new leaders, new sanctions. But the basic tone was amazingly similar to that which he could recall from his last assignment. The first three brothels consumed twenty-seven hundred American dollars without so much as a cup of coffee to show for his efforts. One thing he did discover, however: Be sure to pay the bouncer at the door before anything else. A custom that was probably begun by some high-flying drug dealer in the late seventies, doorman bribes had become a commonplace transaction. Cross was instructed by his first host that a double compliment should be paid to the stern-faced gentleman he had ignored on his way in. Otherwise he might find himself relocating his kneecap halfway up the street.

119

Cross paused at the door to his fourth stop and paid the "doorman" an exorbitant one hundred American dollars. Without raising an eyebrow, the burly, dark-skinned bouncer grasped Cross firmly by the elbow and led him to a corner section of the house. Cross was not alarmed. In fact, it was exactly as he had expected. He was led straight to the person who would know where any information or diversion could be bought by a person with money. The bouncer was paid well and effectively saved Cross time and effort. Maybe an increase in funds would save time on this end as well.

"Yes sir? What can we do for you to make your visit memorable?" From a position behind a round table a man of surprisingly western features glanced up from counting money and addressed him. Cross was direct.

"I'm looking for information that is important to me. Information that will earn you one thousand American dollars just for speaking with me. Ten thousand more if it is at all helpful."

The man studied Cross, his eyes squinting slightly against the rising smoke from his thin cigar. "You are speaking the truth, Mr. American. My friend is very particular about who he escorts to my private quarters. Speak up. What kind of information?"

"I'm looking for trouble."

The man pulled the cigar from his mouth and laughed hoarsely, coughing a mixture of dust and thick smoke that was part of his livelihood, from his lungs. "I daresay you have come to the right end of town for that. What kind of trouble are you interested in?"

"The kind even you wouldn't want to deal in too often. Political trouble. The people who pay me to make men like yourself very rich, want to know if anyone has spoken to your people about a 'glorious' or 'memorable' occasion to occur in the next two or three days. My sources tell me there will be major trouble in Istanbul. This kind of trouble may not even be good for your business."

"You make it sound like a military coup, Mr. American." The man snubbed his cigar on the edge of the ashtray and stood. He moved to the front of the table and eyed Cross carefully. "Perhaps this information would be worth more than ten

120

thousand dollars. Suppose—though I promise nothing—suppose this information was priceless. How much would it be worth to you, Mr. American?''

''One hundred thousand dollars,'' spoke Cross simply.

''You have come to the right place.''

Cross was led by the elbow again, this time by the owner of the establishment. A path was cleared. When the man from the corner left his banking and escorted someone to speak with one of the ladies, even the most hardened among them were curious. Only the most bizarre fantasy would merit such treatment. The same process of deduction occurred in the pillow-laden chambers of the lady Cross was brought to speak with. She seemed paralyzed with fear at the prospect of what she might be required to provide in return for the rare escort.

''Relax, Charlene. This is an opportunity for both you and me to rid ourselves of the pus and corruption of this hellhole. He doesn't want flesh. He is looking for information. Give him what he wants and you'll never have to drop your pants again.'' The man gave her no time to respond. His message was clear. He left abruptly, the beads covering the entrance to the small room swinging in his wake.

''Hello, Charlene. Your boss is telling the truth. I'm looking for information, that's all.'' Cross was beginning to believe he was a Turkish mockup from downtown Las Vegas. With light brown hair and blue eyes, Charlene was as ''back home'' as they come.

''You sure have a way of making an impression, fella,'' said Charlene, reaching with shaking fingers for a package of cigarettes on a corner table. ''The last time that man set foot back here with a customer the girl wasn't seen for nearly a week. She lost two fingernails, I mean completely, and the hairs on her head were burned to the scalp one at a time. She said the fucking animal used fourteen boxes of matches on her. Fourteen fucking boxes of matches.'' There was a moment's silence as Charlene tried to calm herself. She lit a cigarette and drew hard on it. Letting her eyes roam over Cross through the smoke rising from her mouth and nostrils as she exhaled, she ran through her mind the kind of man this might be. He didn't look like the type who was afraid of women. He wasn't out to save the world on a white horse and he dressed well. She chuckled lightly to herself as she took another drag and blew it toward the ceiling. He's probably the type that still believes there's more to a good fuck than just a pretty face between your legs. Just the kind Momma would have wanted me to marry. Just the kind I should've settled for, myself.

"So why the big hoopla?" Charlene said finally, her curiosity piqued. "What's so special about your dick that Franklin felt he needed to carry it in on a silver plate?"

"Your boss seems to think that you can tell me something that's worth a lot of money."

"A little gal from Tennessee? Shit. What you see is what you get. Most don't complain. I'm Buddhist, you know? See nuthing, hear nuthing…"

"There's going to be trouble in Istanbul, political trouble, in the next couple of days. I need to know what it is and where it's supposed to happen."

"And what if it's hard to talk about? What if I struggle through and that shithead that brought you in here doesn't give me a damn thing?"

"Free enterprise, Charlene. Here's five thousand dollars. Do what you want with it. Whatever he gives you is bonus." Charlene grabbed the money and threw herself at Cross, smearing his chin with cheap lipstick.

"Why you goddamn all-American hero! That's enough to put me back home and enough to vacation for a few weeks after! You just bought yourself front-line highlights, buster.

"A man came in here two days ago lookin' for a blowjob and somebody to show his muscles to. We get it all the time from the younger ones, but usually when they're drunk and their imaginations are in high gear. Not this one, though. He was sober and older lookin'. Your age maybe. But he still had enough energy to get it up three times in an hour and every time he finished he was laughin' about history or some damn thing. 'This is how men were meant to be treated' he kept sayin' and some bullshit about 'the Roman man will soon have much to celebrate.' I dunno. Figured he was Italian maybe. Didn't seem to make much sense at the time, so I paid no attention to it. Just before leavin' he started talkin' about how I should be proud to service him in partic'lar. Said he was gonna play a big part in the future of the world.''

"What else? Was he specific?''

"He sure as hell was,'' Charlene said, pausing for another drag on her cigarette. Cross could feel the sweat beginning to gather at his temples. Sweat from the heat. Sweat from apprehension.

"Well?''

"He said he was gonna kill somebody. He said he was gonna kill hisself a Russian fucking diplomat.'' Cross stiffened. That would be the last move, he thought, his mind racing ahead, visualizing the possible consequences. There was no doubt. If an assassination was successful, there would be war. He had to find out more. He had to find out quickly.

"Did he say when or where?''

"Nope. I just stared at him when he said it and he must have known he said too much. He got angry as hell and slapped me around a bit. Told me if I spoke to anyone in or outside the brothel he'd slit my throat and pull my tongue down over my belly.''

"Think, Charlene! Are you sure he never mentioned a time or place?''

"Sorry. But I wondered, you know, with the anger and all, if he might be tellin' the truth, so I told Franklin out there. He told me to stay inside for a few days and to keep my mouth shut. Except for customer service, that's just what I done.''

"Was there anything else?''

"The only thing I'd tell a nice dressed fella like you is to watch your ass. There was somethin' about the look in his eyes. Kind of glassy and crazy-like. My guess is he and his friends are bad shit. I mean very bad.''

"Here.'' Cross passed her another thousand.

"Hey man, I owe you,'' Charlene said, shaking her head and smiling as she recounted the cash. "You've just made me one happy lady....''

Cross would remember that line for a long time. Just as Charlene was reaching out to shake his hand, Cross could hear something that sounded like a battering ram from the bar room outfront. The whole building seemed to shake; shells hanging in the corner of Charlene's room tinkled ominously. Shots were fired. Rapid fire. People started screaming. Instinctively Charlene leaned in toward Cross. He took her by the arm to the far corner of the room and told her to stay put. Pulling the revolver from his belt, he swung at the light on the corner table and busted it. As the room fell into darkness, Charlene whimpered, "I'm scared, Mister." Turning, Cross saw the dark outline of a man rip through the bead curtains, flaring a sawed-off shotgun. Three shells were fired in rapid succession. Cross threw himself against the side wall just in time to miss catching a hot burst of lead full in the chest. He emptied four rounds from his pistol at the red flames that had exploded from the end of the shotgun barrel a second before. There was the sound of metal hitting the floor and someone stumbling down the corridor. Cross threw himself through the bead curtains and followed the retreating gunman. He stopped at the entrance to the bar and leaned his back against the wall. Breathing heavily he reloaded four shells into the revolver and, snapping the chamber into place, pushed back the partially open door slowly with one hand. The bar room was in chaos. He could see two men leaving by the front, the second one holding his right arm. Tripping over tables and toppled chairs, Cross made it to the exit and whipped open the door. He listened for a moment. Shoes on pavement. Up the street he could see one man encouraging the other to speed up. The man in the lead was waving frantically at something, screaming "Start it up! Start the goddamn boat..." Cross skipped three steps at a time down to the street and raced after the gunmen. They had at least half a block on him, possibly more. He stopped. Trying to control his breathing he braced his feet and took aim, letting the point of the pistol fall slowly. The tip came down along a lightpost, across the bow of a tugboat and rested on the broad outline of the man holding his arm. He fired.

Just as the lead man turned to jump into the belly of a boat that was already moving, his partner crumpled on the wet cement of the dock, loose bits of gravel grinding their way into the side of his face. He wouldn't have to worry about scars. The man was dead.

Cross checked the man he had killed for I.D. Nothing. This one had no ring either. Probably a hired hit. For Cross there was no remorse, and in the pit of his stomach, he knew why. Racing back along the slippery street puddled from the day's transfer of fish, Cross reached the brothel and forced his way through the maze of frightened and confused men and women who were just beginning to re-orient themselves. He arrived at Charlene's room just in time to hear Franklin speak, his voice strained and heavy. "Holy shit..." The owner of the establishment turned away and Cross tore the flashlight from him. Focusing the light on the corner of the room, Cross cast a shadow of Charlene's natural curls on the back wall. The right side of her face was frozen in fright, the makeup untouched, the powder on her cheeks marked only by the trail of a single tear. There might have been others, but the left side of her face and skull had been hit by a shotgun blast and cleanly severed from the rest of her body. Charlene would share herself no more.

XIII

"Vlademir, really. Must you always take an ounce of flesh every time you ask the boy to bring you something? He's been a model Communist since the time he could crawl. You know he would walk on burning coals to please you. Lighten up a bit. The Americans are no less anxious than the Politburo. Everything will go fine." The diplomat's wife talked over her shoulder at her irritable spouse while watching him struggle with his cravat through her vanity mirror. For the second time that afternoon he had scolded his nine-year-old son with little provocation, venting pent-up frustrations that had accumulated over the past six months.

The media had managed to focus only on the tip of the iceberg. Both the United States and the U.S.S.R. were grappling with an inexplicable rise in desertions, stolen documents, interrupted transport convoys and logistic stresses that numbered in the hundreds, possibly thousands. An emergency meeting had been called in Geneva in mid-July to discuss what both superpowers had come to believe was an international political catastrophe of unfathomable proportions. Two of Russia's highest-ranking members of the Polituro left the country and the U.S. President had been given notice that his chief political advisor was resigning, effective immediately.

It may have been somewhat easier to comprehend if either side had gained from the other's loss, but such was not the case. These men, as countless others had over the preceding eighteen months, seemed to disappear without a trace. Two days of talks brought both governments closer to the same conclusion. Under a seeming impenetrable shroud of secrecy and with an astonishing ability to gain access to information that was guarded by the most advanced technological protection services available, someone somewhere was systematically sabatoging both governments in their traditional areas of influence and their hard-won, albeit tenuous, political relationship to one another. The degree to which both superpowers had begun to feel manipulated was beyond anything either of them had ever before experienced. Like strangers falling into the same foxhole, they had learned to put aside their polarized ideologies in an attempt to uncover the common enemy.

Cooperation was still very difficult. Occasionally a situation would arise where no other explanation would be as simple as believing the godless Russians of blood-thirsty Capitalists were to blame. But each time, candid, emotionally-charged confrontations had succeeded in maintaining the perilous alliance that kept each country from declaring war on the other. The last incident in West Germany, however, had been the worst. Every intercepted communiqué, every scrap of electronic wiring remaining from the explosion that had killed General McDonnell had been traced to the Soviet Union. There could be no other interpretation. For NATO Intelligence to assume otherwise would be lunacy. It *had* to be the Soviets. Only the fact that both superpowers had experienced so much recently that was unexplainable prevented a violent retaliation by the NATO Alliance.

Whoever was to blame, the present state of tension could not be endured for much longer. Both governments had begun to mobilize troops and armaments. There was no other choice. They had tried to elicit some agreement from each other that nuclear weapons would not be used if the situation ever came to that, but it was useless to debate. Something had to give somewhere. And soon.

Vlademir Nowroskov's summit with the American ambassador in Turkey was aimed at giving the media something less volatile to focus on, for a change. It was difficult to determine what impact newspapers, journalists and international analysts would have on the psyche of the common labourer, but it was estimated that three out of five people expected war within the next twelve months if the political climate did not adapt quickly to alleviate the innumerable stresses that had been put upon it. For such a large proportion of the population to assume there was no other alternative for their governments than to declare war meant that· the situation had truly escalated to a dangerous level.

The decision to welcome Ambassador Nowroskov came as part of a joint publicity move organized by members of the U.S.S.R. propaganda specialists and the FBI. In an unprecedented and thoroughly cooperative effort, both governments had designed and were preparing to implement a three-leveled approach which would hopefully offer some alternative focus for the media over the next six to eight weeks. This would give politicians and tacticians time to deal with the tremendous backlog of intelligence information that left so many unanswered questions. Lately there seemed to be so many holes in the net that no theory of any substance on either side of the Pacific could be formulated and tested without another incident of international significance demanding immediate attention. Surely, a number of benign international meetings, economic agreements and exchanges would add an element of doubt, a moment of respite to the theme of impending doom that prevailed the highest echelons of power in both countries.

And so, on a warm Monday afternoon in the month of September, the Ambassador of the United States travelled from his seat in Turkey's capital of Ankara to Istanbul to prepare an appropriate welcome for the Russian diplomat. Ankara might have seemed a more likely choice for their meeting, but Istanbul was chosen because of its historic importance in the trading routes between Soviet Bloc countries and the Mediterranean. Every choice had to be sensitively orchestrated. Every level of government in both arenas prayed earnestly for a meeting that would remain simply, an international courtesy: a time to shake hands, make a show of earnest concern and bid one another good-day, hopefully, the first of many such successes.

Ambassador Nowroskov had given his government every reason to believe that he could easily handle such a task. He was accustomed to stress and had managed to communicate a sense of confidence and easy self-assurance that had not lost its effect in many areas of international scrutiny. This task would be no different, he had decided. Speak no evil, promise nothing, display appropriate frustrations and the newspapers with their little-boy photographers and manic journalists would have nothing but smiles and handshakes to report to their anxious public. But somewhere inside, he was afraid. There is a Russian saying: "He who stands near a hot stove will eventually get burned". Nowroskov had avoided many serious scaldings. Why, then, did he feel so nervous today?

Scolding his son for the third time while carefully pulling on his gloves, Nowroskov kissed his wife on the cheek and headed for his staff car. How precious those moments of farewell become, those last moments. How different they might have been had he known...

Warren Cross had spent the remainder of Sunday evening and most of Monday morning trying to pin down the address of the stranger who had talked to Charlene about killing a Russian diplomat. He was worried. Clearly Nowroskov would be the target; his timely meeting with the United States Ambassador and the social gathering planned afterward would provide any number of opportunities for an assassin to place a lethal bomb or aim a high-caliber rifle. It did not take much to kill a man once the decision was made. What was Cross to do with the information?

Cross still wasn't sure whom he could trust and whom he couldn't. Had he been thinking more clearly the day he met with McKay in Washington, he might have been able to spot Wallace whose manner was noticeably tense, like a man who had a lot to hide. Apparently Wallace had vacated his desk the day General McDonnell was murdered and was suspected by a number of people in the Agency to have been directly involved. But what about the President's chief advisor? Who would have expected that a man who had spent nearly forty years serving his country would decide to leave without any prior notice, possibly in conjunction with the crisis that had developed over the year? Could that mean that the Secretary of State or Vince McKay at Level One might also be involved? How could he know for sure? No. There still weren't enough cards on the table for Cross. The information about the assassination attempt would have to remain with him until the visit was complete. The last time the

129

Caspersan theory was shared, that call cost General McDonnell his life.

Cross provided McKay with enough detail to ensure the serum for his father would be continued, as well as buy himself time to keep digging. Earlier in the morning he had heard talk on the wharf of a stranger who had been offering huge sums of money for information about the American who had spent the last few minutes with Charlene. His description fit the one Charlene had provided. Cocky, full of himself, brusque. One fisherman even said he had that crazed look about him. He was said to have arrived in a taxi from the United Cabs.

The taxi driver was uncooperative at first. Full-time employment in Istanbul was hard to come by for the twenty to thirty percent of the rural population who were illiterate. This man had hoped to bring his young family a better standard of living than that endured in the harsh eastern climate of their village home. Thus far Allah had smiled on him. He did not want to betray the confidence of a client or his employer when things were going so well. Cross finally won his favour by offering him what amounted to well over five times his annual salary. Every piece of information had its price.

"He was a strange man, good sir. I do not understand what could be so important about such a solemn person. He would not talk. He told me to stay quiet and watch the road. Then he warned me that I must keep his address to myself." Cross handed him another hundred dollars.

"Allah Himself has sent you to me! Very well. I must follow the destiny He has chosen for me.

"Go to the end of the Galata bridge next to the Blue Mosque. Four blocks east of the bridge is a small hotel called the Sea of Marmara. They will know how to find him."

Crossing the Galata bridge with noon-day commuters reminded Cross of downtown Manhattan. The only difference was the language. Spires along both rails of the bridge advertised radios and candy, but not in languages that would influence anyone from North America.

The Sea of Marmara is appropriately named. Facing the body of water whose name it bears, the small hotel fronts a constant stream of pedestrians. Near its doorways can be seen still standing, a portion of the sea wall that once served as a bulwark

130

against naval invasions. The tall minarets of the Blue Mosque are clearly visible from the entrance.

"Yes, sir. Can we help you?" Cross placed five hundred dollars on the desk in front of the man. He paused and allowed the frightening and irresistibly seductive message of the small fortune to sink in.

"Answer one question and this money is yours," began Cross. "Tell me where I can find a man..." Cross described to the hotel registrar the same clear physical traits the taxi driver had given him of the man who had met with Charlene. He tried to remain calm. Cross had awakened from a light sleep with Charlene's words in his ears 'you goddamn all-American hero!...' and the image of her severed face in front of him. The personal debts were adding up. "...and seems to have a habit of dressing ten years beyond his age. Likes women."

"I know the man, sir. But I cannot tell you where he is. He checked out only an hour ago. Perhaps he is headed toward the park near the Mosque. I have heard that the meeting between the Americans and the Soviets will begin there."

"What? I was told they were meeting on the Princes' Islands. They were not to begin until four o'clock." The Princes' Islands, approximately twelve miles southeast of Istanbul offer a quiet retreat for vacationers and an ideal meeting place.

"That is true, sir. But they have arranged a stopover while awaiting passage to the Islands to pay a visit to the Mosque. Many of our people will be gathered in the park to greet them. The sight of foreign government has not shadowed our doorstep for many years. Sir?" Cross struck the desk with the palms of his hands in frustration and self-criticism. Of course. There would be no way to lose the authorities on the Princes' Islands. The water separating them from the mainland would be like a noose around the assassin's neck. He would do it in the city. He would be choosing an area which would give him an opportunity to leave quickly by boat or by air. Only the city itself would offer these options.

Cross could think of nothing else. There were no streetcars or buses anywhere nearby. Running up to a bicycle that was leaning on a lightpost outside the hotel, Cross pulled it across the grass that separated the beach from the road and hopped on. A young man could be heard calling after him from the sand where he had been lunching with a female friend.

Cross weaved his way through the gradually thickening traffic, stumbling on curbs and narrowly dodging pedestrians. Two blocks from the park it was clear he would make no further headway on the bike. Throwing it roughly aside, Cross broke into a full run, edging himself around the outside perimeter of the slowly moving crowds. Twice he was almost stopped: once by a stand selling fresh water on the street and another by a woman carrying a young child and pushing a baby carriage. Curses followed him in languages he could not understand.

Finally reaching the end of the park furthest from the Mosque, Cross's heart sank. There were hundreds of people gathered along what must have been the proposed route of the Russian diplomat's cavalcade. Even if he managed to make it through the enormous crowd to the front before the procession and formal greetings began, he would have no room to move. He would simply be a spectator to the gruesome event along with the others. Quickly Cross reviewed the situation. If he were an assassin, where would he perch? Would he bomb or shoot? Up front or from far away? Cross decided that injuries to civilians might stir up emotions, but conflicting ones. It would be difficult to pin the blame on any one source. As NATO sympathies clearly lay with Turkey, no one could reasonably believe that the morally conscious NATO nations would ever plan an attack that would also claim the lives of numerous civilians. A bomb was out. Would it be a rifle? A handgun? The assassin wants a way out, Cross reasoned. That's why he's here. A more dramatic stage could be set in the Princes' Islands if he was planning on sacrificing himself as part of the deal. He'd have no way out in a crowd like this. It's got to be long range. Now, where?

It is a curious human phenomenon that crowds will gather to participate in an otherwise benign or even slightly distasteful event. The fear of Russian expansionism was a prime factor influencing Turkey's decision to enter the NATO Alliance during the 1950's. Yet here, on a warm, somewhat muggy September afternoon in Istanbul, thousands of Turkish citizens gathered to welcome the representative of their ancient foe.

From his vantage point atop a nearby five-story apartment building, the man who loved to boast was clearly prepared. He was no longer concerned with flaunting his prowess or impressing strangers. Like the maintenance workers who arrive at dawn to oil their tools and dust off their machinery, this man was preparing to do his job. Along the chosen route below, the sounds of the crowd alerted him to the task at hand. He looked up from where he had begun to lay the pieces of metal and hardwood on the roof for assembly, and stared through mirrored sunglasses into the street below. There he was. Car number four. The small red flags waved briskly in the breeze. The rifleman yawned nervously. Concentration. Breathing. There would be time only for one shot. In reality the mushroom tip would likely cause death regardless of where in the upper body it penetrated. But the end is one thing. Each craftsman takes pride in his task. Implicit in his agreement to kill the diplomat was the unspoken assumption that he would do so in a professional manner.

It may have been the barrel of the rifle, though this could easily be debated. The rifle was well-camouflaged and the steel thoroughly blued. Cross would never know for sure, but undoubtedly the man's taste in sunglasses contributed to his discovery. As the marksman returned to the activity at hand, reaching once again for the pieces to his rifle, the sun cast a momentary glare into the crowd. The path of the reflection covered the full distance of the park. Others may have grimaced, shielding their eyes from the unpredictable dance of the sun on the rooftops. Cross turned quickly. There! Bursting through the crowd of spectators, he began running toward the building, two hundred and fifty yards away.

The emotions of the crowd increased in intensity. Murmurs gave way to spontaneous smiles. Hands waved in places. The diplomat's car was only one hundred yards away.

Moments that are separated by milliseconds cannot be fully understood at their natural pace. *A camera, well-placed, and in slow motion, would have shown clearly the progress of events.* Ahead, the parked car of the American Ambassador is stopped. He opens the door and climbs out, turning to face the crowds, acknowledging their support in a slow sweeping wave, smiling warmly. He thinks of excellent press. The man on the roof yawns. It takes forever at this speed. He slowly wipes a nervous tear from the effect of the yawn and begins to shoulder his high-powered rifle.

Cross's face billows, the air that feeds his heart and lungs pushing him forward. Smiles and anticipation around him turn to frustration and anger as his body clears a path. *Slowly. One frame at a time. One movement passes the baton to another, slowly.* The vehicles stop, one after another. Seconds that seem like hours pass. Doors open on all sides, bodyguards and aides moving to the places their guidebooks suggest would stop a seasoned killer. The rifle is raised now. The manicured hands of the assassin closing the gap between his face and the stock of the rifle. Like an intimate kiss, flesh touches wood. The forefinger creeps from its ready position along the rail of the trigger guard and closes over the trigger. The man sighs. Breath one.

Cross reaches the building and crashes through the front door, the strength of his determination clearly evident on the sweat-lined features of his face.

The Soviet diplomat hesitates. All is ready. *Click. Click. The frames of the film pass, showing no change.* Then, the door opens. The carefully gloved hand reaches through and around the door, opening the world to disaster, slowly, ever so slowly, opening the world to crisis, to chaos. He rises from the velvet seat of the People's Car. The door swings shut.

The shoulders of the man on the roof heave. Through his sights, the target is visible now. Soon it will be time. He lets the air escape gradually from him, fighting the urge to yawn. Breath two.

Cross races along the corridor of the apartment searching for the stairway. Is there a God? A voice continues to haunt him: "why you goddamn all-American hero..."

The gap between the two political officials is narrowing. Bodyguards turn and twist, surveying the crowd, keeping their eyes on the unexpected. *The camera rolls sluggishly. Click. Click.* Smiles, cheers, the crowd waves...heat rises from the pavement...the American Ambassador turns to face his guest. Each begin to extend a hand.

The target is clear. Breath three. He holds it. His forefinger tightens, squeezing, squeezing.

An explosion is heard. A burst of soft lead terrorizes the crowds, the aides and the guards. The Soviet diplomat does not hear any of it. Pieces of his skull and brain tissue are blown violently into the hands of bystanders, unsolicited reminders of the fragility of life. His body is a corpse before it hits the ground. The deep red blood spews forth on the grass, his body's pump still ignorant of the irreversible damage that has been done. With it flows much of what is left of hope for peace in the modern world. Slow motion changes none of it.

Cross couldn't be sure if he heard the shot or not. Somewhere between his discovery of the rifleman on the roof and his flight up the stairs of the apartment house, pandemonium had broken out, terrified spectators emptying into the side streets and causing exactly the kind of diversion Cross knew he could not afford.

The assassin heard Cross first. Perhaps there is a kind of narcissism which leaves a practiced killer under the impression that he will never be cornered the way he has cornered others. At first he could not believe it. He paused only long enough to reach into his pocket and pull out his papers, frantically trying to light a match to burn any evidence that might lead to the Rempal Inquest.

"This is no way to end a distinguished career, Mr. Richards," spoke Cross to a man he had known for almost twenty years. The man was holding a gun in one hand and burning papers in the other. He looked up, surprised at first, then unbearably humoured at the recognition of a fellow field agent.

"Mr. Warren Cross. Do me a favour?" said Richards. "Don't give me any of that horeshit about who sent me here or why I did what I did. This one's above and beyond you and me and the little bureaucratic janitors in Langely or Washington."

Cross was stunned. This man had Omega clearance. As close as you can get in the trenches, they had been almost friends in the field. He was confused as hell. Answers would be needed. The bedlam in the park below them seemed far away. As far away as trust, and understanding.

"Talk, Barney. And for fuck's sake, don't make me shoot you."

"That's very compassionate, Cross, considering I just wiped out a man from fifty feet above his shoulders. Don't waste time. I can't go with you."

"There's a reason for. all this," muttered Cross, suddenly aware of a tremendous headache welling up.

"Yes, there is. I'm part of it, you're part of it and poor ole Nowroskov was part of it. No going back. No going away. This is the way it is."

"Okay, Richards, we're going to handle this, one thing at a time. You can begin by dropping the gun and moving from the edge. When I've got some space, there are going to be some specific questions for you to answer. This shit is getting more fucking confusing every minute."

"You don't really think I can just drop the hardware and go for coffee, do you? I can't leave here, Cross. There's no time for catch up. It's check-out time."

"Speak your mind."

"Will it be you or me?"

"What do you mean? Drop the fucking gun, Barn, or I'll shoot, I swear to God." Moving his pistol from his waist to his temple, Barney Richards shrugged his shoulders and sighed.

"See you, Cross. Cover your own ass. This one's a dead end." He pulled the trigger.

Shaking with emotions and questions he could not deal with, Cross closed down. All of it. The last resort. The shutdown. He walked over to Richard's body and frisked him. Picking up the charred remains of a passport and what looked like an airline ticket, Cross turned his back on his friend, and fled.

XIV

"I can't really talk about it now, Mother, I've got a gang of strangers running through my place...Hey! Leave that on the table! I don't care, I'll box it myself. Hello, Mother? Sorry. Oh, I don't know, around eight this morning I guess. They've been packing and throwing things around. I'm supposed to be home by tomorrow evening. Can you wait just a minute? I'm going into the bedroom. I can't hear myself think out here." Dressed in her jogging pants and a sweatshirt Claire Monty looked like she hadn't slept in a week. The notice from the Base Commander that she was to be transferred back to the United States immediately came as more than a surprise. She was accustomed to getting into trouble by tapping sources that were none of her business. She had no idea that her initiative would cause such unprecedented reactions from people who obviously held tremendous influence. Her boss had made it clear to her the day before.

"I'd like to tell you there's something I can do about it, Claire, but this one's way out beyond my reach. The regional supervisor was called by the Vice-President in person this morning to confirm the order. You know how much money is tied up in Defense contracts. There's not a damn thing we can do. Especially with the General's assassination hanging in the air. I'm gonna hate to lose you, Claire, but you've got to go."

Claire had spent the remainder of the day trying to figure out what options she still had. Three days ago, she was sitting at a blackjack table losing some jerk's easy money when a charming stranger walked up and stuffed a book of matches in her hand. Today she's got soldiers in green T-shirts throwing her personal belongings in cardboard boxes, and a one-way ticket to New

137

York. She had asked the Base Commander why and all he would tell her was that she had invaded confidential files. With the Vice-President of her own country calling her regional supervisor, and Canadian soldiers doing her packing, she wasn't sure who she was supposed to be angry at. All she knew was if she heard the phrase "sorry, ma'am, we have to follow orders" one more time, she'd have a nervous breakdown.

"I know, Mom. But that's not the point. Even if they promise to pay for anything that gets damaged it won't be the same just getting money in return. Besides it takes weeks to get those claims adjusted.

"I'm trying to arrange a few weeks vacation before actually returning to the States," Claire said, misleading her mother deliberately. "There might be a chance I can join a tour if I make a firm commitment not to go near any military establishment. Maybe the timing is not so bad on this after all. You've been bugging me to take a real break for years. Okay, I will. Give my love to Melissa and the kids. Love you too. Bye."

In the confusion Claire was able to keep one priority clear in her mind. She would be asking Warren Cross some very up-front questions face to face or she would be arrested trying. As soon as she had been told of the transfer, Claire headed for the office and sent a message to the telex where Cross had registered his last Gold Card transaction.

The hardest part now was lack of information. She needed to know more, and very quickly. The unfortunate experience of being so easily caught by the monitoring team at CFB Baden Communication Headquarters resulted in one positive outcome. She now knew not to ask for information. The military likes it best when you tell people to do things. The higher the rank, the better.

From the administration records, a list of officers on leave provided Claire with a name and an excuse. The rest was determination and stubbornness. Three hours and four cups of coffee later, there it was. Cross had registered his passports with General McDonnell's confidential files. Each alias had a full name and birth date—all she would need to track him down if he had booked a flight anywhere in the world in the past twenty-four hours.

138

Claire was disturbed when she had heard of the General's death. But in the strange way that one person's tragedy becomes another's blessing, Claire was amazed at what she was given once she succeeded in tapping the Base's computer system. She assumed that there must have been hundreds of demands from every level of government for information regarding the details of General McDonnell's death. She had barely typed two sentences into the computer when her message was interrupted and the following statement received:

"Sir: Regarding the incident in question, there have been many inquiries and a personal reply is not possible in every instance. The Base Administration Officer has been given clearance to formulate a text which covers the basics of the incident. More urgent inquiries can be priorized through Echo 90 AM frequency. Please provide sheltered code and key when requesting individual service."

The text was thorough. As the role that this Cross, alias Market, Jones, and O'Brian played became clearer, Claire considered dropping the whole plan. Intrigue was one thing and risking your life something else. It was her dear old office buddy, Forester, who helped her decide. After all, she had to confide in somebody.

"I have to be honest, Claire," Forester had begun. "I'm more than just a little jealous. I've liked you for a long time." Claire smiled. Usually a warm moment for Bobby, but this time her understanding felt painful. "But I like you in other ways than just wanting to go out," he continued. "I think you deserve somebody that's really special. I personally think you've lost a bolt or two to be chasing some guy all over the globe just to hand him back a book of matches that ended up practically ruining your career, but I have to admit I've never seen you this excited over anything to do with a man before." Claire was touched and surprised. Bobby wasn't only pleasant, he was also perceptive.

"So what are you saying?"

"Two things. One, I think you're crazy. Two, do whatever makes you feel alive in the morning. If you want to see this guy, follow the fucking eel to Siberia. Sorry about the pejorative description, but I really would have liked to take you out."

Claire did something else she had been wanting to do for a long time, and kissed the glasses right off Forester's face.

Whatever else he had failed to accomplish, he was one thing for sure. Robert Forester was a true friend. His honest encouragement was all Claire Monty needed to hear.

For the next six hours, Claire poked and prodded the console in front of her. She had a plan. The hardest part would be getting a very busy administrative system on the Base sufficiently convinced of its validity to act on it. Another complication had been finding out where Cross had headed after hijacking the CF jet pilot to Italy. A telephone call registered at the message address in Strasbourg provided the answer: Istanbul. Shit. How much more exotic can this thing get? she wondered.

Twenty minutes into the seventh straight hour, Claire touched the enter button and waited. "CONFIRMED". Good. She rose from her desk. God, what a mess. There were empty coffee cups strewn around her console and by the telephone. The pizza box where she and Forester had shared supper a few nights ago was still open and gathering dust by her In-basket. A stack of unanswered messages and unopened wish-you-well cards was leaning precariously on her purse, the slightest movement threatening to topple the whole structure. The situation seemed hard to believe, but the proof was scattered all around her: Claire Monty wanted to find Warren Cross, no matter what it cost. Already she had paid for her curiosity with the loss of her position in West Germany. What would be next?

The day before, Claire had asked her local bank to prepare the closure of her accounts with half the considerable savings she had accrued in cash and the other in travellers cheques. Everything was ready. It was now or never. Turning off the computer monitor, Claire half leaned, half sat on the edge of her desk and looked around. This office represented to her all she had worked so hard for most of her life: the degree in computer programming, the competitions she had entered to find the best paying jobs, the most promising career. Now there were two military policemen sitting just outside the office in the corridor, their whole existence focused on keeping her out of trouble and seeing her onto the plane to New York the next evening. That's it, she decided. No use crying over spilt milk. I'll know in an hour if all this is going anywhere. Without a tear or a sigh, Claire picked up her purse, leaving her cards, her messages and her predictable but somewhat stale lifestyle behind.

Master Corporal Stewart had seen a lot in his fourteen years with the Canadian Forces. On a tour in Cyprus he had watched one of his best friends stumble on an old mine that blew his leg and hip right from his body. In Quebec City in 1983 he and four companions had saved the life of three people in a burning vehicle after returning from a retirement party at a local pub for one of their senior officers. There was the mundane as well: the endless patrols that had to be made, the security checks and the reports that couldn't wait until the following shift. But all in all, he was happy with the military and did what was required of him without complaining. The last six months had been hectic, however. Poor Jim Carmicheal had received an awful trouncing by the staff sergeant on the weekend for letting the American Colonel make off with his police vehicle. Then there were the endless interviews with Captain Morris on his return from Turkey. And none of the activities which required so much intense work was completely explained. Top Secret, they said. Eyes Only or some other bullshit which basically meant politicians had access to information they didn't know what to do with while the boys in the trenches had to carry the load without knowing what the hell for. THERE'S NO LIFE LIKE IT the poster says. Hmmph. Then of course, there's Miss Claire Monty. What a peice of ass that one is, he thought. I wouldn't mind being twenty-four hour escort if it meant I had to tuck her in and keep her comfortable at night too. Stewart let the legs of the chair ease to the floor from its tilted position and put down his magazine. He checked his watch. Seven fucking hours. She said she had last minute paperwork to do, but shit. Stewart yawned and tapped his buddy on the arm for a smoke. Just as he was placing the butt of the cigarette in his mouth, the lights of the office went out and Claire Monty opened the door. She closed it behind her and turned the lock.

"All finished, Ms. Monty?"

"All finished."

"Are there any stops you'll need to make before heading back to your apartment?" Stewart liked the sound of that. Christ, what a body.

"I called one of my friends who borrowed some tapes from me last week. I'd appreciate a ride to her apartment if you don't mind."

"No problem."

Stewart and his companion were sitting outside her friend's apartment waiting for her to return when the message came over the radio.

"Car nineteen, come in."

"This is nineteen, go ahead."

"Pete, this is Linda. Sarge just got a note from Com HQ that says your parcel's got an urgent message waiting for her from overseas. It's family, I think. She's supposed to call a number in Italy. Sarge says it's pretty important. A car accident or something. 02-94-63-69. Get that?"

"Got it. I'll get her to phone as soon as she comes out."

Claire had never taken a serious interest in drama. She soon found it had its place, like everything else.

"I don't understand. Call Italy? What's the problem?"

"I have no idea, ma'am. All I know is that you are to call this number for an urgent personal message." Claire explained that her friend's phone wasn't working. Was there a telephone nearby they knew of that she could use? The ride to the phone was appropriately tense. She dialed the number. Time and temperature for Rome repeated itself over and over while Claire played her role, hoping it looked authentic.

"Hello. My name is Claire Monty. I'm calling from West Germany. I was told I should call this number...No. Yes. My mother?! What do you mean? She was leaving Rome last night. Is she all right? I'll call back...no, wait! Can I talk to her? Okay. Thank you." Claire started to cry.

"I'm sorry, ma'am. Anything we can do to help?" Stewart was sincerely supportive.

"My mom was in a car accident. A limousine van on the way to the airport or something. She's in bad shape. They want me to go to the hospital; my brother and my dad are already on their way. I-I don't know what...."

"Just hold on, Ms. Monty." Stewart picked up his microphone.

For all his shortcomings, Master Corporal Stewart knew the system, and he was as gallant as any knight in shining armour. Here she was, this poor woman, stuck on a roller coaster she had no control over and she gets news that her old lady is dying in Italy. No sense sending her home right away.

Something's got to be done.

"I'm telling you, Sarge, I was right there when she made the call. She says they want her in Italy as quickly as possible. I guess her mom's not expected to live. Okay. I'll let her know.

"Looks like they're going to try and arrange something, Ms. Monty. Under the circumstances I can't see us doing anything else..."

It wasn't until Claire was actually off the ground that she managed to stop sniffling and compose herself. So that's how actors do it, she thought. I damn near convinced myself I had better check in and see how's she making out at the hospital by the time they changed my flights. Opening her purse she let out a little laugh. Hoping to find a clean kleenex she discovered twenty others rolled up in little balls of sorrow and grief. She sighed and looked out the window, the West German landscape shrinking beneath her. Letting her head fall back on the head rest, she reached up and pressed the button for an attendant. That exercise deserves a drink. And by God, Warren Cross, like it or not, I'm on your tail.

Claire knew it would be only a matter of time before her tampering would be discovered at the Base. She had a classmate from university who worked in Rome for the same company Claire had worked for in Germany. Claire lost little time. Within two hours of her arrival in the city, she was sitting at a console again, this time in another country. Her girlfriend had gone out for sandwiches and left her the keys to her office without any questions. Claire and she had been close long enough for her girlfriend to know when it would be fun to pry and when she should mind her own business. One look from Claire said it all.

Claire had heard the terrible news about the Soviet diplomat's assassination in the taxi from the airport to her friend's home. News reports confirmed that the body of a middle-aged man, assumed to be the assassin, had been discovered on the roof of a nearby apartment building. Apparently he had taken his own life also. The news agency mentioned a second man seen running through back alleys away from the scene. Istanbul. She was surprised at her response to the news. Surely to God the dead man would not be Warren Cross? At least Claire hoped it was not. She told herself it was because he owed her something. Her emotions said something else.

At 10:30 A.M. local time, Claire's girlfriend returned from the supermarket with pita bread and vegetables. She was excited to see Claire again. It didn't look like they would have much time to talk, but for now that didn't really matter. They hadn't kept in close touch for several years and a real visit would need to be at least a few days for any catching up to be done. There were memories, though. One weekend they had teamed up with two girls they had met at a volleyball tournament in Mount Vernon College. Through two sleepless nights they wandered in Las Vegas, looking for trouble and snatching young available men off the street for snacks and some laughs. That was the kind of person Claire had always been, she recalled. When there was a job to do, she was as serious as anyone she had ever known. But when she got an idea fixed in her mind, she was obsessed with it until she followed through or came to an absolute deadend. She wondered if the trouble she had mentioned was part of another obsession. She shook her head and smiled. Some things never seem to change. Shifting the groceries from her right arm to her left and fumbling with the keys to her office, she tapped on the door and opened it to see Claire scrambling to fold several sheets of printout paper and stuffing them into her purse.

"What's the panic, sister? You look like you've just been hit by a front-end loader."

"I've got to go," said Claire, glancing up only long enough to recognize her friend. "I've only got an hour before my flight leaves."

"Whoa, cowgirl. What's this? I'm loaded down with cheese so old it moves when you reach for it. Stay for a bite?"

"You've been really kind, Melanie, but I can't. I've got a blind date I have no intention of standing up."

"With who?"

"With a man I only spoke to for three minutes over a blackjack table about four days ago."

"And where might this mysterious man be drawing you off to?"

"The great Down Under. I'm flying to Australia through Singapore tonight."

XV

"There are thiry-four new recruits. The average age is twenty-six. Fourteen North American. Six from Soviet Bloc countries. Three from Africa. Three from China. Two from Brazil. Two from Japan. One from each of the following countries: Afghanistan, New Zealand, Taiwan, Greenland.

"AVERAGES: Entry code: seven. Experience level: three years university. Physical suitability for implant and reprogramming: excellent. Commitment: final. Do you require a printout, Senator?"

"No, Augustus. That is fine."

"Is there anything else?"

"Have Quintus come to my quarters immediately. Also, relay the photographs and recordings from our fallen colleague in Istanbul along with the address where Mr. Cross is staying in Sydney."

"Yes, Senator."

"That is all." With a soft beep, the intercom switch light faded and Senator Caspersan was left alone with his thoughts in the sparsely furnished but comfortable room which served as both bed chambers and office.

Caspersan had paid little attention to the portfolio that had been initiated by AUGUSTUS CENTRAL COMPUTING COMPLEX on Warren Cross, CIA retired, until shortly after the death of the envoy in Strasbourg the week before. It was accepted as inevitable that the State Department would make some attempt to find the missile that had been stolen from the military stockpile in the United States just prior to the planned shipment overseas. It was also assumed that they would choose someone who had the experience and creativity to design a plan which would bring some initial success. No one in the Senate would have envisioned, however, how one man would succeed in tracking the elusive Rempal Inquest as far as Australia. Two envoys had terminated in order to protect the system from him, an action which is designed as the last resort. Their human capacity to redefine, restructure, plan and initiate interventions based on their intellectual and emotional intuition had reached the same conclusion in each case. Fascinating, thought Caspersan. This Warren Cross would have been a shining addition to our Legions.

"Senator," the clear, slightly mechanical voice of Augustus interrupted Caspersan's thoughts.

"Yes, Augustus, what is it?"

"Quintus is standing by. Also, there are problems with the photographs from Istanbul. Legionnaire Richards terminated by shooting himself in the head. The bullet destroyed most of the recordings. We have only pieces of the conversation and a broken outline of Mr. Cross."

"Very well, Augustus. Copy what you have to my desk on line four and send in Quintus." At almost the same moment, there was a light knock on the door to his room.

"Come in, Quintus."

"You called for me, Senator?" The thirty-year-old man was dressed in gym clothes and covered in sweat.

"You have been in the training compound?"

"Yes, Senator."

"It's heartening to see that the instructors find it important to show a good example." Quintus acknowledged the compliment with a slight nod. He continued to face the wall opposite the door, not moving his eyes or his stature without word from his superior. "Please relax, Quintus. I will need to speak candidly with you on an important matter." The man relaxed his posture and turned to face Caspersan. Walking over to the desk which housed his computer console and the centralized communication link for the entire two-kilometer-square complex, Caspersan pressed a button marked "4" and immediately a laser printout of Cross's last encounter with Legionnaire Richards in Istanbul was slid into his waiting hand from a slit in the desk top.

146

"I hold in my hand the last communication, postmortem, from Richards in Istanbul. Our organization has much to honour him for. The assassination was successful, but an encounter with a man by the name of Warren Cross necessitated ending his own life soon after his mission was accomplished. You are to travel to Sydney and bring this man back to the complex. He is to be brought in alive. There will be no intention of him ever leaving us the same way he arrived. He is travelling under the assumed name of Arthur O'Brian. Augustus will provide you with his file and the hotel where he will be staying."

"Yes, sir," responded Quintus, his voice strained. The tension in his face did not go unnoticed.

"Quintus, listen carefully. You are aware that Richards chose his duty as well as his mission. He was a Legionnaire as you are and he could have done nothing else under the circumstances. Had he been taken in by Mr. Cross there are drugs which would have given the world information they cannot yet have access to. There was no other way."

"Yes, sir."

"I know too, Quintus, that you and Mr. Richards had been intimate for a number of months prior to his departure. The sexual preference of my men is none of my business. But I must make one thing clear. You are being chosen for this task because I feel certain you will be successful. Do not let your emotions cloud your judgment. He is not to be harmed." Quintus's eyes had begun to swell with tears, his desire to be strong clearly battling with the affections he held for Richards, a lover, a friend, a comrade.

"I hear you, sir. I only ask one thing."

"Speak up."

"When the time comes, I request permission to be assigned the task of killing him."

"Very well, Quintus, but remember. That time will be chosen by the Senate. Do you understand?"

"I understand."

"Good. Carry on." Quintus stiffened his posture and saluted Caspersan, his forearm thrust broadly across his chest in the ancient Roman salute. Poor man, thought Caspersan as his subordinate turned to leave. His relationship with Richards had

147

been long-standing and envied by many of the men at the complex who had to settle for weekend leaves or long-distance affairs with their girlfriends, sometimes not having sexual contact with them for weeks at a time. It would not be helpful for Quintus to be further hurt without reason, either. Richards had not always been singularly homosexual.

"Augustus."

"Yes, Senator."

"Before giving information to Quintus, insure that Richard's evening at the brothel is withheld from him. I do not want him to have access to Richard's exploits with that woman near the wharves in Istanbul."

"As you wish, Senator."

"You may inform the residential director that I will speak with the recruits in the theatre in twenty minutes."

"Yes, Senator."

The theatre was designed after the theatre of Marcellus which was erected by Emperor Augustus as a monument to his nephew. It was much smaller, of course. But Caspersan was steadfast in his belief that architecture was like music: it created a mood in people that predisposed them to receive or reject, to be open or closed. He may have been right. None of the thirty-four men awaiting Caspersan's welcome as they sat stiffly on the spartan benches, could feel anything other than Roman.

Caspersan refused any unnecessary shows of pageantry. Entering from the side of the stage, he walked to the centre and stood calmly behind the podium. He did not raise his hand nor call the recruits to attention. He simply waited until his presence was remarked and they quieted of their own accord. Once he was seen, this did not take long.

"Welcome, recruits. My name is Roman Caspersan. For those of you less familiar with the English language, Augustus will translate my talk with you in the language of your country. Headsets can be found beneath your seat." Various members of the group aided their new companions in discovering and activating the headphones. Caspersan began.

"I have much to tell you today. The history of mankind is long and complex, rising and falling with the seasons of the sun, returning again and again to help us evolve gradually from the foraging primates to the fully integrated beings we are destined to become. There have been theories, religions, philosophies and cultures throughout the eons which have attempted to answer the most basic of man's anxieties about the meaning of his existence. It will be my task to begin emancipating your minds from the rules and rigidities that have influenced you throughout your life, filling them with reality rather than fear.

"The first thing, therefore, that must be understood about human beings is that they are afraid. From the moment you were born to the moment you finally relinquish your frantic hold on the breath of life, you will be moved and motivated toward objects and people who can offer you security, a sense of belonging, of continuity. This is not only because we have inherited the primal instinct to socialize throughout the centuries, but also because we are conscious of our finiteness, aware that our experience and integration of sensory information will one day come to an end as we know it. Your bodies, the receptors of this information, will rot and decay, just as the corpses of plants and animals of the distant past are burned as fossil fuel in our factories and machines today. And because reason has imprisoned us with this knowledge, we distract ourselves from our fear by addictions and fleeting pleasures, sharing amongst ourselves anything that will dull the pain of our conscious awareness that we are insignificant, fragile, finite. The majority of mankind cannot reason the end of physical life without extending it in their minds, and so we have God or Nirvana or the legacy of children to believe in. Something that will extend us beyond ourselves, another social hiding place. We are bands of frightened beings huddled around any ideal that will give warmth to the cold reality of death, the ultimate enemy. The world is full of idols which represent our fears: nuclear and conventional armaments, the incessant scramble for personal wealth and financial security. And those who have power and influence prejudice their decisions in order to remain in control. They too are afraid of loss, of being human, of death.

"The second thing that must be understood about humanity is its sexuality. You will have noticed there are no women present. Do not delude yourself with grandiose reflections of superiority. Men and women differ in their abilities and in their limitations, but they are equal in their rights and their degree of importance. No garment can be sown without both needle and thread. The

149

needle of steel is no more essential than the cotton thread that follows its lead. They must work together to bind and to heal and to shape the cloth. So it is with men and women. Men were designed in their bodies and their biological dispositions to penetrate, to lead, to protect and to conquer. Women open themselves to maleness, receiving leadership, submitting to the other, comforting, soothing, encouraging. One of the greatest tragedies of the modern era is that its men have become weak. Physical and mental brutality have replaced the secure, firm direction of male self-awareness, and women have reacted to their social degradation by providing for themselves the comforts and security their lazy bedpartners can no longer supply. In the process of gaining this autonomy, women have lost touch with the sensitivity and receptiveness that creates a wholeness in the environment of the young who now grow in a society which promotes equality but which, in fact, denies the basic human drives that are innate in each sex. The two greatest civilizations of the world—Greece and Rome, succeeded for a time in marrying the strengths of masculinity and femininity, the conquered Greece adding her mystery and sensuality to the harshness and inflexibility of her Roman partner. But, unfortunately for the generations that followed, the leaders of those times became soft and failed to remember their purpose. Losing their vision, becoming mired in self-centeredness and conceit, Emperors deified themselves and lost perspective of the goals of true humanness, destroying literature and science by burning libraries and killing philosophers.

"But history is a stubborn teacher. A thousand generations have passed and still the man climbs upon the woman, the scratches on his back a symbol of her angry need to be conquered and the price he must be willing to pay to stay there. There is great power in dominance. But the lesson of history for men is clear. With power comes responsibility. He who cannot provide for his woman or protect her is not worthy of her. Eventually another will take his place, or she shall replace him herself with illusions of independence. Any man here who is not willing to take civilization as his own and continue to provide for her does not belong. This new age requires men, not children.

"The third aspect of man's destiny that stands out is science. The curiosity of people is such that questions must be answered,

150

regardless of the price. But once again, humanity has fallen short of its destiny because of its inability to accept its true place in evolution. The only possible outcome of thought is creation, and one cannot create without knowledge. But man has succeeded in hiding from the responsibility of creation by keeping the discovery and mastery of science at a distance. Like ambivalent children, we have toyed with astrology and physics, never reaching beyond the commonplace for explanations which could change the Universe, not to mention the present-day squabbles of a confused and frightened people. The astrologers of ancient Egypt had theories which pointed clearly toward a time when nothing would limit man's ability to control his future. Yet modern man drools with fascination when the telephone rings or the coffee maker turns on at 6 A.M. all by itself, seemingly blind to the potential of extrapolating the basic rules of nature to their inevitable end. Of all the men I would have liked to spend time with, Albert Einstein was the one I have truly admired. While his contemporaries were playing with heavier-than-air machines that could lift man above the ground, his theories hinted at a reality which would allow people to walk through walls and travel to distant stars in the blink of an eye. Our complex here in the marshes of Australia is a tribute to his type of genius. Leaving behind the competitive market and focusing on results rather than marketing potential, we have succeeded in constructing a network of information gathering and analysis which gives us control over the weather, access to an almost infinite band of communication and information sources, and an ability to link the biological with the machine; computers that understand; people who can process and retrieve information with infinite speed and accuracy.

"It is not expected that you hear my words this morning and grasp each syllable like some treasured relic. Each of you has been screened and accepted as part of our organization because you show potential to understand. Even if you did understand completely, there would still be a gap in the process if one last item was not present. This item is belief.

"Human beings choose to believe what they feel will allow them to remain safe, creative, popular, healthy and strong. It is rare that a truly independent thinker is born. Most people are looking for others to lead them in how they should process their experiences, to give them a system of beliefs which will allow them to strain out the disappointments of life, leaving only fresh water and clean food for their minds. Humans have difficulty with challenges. And so we have sub-cultures and religions and fads which attract any number of followers, guilt and tradition monitoring and determining the extent of a man's righteousness, worth and morality. One of the greatest secrets of living is that there is no right or wrong, therefore no guilt. There are only consequences. Each person must choose how to believe in a world that is basically chaotic and haphazard, without becoming bogged down in the expectations and sanctions those beliefs inevitably demand of him. In our modern day, we see the inherent danger in conflicting beliefs—for example, those born Catholic fighting with those born Protestant simply because they have been dropped into a system of beliefs that neither has ever stopped to question. In this type of believing world there are only winners and losers. There is rarely cooperation.

"Therefore, our complex has been designed to give you a set of beliefs, a background of knowledge and an education in responsibility which will at once free you from your past principles and demand a lifetime of commitment. In the past year, fourteen men from our Legions across the world have terminated their lives in order to protect the projects we have begun. Microscopic surgery gave them a potent and irreversible program of electronic priorities which clarified for them their choices based on what they had chosen beforehand. Trembling with fear, dreading the unknowable, each chose freely to end their lives because the implants they had been given did not let them down or change conveniently to fit the occasion. In the clear-sightedness of training and indoctrination, they decided to hold firm to their belief, to carry out the task, regardless of the cost.

"So, then, this is the beginning. You are human. You will fear, you will want, you will search and be ambivalent. History will tell you that the Rome of an ancient civilization almost succeeded in bringing direction to the world. In respect and honouring its example, we invite you to greet history face-to-face. We invite you to scrutinize, to listen and to train your bodies well. Then, if you accept and want to believe, if you decide to join the ranks of the new era bringing some hope to the

152

world in its frantic race to self-destruction; then we will give you the keys to power and responsibility that belong only to the chosen few: The Legions of the Rempal Era.

"And for those of you who are too curious to wait, your computer monitors in the dormitories will give you a head start on the lessons beginning tomorrow morning. I would respectfully suggest you begin with the Songs of Rempal. This little-known but highly creative poet of Augustan Rome has been an ongoing source of inspiration for both myself and many other members of the Senate. I look forward to working with you all in the near future. Good day."

In the same quiet and unremarkable way he had entered, Caspersan turned and walked toward the side exit of the stage, leaving the thirty-odd men seated below, alone with their silent excitement and anticipation.

XVI

Descriptions of the man running from the scene of the assassination were not clear. Some said he was wearing a suit. Others could swear it was a light leather jacket. Most people said he looked between thirty and forty years of age. Average height. The authorities in Istanbul did not have a hell of a lot to go on. This fact gave Cross time, and he took advantage of every minute.

Cross figured catching a flight to Australia would be easy enough once he had passed the careful scrutiny of the road checks. He had abandoned his hardware and played the confused, frustrated or angry tourist depending on whom he had to confront at each stop along the way to the airport. It became obvious at one area that they were looking for a man who would be travelling lightly. Middle-aged men with only carry-on luggage were being detained on the highway from their international connections at the airport for questioning. As people moved to the front of the traffice jam to question the holdup, Cross managed to confiscate several pieces of luggage from various vehicles and passed unnoticed.

The plane ticket Richards had tried to burn had Sydney, Australia as its destination. Only five numbers remained of a telephone number written on the back of the attached agenda sheet, but that would be enough. Cross reasoned there could only be a certain number of internationally organized terrorist groups with a fanatic twist for Roman history in the Sydney telephone directory. Humour helped keep him from becoming too tight to think. And there was plenty to worry about. The radio stations had been very busy in the three hours since the assassination, first denying and then confirming reports of the murder of the

Russian diplomat outside the Blue Mosque. Several factions of Muslim extremists had already begun to claim responsibility for the assassination, while the Soviet News Agency attempted to focus international attention on the NATO broadcasts following the death of General McDonnell in Germany which promised his death would not be easily overlooked. It was easy to predict the outcome. Once the stunned international community gathered its wits, both the Americans and the Soviets would step up their mobilizations, calling for more "exercises" and "test patrols" on both sides of the German border, not to mention increased submarine activity and hot-line confrontations. One American news agency broadcasting out of Istanbul said that a considerable number of Beverly Hills inhabitants had begun an exodus to personal bomb shelters, well-to-do families concerned that the tensions between the two superpowers could tolerate nothing more. Doomsday revivalists were enjoying a heyday. Jesus was coming soon, maybe before the weekend, they spouted—"get your seat on the bus to glory before it's too late."

Cross had tried to sleep during the long series of hops and jumps from Istanbul to Sydney, but with little success. His system had only begun to adjust to European time and he was thrown another seven hours back. His haggard beard of forty hours and bloodshot eyes told a story of their own to the receptionist at the desk of the Royal Markum Hotel in downtown Sydney. If he has the money for a room, she thought, this man needs some sleep.

Cross also knew he could not function much more without some rest and some food. Even in crisis, the body has limits to what it can endure without breaking down. Declining to use the elevator out of habit, Cross climbed the three flights to his room and dropped himself on the bed, his mind asleep before his head hit the pillow.

Four hours later the only change in Cross's position on the bed was that one arm was now hanging over the edge, his mind still floating through REM sleep, his body twitching involuntarily in its state of slowed consciousness. In the lobby below, the receptionist was preparing to change shifts with a girlfriend when the phone buzzed.

155

"Hello, Royal Markum, can I help you?"

"Yes, I think so," the tired voice on the other end responded. "I'm looking for a couple of friends of mine. We kind of lost each other at the airport, and I don't know which hotel they're staying in."

"One moment, please." The young woman stopped to point out a correction to a man who was signing the register.

"Yes, ma'am. What were their names again?"

"There are three of them. I don't know if they're together or not." The woman named her three friends.

"We have a Mr. Arthur O'Brian staying with us."

"When did he arrive?"

"About eleven A.M. Would you like to have me leave a message for him?"

"Yes, please. Could you tell him that Claire Monty called and that she'd like to meet him for supper in the hotel restaurant this evening around eight? Thank you very much."

At six-fifteen, Cross awoke with a start. He lay frozen on the bed, his mind fully alert. He looked around: It seemed like a hotel room. He sighed. Sydney. The Royal Markum. He had been sleeping. Cross was relieved and disappointed. He felt relieved because he was having a vivid nightmare. His father had died and when he went to the funeral he was not allowed in. Family relatives blocked the entrance and said he couldn't enter because he hadn't been a real son to Mr. Cross in twenty years. How dare he show his face in the family's hour of sorrow? Disappointment flooded in to take the place of his relief. This hotel room signified that he was halfway around the world from anyone who meant anything to him including his father who was right now dying of cancer in some hospital ward. Worse yet was his realization that a little over a day ago he had witnessed what might prove to be the terrorist act that would signal the end of the modern world. Sometimes nightmares can run a close race with reality in a person's quest for sane experience.

Cross turned over and sat upright, running his hands over his face to bring blood back as he had done every day of his adult life for as long as he could remember. A small red light flashing on the phone to the left of the bed went unnoticed at first. Then it occurred to him. A flashing light means messages. Someone in Washington was taking a fucking risk tracking him on his

156

aliases, Cross thought. Maybe the two governments have finally done it? Maybe they've declared war and it's too late for anything to be done?

"Good evening, front desk."

"Yes, this is Mr. O'Brian in Room 311. I have a flashing light at my phone. Are there any messages?"

"Only one, Mr. O'Brian. A Ms. Monty has called. She says she would like to have supper with you this evening at eight o'clock in the dining lounge."

"A Ms. who?"

"A Ms. Monty, sir. She said her name was Claire Monty."

At first Cross was shocked. It frightened him to think that a civilian could find him so quickly and follow him ten thousand miles across three continents to a hotel in downtown Sydney. Then he remembered another message he had received from his answering service in Strasbourg. He smiled. So Claire Monty is on the trail of the bastard that left her high and dry in Baden-Baden last Friday. Sonofabitch. How did she know I was on my way to Sydney?

Cross mulled over a handful of possible explanations. His thinking was dulled somehow. He finally realized he was having difficulty concentrating on the question because he was feeling something—something he hadn't felt in over a decade....

"Tell me, sir, do you know the way to information?" Bridget's voice in the O'Hare terminal came back to him. Cross felt a wave of anxiety. Now now. Not fucking now. Why is all this coming up? Why the guilt? The memories would not relent. "Tell me you'll never love anybody but me, Warren? Promise me there'll never be anyone else?" Bridget's high school tone of voice brimming with vulnerability and love had made him feel like he was the only man in the world. Twelve years ago. A lifetime ago? Or was it yesterday? Why would he be thinking these thoughts about dinner with a woman he didn't even know? He had slept with many women since Bridget's death. He had never thought twice. A human being has needs. So did he. Still Bridget's voice would not go away. "You shithead. You're just saying that to placate me! Then next week you'll fly off to a job somewhere in the Orient and tie yourself up with a dozen Chinese teenagers looking to book passage back to the States.

How can I trust you when I love you so much?'' Bridget's voice was clear, ringing with love, humour, affection. Then the unthinkable occurred to him. He paused and walked to the sink in the corner of his room, gazing at the man in the mirror. Look at you. You've just purchased a new sport jacket and pants at the men's store down the street. You're fumbling with a knot for your tie and can't decide whether or not to wear aftershave. Claire. The stranger from Baden was touching a forgotten place, a place that Cross had buried with Bridget over a decade ago. His feelings for this stranger were meeting his memories head on.

Cross finished cleaning up with his usual defense against feelings. Within a half hour he had created a business agenda for his meeting with Ms. Monty that had nothing whatsoever to do with sexual attraction. He now knew his responsibility was to concentrate on finding out how the hell she found out where he had flown to and where he was staying. That little bitch. How dare she take it upon herself to corner me like this? By the time I'm finished with her, Cross told himself, her interests will be redirected. This is the wrong time and the wrong place for playing detective.

At five to eight Cross walked down the winding staircase of the Royal Markum and seated himself in the dining area. He chose a table next to a bay window, giving him the widest possible view of the room. Concentrating on the wine list, Cross suddenly felt a strange twinge at the back of his neck. Reluctant to think about it he simply looked up. He was not surprised why his peripheral vision had made him react in such a strong way. Walking toward him in an elegant evening dress that gathered at her slim waist and separated at the side six inches above her knees, Claire Monty approached his table. He tried to read the expression on her face, but couldn't. Arriving at the chair next to his, she looked down at him a moment. Placing her small purse on the table she paused briefly and then slapped him in the face.

"The next time you choose to communicate with me, Mr. Cross, be damn good and sure you know who you're fucking with. You have made me very angry." Several diners had turned in their chairs at the sound of Claire striking her dinner companion. Cross listened until she had finished her sentence.

Then he placed the wine list gently on the table, rose and slapped her back.

"The next time you raise your hand to strike me, be damned sure you're carrying a horseshoe in your glove because I'll nail your face to the carpet and you'll need a plastic surgeon to clean it off. Do YOU understand?" They stood there regarding each other, Claire holding the side of her face and Cross straightening his jacket. "I suggest we sit," said Cross, looking around as he left his chair to push Claire's into place. Those who had turned to watch were encouraged by his stern gaze to mind their own goddamn business and seemed to understand. By the time he had returned to his own side of the table and seated himself, the dining area was pretty well back to normal. At most tables, that is. The table next to the corner bay window endured a strained silence while Cross continued his perusal of the wine list and Claire stared at him.

"Sorry," Claire said simply. Cross sighed and shook his head, placing the list to one side.

"That is the most abrupt introduction to a dinner for two I have ever experienced," he said with a touch of lingering disbelief in his voice. Claire tried to hold back a smile, but it crept up and the tension began to dissolve.

"I was really angry with you."

"I believe it. The last person to slug me like that thought I had rear-ended his Ferrari at a garden party," Cross returned, "but we eventually made up." Claire leaned forward, realizing when it was too late that she looked much too interested in his answer to the next question.

"And you stayed friends?"

"No. I threw him in the pool and took a shovel from the tool house to his car." They laughed quietly. "It's too bad you didn't give me a chance to speak first," Cross teased her, aware now that the attraction was definitely mutual.

"Why?"

"I was about to say you looked very beautiful in your dress. I guess you must have been planning to drop me here with the first punch and move to another table."

"No, I just wanted to...Okay, so I dressed up to meet you. Maybe my memory didn't serve me all that well and I was

159

expecting to have supper with a gentleman. Not someone who spends enough time connecting at a blackjack table to send his acquaintance on a suicide run over the Autobahn to meet with some foreign general at three-thirty in the morning without so much as an explanation or even a thank you.''

"I was very grateful, believe me. I am indebted to you—you may have saved my life..." The sincerity in his voice made Claire flush. She was aware there may have been other reasons why she spent so much time and energy following this stranger. He seemed gentle somehow, yet unyielding. "...and thought the least I could do was take you up on the offer for dinner. Are you listening, Ms. Monty?''

"I-I'm sorry, Warren, I mean Mr. Cross. What the hell do I call you anyway?''

"That gets complicated.''

"So I've learned. Maybe O'Brian is your real name and Cross is just another alias?''

"I think we're going to need to talk about one thing at a time. I still don't know if you heard me explain why I didn't make any attempt to contact you after that night at the casino. I haven't exactly been on vacation.''

"No, I realize that. In fact, you can save yourself a lot of time and effort. There's no need for games. I'm a computer programmer, Mr. Cross. That means I know how to make machines do things for me, give things to me..." I wouldn't mind a chance to do things for you myself, thought Cross. "...and when I got stuck, I just kept plugging. The military needs more protection devices. Their computers are slow and to be quite candid, considerably outdated.'' Cross knew that wasn't completely true, but her tenacity showed one thing for sure. The systems didn't keep her from getting what she wanted. Whatever that was.

"Answer me one question, Ms. Monty.''

"No need to be formal. Try Claire.''

"Okay, Claire, answer me this. Your explorations and antics have succeeded in gaining you a whole lot of information that could prove dangerous to you—a fact you probably haven't stopped to consider. You've travelled half way around the world to slap me in the face and get belted in return, and one thing is still not clear to me.''

160

"Shoot. I mean, well—go ahead."

"What do you want from me?"

In the intensity of this moment, compounded by the hours spent at her computer, by her two-step moves to ger her away from the military and by the drama of their first meeting alone, Claire Monty felt very close to asking him to take her to bed after supper and then fly home to meet her parents. She didn't understand the feelings, but was very relieved when the waiter arrived only seconds before she blurted it out.

"Pardon me, may I take your orders?" It was good timing. Pleasantries were exchanged, thc waiter showing no sign of having seen or heard any commotion beforehand. Claire was impressed by Cross's choice of wines. For all the commotion, he seemed relaxed, comfortable with himself. I like that, thought Claire. I really like that...Whoa. Too fast. Back up a step or two. You don't even know this character. The waiter picked up the menus and left.

"What do I want?"

"Yes, that was the question."

"Well, I want to have dinner with you. Get to know you a bit." Hoop-jumping time, thought Cross. There must be a way to make this less complicated.

"Look, Claire, I'll be frank with you. When I first met you at the casino I had no idea I would be requiring any assistance whatsoever. I went to you then because my gut reaction to you was that you could be trusted."

"Is that all? I mean, what made you think I was trustworthy? Why DID you stop?"

"I stopped because you are an extremely attractive woman, and by some miracle you seemed to be alone. I may have played the cool dude, but I was sincerely disappointed when I heard you had a date."

"Who I made clear to you was not prime time company."

Cross shrugged. "Whatever he was to you by the time we met, you had accepted his invitation. It's not my style to cut in when someone I'm interested in is dancing with someone else."

Claire was feeling warm under his approving look. Each word that confirmed he liked her made the risk seem more worthwhile.

"That's honourable enough, Warren...." She decided to try his first name and stick with it, just to see how it sounded. "But you sure wasted no time interrupting my evening when it became convenient to do so.'' Warren looked disappointed. Claire felt bad. Maybe she had said too much?

"Look, Claire. I don't know how to make it more clear to you than I have, without getting into things you're not supposed to know and have no need to know.''

"Oh, that's cute. Information? Like hijacking an aircraft to Istanbul? Like being involved in the assassination of the Russian diplomat?'' Claire chanced the last statement. Nothing she had read suggested he had been, but he was there. The murder occurred shortly after he had arrived in Istanbul.

Warren stared hard at her. How much did she know? He took a long drink from his water glass, not taking his eyes off her. "I think this conversation is getting a bit out of hand.''

Bingo, thought Claire, he was involved. "What do you suggest?''

"I suggest we begin again. Maybe you can start by telling me how the hell you followed me out of West Germany arriving only a few hours after me in Sydney, Australia.''

The hours passed. The conversation flowed and so did the excellent wines. The tensions that had been present earlier were forgotten, though the introduction, both people had agreed, would go down in history as a classic. Once dessert had been served, and the dishes cleared away, Warren and his companion were at a crossroads. They had talked about their growing up and their work, Warren making it clear there were things that couldn't be discussed even with a nosy computer programmer. Warren had even alluded to his relationship with Bridget, talking about why it was difficult to let himself get close to someone. For both of them the evening was special. It seemed natural to want to extend it to the privacy of a hotel suite, but Warren, for only the second time in his life, was surprised when the natural inclination did not seem like the right thing to do. Not yet.

"You're not going to tell me, Warren, after all the wine you've helped me drink and all the warm feelings you've got stirred up in me that you're not really a lady's man? I want to sleep with you.'' That's about as direct as it gets, thought Warren.

162

"That's nice, Claire. That's real nice. But I can't do it."

Claire laughed. "You mean that alcohol loosens you up so much you can't get tense enough to follow through when you've seduced someone?" Warren reddened slightly realizing how the phrase he had used could carry more than one meaning. Clearing the wine bottle, the napkins and the glasses from between them, Warren reached out and took her hands. He had something to say; he wanted it to be taken seriously.

"No. I mean I like you. I really like you, and the first time I want it to be when we're ready for more than sex. Maybe I'm hoping that at some time we could be ready to make love instead." Claire allowed every word to burn into her mind. Did he say he wants to learn to love me? I need another drink.

"Okay. I think. Warren, I'm a bit afraid. What about the job, the task, or whatever in hell you call it? We've danced around the subject all night and I still have no idea what's going to happen to you in this thing. Is this what falling for a field agent is like? Where do you see me fitting in to all this?" Warren gave her hands a slight squeeze and pulled away. He reached for a plastic stir stick from an empty glass and scratched a piece of wax from the candle that was slowly expiring.

"I don't know, Claire. That's going to be a question we both work on. It's going to take some time...God knows none of us may have much time anyway. I heard on the radio this afternoon that NATO forces have warned the Soviets not to approach the West German border closer that twenty kilometers with their 'exercise tank maneuvres' or there would be a formal declaration of war."

"Don't tell me that Warren Cross is going to turn in his badge just because it looks hopeless. I'm talking about tomorrow and the day after that. I want to spend more time with you, do things with you. I want a chance at making that kind of relationship we've been alluding to. You can be straight. Is there room or not?" That's a damn good question, thought Warren. How do I answer it honestly?

"I want to spend time with you too, but the reality is I can't be split between the people I'm looking for and a schedule that has us booked for boating in the harbour at two P.M. every second day. I'd let you down, Claire. I can't be predictable or reliable when I'm working on this type of thing."

"What about your feelings? Are they reliable?"

"Yes," answered Warren, looking directly at her. "My feelings you can count on. This is the most I've shared with a woman in over ten years. It's because there's something here that's missing in my life, something I need, something...something I really want." There was a lengthy pause. Claire sensed he hadn't finished. She waited. It was the right decision. "Claire, listen. The choice over the next two to three weeks has to be yours. I don't want you to decide over supper with your mind full of questions and wine and cordon bleu. Take a day or two. Leave me a number where I can get back to you from time to time and we'll talk. It's you who needs time to decide where this thing goes, because for me the cards are already dealt. I have to continue and that might mean leaving you in Australia for a flight to the Amazon at four in the morning. The question is, can you wait? Is it worth it to make the emotional investment when I can't promise anything right now?" Claire looked like she was about to answer. Warren interrupted her. "No. Please, Claire. I'm dead serious about this. I want you. I want to have a chance to see where things go between us. If I get out of this alive or the world is not vapourized by button-pushing neurotics on both sides of the Pacific before I have a chance to come up with some real answers, then I know there would be time for us. I'd make it. We'd have the space and leisure to really look at things clearly. Do us both a favour. Sleep on it? Think about it for a day or two. Wander around Sydney. I'll call your room in a couple of days. We'll talk. What do you say?"

Claire had wanted to say a lot of things. She wanted to talk openly and freely about the kind of feelings Warren Cross had awakened in her. She knew she wouldn't be able to sleep. God, she felt like a school girl. He kissed me goodnight, she thought. A light, sensitive, I-really-like-you kiss on the lips.

With these and a thousand other thoughts racing through her mind, Claire threw her purse on the bed and let out a little squeal. It was worth it! To hell with the job in Germany and the military assholes who packed my china in two sheets of newspaper. HE is worth it. Talking to herself, wondering, dreaming, Claire entered the bathroom, reaching behind to catch the zipper at the back of her dress. She tried her right hand, then her left, finally nabbing it between her two hands midway between her shoulder blades. She zipped it to her waist. Slipping the shoulder straps over her shoulders and pulling the tight-fitting dress down to her ankles, she stepped out of it, a small pile of seduction on the bathroom floor. Thinking how it had served its purpose, she picked it up and hung it over the shower curtain bar above the tub. In front of the mirror she removed her bra and threw it in a corner. She looked at her breasts and cupped them in her hands, fantasizing Warren's firm hands on her. She ran her right hand up along her right breast and along her neck, pushing her short hair to the top of her head. "You are kind of cute, aren't you, Claire Monty? Warren Cross had no chance when you sauntered in with half your leg swinging, did he?" She giggled and faced the tub, reaching for the taps to start a bath. A nice hot bath. Maybe she'd relieve some sexual pressure and touch herself for a while tonight?

There was frustration for Quintus when Claire moved out of sight, though there ought not to be. Quintus had always been sure of his sexuality. Maybe it was because he wanted to do things to Cross's new girlfriend that might hurt Cross the way he had been hurt? Quintus listened to the young woman talk to herself as the water poured into the tub. The phone rang. Claire Monty came back into the bedroom fully naked. He noticed in a detached kind of way that she had a beautiful body. No stimulation there, no sexual stimulation. But there was anger.

"Sorry, you've got the wrong number." Claire hung up. She was smiling. Too bad, thought Quintus. The bait has to be living if it's going to catch a fish. Maybe I could just hurt her a bit? Maybe Caspersan would let me hurt her a bit when I get back? Quintus watched from the crack in the closet door as the door to the bathroom closed, Claire seeking the privacy of the small room out of habit. Quintus waited. She would come out, he reasoned. There would be time. Time to think of Cross's expression when her pretty body is scarred with a rusty nail. Time to think of throwing pieces of Cross into the swamp outside the complex and watch the neighbouring 'gators munch on his bones. When she slips into bed, there will have been enough time to enjoy the thought of it all.

Forty minutes passed. Quintus heard what he imagined was a practiced hand touching, searching, putting pressure in the most sensitive places. Strange, he thought, as murmurs and soft moans drifted into the bedroom; quite strange, the private sounds people make when they feel they're not being watched. He smiled. The plug from the tub was pulled. The water began to drain. Moving more slowly now, her hair wrapped in a towel to keep it dry, Claire returned to the main room of her suite. She yawned. Dropping the towel on a seat near the bed, she turned toward her closet. Quintus pulled back instinctively. She reached for the clock on her night table. She took a moment to set it. Walking to the light switch, she turned off the lights and slipped naked under the covers. She tossed once, twice. Her body, relaxed from the release of her orgasm in the tub, soon began to breathe evenly. She was asleep. Now, Quintus decided. Hinges had been lubricated. Shoes were cushioned. She had no idea he was there. He stood over her bed and smiled a moment. A gloved hand extended from the darkness toward Claire's face...

XVII

When he first became a field agent, Cross had been told about the need to develop a kind of split personality, the man on the job complete and apart from affections, ties, romance. As a young lieutenant just out of Ranger operations training, the advice stayed simply that. A note placed in the margin of a long lost manual. Then came Bridget. And with her the knowledge that survival in both worlds would mean a delicate balance of emotions and intellect, that the agent is demanded by the exigencies of his position to remain aloof from his loved ones when cornered or coerced. To think, to do, to accomplish the task. An agent had no time for subjective experience. He must remain emotionally alienated. Then, should the job allow a moment of respite, there would need to be a change of character, a seeming change of energy and priorities. A change in focus. Some guys never succeeded. In recent years it seemed like some of the female agents managed somehow to keep a tighter lid on that kind of thing.

In the early days Cross was given enough assignments to keep him afloat. They met his needs, or seemed to. His work was like a kind of religion: attempting to curb the tide of craziness in the world being for him the only way of coping with knowledge about the extremes of human kindness and human cruelty his experiences had brought him. Then the impossible. Cross fell in love. Another equally powerful desire was ignited and fed. It became obvious with time that both fires could not burn together; coexistence would eventually mean becoming ineffectual as an agent or totally unreliable as a lover, or both. But that first time, love had died before a final decision was made. Somehow Cross had managed to keep both priorities from tearing him apart over the year and a half they had known each other.

Now there was Claire. And at the same time there was a mission which could conceivably contribute to the resolution of a potentially terminal world conflict. Impossible. No time. It seemed inconceivable for him to try and live in one world without losing his mind in the other. Worrying about his dad was bad enough.

Cross was familiar with this type of craziness. After more than ten years of attempting to forget, to put memories behind him, away from him, erased from his mind, now he fumbled and urged himself to recall, to turn on the switches that helped him have as much of love as he could without endangering himself or others in the process. Love? Are you out of your mind? he asked himself. This is not high school. You are not a teenager. Warren shook his head as he headed down the corridor to his room. One fight, one dinner and one kiss. Christ. Maybe a man just doesn't know how hungry he is until the right food is placed in front of him? Time out, he told himself, turning the key in the handle. Dinner was fine. Claire was wonderful. Now what?

Turning on the light switch, Cross began to undress before the door was closed. There were questions to be asked and places to visit. Seven minutes later the man of emotions, the listener, the sincerely interested, had a change of clothes, and to an outsider, a bizarre change of thought process. Dress pants were exchanged for jeans. Tweed was exchanged for a jacket of dark leather and soft-soled street shoes. Okay Sydney, thought Cross, zipping his jacket to just below the neck. Heads up.

Sydney, Australia, the historic port of destiny for the immigrant exiles of eighteenth-century England, is a vast testimony to modern development and traditional stubbornness. Nestled in her arms are immigrants from almost every nation of the world, seeking opportunities and hope. None who have found work and leisure here would want to live in any other world. Its people thrive on the ability to prove that hard work can be accomplished with one hand on the slaughterhouse table and the other on a cool beer. No rush. Do your work and then lie on the beach. Sweat it out, mate, make a fist of it. But don't let life hassle you too much.

Native Aboriginal peoples, who once possessed the land in all her majesty, now have only sadness to replace the pride they once enjoyed. In Sydney's Redfern district, poverty and the struggle to maintain a clear sense of dignity clash with the urban expansionism sponsored by the country's desire to learn and to grow. Cross had known intimately of that sadness many years ago. The story of a man named Jojo had pointed it out.

Cross had been assigned the task of passing on information to agents in Russia through an Australian courier who was home on holidays from doctorate studies in the Soviet Union. The task was simple enough. Two strips of coded messages were bound in the pages of some reference material Cross had carried with him from the States. Four trips a year communicated a considerable amount of undercover software for the Agency, while the Australian student was building a sizable reputation for thorough and discreet service with an organization which promised him a choice of any project, anywhere, once his doctorate was complete.

Jojo was the young man's grandfather. He had spent most of his energy during the last years of his life trying to convince his people of their rights. He had already failed to keep his two sons from marrying white women. He had failed to save his own wife from drinking herself to death. He had three grandchildren. The least I can do, he had told himself, is share with them where they have come from. And maybe, he had said, I can help build something for them to look back on. There can be no future without a past.

On a hot Australian summer day in November, Jojo travelled with his two grandsons and his granddaughter to the wide open bush of Kakadu National Park for a picnic. During his time with them he told them many stories that had been handed down by word of mouth for centuries—stories that spoke of the Ice Age and the purpose of man who shared life equally with the rock and the tree. He drew pictures for them in the sand and showed them how a person could climb a tree that had no limbs and where water could be taken from leaves and roots. Jojo shared all those skills that his people had given to the immigrant settlers over two hundred years ago. He explained to them patiently what made their heritage something to be proud of, something worth keeping.

When the week-long trip was over and the children had returned to their homes in Sydney, Jojo overheard one of his daughters-in-law talking to another on the phone. They were laughing about their black-skinned father-in-law, discussing his traditions and his desire to influence his grandchildren as the muddling of an old fool, the endless dreams of a time that was passed and gone. He should stay in the dust with his dances and leave us alone, one had said. Jojo could take no more. In a rage of hurt and frustration he grabbed the woman and threw her against the wall near the phone where she cracked her temple on a coat hook and was killed. Jojo's grandson watched his mother die and his weeping grandfather hauled away by the city police, later to be convicted of manslaughter and sentenced to twelve years in prison. Refusing to eat for almost a month, the old man died in his cell with his face to the window during the day, his body curled up in a corner at night. The land that had welcomed the white man in exile had sentenced its ancestor to the cell.

In his youth the youngster hated his grandfather for taking his mother from him. As he grew and studied, he understood more and often spoke with Cross about the sadness of the Aboriginal people in the country. Cross could never walk through the dusty Redfern district without thinking of Jojo and his grandson. There remained in the defiant and rainwashed graffiti of the Aboriginal slums the same tone of frustration and sense of powerlessness. And often, Cross had discovered, the same patience and desire to live in dignity.

The sky was bright with stars. Cross walked briskly past video game parlours and late-night coffee shops just outside the Redfern district, remembering and trying at the same time to keep his mind focused sharply on the present. Too much at once, Cross said to himself. Richards in Istanbul, General McDonnell in Germany. Claire Monty following me all over the globe with only a sincere desire to make me feel good as motivation. Shit. A little clear-cut undercover work might help me make sense of the world.

Just as Cross had left it six years ago, the Hawkesbury Tavern flashed its small neon light above a wooden carved door sign. From half a block up the street the buzz from the light could be heard, its incessant crack-fizz gradually losing ground to the more insistent background of laughter and good times that issued forth through the door of the bar. Cross paused only long enough to allow two young men to pass him in the doorway. "Oh, sorry, mate. Me cousin's had a glass too many tonight. I think he's gettin' married." Cross smiled as he held the door for them. Hawkesbury Tavern. Be damned if it didn't sound like the same party he'd left behind.

"What'll be, mate?"

"Scotch."

"Jis up clear and clean?"

"That's it." A friendly nod and the bartender turned away to pour Cross a glass.

There was a system here, as in every place where Cross came for information. It was slightly different from what North Americans might readily recognize. But there were social customs that had to be followed. Urban American yuppies, with their norms and pecking orders would here be compared to reckless partygoers, the one just as strict in its adherence to tradition as the other. Consequently, the first question in Australian bars was usually the same:

"What's the celebration?"

"I don't really know, to tell you the truth," the bartender answered, interrupting his wiping of the bar to place a tray of dirty glasses on a side shelf. "Somethin' about a sailing derby on the weekend. Started out that way anyway."

"I guess it really doesn't take much, does it."

"Hell no. When these boys get on well together over the weekend they usually dull the hangover with a good stiff start to the week. It doesn't take much more than a tennis match on the wide screen to bring 'em in."

"You should know all about that, Mr. Cross. I can tell you've had a hard weekend yourself." The voice from behind Cross's back fused his spine into one rigid rod of apprehension. Only twenty years of experience kept him from whipping about to see who had spoken his name. The impossible had happened again.

"Come now, Warren. Let's not play hide-and-seek. I have a message from someone for you. She says that she feels very thwarted by your lack of sexual ardor. She says she would have loved to share a bed with you tonight and that she's extremely disappointed that you decided to go out drinking alone without

171

her. Especially when dinner was so pleasant.'' God no. Not Claire...There was no choice. In a slow movement, Cross turned and faced his antagonist as the bartender slipped away to leave them the space Cross's expression had insisted on.

"Don't expect to know me, Mr. Cross," began Quintus. "We have so little in common, I am positive we have never met before.''

"For someone who doesn't know me you seem to know a hell of a lot about things that are none of your business.''

"Ah, but they are my business, Mr. Cross. They have become my business just as Istanbul and Strasbourg and Sydney have somehow become your business.''

"Get to the point. What does this have to do with Claire? If she's harmed...'' Quintus frowned and shook his head, turning from the bar to face the rowdy crowd.

"No, Cross. That's not what I want to hear. You're in no position to threaten or coerce. Surely you've learned that those mild pressures don't bother us? We are beyond the frivolous mind games of your profession. Let us speak clearly to one another.'' He paused. Cross knew he had no cards left. He had not been careful enough. If they had taken Claire, he would have to listen. Listen and wait... "Perhaps it is that you don't believe me? Perhaps you're waiting for proof?'' With that Quintus reached into his jacket and pulled Claire's small dinner purse from his jacket. He placed it on the bar and moved closer to Cross, examining his features, fantasizing what one angry man could do to another man's face. Cross could feel the breath of him. He recognized the purse. It was Claire's. Placing a hand on Quintus's chest he firmly and quietly pushed him back a foot.

"I like my breathing room.''

"Really? That's nice. I'll be polite, Mr. Cross. There now. Breathe. In the meantime, maybe you can answer a question for me. Did you know that Claire has a mole on the inside of her left thigh?'' Cross held himself back. He could feel the blood rushing to his face. Quintus smiled. "Yes. We chose the right way to invite you for breakfast, that's obvious.''

"What do you want?''

"Oh, don't be in such a rush, Mr. Cross. We have all night. Think of it. You came here to find out more about Mr. Richards in an attempt to find your little missile and meet the people who

172

masterminded the scheme that has the world arming itself for war at this very moment. I walked into your life to save you considerable trouble. I'm to be your guide.''

"I can find my own way."

"No doubt. This is why I chose to invite your friend first. I was sure you would want to spend more time with her. I reasoned, therefore, that if she were spending breakfast at our complex, you too would want to be included on the guest list."

"So we walk from here to a waiting car and drive casually to your leader."

"In a manner of speaking."

"And if I refuse?"

"Academic, Mr. Cross. We feed your lady in small pieces to the rodents that roam the grasslands."

"And if I go with you she'll be released?"

"No. Probably you will both die. I could tell you differently, but you wouldn't believe it anyway. Here's what you can expect. In five minutes from now, a young man will walk through that door with steel-rimmed glasses and a denim jacket on. If I am holding this drink in my left hand, he will quietly return to the place where Ms. Monty is being kept and kill her. If I have my drink in my right hand, he will bring his car to the door to escort us both to where you can be reunited with her—for a short time at least. You will accompany us to meet people who are curious about you. Then, once your own curiosities and their's have been satisfied, you will be terminated. No need to plan ahead, Mr. Cross. The situation is quite hopeless. Our vehicle is fully monitored at all times, and any irregularities would result in the car being destroyed with you in it."

"And you."

"And Ms. Monty and the driver." Quintus shrugged. "Our deaths are irrelevant, in a sense. I would rather live to be old and happy, but I would have no control over the destruction of the car. A hazard of employment, I suppose. Unless you are totally blind, Mr. Cross, you will have learned that we are prepared to offer that option to our superiors if that is necessary."

"You and your superiors are out of your fucking minds."

"Perhaps. You know as well as I do that psychosis can be perilessly kin to genius. Which is which remains only a matter of society's judgment. The end justifies the means." Quintus glanced at his watch. "Three minutes left, Mr. Cross. If I were you, I would not count on my driver being completely on time. What shall it be?"

XVIII

"Speak up, Terry. Damn long distance. The line is almost as bad as last time."

"How's this?"

"Better."

"You were saying?"

"Ah shit. I don't know. What the hell am I supposed to do? This here's about as clear as axle grease to me. Last I heard he was on vacation. I knew there was something fishy about the whole damn business the day those government fellas drove in and he showed up."

"Well, what did the man say exactly?"

"You mean word for word?"

"Well, yes. He sent a telegram, didn't he?"

"Yeah."

"Read it to me. Maybe it isn't so complicated as it looks."

"Okay. It says here: GARY STOP I'M IN TROUBLE IN SYDNEY AUSTRALIA STOP NO ONE STATESIDE CAN BE TRUSTED SO KEEP THIS MESSAGE TO YOURSELF STOP KEY ABOVE WATERBOWL IN TRACY JOS STALL TO BOX AT FIRST NATIONAL IN TOWN STOP TAKE FIFTY THOUSAND AND FLY TO SYDNEY STOP KNOW YOU HAVE RELATIVES HERE STOP INFORMATION WILL BE WAITING ROOM 311 ROYAL MARKUM HOTEL DOWNTOWN SYDNEY STOP. That's it. That's all he wrote."

"What do you know about him? Was he into drugs or a convict maybe?"

"I don't think so," Gary Fletcher answered, holding the telegram in one hand and his home telephone in the other. "In

175

fact, as far as I could tell he was in the military for most of his career. Said he was retired for asking the wrong question at the wrong time. I never pushed him for more than that."

Terry Farnham, a friend of Gary's since they were school children together in Sydney, spoke in a challenging tone. "Well, reach deep down, Gary. Personally I'd love to see you again. Delores and Frank, Mark and Charlie, hell, we'd all be waiting at the airport if you did fly down. It's up to you. If he was a mate of yours, you're the only one who can tell whether it would be the right move or not. Sounds like he wants to keep the whole fire under your hat for one thing. Is there anybody who could tend to the farms for a week or two?"

"I'd be pushing it to ask my neighbour, Bob Ferguson, to watch two farms aside from his own. I suppose he might get his sons to spread the load. It's not like there's harvesting to do or anything. Just keep the cows fed and watered mostly."

"Did you check to see if there was a key where he said?"

"First thing I did," replied Gary, picking the small key off the kitchen table. "To tell you the truth, I'm a bit afraid to go and check the bank. What the hell would I do with fifty thousand dollars? He never said what I was supposed to do with it."

"So buy yourself a six-month vacation."

"Ah shit, Terry, I'm serious. What would you do?"

"Well, it'd depend on who it was for. Look, Gary. He knows you're from Sydney, he's checked in at the Markum and figures he could use your help on the island. Doesn't sound all that strange to me. Is he a bloke you trust yourself?"

"No question."

"For me that'd be half the distance right there."

"What about Beatrice?"

"Beatrice doesn't need to know anything. It's not like she harbours any ill feelings anyway, Gary. All that was a long time ago. She's never spoken badly of you and the boy's turned out to be a fine young man. This is going to be your decision alone, mate."

"It's making decisions like this all the time that made me want to leave home in the first place."

"And what did you find?"

"The same goddamn thing every place I settled."

Gary Fletcher had been on an airplane only twice before. Both trips were part of his move to the States in the early sixties. Looking back it seemed in some ways like it had been only yesterday, the jet black curls of his girlfriend's long hair blowing in the wind....

"It doesn't have to be this way, love. We'd make a go. My folks mean well. They just don't see things the way we do, is all." Her eyes brimming with tears, Beatrice tried to be strong. She wanted to tie him to a post, make him stay and try to work it out. There was no holding Gary back once his mind was made up. Part of her knew that was true and would not likely ever change.

"It's like I told you, Bee," replied Gary, shifting the weight of his small canvas bag on his shoulder, "I just can't see it working that way. I've got a mind of my own and I want to raise my family away from people who think they know better than me how to do it. It wouldn't be so bad if it were just your folks or mine, but the four of 'em sticking their hands into the pie every time we bring up the subject of moving or investing in a business. I can't live like that." The two young lovers regarded each other with the same mixture of sadness and longing that had created tremendous agony for them both over the last several weeks. They had been so happy for the years they'd gone out together. Beatrice was four months pregnant. They had planned to marry in the spring, but Beatrice said she wasn't ready to leave Australia yet. She wanted her baby to know family, to grow up with relatives to turn to if need be. "There's still time, Bee. I've got the money right here. Just say the word and the three of us will walk up the ramp and head east. I want you and the baby with me, but it can't be around here. I'm suffocating." Beatrice let forth a small sob. She forced a smile and pulled a kleenex from her dress pocket. Blowing her nose, she tried to straighten her shoulders. This was the way it would have to be.

"You are one bloody stubborn old mule, Gary John Fletcher. I love you more than you'll probably ever know. But I can't do it. Maybe in a year or two, once the baby's born and I finish my accounting courses. The timing's real bad, honey. I can't. You can't. We're best to say goodbye."

And say goodbye they did. They wrote for a time. But Gary had his money and his energy tied up in the farm. Beatrice was trying to finish her courses while working part-time and taking care of the baby. Before too long, three weeks between letters turned to six. Different worlds, different priorities. After a year and a half they wrote their last notes. No hard feelings between them. There would always be sadness though. Some people say the kind of love they had comes only once in a lifetime. Gary assumed Beatrice had remarried by now, but he had never found anyone to hold a candle to her. Sometimes things just don't work out the way you want them to.

The Sydney airport was dusty and dry. Gary expected to feel something important, something nostalgic, as the plane touched down. It wasn't there. This whole business had too many holes in it to make sense. What does he do with forty-seven thousand dollars in American Travellers Cheques? Who does he see? What the hell is Cross looking for anyway?

For a while Fletcher was able to put his questions on hold. Standing in the gateway holding a sign that read "Welcome Home Gary!!!" on a piece of cardboard four feet by six feet, were some of his best friends from high school. Most of them he recognized. There was a bedlam of good cheer when Terry Farnham, the man he had spoken with on the phone, saw him enter the doorway. Questions were thrown at him, pats on the back were exchanged. Gary was deluged with plans and laughter and jokes about the great American adventurer returning to the bush of his home country. There was to be a party that night at Terry's place. Charlie wanted to take him on a tour of the city before he left. Gary's mind was spinning. Then he saw her. At the rear of the small crowd stood a graceful-looking woman, the only telltale sign of her forty-eight years a tightening of laugh lines around her eyes. Her hair was still coal black, a bit shorter but full and tumbling in natural curls, just like the hair young Beatrice had when Gary had left so long ago. It didn't take long for most of Gary's friends to notice him staring at her. When Beatrice had asked to be included in the welcoming, it was assumed they would want to talk. Terry spoke up.

"Okay, gang. Let's not hang about like teetotaling preachers at a football stadium. Bundle your gifts and pocket your questions. Gary, we'll see you in the wagon out front when you're done here. Take your time, mate. It's damn good to see ya." Gary shifted his gaze and thanked them all for their kindness. Fielding last-minute jokes and slaps to the small belly that hung slightly over his well-worn leather belt, Gary walked over to her. She smiled.

"Well, don't just stand there, you migrant devil, give us a hug," Beatrice said, holding out her arms and folding them around her long-ago love. The poignant sadness and bitter-sweet joy of the moment was savoured by both. Gary found it hard to speak.

"Did you learn to hate me, Bee-Beatrice? Are you happy today?"

"I'm as happy as I choose to be, and most days that means something between content and ornery as hell. And as far as hating you because you couldn't stand around and vegetate like the rest of your brothers, God help us, never. I hated loving you so much by times. There were real hard days for a while, and much harder nights. But what we had was good, Gary. My memories have stayed sweet and tender." Fletcher could tell she was telling the truth as she had lived it. He started to cry, silent tears streaking his sunworn cheeks.

"Now see what you've done with your talk of memories!" said Gary, wiping his face with the back of his hand and smiling. "A man does his best to forget what he's chose to leave behind and one look makes his brainwashing out to be a waste of time."

"Yes to that, Gary-John. I learned that early on. I finally realized there was no use trying to erase what had been good and right, and your son has no reason to resent his dad for not loving his mother while he was here. Mind you, I'll be honest. He hasn't shown much interest in seeing you. He feels you left a hole in his life no uncle or cousin or scout-leader would ever fill. That'll be for you to deal with, if you choose."

"I know," agreed Fletcher, nodding his head. He sighed. "I wondered many nights how I could make it up to him. But so far away, year after year, just making enough to keep the farm afloat. It's been hard. Harder still not having the means to really do anything about it." There was a slight pause, each taking a moment to catch their emotional breath.

"Are you married?" Gary asked warmly, curious as to how she may have lived her young years.

"Now how does a girl answer a question like that? I suppose you've been through a litany of women yourself and expect me to have done the same thing to keep my mind occupied. Not a chance. One beer-drinking football player was enough for this lady," Beatrice answered, shaking her head with a smile. "Truth is, I think your charm ruined me for life, Mr. Fletcher. I liked a few and even gave one boy a chance for almost a year, but I knew it'd not work." Gary held back a flicker of hopefulness. How selfish and bullheaded can a man get, he thought to himself. She's truly being kind about it all, I'll grant her that. "What about you?"

Gary shrugged his shoulders and shook his head, reaching for a handkerchief to blow his nose, the white cotton cloth covering three quarters of his bright but shy smile. "No sir, not this farm boy. I knew enough the time you and Mabel had Terry and me picked up for impaired that Saturday, never to trust a woman. They can be more trouble and less predictable than a bad politician."

"That's all we need," returned Beatrice, becoming suddenly more serious.

"What do you mean?"

"Oh, the young fella's got his eyes set on the military, some nonsense about adventure and travel. And with half the world about an arm's length from tossing nuclear softballs at each other over God-knows-what. If I had the power to make some political decisions of my own, I'd start by firing the whole bunch of them from the President of the United States to that Russian mousetrap of a terrorist in Moscow. Then I'd give them each a shovel and demand they be the first to wade through the bullshit they've created over the last year and a half that's got the rest of the world scared to turn on the radio."

"What's it like down here?"

"Just as bad as across the Pacific, I'd imagine. There's rallies at the university and press conferences every second day. One telling you not to worry and another selling his second home to build a bomb shelter on the Antarctic coastline. I don't know. But I'd say Mr. Fletcher has chosen a good time to drop in for a neighbourly visit. Don't get me all excited now, Fletcher. Is there a woman somewhere or not?"

"You're not one to lose time beating about the outback I can see that, Beatrice Campbell. No, there is not."

"Good. Then, if you'll not reject my company, I'd like to ask you to escort me to the party at Terry's. Rumours be damned, you're a hell of a dancer..."

"Once was a hell of a dancer," Fletcher interrupted.

"...and I intend on enjoying the right to your company above all the other girls whose hearts broke and settled for second best the day you proposed."

The word "proposed" was the hardest one yet for Gary to hear. "Beatrice. I need to say it. I'm sorry..."

"To hell with being sorry, Gary. You're here for a day or a week. It's a gift of God to spend time with someone you've loved no matter what has been between. Here. I'll carry some of that. And God bless the man who had you sent back home."

XIX

"I trust your trip to the edge of our Aboriginal wilderness retreat was pleasant, Mr. Cross?" said Roman Caspersan, speaking over his shoulder as he continued to watch the new recruits from his chambers as they tested and trained themselves in the gladiatorial mockup court below him. Ancient arts and architecture, Caspersan believed, would give them a sense of their ancestry and with it a sense of their destiny.

For Cross the trip to the edge of the Kakadu National Park had been anything but pleasant. He was very aware that no precautions had been taken to protect the route, which in his experience spelled out clearly how confident this man was that there would be no need for them. "What, the silent treatment?" began Caspersan anew, turning to face his reluctant guest. "Come now, Mr. Cross. Your diligent pursuit of knowledge has cost our organization a considerable amount of time and money, not to mention irreplaceable manpower. Surely any amenities we have offered you have not gone unappreciated?"

"We were not bruised or tortured. My friend has not been raped. I suppose you might say I am surprised." Cross sized up this giant intellect in the narrow frame. No time will be bought without providing him with a distraction. This man feels success. He feels the glow of sweet and complete revenge in his grasp. International ridicule has become worldwide confusion and helplessness. Yes, thought Cross. There is a voracious appetite for greatness in this seemingly service-minded genius. Perhaps feeding it lightly will buy the time we so urgently need.

"Please relax, Mr. Cross. We are professionals, you and I. Not on the same side of reason perhaps, but equally well-

182

intentioned I'm sure. Come here a minute." Cross walked slowly across the marble floor to the oval window that gave Caspersan a clear view to the wrestling and endurance training that occurred every morning from 6:30 A.M. until 10 A.M. "Do you see those men down there? All of them have been here for just under a week. They will remain here for almost three full months, pushing themselves day and night in an effort to excel in their profession. Do you have any idea what that profession is?"

Cross delayed his response, attempting to show a cool yet discernible interest in the scene of the court below.

"I could speculate. Over the past nine days I have had people from all over the world share with me bits and pieces of a puzzle that have left me both fascinated and afraid."

"Ah, yes. Most appropriate in both instances, Mr. Cross, and to your credit that you should speak so candidly. Men are often fascinated by ingenuity and frightened by the most ingenious. And we are all most afraid of what we cannot understand." Caspersan waved his arm to a chair in a far corner of the room, his ceremonial robe reminding Cross of Julius Caesar. As Cross took his seat, Caspersan walked to a mantle that supported several huge volumes on both ends, framing a glass-enclosed scroll in the middle of the mantle which appeared to Cross to be written in unfamiliar scribbles or signs.

"The many questions in your eyes will soon be answered, Mr. Cross. I'm sure you have no delusions of ever leaving here, but I hope to provide both you and your playmate with some incomparable diversions in the meantime. I will be honest with you and say that your visit will also give me a rare chance to grasp some human sense of what the world is experiencing at this time. Our sources are irrefutable, but mechanical in many instances."

"And why should we talk at all?"

"Because the natural human propensity is to live as long as possible, Mr. Cross. You have heard of the 'thousand and one Arabian nights'? I will offer you several more brilliant and intellectually stimulating days than stories from the ancient Middle East may have alluded to, but you will be expected to reciprocate in full measure." Caspersan walked near his console and spoke firmly but not harshly. "Augustus, bring Mr. Cross his scotch straight up and I would like ice water."

"Yes, Senator," spoke the computer. Cross feigned a mild interest.

"Augustus? Augustus is the brain at the centre, Mr. Cross. Around the world we have planted a network of over seven hundred satellite dishes which constantly relay information to our centre here in Northern Australia. We have also designed the means and equipment to effectively control ninety-four percent of the earth's atmospheric conditions, a feat which rivals creation itself in my estimation."

"I saw the results of one demonstration before leaving the U.S."

"Yes, you did. Can you imagine, Mr. Cross, what it's like to decide exactly what kind of weather you want to experience today? Or possibly what weather would be most conducive to a cooperative alliance between, say, your headquarters and a stubborn Tibetan city? God has truly been selfish and playful over the centuries keeping the amusement and power of weather to himself. Rainstorms, tornadoes, tidal waves. I must admit we are somewhat reluctant to play with tornadoes too much. A tidal wave will destroy a waterfront, if one feels the need to make a point. A whirling, twirling tunnel of madness is much more difficult to contain. So much property can be uselessly destroyed."

"Your pragmatic appraisal of the effects of atmospheric chaos in the lives of people leaves much to the imagination, Caspersan," Cross replied. "It frightens me to think what kind of anguish would be endured by the common man or woman if you ever succeeded in your plans."

"You are being hopelessly melodramatic, Mr. Cross. And fully inappropriate. There is no question that we will succeed. It is only a matter of time. There is a time for everything under the sun."

"The fact that you would be quoting Scripture strikes me as greatly ironic considering your motives."

"That is entirely a personal judgment on your part," said Caspersan, pointing a corrective finger at Cross as a teacher would at a mischievous schoolchild. "God, if there is a god, was not known to be milk and honey all of the time. He was revered because He could see all, do all."

184

"And you purport to possess these same supernatural abilities."

"That is the beauty of it, Mr. Cross. There is nothing mystical about power at all. Knowledge is power. Access to information is power. The genius lies in one's ability to procure it.

"Take for example, the film of the tornado you were viewing in McKay's office. Although neither you nor your superiors could possibly have known it at the time, we were watching your backs hunch with horror as the farmhouse was demolished on the wall of the room. How? Mr. Wallace is on another assignment in the southwest corner of New Guinea at this moment. Watch this screen." As he spoke, Caspersan typed in a code and turned on the monitor above his desk. The figures on the screen were dusty, but easily distinguishable as people sitting and conversing in what appeared to be a police installation. Caspersan turned up the volume. For several minutes he and Cross were spectators to a live transmission of Wallace's visual stimuli. "In the recesses of his brain has been implanted a gathering device which emits signals from his wristwatch at ultra-high frequencies. These signals are so minute that the most sensitive military equipment would interpret them as random microwaves, useless and harmless. In several well-chosen geographic locations, high altitude boosters bounce his field of vision across continents where Augustus breaks down the messages and interprets them. The picture you see is not of high quality, but the technique does not need to be in order to be effective."

"I am impressed," said Cross sincerely. Who wouldn't be? "But why would the autopsies not show any sign of these implants on x-ray or internal searches where your men have been killed or have killed themselves?"

"I personally had almost neglected that point," returned Caspersan, turning off the monitor and sitting on a chair near his desk. Cross could tell it was difficult for the man to admit he might have forgotten anything. "Fortunately one of our other Senators brought it up and our people were recalled, one might say, before any were killed or terminated. Small but potent capsules of acid were implanted alongside, programmed to release the acid only upon complete brain death of the carrier. So far we have not heard of any untoward publicity being generated by them. The relatively safe assumption would be that this too has proven foolproof as much of our technology has

185

been. This has been the reward of hard work and brilliant investment.''

"You speak of Senators. I'm far behind in my recent history, Caspersan. Any true diversion would have to include facts and figures for it to be of benefit to me.''

Caspersan smiled and walked to the door where a recruit had been sent by Augustus to bring the drinks requested earlier. Closing the door he passed Cross his scotch and pulled another seat close to the mantle, sipping his water as he sat.

"Of course. But there is some time, Cross. I can't see your being impatient as providing any solace for you. The longer it takes to explain the process the longer you will be alive.''

"It's my nature.''

"Quite. And I have seen the ability of your nature to outwit and dangerously threaten this operation, Mr. Cross. It's a pity of sorts you had not been in a more convenient position at the right time. We might be conversing across a Roman Magistrate's desk rather than the dim but very real mist of the gallows.''

"Your analogy doesn't help me understand anything.''

"You are correct. Allow me to refresh my experience.

"It actually begins long before any of us were alive or even a shadowy design of nature. On the mantle here you see a glass case. In it are papers that I prize almost above everything else in this complex. The original hand-written Songs of Rempal.''

"You'll forgive me if I don't gasp and applaud. I haven't a clue who or what Rempal is.''

"Rempal is history, created by the magnificent mind and harmony of a simple slave to a Roman Senator in the first century B.C.''

"During the reign of Augustus.''

"Score a point for ancient Roman trivia, Mr. Cross. This obscure little man was, in my biased judgement, the finest writer/poet of his time. He had a vision for Rome. He saw the conquest and protection of Roman civilization as a model of human accomplishment. He encouraged the governments and their soldiers to stand fast in their roles, to remain simple and strong, male and dominant, leaders and builders. The decadence that led to her collapse might have been avoided had the schools embraced his lyrics, listened to his verses and memorized them. An archaeological find in the mid-eighties unearthed this treasure

186

near the Gulf of Taranto in Itlay. I have, myself, memorized the better part of half of everything he wrote. It has been a constant encouragement and brace when my dream was difficult.''

"There were difficulties, then?'' Cross ventured, hoping in the speaker's romantic indulgence to uncover some information that might benefit their attempts to plan an escape from the complex.

"Yes. Considerable ones. Finances were rarely a problem as my own investments and designs accumulated millions for me within only a few years of my being retired from formal education. But I needed people. People willing to sacrifice dogma and indoctrination. People willing to dream beyond what we as a twentieth-century population had come to accept as normal living.''

"And where did you find your disciples?''

"Disciples is not the proper word for them, Mr. Cross. Disciples adhere to a religion, they do not actively create one from the ground up. I enlisted men who would cooperate with me in the building of a New Empire, a technological and political force that could mold and shape the future of the world.''

"Then you walk in and take over. Kind of dictating history, I take it.''

"Oh no, Mr. Cross. That type of conquest is almost vulgar. Strides in intellect insist that true brilliance be more sensitive and premeditated. Machiavelli insisted on fear as an adjunct to leadership. But he felt one who was both loved and feared would be the best.''

"So why not hold an election?''

"People are not informed of their own accord, Mr. Cross. They are informed according to what they believe to be true as interpreted by the various media. No. We knew there was one sure way to present the world with its destiny. That was to help it confront itself. We decided the answer was to make them deal with the consequences of their own incompetence. Thirty men from every conceivable power position in the world, and from every major industrial nation, gathered with me to form a new Senate, a seat of judgment which would decide how and when and if there was a need to intervene directly in world affairs. With the Songs of Rempal to inspire us, we have called our task, 'The Rempal Inquest'. Poetic, is it not?''

187

"You said something about direct intervention," said Cross, ignoring Caspersan's question. "What did you mean?"

"Well, knowledge can be used in many ways," answered Caspersan. "Subtle influence can sometimes be the most potent form of direction. We could have simply pushed and prodded the various governments of the world toward a management of her resources and people that would be more conducive to planetary survival. But instead, we chose the Rempal route, as I have coined it. That is to say, the direct route."

"Coercion, extortion, murder. Sounds like the classic route to me." Cross couldn't help himself. This man was dangerously enraptured by delusions of his own abilities.

"That is a coarse and thoroughly unfair assessment of the procedure we have outlined, Mr. Cross. It is also highly premature. Somewhat like the grade two student who feels he understands everything about electricity when shown how to make a light switch, you have outdistanced your knowledge by your desire to provoke me. Don't waste your energy. These men gathered with me to form a judicial Senate which agreed to preside over the affairs of the world in response to a number of well-planned and intricately detailed 'exercises', each stress designed to place world leaders and government ideologies into positions where decisions would need to be made for the survival of the human race. Look about you, Mr. Cross. Regardless of the political impact, tell me how rational and secure the world can be with governments pointing nuclear weapons at each other this very moment, simply because two famous people have been disposed of. Regardless of the perceived implications, the very idea of such an option as nuclear war is impossibly suicidal. This is the very scenario we had anticipated. Although a formal declaration of war has not yet been proclaimed, we expect one in the very near future. At that time our Senate will take command of the airways and confiscate the dangerous toys of the idiots that call themselves leaders. Their golden toilet seats and expensive hairdos will not save the world. Rational intervention will be the key to the New World, Mr. Cross. The Rempal Inquest will have proven beyond a doubt that the world needs direction, and I will have the privilege of watching the magnificence of her future blossom into the annals of history."

"It sounds like basic manipulation to me, Senator, with all due respect. Rhetoric has never impressed me. I believe Winston Churchill once said that democracy might not be much of a governmental institution, but it's the best we've got. I agree with him one hundred percent. The people have a right to decide their own future.''

''I agree entirely, Mr. Cross. But perhaps your education in sociology is as limited as your ability to rationalize and comprehend the obvious. History speaks for itself. There is no such thing as individualism on any grand scale. The vast majority of people want to be led. We are born into a world of sheep, with the very few destined to lead and to direct.''

''Supposing,'' Cross began in a new direction, ''just supposing you were correct. And let's further extrapolate the present situation. What then? The world is dominated by one council, one party of ideas, one man perhaps? Where is the fresh water to wash out the natural impurities of human limitation? Where is the healthy competitiveness of expansionism? Rome died because it could not administrate its government to the extent it had conquered. Maybe your ambition has exceeded your ability to follow through and history will truly repeat itself? What makes your organization any different from a Hitler's dream of a third Reich or Communist move into Afghanistan?''

''Whoa, whoa, slow down, Mr. Cross. I am pleased that you have allowed yourself to think and challenge my assumptions. In fact, I would love to spend many more hours with you debating just these kinds of questions. But I also have other duties. I would ask you to content yourself with what I have shared so far. In the next few days, look around. You will be accompanied of course, but take some time to formulate an opinion. I may be persuaded to let you attend a Senatorial debate before your demise. After all, even Senators require an occasional diversion.''

''Come on, Claire, stay on track. This friggin' unit has too many buttons.'' Claire chided herself for not making more progress in the three hours she had spent at the computer console in her room. Claire knew that chauvinism had maintained a firm foothold in the social psyche of the modern world, but she never encountered the kind of male-dominated atmosphere that clearly pervaded the halls and chambers of the complex. Beyond fascination and simple lust for her, the crowds of men she had encountered since her arrival early in the morning had shocked her, then raised in her an almost uncontrollable loathing and hatred. She was afraid that she wouldn't be able to contain and direct her emotions away from Warren, who she had begun to see as a healthy mixture of male energy and female sensitivity. Roman this, world destiny that. To hell with all that garbage. If this kind of social attitude is destined to control the twenty-first century, I'd just as soon not be around to experience it. She assumed early signs of boredom with their explanations and chest beating and asked to be assigned to her room; being a computer programmer, she told them, the computer monitor (available in every room of the Complex) would save everyone a lot of trouble. No trouble they insisted. She smiled and insisted in return. Male dominance. Humph. A little well-placed sexual innuendo and puff, back to my room.

The going had been tough though. Augustus was phenomenally polite for a computer. At one point Claire was tempted to talk to it about her frustrations, it seemed so capable of communicating a sense of understanding.

"THAT'S TOO BAD, CLAIRE. THAT MAKES SIXTY-FOUR DIFFERENT ATTEMPTS TO ACCESS CLASSIFIED MATERIAL. IT MUST BE VERY FRUSTRATING TO WORK SO HARD AND GET PRACTICALLY NOWHERE." How does a programmer work with that?

It was almost time for lunch when Claire stumbled on something. It was so simple and ridiculous that she was embarrassed to try it. But the reasoning fit: 1) the computer is a machine; 2) machines are designed to work according to commands; 3) machines will respond to the proper command if it is used; 4) the language of the computer program must be used. Claire had applied every aspect of the basic rules of computer keyboarding, yet she met with no success whatsoever. Then it occurred to her. What language would most make sense to this machine? An interruption at the console by the guard who had been assigned the pleasurable task of escorting her gave her the idea. His helpful contribution came as part of the ordinary, as are most prefaces to brilliant discoveries. A knock on the door.

"Yes?"

"It is your guard, Ms. Monty. Augustus has just informed me over the intercom that lunch is ready. Please shut down your keyboard and come with me."

Augustus. A Roman Emperor. Holy cow. Rome. The language of Augustus? *LATIN.* "I'll be right there," she answered.

XX

In the wilderness of Kakadu National Park lives a small group of people. They, like Jojo, grandfather of the boy who studied in Russia and smuggled for the CIA, are people of the land. People of the dreamtime. The Gagudju. Aborigines of a quiet and ancient culture that has left enduring legacies of art and mythology among the rocks and caverns of Australia's coastal Northern Territory. Amid the heavy foliage of the paperback trees the elders of the tribe live in harmony with their surroundings, passing on to the young ones who will listen, the ancient stories of the wind and the water, the crocodile and the eagle.

"To us the crocodile is Ginga," said Barratumi, oldest of the elders, speaking with hand signs and the frown of serious work. "Once Ginga was man. Man caught fire and ran to the water to soothe his burns. Now see, young ones, the bumps he carries. These are his scars, the blisters that hardened."

Gerigi watches from a distance. He smiles. Dressed in the khaki uniform of the Park Warden, he feels torn and weary. But he is proud of his job. When the Aboriginal peoples leased this land to the government to create Kakadu Park, he knew he wanted to be part of the group who would keep it safe from poachers and help ensure that its natural beauty remain despite the tourism that brought hundreds of thousands of curious Balanda, or white people, every year. It was very hard to work and live being so tied to the rules of government while so steeped in the ancient customs of the Gagudju. His own past was simple, part of the land. Yet time changed things quickly. Although he did not even know his own birth date, his daughter would be expected to use computers in school. He sighed. One must go with the world as it is. There is no other way. Still at times he would like to turn in his gun for a spear and be given the wilderness to tame as in the old days.

Gerigi has many relatives. Some live far away in Sydney, others close by in Darwin. His brothers chose to move to the city when they were very young, hoping that progress—with its promise of factory jobs and urban entertainment, would give them comfort and hope. The slums and closed doors of modernization were all they were offered. Gerigi is grateful for his job. It is hard, but it is near the land at least.

The job would be much easier also, if the Chief Warden were not so touchy. Go here, go there. Watch for this one, ignore that. He could never understand what was right and what was wrong, sometimes. As a child it was easier. His father had told him that speaking truth simply was the easiest way to live a long life. There was no need to make up stories that weren't true and then spend nights worried about who would find out. Say what you know. Say when you don't know. But Warden Beechum insisted that life wasn't run that way. He insisted that sometimes one has to overlook some things. He never gave any reasons. He said it was not Gerigi's job to ask questions, but to do as he was told.

Gerigi climbed into his government 4 by 4 and turned the key. He paused for a minute, relishing the spectacle of Barratumi telling the young children of the old way, his hands weaving and drawing the animals and people of the dreaming times, the creation of the ancient Gagudju and their culture. The children sat obediently, though maybe only one or two seemed truly interested. Perhaps the others wanted to watch television instead. Sad, thought Gerigi. There was once such harmony. Now we learn to lie and compete like the Balanda.

Gerigi thought about his Chief Warden. Perhaps Warden Beechum had forgotten to explain something that would make it easier for him to understand? Maybe there was something simple and true that made his stories about the visiting Balanda in central Kakadu right for the Park, and natural? He thought and thought. The orders were clear. Anyone with the eagle ring, he was told, was allowed to roam. Anyone with the eagle ring could cut trees or put up signs or destroy wildlife. There was a reason for it, and the Park Wardens were not to ask questions. That was how it was. Hmm. There must be sense to it, decided Gerigi.

There is sense to the rest of the things in my life, even the computer my daughter needs. The world is a big place outside the bush, but not so big that Gerigi could not understand if someone took the time to explain things to him. It is decided, then, Gerigi told himself. I will ask Warden Beechum as soon as I get back to the station house. It doesn't seem right that anyone could build and chop down trees and make long roads for planes to land and walk through sacred burial places without some reason.

It has been said that reality is often the thing that is most unexpected. Others quote the saying: "truth is stranger than fiction". Neither method of coping with the extraordinary facts that sometimes bewilder the common person helped Gary Fletcher with the letter he found in his name at the Royal Markum Hotel.

> *Gary,*
> *I left a message at the desk that your telegram be wired if I didn't return before 6 a.m. If you're reading this it is because your greenhorn farmer is caught in a fucking major situation.*
> *I set up your telegram because I knew, if I was going in over my head, it would happen in Sydney. I believe the people I'm looking for are based in Australia. They're ruthless and smart. If you decide to try and find me, watch your back.*
> *I know this whole thing makes no sense to you. You'll have to believe me when I say that I'm not in trouble with the law although there's no one in the official areas I can work with right now. I need help from someone I can trust, Gary. All I want you to do is follow my tracks. I'm heading into the Redfern district. I'll probably start at the Hawkesbury and work the south end most of the evening. If you find a lead to me, don't play hero. Let me know you're around and I'll take the risks. The people I'm looking for would just as soon shatter your kneecaps with a hammer as ask you your name. Another thing: if you decide not to look for me, no hard feelings. Take*

whatever money is left and enjoy, I mean that. It may
be too late anyway. The key in the envelope is for
another safety deposit box at the Westpac Bank.
There's more money there in case you need it, or I'm
no longer around to use it myself.

Warren C.

Sitting in the luncheon area of the hotel, Gary reread the letter
several times, nibbling on some toast and pausing every few
minutes for a sip of coffee. Warren Cross. You got yourself in
one deep pile of shit. My head says run in the opposite direction.
My gut says you haven't told me the whole story, but you
wouldn't have asked for help unless you needed it. Can't hurt
much to take a walk down to the Hawkesbury. But I will reserve
the right to check out if it gets too dangerous. It's strange. You
call me over to help you and here I am thinking most of the time
about Beatrice and what it's like seeing her again. Okay
farmboy. I'll do what I can, thought Gary, folding the letter and
slipping it with the small key into his shirt pocket. But don't
blame me if all I come up with is a handful of dust and a sore
throat from asking questions.

Gerigi was happy to talk to the stranger. For one thing, he
needed the money. It had been almost six weeks since Chief
Warden Beechum had arranged to have him fired for
insubordination. All Gerigi had done was to insist on an
explanation about the Balanda with the eagle rings and their
planes and electric machines. Chief Beechum had exploded in
anger. He told Gerigi that he was finished, that a man who can't
follow orders shouldn't work for the Park. He was fired. Gerigi
pleaded with him. He explained how his family had come to
depend on the small salary he received. He promised not to ask
any more questions about the Balanda. He would be quiet now.
But it was too late. Gerigi and his family had to leave the quiet
wilderness of Kakadu and travel to Sydney to live with his
brother while he tried to find other work. It had been very
difficult. Tempers were short. His brother was poor and the
small amount of food his family lived on had to be split even

more. Everyone tried to be patient. But Gerigi was dejected. He felt hopeless. One night, he saw Chief Beechum here in Sydney, far from the Park and Gerigi's home, leaving a gambling house. Gerigi knew that gambling was an evil thing. His father had said that more money was spent on gambling in Australia than on all the Aboriginal people of the country. Gerigi didn't know how much that was, but he knew it was a lot, and he believed it was wasted. That Warden Beechum should throw away his money on gambling when his family had none...Gerigi attacked him on his way to his car. It was useless. A friend of the Warden's called the police and Gerigi was held overnight in jail. No charges were laid, but Gerigi's pride was deeply hurt. Now there seemed only drink which could dull the frustrations. Drinks for cleaning tables, drinks from friends who had a little understanding and a little booze to share.

Then, two nights ago, Gerigi had seen one of them. At first he wasn't sure. But when the man turned from the bar and smiled in the light, Gerigi was certain. He had a little ring on his finger too. Like the Eagle ring. Yes, Gerigi told Gary Fletcher, I saw the man you talk about. He left with one of the Eagle Balanda.

"Those people, they bad. I see many where I worked in Kakadu. They kill animals, set up tents and buildings. Sometimes planes come. Once I ask my boss, I say Chief Beechum, how come they kill animals and walk through the sacred caves where no tourists are allowed and carry guns and we don't stop them? Chief Beechum he cut my throat for asking questions. My family's kicked out and we starvin' here in Redfern. I'm so angry. Life shouldn't be like that."

Gary Fletcher couldn't believe his ears. This man had actually seen Cross, seen him leave. And he knew the man he was with. "Do you think, Gerigi, you could recognize the man who took my friend away?"

"I know him, if I see him anywhere, I know him for sure."

"Where is Kakadu? Your people are from the North, aren't they?"

"The land, we lease to the government a few years ago. Bad deal, I think. But then I worked. I see the caves when I want to...." Gerigi's eyes brimmed with tears.

"Do you think you could take me there, Gerigi? There would be much money for your help. I must find this man, my friend."

"Money? You pay me for guide? Oh, man, you got yourself a guide. But I want something too. I need to find out something for Gerigi."

"What's that?"

"Need to find out where Chief Beechum sleeps at night. I know he lied. He's bad. I want to hit him hard, maybe break his head."

"What you do is your own business."

"And you pay money now?"

"Now."

"How much?"

"How much does your family need?" answered Fletcher.

XXI

"This won't work," said Claire Monty to Warren Cross as he entered the room where they had bunkbeds. Warren had just returned from the fifth meeting in three days with Roman Caspersan. Caspersan was open about the Senate's plans, its strategies and its accomplishments. Cross felt sure that he would never want to set foot in Rome, maybe Italy, again. He had heard enough poetry and philosophy and debate to last him a lifetime. Senator Caspersan appeared bored that morning as well. There wouldn't be much more time. Warren knew what Claire was speaking about. The complex was like a steel vault. Seventy-two hours with wide-open eyes and ears showed few, if any, opportunities for escape.

"What won't work?" Warren threw a collection of Rempal's poems on the bed and pulled up a seat beside her. Claire looked up from the monitor and smiled.

"It won't work for you to walk in and disturb my review of the library here. Did you know they have almost one half of the world's total literary works on microfilm? One computer like this and I'd have been able to complete my degree from my bedroom, a thousand miles from the university."

"Is that so?" Warren answered, understanding completely. Both he and Claire had known from the first day they were locked up that they were being watched twenty-four hours a day. They had found a way of communicating by writing on a pad on Claire's desk. Then, once the message was read, Warren would burn the slip of paper with a match and drop it in the metal waste basket. Warren once joked about how the room would not be so full of smoke if they weren't so hot for each other.

Claire had stayed almost nonstop at the keyboard since their arrival. At one point she thought the Latin language would allow her to reprogram and direct the computer. The idea seemed so simple, logical. But the computer didn't respond. Her first real break came when she learned the word L-A-T-I-N would, however, open the doors to a menu that gave her access to the main computer banks. Since then she had fought a computer war with Augustus, asking, asking again and trying to add or take out without disturbing the seemingly endless defenses against tampering built into the system. On one occasion she had tapped into a message from a grocery store owner in Milwaukee who appeared to be carrying on a computer-letter love affair with an office secretary in New York City. She indulged in a little hanky-panky by imagining the scene she'd create if she could type a letter to both parties stating the man's wife had found out and was suing her husband and calling the secretary's boss. She laughed so hard the intercom asked if anything was wrong. She needed that.

"Yes, that is so," Claire said to Warren, smiling. She stretched from the chair, her arms reaching for relief above her head. "I suppose you'd be embarrassed again if I told you something out loud."

"That depends."

"Depends on what?"

"As usual, on what you have to say."

Claire stretched again, this time letting her hand fall onto Warren's shoulder, a light caress down his arm accompanying the warm grin. "Okay, Mr. shy person. I never would have thought a little electronic surveillance would bother you at this point in your career. We're not likely to get out of here, and I can't see how it makes any difference."

"Just old-fashioned, I guess," answered Warren. "They can watch me say hello if they want, but if you've got something personal to say, Claire, I'd rather it be private." Claire smiled as if she was indulging the whims of a schoolboy. She slid the pad from the top of the desk where she sat and began to write.

"I'm still working on the door code to the gate. Seems like Augustus is programmed from the inside out. There's no use trying to make a change to the internal security until I can get

199

clearance to 'walk in the front door', if you know what I mean. I've figured out a way to cut power in some areas and I've got access to the Caspersan's itinerary for tonight and tomorrow. Not good. Looks like the Last Supper tonight. Some kind of games for you starting this evening and 'dismissal' written for tomorrow afternoon." Claire finished writing with a flourish and pushed the pad to Warren where he read and shrugged his shoulders.

"What if my father still insists you're too young for me?" he said, mocking a response to her writing. Claire tore the pad from him and continued writing.

"Then screw your father," wrote Claire. Warren looked at what she had written and they laughed. Warren took his turn with the pad.

"I wish I had more to say that could keep us laughing, but it looks dim. Caspersan kept alluding to something this morning about these 'games' you're talking about. Said we should enjoy our evening; that it would undoubtedly be our last. He's a very fucked-up mini-dictator, Claire. The whole missile business was a hoax. A test, he said. An inquest into the world's ability to govern itself in times of severe crisis. His mind is full of this kind of rationale. He's got charm and wit too. After spending that much time with him it doesn't surprise me how he's convinced so many influential people to work alongside him. He doesn't seem to indulge in any luxuries. The most dangerous kind of fanatic is the honest kind." Warren drove the pencil into the pad, emphasizing his own frustration. Claire read what he had written.

"So what now?" wrote Claire. "It's going to take me at least another ten hours to do anything concrete. Picking out itineraries is not so hard because the computer field it's written on has a low security defense in the computer. There won't be any miracles here. I'll be able to bring on a few distractions at the most."

Warren read the pad and nodded, leaning across the table and kissing her lightly. Claire was surprised and delighted.

"That's fine with me," Warren said. "The best you've got will be the best I've ever had."

***

Gary Fletcher had insisted, but it was useless.

"I suppose you think, after nearly thirty years of pining and keeping myself occupied, I'm going to let you go off to the Aboriginal wilderness looking for some bloke with money to burn and dingo brains to spend it with. Forget it. You go north. I go north. You have me now, Fletcher, and you'll not lose sight of me again."

Gary couldn't argue with her. He had no intention of turning down the offer either. He was surprised, alarmed almost, when Beatrice had asked him to sleep with her the first night he arrived. There were tears. Many tears. This night was much the same. With the jet lag, Gary still couldn't sleep well. At least that was his excuse every time Beatrice looked up from where she lay on his chest and saw him staring off into a corner of the room, the light from a lamp post outside her small two-bedroom home casting shadows against the far wall.

"Really, now. Why can't you sleep, love, what's ailin' ya?"

"It's the time, Bee. The time that's been spent diggin' post holes in the ground and raising beef. The time where we could've been raising a family." Beatrice didn't answer right away. Some things change. Some stay the same. Gary Fletcher was a man who needed to be heard and understood. Advice and difference of opinion had their place, but it was always behind the first two. "It's not like I wanted it this way. God, how I prayed myself to sleep some nights, wishing and hoping things would turn out; that maybe I'd have a lucky year and be able to send for you and Timmy. Then one year was two. We wrote less and less. I've played it over a thousand times, Bee. Seems like there ought to have been a way."

"Yes, Gary. You're right. There should have been a way. And neither you nor I were bright enough or open enough to come up with one. There's a sunny side. We're older. Your farm's running well. Maybe you'll never be rich, but the bills are paid. We still have today, Gary-John. We can still do what we want with today." Fletcher moved to the side a bit, holding Beatrice in his left arm and brushing the hair lightly from her face with the other.

"You're a phenomenon, Bee, did you know that? I move to America to seek my fortune and thirty years later you still want to find a way to make it seem okay.''

Beatrice smiled and kissed his hand. ''I'm not so phenomenal as all that, Mr. Fletcher. I'd be lying to myself and to you if I pretended there weren't times when I wanted to hit you over the head with a billy for making my own choices so difficult. But that's the other half. I could have left when you did. You made that clear. I've had my share of guilt and remorse. Now there's no time to waste, as far as I'm concerned. One day at a time. The more spent with you the better.''

They talked long into the night as they had each night since Gary arrived. He told her about Gerigi and the man seen walking from the Hawkesbury with Cross. How the hell they would approach a dwelling that was supposedly surrounded with cameras and other electronic paraphernalia in the middle of the Northern wilderness, Gary had no idea. Gerigi couldn't be as specific as Gary would have liked. He recognized the cameras because he had seen them used before in a training workshop in Darwin. Other than that, all he knew was that any time a Warden approached the ''area'' marked off by the eagle ring visitors, there was always someone out to greet them and ask their business before they had come anywhere near the fence that surrounded the buildings. Cross needn't have worried about Gary taking too much into his own hands. Just getting a message to Cross, if he was there and if he was still alive, would be an accomplishment.

At seven A.M. Gary stepped out of the house to throw their bags in the car and get ready for the drive to the airport. Then there would be a five hour flight to the middle of the continent and an eleven hour drive by rented jeep from there to Kakadu National Park. His mind on the long journey ahead, Gary just about stepped on Gerigi, who was already sitting on the doorstep, facing the sun. He looked like a new man.

''We gonna catch ourselves a poacher, eh Mr. Fletcher? I'm ready to go. Anytime. You name it.'' Gary knew the money he had promised in exchange for Gerigi's help and advice was much more than one would have paid for a guide. But Gary thought, what the hell? He needs the money. Cross said to spend it. Fuck the government. Somebody's got to give back to the first inhabitants. Even if it's just one at a time.

"Where's your gear?" asked Fletcher, noticing only a small knapsack sitting on the step.

"You see this bag? That got all a man needs. You or another Balanda—you never comfortable without your blankets and your air conditionin'. Not me. We goin' home."

The trip to the edge of Kakadu Park from the urban sleekness of Sydney's avant-garde architecture and bustling commercial community was like a voyage back in time for Gary and Beatrice. Each rock face, each water hole, each animal that darted from the side of dusty roads or between parked trucks at the gas stops along the way, were fascinating subjects of folklore and legend to Gerigi who offered explanations and accounts of past civilizations according to his cultural heritage. It was also nostalgic for them. Despite Gerigi's energetic narratives, Beatrice and Fletcher often glanced at each other as they passed a place they had seen before in their youth. They shared together moments from their past, memories of a time when a stolen truck and a tank full of gas would bring a weekend full of mischief and laughter, when the carefree enthusiasm of youth mixed with the lingering bliss of ignorance granted those who had not yet left home on their own.

"What this man want, Mr. Fletcher? How come he went out to Kakadu with that eagle man?"

"Hard to say, Gerigi," answered Gary truthfully. "All I know is that he says he needs our help. Once we find him, you can ask him these questions for yourself."

"I'm not interested in talking with nobody from that place," said Gerigi, a deep frown forming on his face. "I got me a job to do. I work hard. I listen good. But all I want is to see my home and take money back to my family. Maybe move there again. But for sure, before we go back, I wanna visit somebody."

"The guy who fired you."

Gerigi nodded. "What he did wasn't right. He lied to me. He wanted me to not talk about the Balanda killing the animals and burning bush for their planes to land. I don't like him."

Gary debated whether or not to talk to Gerigi about his obvious plans to deal with the Chief Warden. He knew it was not his grudge, but he hated to think what would happen to Gerigi's family if he got carried away. Honour doesn't feed the children.

"Even if Chief Beechum said why and said shutup. But he just threw my family out. That's not kind. No reason why not he coulda just been more kind."

By the time supper rolled around the next day, both the rented 4 by 4 and its passengers were covered in dust and ready for some rest. Gerigi seemed more excited than tired though. Even two days travelling didn't dampen his spirit. One would think he hadn't seen the bush in twenty years. He was like a kid at the fair, pointing out familiar places and calling them by nicknames shared by his friends and his elders.

They stopped at Jabiru, just outside the park Headquarters. Gerigi was restless and Gary knew why. His enemy was close by. The feelings were raw and insistent.

"Gerigi?"

"Yes, Mr. Fletch-man?" Gerigi had decided on his own during the day that "Fletch-man" better suited his new boss. Gary did not argue.

"I feel like we need to talk."

"Sure." Gary walked thirty yards away from the truck where a number of young children from the community were busily playing up against it, shyly advancing on the white woman with the long black hair. Gerigi followed.

"I need something from you," said Gary.

"What's that?"

"I need you to promise me that you will wait until we find my friend before you go for your visit." Gerigi turned to face his boss Fletch-man, looking for something that made Gary feel he was being read inside out. It was a long moment. Gerigi sighed and turned away.

"You can see me, Fletch-man. Not many Balanda can see good. But you see what I want. Okay. I promise. Kakadu is big park. Many places even outside the place where eagle men go that your friend could be. Could take many days. But you pay me good money. I do what you say." Then Gerigi turned to Gary and demanded something in return. "Only one thing."

"What's that?"

"When we find your friend. I go visit."

"Agreed."

"And when I go visit, Fletch-man stop seeing me so much. Keep busy. Talk to friend. Sleep with woman. I don't like him. My family hurts. I have to tell him why."

"It's a deal."

XXII

"You are out of your fucking mind, Caspersan," said Cross, finally unable to withhold his opinion any longer.

"In your eyes, perhaps," answered the self-appointed Senator, returning his gaze to the four huge monitoring screens that covered the wall in front of him and relayed constant updates of the world's escalating pressures. "It is all in the mind of the beholder, Mr. Cross. There are many paths to enlightenment. We must each be the prophet of our own experience."

"Look around you," said Cross, his tone angry as he watched the men one floor below them scurry among consoles that were aligned like NASA terminals. "These men you've got trained to believe what you believe. You've made your experience their experience. This isn't enlightenment. This is dictatorship."

Caspersan smiled and walked to a corner of the balcony which overlooked the control centre. Instructing a young recruit to pass word to one of the console operators about something he had noticed on the screen broadcast from the United States Congress, he sauntered back to his position against the railing. Cross stymied the almost irresistible impulse to reach out and strangle the man.

"Don't delude yourself into thinking that you have grown into manhood without being influenced yourself, Mr. Cross. My men were not bribed or coerced into joining our organization. They were volunteers. The experiences they have participated in were chosen by them toward goals they freely selected."

The endless back and forth had become tiresome. Cross had begun his debates with Caspersan to buy time. The man's incessant rebuttals and egocentric narrow-mindedness had left Cross infuriated. It felt good to say what he had been thinking since the first day he was brought here. There didn't seem much sense in pretending to be interested when the end was fast approaching anyway. "The truth," said Caspersan. "However you dress it, the truth is simply a design of the mind. I have chosen the truth that has worked in the past and is destined to work in the present age. There is no other reality."

Cross decided to speak his mind clearly. Enough is enough. Time to get to the point. "And your little game. Where's the design in that? You don't really expect me to believe you would let Claire and me leave if I succeeded? Why the charade? I had begun to see you as an honest man, Caspersan, regardless of how you picture the world." The Senator frowned. Hurt pride, thought Cross. I have injured the pride of a lunatic who takes himself to be the reincarnation of Roman history.

"I can answer your insult clearly, Mr. Cross," said Caspersan, turning to look at Cross directly, a rare move. "You can see as well as I that both major powers have begun the final perilous journey toward self-destruction that has been predicted. It will not be long before the Rempal Inquest is complete and we intercede. At that time it would not matter what you had seen. It would be too late for anyone to do anything anyway. But I owe it to those who have died for our cause to deal harshly with the enemy. There is no way I could simply release you and still call myself Roman. So I have chosen a route that I feel will do justice both to your tenacity and courage as well as my conscience. It would be most honest to say I enjoy being entertained as much as anyone."

"I never would have believed I would meet someone who personifies the full range of human extremes. You, Caspersan, approach that unique place in my mind reserved for someone who offers a flower with one hand and a snake with the other. The scariest part is that you truly believe what you say."

"Indeed I do. What is scary and unreasonable to you is salvation of mankind to myself and my contemporaries."

"When does this game start?"

"Soon. It's a pity you are not a man who enjoys literature."

"It has always put me to sleep."

"Quite. I wager tonight will make you wish you had read at least one short story in your lifetime and perhaps learned something from it."

"For instance?"

"In my mind the greatest single short story adventure ever written was created by a man called Richard Connell. He composed a story called 'The Most Dangerous Game.' What do you suppose it was about, Mr. Cross?"

"Let me guess—Roman gladiators," said Cross sarcastically.

Caspersan allowed himself a rare chuckle. "Not quite. It is the story of a famous hunter who falls overboard while cruising past an island near the Amazon River. It's dark and cold. He makes it to shore. What do you think he finds?"

"A bunch of fucking Senators playing with themselves."

"Are we getting nervous, Mr. Cross? No. He is taken in by another man who enjoys the hunt. A meeting of minds, one might say. The visitor is invited to hunt game the next day, great and dangerous game, but the famous hunter declines."

"This is where I ask why."

"Yes. And the answer is delightfully dismal. The visitor chooses not to go because his host has developed an insatiable taste for the smell of human fear. He hunts people. There is nothing to equal it, so he says."

"I would also decline. If you're planning that kind of game, think twice, Caspersan. I've never killed a man without reason. You're sick, that's all there is to it."

"I'm sure the man's visitor thought much the same. The resulting game was charming. The host had no choice but to offer his visitor the chance to be hunted instead."

"So where do I and Claire fit into your fantasy of playing out your favourite bedtime story?"

"Be patient. The story ends with the visitor managing to win his freedom from the island in a manner that would not have been foreseen. Therein lies your chance to live. If you succeed in dodging the efforts of my best soldier to find you and apprehend you on the grounds outside the centre, you will have won a fair and difficult contest. The pride of those who died serving their ideals will be honoured, and you will live.''

''And if I don't?''

''Funny you should ask, Mr. Cross. The man in Connell's story asked much the same question. I will not be quite as indirect in my answer. You and the girl will be shot.''

***

Rempal Senator Williams had never been totally sure. As chief political advisor to the President, he had ample opportunity to inform his Rempal colleagues of the political reactions in the White House, and had as well, influence with the President which would contribute directly to the Inquest. He had even been commended by many of the Senators for his ability to play both roles, faithfully serving the bureaucracy of the United States government while continuing to advance the cause of Rempal Inquest. But the last several days had been especially trying for him. He missed his wife and two teenage daughters, of course. Almost every man in the centre had a similar kind of emotional struggle that took every ounce of dedication they could muster as the final steps of the Inquest were implemented and carefully monitored. But it was more than that. Much more. He had decided for himself that before the actual takeover, he would need to be absolutely sure that the Senate and its magistrates truly had the best interests of mankind at heart. He had heard some disturbing stories. The stoic and frugal Caspersan was rumoured to have an insatiable sexual interest in young boys, most of whom he would pick off the street if necessary. The story had been passed to him through the informal grapevine. Apparently a recruit had somehow stumbled onto a tape in Augustus's library of Caspersan ''playing'' with two boys, both under ten years old, and neither consenting, although to Senator Williams that would not have meant much. It started there. When this recruit was ''accidentally'' killed in the training compound Senator Williams became truly concerned. If there were cover-ups of this kind, there must be others. For many nights he tried to concentrate on destiny, on history and on the selfless investments of time and money Caspersan had given to the Rempal Inquest. But he couldn't shake the feeling. It seemed too much like what had sent him looking for a new ideal in the first place. And now it made him sick to his stomach with the possibilities.

Senator Williams had watched with a number of the other Senators through monitors as Claire Monty dressed and undressed for bed. The lack of female contact had heightened the desire of all the men to see a real living woman. Claire assumed this by their reactions to her in the halls and would sometimes hang a towel over the camera which was useless as there were at least four others hidden in her room. He had watched too as she typed hour after hour into the console, refusing to give up on Augustus. Every word she typed was monitored by a recruit who was ordered not to interfere unless she got close to discovering something potentially damaging to the complex. She had approached some brilliant moves toward extricating herself and her partner several times during the past three days, but each time the recruit would consult with Caspersan and parry her initiative. It was almost as if Claire had become some kind of fascinating study for Caspersan and, Senator Williams admitted with some shame, for him and other Senators. Only the notes that Warren and she passed back and forth were truly private. It was that observation and the nagging sense that his ideals and those of the Senate did not seem as pure and well-intentioned as he had first believed, that led to his difficult decision.

Coming back to his room after supper, Senator Williams locked the door behind him, and closed the drapes. Walking to the light switch, he turned off the lights. Pitch black. Good. There were infra-red cameras on the grounds, but there had been no need to have the expensive devices installed in the bedrooms. A black room meant a black camera picture.

Williams knew that trying to communicate anything to either Ms. Monty or Cross directly would be immediately foiled. The visual/auditory transmitters implanted in his brain would result in his being disposed of immediately once the contact was noticed. Even writing a note would be out of the question, as long as he could see the paper he was writing on. But if he could not see the paper and did not talk, Augustus would be deprived of the information. The Senator had made his decision. Even if he could just slow things down a bit. Give him and the others more time to analyze what appeared to be happening so quickly around them. It was the only thing he could think of. It was worth the risk, if it was the right decision. It would be fatal if it was not.

Feeling his way to the desk opposite the side of his bed, Williams felt for the handle on the drawer. He realized his hands were sweating. His heart was racing. Would this work?

The programmed messages that had given other members of the organization the mental strength to suicide in order to protect the Rempal Inquest began now in him, his mind battling to gain control over his emotions. His intellect tried to fight the onslaught of messages which would steal from him the most precious of human freedoms: The freedom to choose. Fear welled up in him. The internal circuits understood. Senator Williams was a threat; his beliefs had become dangerous. THOSE BELIEFS MUST CHANGE. DON'T DO IT. YOU ARE WRONG. YOU ARE A TRAITOR TO YOUR IDEALS. KILL YOURSELF SENATOR. DON'T BE AFRAID. YOUR IDEALS WILL OUTLIVE YOU. YOU HAVE WORKED FOR THIS. YOU HAVE GIVEN UP YOUR LIFE FOR THIS. THIS IS FOR MANKIND. THIS IS FOR THE FUTURE. THIS IS FOR YOUR CHILDREN'S CHILDREN. Children. My God, thought Williams. My children. Senator Williams pulled on the drawer. It spilled onto the floor. "I'm all right, Augustus. Just dropped something." Checking his voiceprint Augustus recognized the man.

"Very good, Senator Williams."

The messages from the implant continued. There seemed no way to avoid them. There seemed no way to stop them. KILL YOURSELF. SENATOR. KILL YOURSELF. THIS IS NO TIME FOR THOUGHT. IT IS A TIME FOR ACTION. KILL YOURSELF YOU HAVE GIVEN YOUR LIFE TO THE SENATE. YOU ARE A ROMAN. BELIEVE. THIS IS NOT WHAT YOU WANT TO DO SENATOR. YOU ARE

DANGEROUS. DEATH IS HONOURABLE. CHOOSE
HONOUR. Senator Williams held his hands to his head. It felt
like he was going out of his mind. As the messages became
louder, his attempt to fight them increased. He moaned, "No!
Goddamn it! No! I-I want to change my thoughts! I-Fuck. No.
Okay. I-I understand. Kill myself? But my wife...Marjorie! Oh
my God..." Crashing against the side of the desk, Williams
reached for another drawer. He pulled it open. A revolver slid to
the opening from the back of the drawer. THAT'S RIGHT
SENATOR. YOU MUST SHOW THE EXAMPLE. YOU
HAVE BECOME DANGEROUS TO YOURSELF. THE ONLY
WAY TO PRESERVE YOURSELF IS TO DIE. YOU MUST
KILL YOURSELF SENATOR. THAT'S RIGHT. THERE.
YOU HAVE IT. YOU ARE AN HONOURABLE MAN.
THINK OF THE GLORY. THE GLORY OF RO...

"Holy fuck, what was that?" Two recruits in the secondary
monitoring chambers heard an explosion that sounded like a
gunshot. They both switched channels to the area from which the
sound had come. It was dark. The only sound Augustus
could pick up sounded like a small animal, scratching his paws
in sand. Mice? In the complex? If the camera had been infra-red,
it would have provided a simpler explanation for the sound.
Williams was lying on the floor of his room, his head and neck
surrounded by an ever-widening circle of blood. All that
remained of his nervous system were tremors that made his arms
convulse and his fingers twitch, his fingernails and the ring on
his small finger scratching the writing paper that had fallen on
the floor.

In her room, Claire noticed something. There had been what
sounded like a door slamming down the corridor from her suite.
It startled her. Almost immediately afterward, Augustus had
typed the following message onto the screen. "Command
schedule interrupted. Please activate primary command list for
continued monitoring." Monitoring. Command schedule
interrupted...Then it came to her. I'll be damned, thought Claire.
Somebody's looking in another direction.

Claire had begun to suspect her work at the keyboard was being
closely watched. At first she tried to make herself believe that it
wouldn't be, that somehow the rest of the complex and the world

212

itself could be under close scrutiny and that her frantic attempts to manipulate the world's most complex computer system would have some chance at success. But there were times when it was hard to believe that someone human wasn't watching somewhere. There were pauses in response to commands she typed. Once there had been a typing error that appeared manually erased and retyped before her eyes. Yes. There had probably been someone playing cat and mouse with her since she first sat down. So much for feeling like she could accomplish anything beneficial at all. But this was different. Augustus was asking her for something. Augustus was asking SOMEONE for direction. That could mean only one thing. Somehow the sound she had heard either distracted the people who were monitoring her efforts to manipulate the computer or the event itself had caused some timely distraction. No time to figure out what or why. An opportunity was presented. Time for action.

Her mind moving swiftly, Claire sensed herself thinking far beyond her ability to type. She tried to calm herself; errors are too time-consuming. Each word, each directive would have to be clear and correct. She began by testing her hypothesis. She asked Augustus for a record of her typing for the previous three days, scanning the library records. There it was. The times and computer memory space used were clearly identified at the computer's main banks. She then asked where it was being relayed to. Once again Augustus obliged her. "Monitor 40-336 Rm 17." Then an idea came to her: If she could have the thirty-odd hours of tampering replayed to the monitor numbered 40-336 while her screen kept clear of interference, there would be no telling what she could do over the next few hours. All this time at the board had not been wasted, in a sense. She knew a lot about what Augustus could accept and what he could not. She had learned short cuts and banking codes. Holy, Claire thought to herself as she pressed the enter key and waited for Augustus to respond. If this washes we might have a chance. We might just have a chance.

In Room #17, Caspersan had spoken to the young recruit who was monitoring Claire's chambers. Do not be alarmed, he had said. There has been an accident. Continue monitoring Ms. Monty and await further instructions. "Await further instructions?"

Fucking recruit school, he thought. Not much different from my winter exercises in Siberia. He sighed as he switched to the information coming from Claire's room. The same old thing. Try this, try that. She's persistent, you have to give her that, he thought.

Quintus had spent a lot of time in his room since the arrival of his two captives. He looked at the photographs and notes which reminded him of times he and Richards had spent together. Their relationship had been special to him. He had known in junior high that his tendency to fantasize about having sexual encounters with his gym teacher, Tony Laver, was more than simple experimentation. Quintus's physique and good looks made him immensely popular with young women. He avoided having to go public with his orientation by dating the most exclusive females and finding reasons not to become more seriously involved with them after a few "dates". No one at home or in his community suspected at all that he was homosexual. Then there was Clark.

He used to tease Clark, along with his college friends, about the glasses he wore and the swimmer's body he hid under the jeans and T-shirt that made up most of his college wardrobe. Superman, they called him. Clark Kent. On a return trip from a basketball tournament in Kansas, Clark and Quintus, then Steve Pearson, roomed together in a dive called Pearl's Harbor. Clark must have suspected Steve was gay. While taking a shower Clark volunteered to help him "relax" after the long drive and proceeded to give Steve a series of terrifying and totally fulfilling orgasms in the hotel shower.

Clark was also respectful. Never after that time did he mention to anyone what had happened, understanding that the time to "come out" has to be a personal thing. In his fourth year Steve decided to attend a gay support group on campus. Since that time he had never regretted disclosing his orientation or investing in its pleasures, despite the still prevalent although more socially subdued reaction he encountered in his daily life. The years had clicked by, his work with the FBI filling his days and frequent lovers filling his nights. The AIDS epidemic had scared him away from sex for a time. He needed to sort out for himself what taking those kinds of risks would mean to him. But eventually he

214

was back with his boyfriends, each trying to candidly support the need for disclosure and sharing safety precautions.

The move to work with Caspersan had been part attraction, Quintus had known that. The leader's lofty ideals and charismatic speeches made Quintus excited just to be around him. But Richards had changed all that. He had brought Quintus intimacy, each sharing feelings and frustrations as well as sexual joy. Quintus had tried hard not to pressure Richards into a more permanent commitment. Neither knew how it would work in the organization anyway; but he knew that he wanted more and more of Richards and more often. No more one-night stands. This was what he had always hoped for.

Then Richards was sent to kill the Russian diplomat while some nobody from the U.S. was chasing after the missing missile causing all kinds of headaches for members of the Senate. And Richards had died. Quintus felt there was only one thing that would allow him to let go of his love. That was to kill Warren Cross, the slower the better. So when Caspersan had asked him the day before to go on a little hunting expedition, Quintus had to fight the urge to embrace him in tears and kiss him. True to his word, he had chosen Quintus to destroy the asshole who forced his lover into a corner, who forced him to die.

"Are there any restrictions, Senator?"

"What kind of restrictions, Quintus? If you mean are you to bring dogs and tanks and anti-aircraft missiles, the answer is no."

"I mean on how he dies, when he dies."

"That is entirely your business. For me there are only two things. One, that he provide some entertainment and two, that he die eventually. He has twelve hours to avoid you. The compound, although strewn with bogs and trees and wildlife, is relatively small. There are only so many places he can hide. Besides, the heat sensors will make it easy for us to know exactly where he is in case you do encounter any difficulties. Should he avoid you up to the tenth hour, call me. The detectors will pinpoint him for you immediately."

By this time Claire had learned some very important things. She had somehow, between the moment she had left her secure and boring life in Baden-Baden and been brought to the wilderness of Australia's Northern Territory, realized that the people Cross was dealing with were not small-time gangsters. His work was lethal, and she had followed up on his book of matches in the casino to such a point that her own life was in danger. Only she could be blamed for the steps she had taken to find out where he had gone and for following him into this mess. She had also decided that the risks had been worth it. In the last five to six days with almost no sleep and the possibility of being executed facing her every minute, she felt more alive than she had ever felt in her life. Warren turned out to be everything she had thought he was. Impatient, bullheaded, sensitive and strong. The only thing that she avoided thinking about too much was what would be lost if they never had a chance to be together. In a way those fears seemed to keep her going, keep her motivated.

The motivation was beginning to pay off. When Warren returned from his discussion with Caspersan at the balcony above the control centre with the news that he would be spending the night outside, Claire drew a happy face on the pad and wrote:

"I know. I've seen it on the monitor here. I don't know what's happened, but for some reason I've managed to make it through to Augustus. The last time we talked I had nothing to tell you. This time I do.

"They've been toying with us, Warren. My console has been monitored in the same way as everything else. Every time I tried something there was someone on the other end watching and diverting all my efforts to the closest shredder. Even little things I thought I had accomplished were a joke. They were playing with us. Then about an hour ago, something happened. There was a noise up the hall like a door slamming, and the screen bounced up asking for somebody to tell it what to do. They must have turned their attention elsewhere for a minute. The end result is, I've got them looking at recorded entries I made the day before yesterday, printed to their screens at slow speed. Unless somebody does a library check, they're watching a used file and your girlfriend has free access to snoop around as much as she likes."

Warren noticed how Claire had underlined the word girlfriend. What kind of marvel was this woman? Here they were, in the

216

midst of a world crisis, trying their damndest to find a way to survive and she's trying to pick him up. Mind you, Warren thought, for the first time in a long time, I don't mind the rules of the game at all. He wrote back to her.

"I don't know how you did it, but the timing couldn't be any better. You mentioned knowing about the little game Caspersan's got planned. Well, cough up anything that would be helpful, Claire. He's got some fucked-up notion about me being hunted by big blue eyes there, the one who grabbed you from the hotel and followed me to the Hawkesbury. Apparently if I make it until morning, we're free. Besides the fact that this guy is obsessed with some short story and has a twisted sense of honour, we are in a major dilemma here. I don't know a damn thing about animal hunts or about this complex. What does your friend Augustus say?"

"For one thing," wrote Claire quickly, "he says you'll have to wait to talk about your hunting trip for a minute because something else has to be decided. For another, he loves the sound of your voice. In fact, he likes it so much, he'd like to record it as a voiceprint and respond to it whenever you feel the need to use it. The only problem with that is you could use it only once. After the voiceprint is carried out by the computer, a test command is entered and executed. Then a secondary list of control prints is checked out through Caspersan's private unit in his room to prevent the kind of tampering I happen to be doing here...." Warren tore the pad from Claire, a long line from the pencil she was using drawing across the page as he pulled it.

"You'll have to be more clear, Claire. I don't know a damn thing about computers. Voiceprints, secondary control checks....what the hell have you got here?"

"What I've got," replied Claire, repeating for Warren his own impolite gesture of grabbing the pad while he was still writing his question mark, "is what I think is a way of stalling this whole Rempal Inquest for quite some time. In fact, even if we were caught in the act, it might still be possible to short out the transmitters they've got placed around the globe, if I can make one or two seemingly impossible but brilliant interventions here. What I hope to accomplish is this. Once Augustus records your voice, he will treat it as a new entry by Caspersan because I am using the same codes he uses. As part of the voiceprint trials,

Caspersan usually gets the person to request something simple like a message on a monitor. Then, if the print is a positive one, the recorded print 'key' is correlated with a list he is compiling on his unit in his room. He then applies an electronic signature to the print, instructing Augustus to continue operating to the command of the voice.'' Claire looked up from her writing, sure that her explanation would turn on a light for her companion, the blank stare on Warren's otherwise intelligent features demanding a further tutoring. "Look. It's this simple," she wrote quickly. "Only Caspersan's electronic signature will make any voiceprint a permanent key for the computer to work on. But the original test command can be ANYTHING. Get it? You could tell the computer to print 'Good morning' on a certain monitor, OR, you could tell the computer to BLOW ITSELF ALL TO HELL...'' Claire printed the last words. Looking up, she noticed Warren's blank stare was beginning to work itself into a concentrated frown. She smiled. He was beginning to catch on. Warren took his turn at the pad.

"How do you do this voiceprint thing? And what if the test doesn't work? What if the voiceprint is not a good one?''

Claire responded in slow writing. "I don't mean to bring you hope and doom on the same plate, but if it doesn't work the first time, we are screwed. The people hearing the words for the test are going to want to know what they mean. Once they check them, I don't think there'll be much stalling for entertainment outside.''

Warren Cross and his roommate had 'talked' for nearly two hours before he left to roam the compound. A voiceprint was made for Augustus, Warren reading three sentences that Claire had composed which covered as complete a range of vowel sounds as she felt would be necessary for the test command to be processed. Claire also told Warren about the heat sensors. He considered for a moment the possible implications. Finally he shrugged his shoulders. There was no use debating the facts. If Caspersan wanted to find him, there was nothing he would be able to do to prevent it.

They tried to keep themselves focused on their plans, but their feelings for each other couldn't be denied. Once the practical side of things were discussed, there was a long silence, the only movement in the room a thin stream of smoke rising from the waste basket. For the twentieth time since they arrived, the automatic smoke detector buzzed for a few seconds before it was shut off, and they laughed together, sitting on the bed. Claire spoke.

"I wish...I wish there had been time to be alone with you, Warren. No," she said, as Warren pointed to the writing pad. "I need to say some things, and I don't care who's listening.

"I want you to know that I've begun to fall for you," she continued. "Some people say it takes a long time. I'm not so sure."

"I know what you mean," answered Warren awkwardly, knowing that others would be listening. "I'm not great with words, Claire. The whole world for me has been turned upside down in the past two weeks. With my dad in the hospital and meeting you and trying to survive this nuthouse along with everything else. It just doesn't make sense that I should be caring as much as I do for you when things have been so insane."

"You mean you wish you hadn't met me?"

"No! No! Aw, shit. I knew this was going to happen."

"What?"

"I knew from the moment you walked into the dining room that I was going to get attached and I'll be damned if I haven't. Claire Monty, I really care for you too much to be scratching in the bushes all night while you're alone in here."

"What?" exclaimed Claire affectionately. "That's it! Caspersan and his stormtroopers are one thing, but a sexist secret agent I cannot handle! Get out of my room and don't come back unless you bring flowers and an apology."

Warren smiled. He looked like he was going to say something, but didn't. Reaching out he pulled Claire's head gently toward him and kissed her. She reached up and threw her arms around his neck.

"Be careful, Warren," she whispered. He kissed her again and left.

If he doesn't make it, Claire thought, then I haven't a snowball's hope in hell. Augustus, in its male-oriented circuitry, would not accept the voiceprint of a female. The nasal frequencies are highly distinguishable, and attempting it is not worth the risk. Warren HAD to make it back. They had agreed, however, if he were in a place where there seemed no way out, rather than losing the chance of stalling Caspersan's takeover altogether, he would call out to Augustus from the compound where numerous intercoms were placed for personnel working on the electronic equipment. Chances were that such a call would be mostly garbled by the breeze and any distance Warren might be from the intercoms, but at least it was Plan B.

They both knew that making it through the night would have more than just the immediate benefit of prolonging Warren's life. With only one chance, optimum conditions were necessary.

Quintus was beginning to get nervous. It had been almost four hours now. Even though it was spring in Australia, the nights were still cool. The sweat from his fast-paced walk contrasted with the coolness of the breeze that make the paperback trees weave a quiet dance above his head. He checked his watch. Caspersan had promised him ten hours of non-interference. Senator Caspersan was a weird mixture of integrity and stealth. If he said he would give Quintus ten hours, Quintus knew there would be no communications or interference for ten full hours. Yet Caspersan wanted so badly to be assured that Quintus would win his quest that he told Quintus he would pinpoint Cross through heat sensors if necessary.

Cross, on the other hand, had expected the chase to be more difficult for him than it was turning out to be. Obviously Caspersan must have been counting on the heat sensors to corner his prey only if nothing else succeeded, and, in the meantime, had been enjoying the thought of his captive being stalked by one of his men. Quintus had not been a problem. He was loud and easy to avoid. In some ways, Cross was surprised that his years of training in the field would have prepared him so well for this type of hide-and-seek. The only difference was that his cover was usually the concrete type: walls and doors and fire escapes with traffic to bustle in and crowds of people to walk through and use as a camouflage. Another thing that didn't help Quintus was his obvious difficulty in separating his emotions from his job at hand. His anger made him careless. Cross had assumed there must have been something more than fraternal affection between Richards and Quintus since their trip by private jet to the dusty flats of Kakadu Park. Quintus had wanted to know what Richards had looked like, how he died and what he said. There were both tears and anger in his eyes, a mixture that had spelled revenge to Cross more than once in his long career in the field.

Cross was huddled beside a fallen log, its branches not fully dead. He could see Quintus walking slowly with a rifle in his hand, the half-moon in the clear sky showing him in shadowy profile.

From an area about fifty feet behind him, Cross heard a loud crack. Quintus heard it too. It sounded like a large animal stepping on a dry branch. To Cross it was a deadly sound. The kind a second or third man makes when the hunted is against more than one. To Quintus, it was the prey: The slippery Cross, who had avoided him for hours, had finally made his presence known. To Gerigi it was a big mistake. The kind he could understand, but knew it would cost them their lives if Gary Fletcher were not more careful.

XXIII

"You gotta be more quiet, Fletch-man," whispered Gerigi, his eyes peering over the bushes that surrounded the outer fence of Caspersan's compound. "We ain't visitin'. We lookin' for your friend."

Fletcher had scolded himself thoroughly for the broken branch that made Gerigi jump half a foot. "I'm doing my best, Gerigi. The last time I walked in outback swamps I was throwing rocks at gators with my teenage buddies."

"Best got to be better, Fletch-man. We gonna be in deep shit soon. A man comin' our way. Hell no. There's two."

Gary crept up beside his native guide and watched as a man raised a rifle to his shoulder. Fletcher realized with a hollow tightening in his stomach and dryness in his throat that the man was pointing the rifle in their direction. At just that moment, Gerigi pulled Fletcher by the arm. The air was knocked out of him as Gerigi threw him to the ground and Fletcher heard two shots fired, one raising dust only a few yards ahead of the bushes where they were crouched. Fletcher struggled to get up, his first instinct to get as far from there as possible. Gerigi held him firmly, motioning to him to be quiet. There was a long pause. Fletcher could hear his heart beating in his ears. He strained to listen in the direction of the gunshots. He could hear the breeze in the bushes. He imagined seeing the person walking right up to the bushes where they were. He struggled with panic. The taste of bile rose in his throat. Gerigi prodded him with his elbow.

"Don't worry, Fletch-man. I been hunted by poachers for a long time. I know when they want me dead. I think that man is shootin' at the noise you make. But he's huntin' for someone else. Look."

Nervously peeking through a break in the bushes, Fletcher saw something that filled him with emotions he had no idea what to do with. There, no more than fifty yards from him, crouching beside a fallen tree was Warren Cross. He had obviously heard the crack of the branch too. But he seemed frightened by it. He was looking through the branches of the tree at the man with the gun who was rapidly making his way in their direction. Every once in a while, he also cast a look behind him toward the bushes.

"That's the man I'm looking for!" Gary finally said to Gerigi in a whisper that was desperate and strained. "Shit. He's moving away. What do we do?"

"He's your friend, Fletch-man. You just ask me to bring you to the place where Balanda run about. You decide."

Fletcher had no idea how big the compound was or what was happening with the guy who had the rifle. He did know that Cross had sent a telegram halfway around the world asking for help. Fletcher made up his mind. When you don't know what to do, don't just stand there. Do something. Anything. He lifted his head three inches above the bushes and cupped his hands around his mouth. Calling in a half-whisper half-normal voice, Gary spoke.

"Warren!" There was no response. If Cross was going to hear him, the man with the gun would too. Cross had begun to creep away in the opposite direction. Gary made up his mind. Standing almost at full height he called out: "Hey! I got a cow named Tracy-Jo! Do you hear me? TRACY-JO!"

Gerigi had still been watching from the protection of the bushes when he heard Gary call out in a clear voice. He looked up at Fletcher with a mixture of stunned surprise and burgeoning terror.

The response was immediate. Simultaneously Cross turned and called out "Gary??! Holy shit, is that you, Gary?" while Quintus fired another two rounds in their direction.

What happened next became a legend of its own in Kakadu and throughout Australia.

"Hey man, what you doin' firin' guns in my park? The warden Beechum, he said to me, Gerigi, don't let no one fire guns at night. You gonna have to come with me." Gerigi had moved from his place in the bushes and walked right up to the fence. He had his hands on his hips and sounded like he didn't know this situation to be different from any Saturday can-shooting he had seen while working for the Park. It was a piece of work that deserved an award from every theatre company in show business. Quintus was struck dumb. He was within firing distance from Cross now, Cross's exclamation to Fletcher clearly pinpointing his position for the man with the rifle. Cross didn't know how the black man fit into the picture, but his gut said wait. Was Quintus going to shoot both him and the stranger? The three of them stood within shouting distance of each other. The lack of information worried Quintus who knew some kind of arrangement had been made with the Park Warden...was this guy really a warden too? He looked dark enough.

"What's you doin' jes standin' there? I ain't got no gun with me, but you makin' big mistake takin' me for prize game," continued Gerigi, shaking his head as if he couldn't believe how the man just stood there and wouldn't turn himself in. "I work for the government. They's laws against shootin' in the park. Go down the valley in the east if you want, but stop makin' noise around here. You there," Gerigi said to Cross who had straightened fully from his crouching position by this time, "take this friend someplace else. He gonna hurt somebody jes firin' around in the dark like that."

Quintus had regained his composure somewhat from the initial shock. He couldn't believe the man he had been chasing for the last four hours was standing right there in front of him. Cross saw the absurdity of it all as one of the funniest things he had ever experienced. He was actually smiling while Quintus tried to sort things out.

"You can see I'm in the fenced-off area," started Quintus, feeling partly frustrated and partly unsure as to whether he was actually being caught doing something he shouldn't. "The Chief Park Warden says we do what we want in here. Get the hell away before I fire a shot through your neck."

Gerigi walked closer to the fence.

"Warden Beechum, he never said nothing about fences. He said to mind our own business with men who got eagle ring on their finger. You got no eagle ring, then you get the hell down into the valley," Gerigi continued, his voice rising in anger and intensity. Fletcher later swore he had never seen anything said with such conviction in his entire life. Gerigi sounded like a warden who would have taken on an army if they were shooting shells on his land. "My partner's just the other side those trees back there, and he'll be comin' by shortly, after them shots. We can wait all night, or you get on your way."

"Eagle ring? What fucking ring, this thing?" Quintus was almost in a rage now, holding his right hand up. Cross's smile began to wane. He's getting hooked, Cross realized. He's buying it. I can use this.

"I don't know," answered Gerigi, equally frustrated. "I work twenty-hour days, man. I can't see three feet ahead by the time I go to bed. You wearin' a ring?"

Quintus must have decided he had had enough. Throwing the rifle to his shoulder, he aimed it at the dark man with the biting tongue. Gerigi noticed the move and took off toward the far right of Quintus, bravely giving Cross the opportunity to attack Quintus on his open and vulnerable left side. There was no wasted time. Quintus fired one shot that missed Gerigi but took his attention fully from Cross who covered the fifteen yards between them just as Quintus pulled off a second round. Cross fell into him from a dive four feet away. He heard Gerigi scream as the bullet tore into him. The sacrifice made by the stranger and Quintus's disregard for the unarmed man, pushed Cross to strike his opponent twice as hard as he might have. It was over almost as quickly as it had started. The butt of the rifle caught Quintus fully in the side of the head. He would be unconscious for hours.

Fletcher had reached Gerigi by the time Cross jogged up to the fence.

"How is he?"

"He's hit in the leg," called out Fletcher, "but he says he's okay." There was a long moment as Gary tore pieces of his shirt and applied a makeshift pressure dressing to the oozing wound. Propping Gerigi's head with his boot, Fletcher then covered him with his own jacket. Cross called out to him.

"Throw these on him too, Gary," he said, tossing his jacket and Quintus's over the fence. Fletcher did so. Only when he was assured by Gerigi that he was as comfortable as he could be for the moment did Gary return to the fence. He glanced for a moment back at his guide and then spoke.

"You got yourself in one hell of a pickle, farmer."

"It's worse than it looks, Gary," answered Cross. "I know you've got lots of questions, and so do I. To tell you the truth I'd have never come if I were you. You've surprised the hell out of me, and right on time."

"Forget it, Warren. What's happening? How are we gonna get you out of here?" The question did not appear to have an easy solution. At least not by the look of the fourteen-foot high fence that had "DANGER-HIGH VOLTAGE" written every seven feet along the side.

"The first person you need to get out of here is that man who saved my life," said Cross pointing in Gerigi's direction. "How bad is the bleeding?"

"I've got pressure on it. That's slowed it up quite a bit. But he's not going to be able to walk on it very quickly. It's been badly bruised; along with the blood loss, the bullet might even have broken his leg."

Cross shook his head. He glanced over his shoulder at the main complex and checked his watch. "What's his name?"

"Gerigi."

"Gerigi," repeated Cross as if to impress the name firmly in his memory. "Tell Gerigi I owe him. I mean it." Gary knew what that really meant. Cross was in trouble. A stranger had taken a big risk for him. Cross would repay the debt. Gerigi had no way of knowing it, but Gary sensed the ex-warden could probably write his own ticket right now for a future in the Park or anywhere. Money would not be a problem for him or his family for a long time. "Who else knows about you coming here?"

"Just one other person," said Gary, pausing to consider whether or not to say who it was. Cross looked down at the ground and smiled broadly. Gary had shared a few memories of his own when he and Cross had gone out for the occasional beer. Beatrice. Long lost Beatrice. "You son-of-a-bitch," teased Cross, drawing out the words for emphasis and shaking his head. "I bet you planned this whole fucking fiasco just to get me to send for you so that you and Bee could walk off into the sunset." If there had been more light, Cross would have seen his friend blushing under his remarks.

226

"You don't need to worry," said Fletcher, quickly changing the focus of the conversation. "She'll keep any and all information to herself. I can speak for her as well as myself." Cross nodded. He didn't doubt it.

"There's not much time for lengthy explanations," Cross began. "None of it would make much sense to you anyway. I've been part of it for nearly ten days and it's still fuzzy as hell in my own mind."

"What do you want me to do?" Gary asked. Cross gave a short sigh, nervously glancing at his watch again. Time. There was no fucking time.

"There's no use trying the fence bit unless the power's off. We'd get fried. There's someone inside I need to bring with me as well. I'm going to have to go back in."

"What was this ape after? Looked to me you had already escaped."

"What you saw was one very disturbed man's idea of late night entertainment. He's probably back in his room reading poetry and waiting for the gory details of my execution." The puzzled creases on Gary's forehead deepened. "Forget it," said Cross with a wave of his hand. "Listen. Here's what I want you to do..."

"Are you certain you have not read the story?" asked Caspersan from his chair by the window where he sat with a scroll of Rempal's poems on his lap. Cross smiled a wry grin: He WAS reading poetry. "It's been barely five hours and here you stand at the door to my room. I also hear that Quintus is not likely to be joining us again. The guard who brought you in from the compound says you left him leaning on the fence."

Even for Cross, with years of hardened field experience behind him, it had been difficult. He was consoled by the fact that Quintus was unconscious at least when he had carried the body to the fence and thrown it against the high voltage current. Gary had been told not to look back. The smell of burnt flesh hovered for a long time along with the burden of the decision. Quintus had to be silenced if Warren and Claire were to have a chance of escaping. And so the world consumed another mortal in the incessant quest for survival of the masses. Unfair. Unjust. Reality.

227

"He was not left leaning," said Cross with sadness and anger in his voice, "he was left convulsing and screaming. Your game has cost another man his life. That must touch off something in you somewhere, Caspersan. Or is Augustus truly a brother of yours? Maybe there's no heart beating in there at all."

"Come now, Mr. Cross. Let us not wax dramatic, shall we? I need to relax. I'm having a very long and trying day myself. Surely his death is only a boon to you. Look. Aren't you delighted? You won. I told you that would mean your freedom."

"That is dramatic. And I believe, most unlikely."

"Your tone of voice suggests to me that you assume my intentions were not honourable, Mr. Cross. That hurts. Really. I was fully prepared to free you if you succeeded."

"So Claire and I pack a lunch and go through the front gate."

"So it would have been, yes."

"Would have been..."

"The world is fascinating simply because it is so full of surprises, Mr. Cross. One of the biggest surprises of my lifetime occurred while you were in the marshes. The two governments have managed to avoid the apocalyptic climax I predicted. Do not ask me how. Perhaps we led them too gently over the months preceding the assassination of the Russian diplomat. They have decided on a two-week adjournment to their mobilizations for war. They are suspicious of a third force in the world, although they have no idea who or what that could be. I'm afraid you might yet be a threat to our plans. We cannot let you leave."

"Ask me how devastated I am. You bring me great joy, Caspersan. I love to have my judgment of human nature confirmed. A snake is a snake is a..."

"Please, Mr. Cross. Respect. A little respect, if you don't mind. For all your concern with your own immediate future, we are talking about world priorities. The general populace must be considered. They cannot yet see, they refuse to see, the truth. We must concern ourselves with history, not whimpering over lost time, money or freedom."

Cross sensed something in Caspersan. It would be a mistake not to follow up on it, test it out. "I'm sure the other Senators agree with you. Who am I to say? Maybe you're right. It's a pity. I've seen what your weather conditioners can do. Imagine how much produce could be harvested, how many natural disasters avoided with the brilliance of what has been accomplished here." Caspersan seemed caught off guard.

"You are brighter than I assumed, Mr. Cross. Please don't take that personally. I compliment you because a number of the Senators have begun to forget the very things you bring to mind. Several of them are of the opinion that the Rempal Inquest has now proven that the world IS capable of governing itself. I am in a difficult position."

"I'm sorry, Senator," Cross said convincingly, "I don't really know what you mean." Cross could see it clearly now. Caspersan was troubled. Things had gone awry, somehow. It was supposed to be over soon. Very soon. War was to be declared and the Rempal Senate would take over with Caspersan leading the New World. Humbly. Modestly. Now it appeared the game plan had become complicated; the unity of the Senate was being threatened. The helpless world was thinking of ways to avoid nuclear war. Caspersan's dream of sweet and uncomplicated revenge on the world was slowly being pulled from him, it seemed. He was not taking it well.

"Well, look at it, Cross! See it! I cannot have people fighting with each other in the Senate Chambers for the next week over when and how and if we should move into our place in history. That would be treason. Treason to mankind, to destiny!"

"Whatever you decide, it will be difficult, Senator. I know that Ms. Monty and I are insignificant. The soldier at the fence is insignificant. The world, and history I suppose as well; these things are important. They will be here long after we have gone, all of us. I'm shocked. I came here six days ago repelled, disgusted. I still do not believe what you believe, but at least I see the common sense of it. I find it difficult to understand how the other Senators have managed to turn from their stance of only a few days ago..."

"That's it. By Jupiter, you've given me food for thought, Cross," said Caspersan walking to the mantle where he replaced the scrolls on the stand and lowered the glass over it.

"What? What are you doing? What about Claire and me? Senator?"

Caspersan moved to his console. "Augustus."

"Yes, Senator."

"Call a general assembly. We will meet in ten minutes."

"Yes, Senator." Turning to Cross, the brilliant, confused and emotionally drained man smiled a tight smile.

"You will die soon, Mr. Cross. But perhaps you will be comforted knowing that your simple challenge has given me the wherewithal to plunge forward again. Yes. At all costs. What is leadership if sacrifices cannot be made? Augustus."

"Yes, Senator."

"Have Mr. Cross escorted to his room. Tell recruit Barnabus to take him and his friend to the back lot and execute them."

Claire tried not to dwell on him. In college she had learned how to sleep in class, her eyes wide open, staring at one fine point on the far wall. She had learned how to go through a week on less than three hours sleep a night, preparing for exams. She had learned concentration. Concentrate on what you're doing, she said to herself over and over. If he makes it back, WHEN he comes back, this thing has to be prepared.

There was no indication that Augustus or the people monitoring her had yet discovered she was literally operating on the open bowels of the complex, Augustus cleanly split down the middle for her to forage with her electronic scalpel. Cutting, reshaping, grafting, rewording. At first she could not clearly define for herself how to go about it. She wanted Warren's voiceprint to activate a series of events in the complex which would startle, confuse and occupy the minds of the majority of the occupants. At the same time, she understood that her life, their lives, were not the primary consideration. There were people here who were actively planning the takeover of the world, the manipulation of governments and peoples by weather control, coercion, dictatorship. Still, she reasoned, we have a right to try and make it, just like anybody else. And if distractions can be worked into this thing, the timing guessed at with any kind of accuracy, maybe there's a way....A knock could be heard at the door.

"Ms. Monty, you'll have to come with me." Claire's heart sank. The words echoed in her mind "...come with me...come with me...have to come with me." She looked at the terminal. It was over. Warren didn't make it. That meant he was dead, and so was she.

"Ms. Monty? I'm sorry, ma'am. You'll have to come. I'm afraid…"

"…I've got my orders," finished Claire for the young soldier in a whisper as he said the very same words. Funny, she thought. Where's the hysteria?

"I'm coming." She turned to the bed and picked up Warren's sweater, the one he had lent her before leaving. She was chilly. Death. Life. Walking to the door she remembered with heavy sadness that she had never told Warren clearly that she loved him. She opened the door. Warren was standing there. Claire looked at him, and fainted.

XXIV

"The realm of human endeavors: thought, creativity, culture, religion, philosophy, science, each is a court of its own, a place of judgment. Those who have studied or discovered or invented in each arena; those with laurels to prove their superiority, the authority that should be granted them; they confer on the people who look up to them for guidance and wisdom, decisions that effect the lives of millions, sometimes billions of people.

"The idea of a god, a being beyond this world, whether true or false, is a message to us, a message that must be heard. Human beings seek guidance and security. It is not right, not human, to deny each and every individual a life free from worry, to deny the kind of direction and freedom we can provide..." And so Caspersan spoke to the Senate. They listened. For a time there was debate. But each man knew there was little sense in it. Senator Williams' death spoke clearly of the corner they had painted themselves into. To pretend they had power to disagree was useless. Long ago their fervour to create destiny for mankind had sealed their own destiny. The man who spoke to them, and his machine, Augustus, had captivated them with his implants and ethics as securely as his genius was planning the takeover of the civilized world. Another Senator had tried sabotage. He too, died by his own hand, the messages protecting the Ideal dealing mercilessly with him when he began to choose for himself. All that remained for those who had began to doubt was the debate. And the debate, with Caspersan at the head, was useless....

In a corridor at the opposite end of the complex, Warren Cross and Claire Monty walked solemnly with armed escort to the place where they were to be executed. Once she regained consciousness, Claire was overcome with relief and an emotion bordering on joy. She did not hesitate to tell Warren the depth of her feelings. The mist in his eyes showed appreciation. He asked if everything was ready. She said, "As much as it ever will be."

The greatest moments aren't always preceded by fanfare. Passing an intercom near the doorway to the outside, Warren spoke loudly and firmly, Claire squeezing his hand. There would be only one try.

"Augustus. Run test Cross." The guards were confused for a moment. Then one realized what Cross was trying to do and laughed.

"It's not quite that easy, old man. Talk about not giving up until the last minute." The other joined in, jabbing Cross with the point of his rifle to move ahead.

Then it happened; it all happened. The same laws that brought rain and started forest fires and propelled torpedoes, reacted predictably and surely to Claire's programming. It started with the lights. Blackout. Along the top of the walls auxiliary beams were activated. Cross wasted no time. Pulling the rifle from the arms of one guard, he struck the other fully in the face, jamming the stock of the gun in a swift second movement into the stomach of the first. Flipping the rifle end over end, he fired four rounds in quick succession, killing both guards while Claire stood by in shock. Sirens began howling. In the Senate chambers, Caspersan ordered Augustus to explain. Augustus was patient with him.

"Presently processing voice test Cross. Please wait."

In the main monitoring room, sixty-four men of all nationalities and ages jumped in unison, their hands ripping the headphones from their ears. The mercilessly tearing high-frequency sound bursts that Augustus sent to their monitors caused eardrums to break. Some fell unconscious, the blood from busted membranes in the ear canal seeping down the sides of their necks.

Caspersan became frantic. Voice test Cross. That meant someone was running a command for the test of Cross's voiceprint. The woman, he thought. The woman at the computer. She's programmed the computer to test Cross's voiceprint through a command. Just as Caspersan reached the exit of the Senatorial Court, the sliding door snapped shut.

Not every command was smoothly executed. The kitchen exploded into activity, stoves and burners turning on, the dishwasher spraying into an empty bin. Intercoms began buzzing all over the complex. The monitors started slowly changing channels, as Augustus reviewed information from each source around the globe. The changes became more frequent each second. By the time three minutes had passed, the images being sent to the individual monitors as well as to the split screen on the wall of the main monitoring room were changing over four hundred times a second. Finally one exploded, its sensitive circuitry overloaded. It began to burn, small flames jumping from the jagged opening which was once the face of the monitor. The flames caught registration forms strewn on the desk. Another monitor exploded. And another. Seven minutes passed. The fire alarm in the monitoring room sounded. Soon the entire complex would be engulfed.

One complication Cross immediately encountered was the fact that the program Claire had created, which shut off the exits from the Senators Court and the monitoring room, did not discriminate and leave a convenient exit for the two fugitives. Warren Cross was running. Claire was not far behind. Fires in several compartments had begun to send steady streams of smoke into the corridors making vision and breathing difficult.

"Warren," Claire called out, her message cut short by a rasping cough, the air a burning mixture of precious oxygen and rising smoke. Warren turned and waited. It was obvious they would not find an open exit at this rate. There was too much smoke and not enough clean air. Warren had been running ahead hoping to spot an exit they hadn't seen, trying to find a way from the corridor that would not box them in as the fires got worse. There was no sign of anyone other than the guards that had been escorting them. Warren grasped Claire by the hand and pulled her to the floor. There was still some space to breathe close to the carpet if they took short breaths. With his eyes stinging and Claire constantly coughing, Warren noticed a sign about three feet away that he was sure he had seen before. For some reason he had a sense it could mean help. He couldn't quite make it out. "L-un--y...Lau----..." The smoke passed in billows and the emergency lights left little to see by. Then Warren made out the full word. "Laundry..."

A laundry chute! In the complex Caspersan insisted that nature could not be improved upon. The greatest genius, he had said, does not look for expensive or complicated ways to do work. He makes the Universe work for him. And so, three hundred and sixty-five days a year, soldiers, recuits and Senators alike would walk to one of any twenty-three laundry chutes throughout the complex, open the hatch and let their dirty clothes slide down a stainless steel tube to gathering bins in the basement.

Without explanations, Warren pulled Claire to a place near the opening to the chute. Claire's coughs had become gagged and Warren could tell there would be no time to try anything else. With little strength left for resistance, Claire allowed herself to be picked up. Using one arm to lower the chute hatch until it clicked into its open lock, Warren unceremoniously dumped his companion feet first and climbed in after her.

Caspersan was human. As a human being he had a rationale that served to protect himself first in severe crises. This was such a crisis. When he noticed that the doors to the Senatorial courts had been closed and locked, he walked to the centre of the room and told the other Senators to stay put. He would return momentarily, he said. Walking to a door in the back of the auditorium that had one of the few mechanical hinges of the complex, he opened it into a passageway that led straight to his chambers, then turned and locked the door behind him. His thought process was simple. The girl must have had help. It must have been one of the Senators. He had known that some were not one hundred percent loyal. It could have been any of a number of them. So be it. There was no time to interrogate them individually. If they find another way out, more power to them. If they do not and the smoke or the flames reach the auditorium, then they will all die. Caspersan was now convinced that good intentions mean nothing. Let the purifying flames burn them, he thought. The world is turning against me again. But this time, he reasoned, with tears of anger and hysteria in his eyes, this time I will leave the world with a memory of my own strength. This time, I will be remembered for the genius I am...

It is inevitable that even the best laid plans will falter in some way. Caspersan had firmly believed that his complex and his destiny were assured as if cast in stone, in glorious Roman marble. He had dreamt at night of seeing his name and his initiative boldly praised in countries around the world where famine and despotism ruled, where the common labourer could never expect to satisfy even the most meager expectations of a struggling family. All the time and effort, the organization, construction, recruitment and training, all of it was burning because someone had told Augustus, in his mechanical innocence, to destroy himself. Caspersan was devastated. It was not so much the loss of Augustus or the complex that troubled him, as he walked the last hundred yards to his bedchambers, but the pervading sense that he was misunderstood. It was now as it always had been. The bright child in school who had been scapegoated and ridiculed, beaten, teased and excluded from the social circles so necessary to a child's sense of self-worth—here he was again, his dreams being destroyed, and still there was no one who could understand, who might offer him that precious human gift of understanding.

Caspersan wiped his eyes on his sleeve as he closed the door to his chambers behind him. At the far end of the complex where the chaos had begun, explosions and the screams of trapped men could be heard. In an effort born from years of persistent research, he turned on the computer console at his desk and tried to interrupt the process Claire had begun, but with no success. She may have been a primitive hacker in comparison to Caspersan's own abilities, but her mindless criss-cross of commands and countercommands were producing in Augustus what amounted to an electronic nervous breakdown. It would not be long and everything Caspersan had created over the last twenty years of his life would be lost.

He pressed the "clear" button on his console out of habit and sat in his armchair. He glanced about the room. His eyes fell on the scrolls that were encased on the mantle.

"Rempal," he said. "How is it that destiny would bear you so long before me, that time would have us be so close in mind and spirit and so separate in history?" Rising slowly and walking to the mantle, the weary and broken leader lifted the glass case, dropping it to the floor with a crash that mirrored ominously the fall of his own power, his dream and his organization. "Is it, Rempal, that the world is trying to teach us something?" said Caspersan, seating himself again and speaking to the scroll as he caressed it like a kitten on his lap. "Is it perhaps that the rise and fall of Rome in ancient times was one with this day? Yes, I suppose. Maybe the message needed to be heard is that man is not worth saving at all. Maybe the message for us is that the greatest mercy is death. Death for all mankind." Another explosion sounded, this one much closer to Caspersan's room than the last. He was startled by it, the proximity of the blast reminding him how little time he had to decide, to act. He remained seated for a moment, cradling the Songs of Rempal like a new-born child. As his twisted intellect reasoned his choices, his posture emanated an eerie gentleness, the irony of the human condition poignantly chiseled on his tired face, a sad smile reflecting the stresses and emotions he was experiencing. He sighed. Standing and walking to the mantle, Caspersan quietly placed the scroll back on its stand. He regarded it for a moment. There was another explosion. The sound was like a lightswitch in his mind. His face assumed the expression of determination that had placed him on the road toward Augustus and the Rempal Inquest almost twenty years before. In the same angry and self-assured manner in which he had told the British Ambassador that life could mean more if people were not so lazy, Caspersan walked back to his console. To the right of the keyboard was an area three inches by six inches, marked off by diagonal red stripes. On it were ten keys numbered 0 to 9. Caspersan keyed a numerical sequence into the only electronic component of the complex that was not in some way connected to Augustus. The red-striped panel lifted from a hinge on the top revealing below the thin cover, a red button. There were no words written. There were no cautions. Only one person in the world knew what pressing that button would mean. That person placed his finger lightly on it and spoke his final words to this world. "Goodbye, Augustus. The fight for humanity is over. Bitterness and despair will be no more. I feel good because, in the very least, it is I who have put the misery of the world to sleep." He closed his eyes and pressed firmly.

237

XXV

Everything had gone just as Cross had hoped. The slide from the hallway three stories above them had dropped them into a bin that was over half full of laundry, softening their landing. With increasing concern Cross noticed, however, that the basement was totally blacked out. There were no emergency lights operating, and the only discernible light came from an exit light glowing dimly approximately seventy-five yards from the bin where they had landed. Claire, still coughing and fighting with a pair of coveralls, finally emerged and called out:

"Warren?"

"I'm right here."

"I can't..." Claire coughed heavily and began again, "I can't see you."

"And I can't see you either," answered Warren, grasping the edge of the bin and hoisting himself over the side. "Here. Give me your hand. I don't know how this blind stumble is going to be much better than the situation we just left."

"Are you kidding?" Claire retorted, not able to believe that a lack of light could at all be compared to the close brush with death by suffocation they had narrowly escaped. "I'd much rather try my luck scratching along the walls down here than have no chance in a locked-off corridor. Where are you? Damn," Claire said simply, bumping into him as she staggered gingerly from the edge of the bin. "You're right. It is pretty dark."

"We'll try reaching the exit sign." Holding hands again, the couple walked slowly, Warren waving his hand in front to touch anything that might be obstructing them. Another explosion in what seemed like an endless series echoed through the cool room. Warren noticed with rising anxiety that the door sign was beginning to flicker. Hold on. Hold on for fuck's sake, Warren thought to himself. If the light would burn for only a few seconds. Claire crashed into a scrub bucket on the floor and let out a howl, half from surprise and half from pain, the metal rim of the bucket leaving a rising welt on her shin.

"Are you okay?" Warren asked.

"I-I think so," answered Claire, biting her lip to hold back the tears. "Warren!"

"Yeah, I know, I see it," Warren said as the exit light, still fifty yards ahead, flickered for the last time. They were alone in total darkness, with no idea of how large an area they had to work with, or even a clear sense of where the door light had been, since Claire had met up with the bucket and Warren had turned to see she wasn't hurt. They were disoriented and Warren, for one, was running out of ideas. He could also smell smoke. The basement would not be safe forever. They had to do something.

Suddenly there was another surprise. This time it was Warren's turn. "Ugh! Fuck!"

"What is it?"

Warren rubbed his elbow where he had run into something himself. He was about to answer that he thought he had hit a box of some kind, when his hands, exploring curiously the length of the "box", discovered it was supported by at least two wheels. Warren had introduced himself to one of the six vans that delivered laundry, equipment and paper supplies over the dirt roads built around the perimeter of the complex. Leaving Claire and running his hands along the edge of the van toward the front, Warren reached the door and opened it. Like emerging from the suffocating darkness of a cave that has collapsed and left no way out, the little interior light filled Warren and his partner with a tremendous mixture of relief and hope. Could it be possible? Could they expect anything more?

"Are the keys in it?" Claire asked as Warren climbed in and searched frantically. Checking the position of the gearshift on the steering column, Warren answered her by pressing the gas pedal to the floor and turning the ignition. The engine roared to life. Warren turned on the headlights and stretched across to open the

239

passenger door, as Claire sped around the front of the van and climbed in. It was only when they were seated and Warren began a sweeping circle of the area that they realized how incredibly fortunate they were to have walked into the van. The basement area was huge, its only structural definition marked by several cement columns that served as supports for the entire complex. Approximately fifty yards to the left of them was another van. Apart from that, the area was strewn with laundry bins, wheeling carts and along the edges, huge industrial washers and dryers. They could have been stumbling for hours without ever finding a door. They said nothing to each other, but the understanding was clear between them. Coincidence or grace of God, they were immeasurably grateful.

Two circuits of the area revealed yet another roadblock. As the electrical systems degenerated steadily throughout the complex, the first mechanisms to seize in the laundry area were the electric doors. There were two perceivable exit ramps. Both were fully shut. Warren chose one at random and told Claire to fasten her seat belt and close her eyes in case the window shattered on impact. There was no other way out than straight up the ramp, door or no door. The moment Warren turned the van toward the door, an explosion behind them served as a reminder of the creeping proximity of the chaos that had begun on the upper levels. Gunning the engine and sparing nothing, Warren floored the gas pedal and headed straight for the door. As the engine screamed, Claire braced herself. Warren yelled just before they hit the door.

"Hang on, this is it!" With a deafening crash the van broke through the aluminum door, ripping a hole in the centre and blowing the left rear tire. This would slow them down, but at least they were outside. Claire opened her eyes and noticed with immense relief that they had made it. The sun had begun to spread a crimson hue along the edge of the eastern sky, the brilliant orb beginning its cycle as if nothing in the world had changed since it descended the night before. Claire motioned to Warren to look at the rising warmth of another Australian spring day. But Warren had pulled the van to the side of the dirt road two hundred yards from the ramp exit and had his eyes fixed on another glowing sight near the rear of the smoking complex. A roaring sound like the murderous growl of some medieval underground fantasy creature shook the ground where they sat. Lifting slowly at first, then rapidly picking up momentum as it emerged, was a rocket booster. Attached to it was an article unknown to Claire but clearly recognizable to Warren. A desperate and highly frightened man had just relinquished his last hold on sanity and reason. As they stood hopelessly entranced, the missing nuclear missile stolen from the American shipment began its skyward arc. Within thirty minutes, someplace somewhere, would be no more.

XXVI

Southern Colorado with its mountains, monuments and sand dunes had been home to David Woods since he was nine years old. His father had travelled extensively throughout the United States and Europe during his thirty-year career with the U.S. Airforce, but to Dave, Colorado was, and always would be, home.

When he and Kathy had first married, they had sometimes talked of moving out to New Jersey where Kathy's folks lived. Her father owned a chain of sporting goods stores and would have loved to train Dave to take over for him when he retired, having no sons of his own. But Dave insisted that the military was the only lifestyle he'd ever feel comfortable with and Kathy relented. Fact was Dave wanted to retire himself in Colorado. There were more military retirement dollars in southern Colorado than anywhere else. He wanted to be one of the people who cashed in on them, maybe running a bookstore or a gym for the guys from the forces who were looking for ways to keep their minds and bodies occupied now that they had time on their hands. He figured his own military experience would make his business a popular place. Yeah, thought Dave, turning to the exit toward NORAD Headquarters located a mile beneath Cheyenne Mountain, four more years in the hole and it's easy street.

Dave stopped his car at the gate, snapping his security card to his lapel as the guard, a young corporal, came to his window.

"Good evening, sir," said the Corporal with a smile. "How's it feel to be working graveyard again?" Sergeant Dave Woods yawned as if in answer to the guard's question. They chuckled together.

"That just about says it all, wouldn't you say?"

"Yes, sir. By the way. HQ said to pass the word that condition is still yellow in the trenches. You've probably heard there's a two-week stay for negotiations but the Starboys aren't taking any chances. I figure there'll be more than one pilot's wife chewing her nails tonight."

"Might well be, Corporal," agreed Sgt. Woods reaching for the handle to close his window. "You be sure to run on down if there's any fireworks and let us know, okay?" The Corporal laughed and saluted Woods. It was a running joke at NORAD Headquarters that someone in the gatehouse would probably see the missiles flying overhead before a sighting was confirmed by the Chiefs of Staff. Over the years there had been a number of false alarms due to computer foulups. The other thing was, no one really wanted to believe that things would come to this. Especially since the assassination of the Russian diplomat in Istanbul at the beginning of the week.

In an installation such as NORAD Headquarters the clearance process always appeared more complicated than it needed to be. For the thousands of military and civilian staff that worked here forty to fifty hours a week, endless precautions seemed purposeless and a waste of time. A simulated unauthorized entry in 1986 had changed many people's attitudes, however. Known only to the Chief Security Officer and the Commander of NORAD, three people had managed to infiltrate the complex as far as the Air Weapons Control Room without being accosted. Had they been seeking information about U.S. strategic armament deployment or Operating Procedures, they would have had little difficulty. The screws were tightened and now even some of Dave's drinking buddies went through the motions when he approached a guarded entrance or passageway.

There was an eerie solemnity about working so deep underground from midnight to eight. Dave had always felt that the people on graveyard shift would be the ones to see something if there was anything to see. The darkness outside, the relatively quiet and deserted streets leading to the mountain from the nearby city of Colorado Springs, and the family asleep at home; each of these things gave those late at night the idea they were keeping watch over the bad guy while the rest of the community relaxed.

Sergeant David Woods chatted lightly with night-shift staff as they passed him on the stairs leading to and from the monitors in the Air Weapons Control Room. Everything was quiet they said. It was the end of the month and coffee breaks would be spent doing paperwork. In other words, Dave joked, it was a shitty shift. They nodded and laughed. Everybody hated the endless paperwork.

Dave moved into position at his console as he had done hundreds of times over the last six years in Colorado Springs. The headset was still warm from the ears of his departing colleague. Rearranging the space in front of him and opening his flipchart to begin the checklist, Dave spoke into the microphone running from a thin wire at his right earphone around his cheek to just below and in front his mouth.

"This is Sergeant Woods, Monitor 21, Sector 7. Beginning checklist."

"Go ahead, 21. I have your sheet in front of me."

"Power, headset, communications all okay. Sector 7 from Midway Island to New Zealand clear and unobstructed. Checking frequencies." Woods slowly and audibly ran a spectrum of thirty bands he could broadcast to in crisis, waiting for the send and return which would signal to him that the computer could receive and integrate his communication on those frequencies without unauthorized tapping or interference. "Frequencies check. Heat monitors clear, there is…" Sergeant Woods was interrupted by a jolting screech in his headset. Designed to elicit immediate reaction from an Air Weapons Controller whose attention might momentarily be elsewhere, the loud beeping sound continued unabated as Woods scrambled to find the volume button on the monitor. A thousand things went through his mind as he stared into the screen monitoring Sector 7. He felt nauseous and his heart beat rapidly. There was no mistaking the signal. There, beginning as a pinpoint and slowly etching its way across the screen from the northern tip of the Australian coastline was the track of a rocket launch. Dave knew what raising a false alarm could mean. He also knew what extra seconds would provide if this was a real missile. He slammed his fist onto the ALERT switch at his elbow and like never before in the history of NORAD, all hell broke loose.

***

By the time Cross slammed on the brakes at the edge of the compound and brought the crippled van to a halt six inches from the fence, fully four minutes had passed since he and Claire had first sighted the missile. To his immense relief, Warren noticed as they approached the fence that Gary Fletcher was parked just outside the gate. He was alone, but the two-foot antenna standing stiffly from the roof of the truck's cab suggested Gary had succeeded in commandeering a vehicle with a long-range cellular telephone as Cross had requested. Explosions from the complex continued to remind them of how close they had come to never seeing the outside world again.

Claire was full of emotions she found difficult to separate from each other. Things were moving too fast. She was shaking with relief at having made it outside the complex before the smoke or flames cornered them in a blazing grave. But moments ago a missile was seen lifting from nearby. Cross had not tried to explain what that meant to him, but he seemed somehow even more concerned than he was when they were trapped in the corridors or in the basement. Claire knew she was reaching a limit when she began rummaging through the glove compartment for a cigarette, a habit she had thoroughly broken nine years before. One cigarette. One fucking cigarette, she thought, her mind racing. Is that so much to ask?

Cross whipped open his door and crept onto the roof of the van, using the side mirror as a foothold. Without stopping to consider whether the power was also shut off at the electrified fence, he leapt at it and, scrambing his way to the top, flipped one leg over, then another, pausing before his freefall to the ground near Fletcher's truck only long enough to judge the distance. With a snorting sound Cross hit the ground and rolled. Fletcher was expecting some type of greeting. Cross's mind was elsewhere. Speeding to the passenger door facing him, Cross brushed by Fletcher without a word and tore open the door. Grabbing at the receiver for the cellular telephone, he pressed the tone button for 0 and tried to calm himself enough to communicate clearly. Gary now began to understand. They were out of the complex and apparently out of personal danger, but

245

something big must have gone wrong. Terribly wrong.

"Operator."

"Operator, please listen carefully," Cross began. "This call is a national emergency. I have information regarding a nuclear threat to a highly populated city. Please connect me to the United States Operator Zenith 79442 extension 70. I repeat. Give me Zenith 79442 extension 70." The operator did not question or hesitate. Cross was grateful that someone somewhere had taken the time to train this operator on priority calls. Five seconds later a man's voice in the United States NORAD command centre answered. The missile had been flying now for six and a half minutes.

"NORAD Security."

"Security, this is Colonel Cross, United States Rangers. I am calling from Australia, the site of the missile that lifted five minutes ago. I must speak to a Chief of Staff immediately. It could mean..."

"I'm sorry, sir. NORAD is condition red. All Chiefs of Staff have instructed..."

"Listen to me, soldier," Cross bellowed, "I know who is sending this missile and why. The information I have could prevent a war. Give me a Staff person, NOW!" There was a short pause. Halfway around the world a young soldier spent five precious seconds sorting agonizing priorities. Cross felt a rare kind of gratitude that brought nervous tears to his eyes when the soldier next spoke.

"Yes, sir. I'll put you through." Cross was shaking badly. He quickly passed the receiver from his left hand to his right. There would be no time for second explanations. A deep and terse voice broke through the receiver.

"General Brooks, U.S. Army. What is it, Colonel?"

"Sir, I am on assignment for the CIA," Cross spoke quickly. "I know that there has been a stay in mobilizations as you and the Russians search for clues to the political deadlock that has been imposed upon you both of late. I have found it, sir. The destabilizing factor. I am calling from the place where the missile was launched."

"We're preparing for nuclear war here, Colonel. The President is speaking with Russia on the red phone right now, but Moscow is terrified and very close to pushing the button themselves. We know it's not our fucking missile and they say it's not theirs. We won't know for another minute or two its true trajectory. Could be Russia, could be West Germany. But here's what I propose. I'll hook you to their conversation and you say whatever you have to. Even if we lose a city somewhere, our goal is to contain it to one and only one. Make it sound good. Buy time, Colonel.'' As abruptly as he had begun, the General cut out. The next voice was the low and firm voice that Cross recognized as that of the President of the United States.

''Colonel Cross, there is no time for amenities. Speak clearly and candidly.'' Cross glanced out the window and noticed that Fletcher was working on the gate with a huge pair of wire cutters. He gathered his wits and began.

''Thank you, Mr. President. I am presently calling from the site of the missile launch of ten minutes ago. I have tracked the political tensions, the assassinations in both Germany and Turkey to the same terrorist organization. As you both suspected, their plan has been to play the superpowers off against each other and to take advantage of the instability that resulted.'' Cross knew that talking about the complex details of the Rempal Senate and the ability of Augustus to control the weather would be a waste of time. He had to communicate one thing clearly: The present turmoil was created by an insane mind. It was not American or Russian. It was, however, deliberately designed to look that way. ''I have succeeded,'' Cross continued, ''in infiltrating the main headquarters of the organization and have obstructed any immediate plans for future terrorist acts. Unfortunately, in his desperation, the leader has launched a missile. From what I could see, it was a nuclear missile.''

Almost immediately there was a barrage of questions from both the American and Soviet Presidents. Cross attempted to answer their questions clearly without creating more confusion. Twelve minutes had now passed. The line was interrupted by a torrent of insinuations and threats from the Soviet statesman. He had just received information that the trajectory of the missile had been confirmed: Destination—Moscow, U.S.S.R.

''And so, Mr. President,'' the translator interpreted as the tensions continued to rise, ''my people have less than twenty minutes to leave the confines of their schools and hospitals before

247

the supposed third-party missile strikes my homeland. It is strangely coincidental that this would happen so soon after our exercise began on the East German border. I warn you. If a missile enters Russian airspace, there will be no discussion. For each and every Soviet citizen murdered, two Americans will die."

"I assure you," spoke the President, "that my government has had nothing to do with this incident. It is as frightening for me to hear the missile's destination as you. I do not want war. You can believe me..."

"Belief! Belief!" interrupted the Soviet leader. "I have heard and seen the fruits of moderate diplomacy! Enough of beliefs! If the missile continues its track and strikes Moscow, there will be war." The line went dead. Soon after, the President too, hung up. General Brooks, who had also been listening to the conversation, spoke to Cross.

"That's it, Cross. Last inning. Twenty minutes and it's fireworks. You did your best." Click.

Cross placed the phone gently on its cradle, conscious that nothing else could be done. He looked up to see Claire crawling through a hole in the gate where Gary had snipped wires and folded back an opening for her. Detached and exhausted, he gazed over the western horizon where the missile had disappeared. Fletcher and Claire walked up to the truck. They could see the look on his face.

"Not good?" asked Claire, brushing the dusty locks from her face and spreading a smudge of dirt along her forehead in the process.

"Not good," answered Warren simply. How was he to tell them within an hour the earth itself might no longer exist? A tremendous sense of hopelessness came over him. Just as he was about to speak, the phone buzzed. Cross hesitated at first. His mind was bogged down, brain cells and neurons fighting for the chance to make some sense of the whole scenario. Two buzzes. Cross picked it up.

"Cross, this is General Brooks. What the hell happened?"

"I-I thought you had hung up, sir."

"Fuck no. Somebody cut it. McKay called from CIA Level One. He mentioned the missile stolen from the American stockyard. Is that the one?"

"Yes, sir, I believe it is," stammered Cross, his internal coping mechanisms in overload.

"Very good. Hold the line." There was silence. A minute passed. A minute and thirty seconds. Suddenly there was a loud crackling noise over the cellular phone, like radio interference. It was clamourous, insistent. Then, as suddenly as it had begun, there was nothing. Cross waited. The General's voice broke in. Cross could hear cheering and laughter in the background.

"You deserve a hell of a pat on the back, soldier," the General began. "McKay gave us a serial number and we matched it to an abort code. Took us three tries, but we finally smoked the bastard. Blew the fucking thing right out of the sky. There's some radioactive litter falling over the Indian Ocean, but we're safe now. Hello? Colonel Cross? Hello?"

After hearing the news, Warren let the phone drop to the seat. Opening the door to the cab, he excused himself and walked quietly to the rear of the truck where he bent at the waist, placed his hands on his knees, and threw up.

XXVII

There are some things considered significant and beautiful to people all over the world: music, art, the serenity of nature's wilderness. These things, and others like them, transcend the boundaries of language and culture, touching the soul of humanity where peace and joy, suffering and grief are common traits of mortality. All humans, even those who have isolated or hidden themselves behind walls of nonchalance or indifference, know what it is to feel alive.

Warren stood at the edge of his fields, the blossoms of alfalfa swaying gently in the last whispers of the day's soft breeze. The sun began its evening ritual, spreading lace of gold, red and yellow along the bottom edge of cumulus clouds that seemed reluctant to say goodbye. The sun's last rays rushed to create a work of quiet wonder that was original and beautiful, never to be seen exactly this way again. It wasn't so much the sunset itself or the solitude that delighted him. It was the fact that he had begun to feel again, to appreciate small things, everyday things. He shifted his weight, lowering one foot from the bottom rail of the wooden fence and replacing it with the other. He sighed. It's good to be alive, he thought.

As if in answer to his reflections, the person who represented for Warren the new life he had begun walked up from behind him. Warren knew it was her. He could hear the pace of her footsteps grazing stubble and imagined clearly the graceful stride that carried her from place to place. Claire stood beside him and put her arm around his shoulder. She squeezed firmly with her hand, another of her persistent signals demonstrating her affection for him, the kind of persistence that finally convinced him after ten months of consistent support, that she was here to stay.

Claire brought her hand back from him and crossed both her arms in front of her on the top rail of the fence. She leaned her chin on her wrists, her face and hair capturing the brilliance of the sun, and smiled. To be with him was wonderful. Talking or not. Working or making love. Meeting with friends or cooking him breakfast while he sang his horrible tenor in the shower. She loved him and just being near him made her happy.

Warren glanced over at her. He felt a warmth rise in his heart and body as he regarded her. He could hardly believe it. After all the terror and stress of the Rempal Inquest, the subsequent debriefings and the illness that finally killed his father, ten months alone with her had given him enough strength to survive the process of grief and change as he adapted to the loss of his father and the pace of life on the farm again. He knew there might never be a way to completely heal the feelings of guilt and loss from his father's passing. The cancer claimed his dad before he had a chance to work things out. But Warren found some solace in the fact that he had tried to do what he could. He had picked up his rusty tools of trade and risked his life, primarily because he loved his father; although once involved, for other reasons. If there is a hereafter, Warren reasoned, his father would surely see that. And through it all, Claire was there. They had spread the ashes over the plains of Texas as his father had always wanted, Texas being his home as a boy and a place dear to him.

Gary and Beatrice had been a great support as well. They often joked together about Bee following Gary to the States the second time around simply because she wanted to see how he managed to live alone for so many years without starving or freezing to death. The four had become close over the winter. Bee found the cold hard at first, but a three-week holiday in the Dominican Republic in February helped her adjust to the unfamiliar weather.

Weather. Cross sometimes wondered if there might not have been a way to save some of the weather control technology and still make it out of the complex. But he knew they had made the right decisions at the time. It was sad, though, how much good might have been accomplished if Caspersan had felt less vindictive under the shroud of righteous Roman Stoicism he proclaimed. A man of that brilliance and creativity probably came to the world only once each century. Sometimes to build. Sometimes to destroy. The world is full of "if-only's", Cross reflected.

There had been some talk amongst the four friends of maybe moving back to New Zealand in the fall. But Gary and Warren had insisted they return to the farms when the dust first settled. They each had their own reasons. For Warren it was partly to see and touch and feel that a normal way of life still existed in the world. In another way, he soon discovered, it was to say goodbye. The farm had been a shelter of sorts for him when he was retired by the Agency. The painful ghost of Bridget had haunted him and the farmwork kept his mind occupied most of the time. But now that Claire had filled and expanded that special place in him, the investment of time and energy in the farm seemed more of a hindrance than a desirable option. Claire was getting restless too. As she became more secure in her relationship with Warren, he could tell there were still many things she wanted to achieve in her career in order to feel good about herself and be productive. Warren had seen what her being productive could mean for the world as well. He was supportive of her plans. Gary and Beatrice naturally suggested New Zealand. It looked like maybe the farms would be put up for sale in late September.

Gerigi had written several times throughout the winter and into the summer. He was appointed Chief Warden of Kakadu Park in place of the previous warden. Chief Beechum had met with an untimely accident which broke several of his ribs and bruised up his face and upper torso quite a bit. Beechum didn't offer much of an explanation to the authorities when they asked him what happened. Cross figured he must have considered himself lucky to get out of Kakadu Park with his life once Gerigi cornered him.

Gerigi was a hero to his own people. News of his brave exploits outside the Complex were fully documented by Cross although Gerigi insisted it was not necessary. He was decorated by the Australian government and received the highest commonwealth commendation for courageous acts by a civilian in service of his country.

The wind had become chilly. The sun was almost fully set now. Claire snuggled in closer to her live-in companion. Warren wrapped one arm about her waist. God, how good she felt, he thought. I trust her, he said to himself. I really trust her.

"You know what, Claire?"

"No. Enlighten me," she teased.

"I think you're the first thing in the past ten years that has really made me feel there is goodness in the world, something to be trusted." Warren stared at her for a long moment. Tears came to his eyes.

As usual, his intimate declaration was a gargantuan understatement. Trust. How much has this man seen? How often has he been betrayed, lied to, used? Trust, thought Claire. To him that must mean more than anything else.

"Tell me more, honey. What do you mean?"

Warren sighed. He appreciated the challenge of Claire's digging, but it frustrated him too. The things he had begun to feel were so important to him. He often felt nothing he would say could truly express his thoughts. But he tried.

"It's like suddenly being sure of a religion or a theory that all your previous life's experience has made you believe was false. For twenty years of my life I figured there was nothing at the end. The reason for living was to work. For a while I thought love would be part of it for me, and the Agency took that too. I gave up believing in long-term things. I started to see an attachment as something to lose the moment you get used to having it. Needing someone or something became the most dangerous weakness in the world. I started to think that wanting something or loving something too much would make it go away, and you're still with me. You still say you love me. I don't know. I'm beginning to need you, Claire. It scares the shit out of me. If anything ever happened to you..."

Claire held the tips of her fingers against his lips and smiled warmly. "The story doesn't always have a happy ending but sometimes it does. Believe it, Warren. As long as you don't run off into the meadow with Tracy-Jo there and swap her technique for mine, you'll have a hard time getting rid of me."

Warren wondered if he blushed. Before becoming sexually intimate with Claire, he felt he had seen most of what the sexual world had to offer a man. Her openness and unique ability to walk a fine line between self-confidence and submission kept him

253

looking at his watch like a teenager most evenings, waiting for bedtime.

"I'll not likely trade you in either," Warren said in a low voice, nuzzling his lips and nose into the nape of her neck. Claire giggled. Warren began to feel himself harden as the smell of his favourite perfume mixed with the sweat of Claire's silky skin and the taste of her softness. Claire's laughter gradually lessened, her chuckles displaced by a growing hunger for Warren's body on top of her. It was so often like this—the mixture of trust and intimate conversation leading them into sexual union.

Claire tore herself from him and challenged him to a race to the house. Warren gave her a head start, threatening to catch her at any moment. Claire began to squeal, caught up in the game. They reached the house. Claire threw open the door and sped up the stairs with Warren in hot pursuit. He slipped on the stairs and she turned to throw a stray slipper at him. She tried to hold the door of the bedroom shut. Warren feigned effort. Then he pushed, gently and firmly, Claire shouting at him to stop, but enjoying and feeling turned on by the small demonstration of her partner's physical superiority.

"So you think pushing the door makes you a real man, I suppose?"

"Yeah, I suppose something like that."

"And I suppose," Claire said as she began to unbutton Warren's shirt, "that you think you can make me do anything you want me to, as dirty and low and disgusting as it may be."

"Yes, little bird, I do."

"And," she returned, grabbing at the edge of Warren's pants and pulling his zipper down with one stroke, "I suppose you think I just love providing you with Class A Lays all the time when all you want to do is spend time feeding the chickens or talking retirement with Gary at the pub."

Warren held her firmly and fell with her onto the bed. Their faces were close. His gaze was intense. Claire stared deeply at him. Her smile faded slowly as she felt the power of his wanting her. She lifted her head....

"Shit! Who the hell is that?"

The classic and universal disturbance of lovers around the world introduced itself with grating belligerence. On the third

254

ring, Claire reached under his arm to the bedside table where the phone sat, as Warren rolled off her and sighed.

"Hello?...Yes, it is. I'm afraid he's detained at the moment." Claire smiled and reached out to gently stroke his chest.

"Who?"

"What is it? Just take a note or tell them to wire a fucking message." Claire held up her hand to Warren's interjection. It seemed important.

"I see. Do you think it's necessary to talk about it right now? I mean, the funeral's over. Any financial loose ends are being handled through his executor in Houston....Okay." Claire held the phone to her breast, covering the receiver. She didn't know what this was about, but she suddenly felt nauseous. Please God, leave us alone.

"Honey, what is it? What's the matter?" Claire turned her head and looked deep into Warren's eyes. Was she looking to comfort him or looking to be reassured?

"Somebody from Washington," she said. "He said his name is Bugs, from Information," she continued, pausing and biting her lip. "Says he's got some knowledge about your dad's death that he thinks you've got a right to know. Says he owes you one," Claire finished, passing Cross the phone.